The Watcher Key
The Descendants of Light Series

BOOK ONE

TROY HOOKER

ILLUSTRATIONS BY
Stacy Hooker and Emily Anderson
EDITING BY
Jeannie Wilson and Brittany Renz

Descendant Publishing

Copyright © 2018 Descendant Publishing. All rights reserved.

The Watcher Key, The Descendants of Light Series, or any portion thereof may not be reproduced or used in any manner whatsoever without the express written permission of the publisher except for the use of brief quotations in a book review.

Printed in the United States of America
Bookmasters, Inc.

Cover Illustration By Rosauro Ugang
Interior Illustrations By Stacy Hooker
Map Illustration By Emily Anderson
Editing By Jeannie Wilson and Brittany Renz

Some characters and events in this book are fictitious. Any similarity to real persons, living or dead, is coincidental and not intended by the author.

First Printing, United States of America, February 2018

Library of Congress Control Number: 2017914796

ISBN 978-0-692-95481-2 (Soft cover)

Descendant Publishing
PO Box 340864
Dayton, OH 45434

www.descendantpublishing.com

1 3 5 7 9 10 8 6 4 2

Dedication

I would like to dedicate this work to my wife Stacy, who has endured countless evenings alone while I write.

To my mother Pamela, for her fervor to ensure that I follow my talents from God in all I do, and to my father, Tom, for his model of work ethic and of God's love.

And to my sister Tracy for her wise words of encouragement, and honesty when I am wrong.

Finally, to my daughter Maddison for her creative inspiration, and my daughter Sydney for reminding me to find God in the forest, away from the tempest of life.

I praise God for the blessing you all have been in my life.

Acknowledgments

Thank you, because you saw a glimmer of hope in me.
Thomas and Pamela Hooker
Julie Johnson
Jim and Suzie Johnson
Lindsey Bethel
John Irwin
Rick and Chrys Gayheart

For the one who sinks in sadness,
I pray this adventure brings you happiness.
For the one whose pain is all they can bear,
I hope these words help you find peace from your hurt.
To the one mired in the pits of anguish from sin,
I pray you find the One who created all things.

Contents

CHAPTER ONE
The Commissioning

CHAPTER TWO
A Secret Club

CHAPTER THREE
Timothy Becker

CHAPTER FOUR
wollemia nobilia

CHAPTER FIVE
Jester's Pass

CHAPTER SIX
Lior City

CHAPTER SEVEN
Boy With the Shadows

CHAPTER EIGHT
City Center

CHAPTER NINE
Games and Dark Dreams

CHAPTER TEN
Old Lady Wrenge

CHAPTER ELEVEN
Office of Research

CHAPTER TWELVE
The Lightway

CHAPTER THIRTEEN
The Darkness

CHAPTER FOURTEEN
The Holobook

CHAPTER FIFTEEN
Incident No. 497

CHAPTER SIXTEEN
The Outer Dunes

CHAPTER SEVENTEEN
Amos

CHAPTER EIGHTEEN
Sha'ar Gate

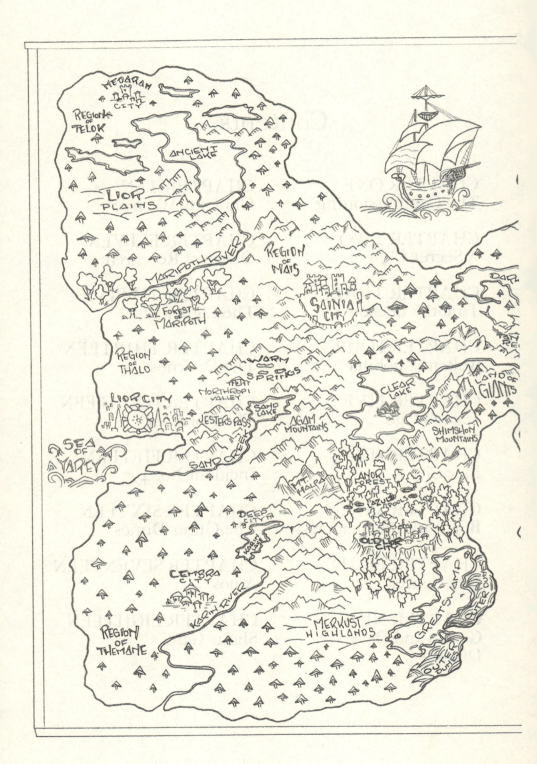

Chapter One
The Commissioning

The clouds on the horizon were burning puffs of black and grey as the young woman stumbled out of the stone structure. In her arms was a tiny bundle wrapped in a dull white blanket, which she clutched in such a way that one could see its contents were of great value.

She was young and slender, and her amber hair drawn up behind her head revealed a soft but tired face. At first glance, with her ornate cream dress and delicate lace patterns that adorned it, she looked out of place in the cavern that surrounded the archway, but a closer look would reveal a dirty and torn garment, the many stains showing signs of a rough journey behind her.

For a moment she looked around, blinking as though just stepping into an intense light, then intently checked the bundle she carried carefully as if surveying it for any harm. Finding none, she surveyed the scene in front of her, and then emerged from the cavern into the forest. The trees were dark and too still, and wisps of the first traces of a storm front were beginning to pass the tall pines overhead.

Chapter One: The Commissioning

Keeping watch behind her, she made for the heart of the forest, keeping the moon to her left as she walked quickly, the bundle close to her chest.

Her brisk pace and need to glance back suggested she was running from an unknown Darkness behind her.

As the woman with the bundle put distance between herself and the archway, she began to move more slowly, as though suffering from immense pain with each step. But she was not giving in to the pain, and she coaxed herself along the path below the trees, using the large pines for support while muttering strange phrases that sounded like prayers under her breath.

Slowly, a dark cloud began to creep up around her, engulfing the trees towering above the needle-laden forest floor. She could barely see which way the path was moving, and now she was doubling over every few hundred meters from the stabbing pain in her stomach. No longer could she spare the strength to look behind her or above her for the invisible danger she expected, but could only move on toward her unknown destination somewhere in front of her—or at least she hoped.

All at once, just as the panic began to set in from not knowing her location, she emerged from the edge of the pines. She stopped suddenly, staring at the little light on the opposite end of the clearing in front of her. High above, the clouds had moved in suddenly, a swirling mass of charcoal against the moonless sky. A streak of lightning bolted her out of her trance. Deep, throaty thunder quickly followed the flash, booming low and angrily through the earth beneath her feet. If she could just make it across the clearing to the cabin, she could rest, and she could find help.

The thought gave her a renewal of strength, and she prodded her body to finish the last part of the painful journey. Her breaths were drawing shorter and tighter, and her knees were beginning to buckle, but she moved along, still managing to hold the white bundle securely to her chest.

Chapter One: The Commissioning

She had put half of the open field behind her when she knew she could not go any further, and her frail body collapsed in a heap in the tall grass. Still, she was able to protect the bundle clutched in her arms as the rain began to pelt her side.

Snug in a small pine cabin from the impending storm, an aging man looked up from his worn leather journal and glanced out the window at the flashes of light. Right away he knew something was odd about this particular storm—something different from most others. The greenish-blue lightning flashed too quickly beyond the trees in almost pattern-like strikes. The thunder that followed boomed long past most normal claps, and it shook the little cabin with tremendous force.

Out in the darkness, between bolts of colored light, a flash of white fell to the ground and then disappeared in the middle of the clearing. The man blinked and rubbed his eyes, not understanding what he saw.

But something drew him to act, to go to the middle of the field where he saw the movement. Immediately he set his pen and journal on the nightstand and grabbed his mucking boots, stepping into them quickly. As a last minute thought, he grabbed a wool blanket from the rocking chair and his rifle on the rack, and then rushed out the thick wooden door into the pouring rain.

The rain soaked him quickly as the huge drops splashed onto his thin cotton button-down, and at once he wished he had remembered to put on a raincoat, but he sensed something was out there, and it seemed to call to him urgently to help. As he drew closer, he felt the urge grow stronger, and he ran even faster, slinging the rifle to his shoulder to free up his arms from the bulk of the blanket.

About thirty meters from the white object, he noticed it was a person—a woman. He sprinted the last few steps almost effortlessly, falling to his knees in the mud beside her. Seeing the tiny bundle in her arms, he pried it out of her grasp and peered at the baby wrapped in the muddy blanket, sleeping soundly. Getting the baby inside was

Chapter One: The Commissioning

most important, so he stashed the bundle in his flannel shirt and headed toward the cabin. Then he would come back for the woman and the rifle. How in the world could this baby be sleeping in this weather? He thought as he ran back, trying to keep the bundle as still as possible.

Once the sleeping child was wrapped in some dry blankets, the man rushed back out into the storm, the edge of the dark cloud now upon the cabin, and hurried back to the woman lying in the grass. He picked her up as gently as he could, draping her over his shoulder so he could move more quickly.

He turned and faced the storm, the eerie lightning striking only a kilometer from where he stood.

It has begun, he thought, searching the trees for signs of other forms. He stumbled while trying to look back while running, and nearly dropped the woman. They will be here any moment.

He quickened his pace, realizing the impending danger he was in. The cabin lights in the distance were his beacon, and again he attempted to move faster, careful not to jostle the woman in his arms too much. A battle was about to begin, and he was in the middle of it.

Nearly at the cabin now, the wind was beginning to blow hard enough to make him have to work to move forward. The last few feet were almost as though he was being pulled back into the gusting Darkness behind him, but he pushed forward until he at last reached the cabin steps. Yanking the door open with his free hand, he rushed inside to find the little cabin groaning and creaking from the stress of the storm. Not stopping to pause, he laid the lifeless woman on the bed near the fireplace and covered her with the grey blanket at the end of the bed, then quickly set about heating up water for tea.

The wind outside began to blow even more fiercely, and the man wondered if the hard work and sweat he had put into building the cabin was going to be soon blown to splinters. But his mind shifted to the two silent guests he had carried in from the Darkness.

Who was the woman? Where had she come from? He stood in

Chapter One: The Commissioning

the kitchen feeling immediately exhausted from the ordeal, his eyes shifting to the bookshelf where he kept many old, worn books with no titles on them. One book in particular caught his eye—a small leathery journal much like his own, which he quickly snatched from the shelf and thumbed through its pages. The woman was wearing a white nightgown sort of dress, no doubt beautiful before it was stained and soaked by the muddy earth. The baby lay still in the little bundle he was wrapped in, and he stared at it in disbelief.

He felt the chill of the wind seeping through the window behind him and checked the latch to make sure it was secured as tight as possible, then checked the door as well, seeing that he would have to do something about the draftiness on cold nights like these. Looking over toward the stone fireplace, he noticed that the fire was blowing more ash into the room than heat, so he picked up a few logs next to the door and put them on the dwindling fire. The logs spewed and sputtered a mixture of ash and sparks up into the chimney, and he stayed for a moment to make sure the flames caught, holding his aging hands close to the fire to warm them quickly before setting about seeing to the young woman.

The tea on the stove began to whistle, and the man quickly set about fixing a cup of tea for his strange guest, keeping an eye out the window for any movement. He knew he was safe where he was, but he was nervous nonetheless. Instead, he busied himself with making the woman more comfortable.

He figured at this point there would be no need for sugar in the tea. She would likely just be satisfied with something hot—that is if she would awaken to his beckoning. She would need proper bedding as well.

He finished fixing the tea and removed the leaves, then sat down beside her on the bed and began to stroke her hair.

Almost instantly she awoke with a start, nearly spilling the hot tea all over the bed and the man that had saved her. The young woman sat up and frantically looked around the room for her child, and seeing

Chapter One: The Commissioning

him, attempted to get up and go to him, but her body would not allow her movement, and she collapsed back on the creaky old bed with an exhausted whimper.

"Don't be afraid. I have your child and he is safe," he spoke softly. "My name is Amos, and you are safe with me here. I am your friend," he whispered now, afraid to cause her any more trauma. "I found you in the field—What is your name?"

She had almost aqua colored eyes, much like the color of the teacup he had prepared for her. She did not speak, but her lips trembled as though she was trying to say something but could not. He could tell she was frustrated from her inability to speak, so he decided to speak for her instead.

"Did you come from town?" he asked, already knowing the answer.

The woman shook her head ever so slightly.

"Another city? State?" he pressed on.

Again she shook her head and seemed frustrated. Finally, she reached for the steaming cup of tea Amos held in his hand, and taking it, gingerly sipped its contents.

He didn't need to pry any further about her origin. The storm outside told him all he needed to know. She was from the other side.

"You should rest," he said gently. "We will talk again in the morning." He knew there was no way he was going to be able to find out any more tonight. She was just too weak.

He set the cup of steaming tea on the little table next to the bed and covered the woman carefully with the quilt. She was opening and closing her eyes heavily, and Amos knew she would be out at any moment.

Getting up from beside the bed, he walked over to the door and secured the latch, even as the wind rattled against the door. He scooped up a spare blanket kept on the trunk at the end of the bed and settled into the chair across the room. The fire was happily licking up the side of the logs in the fireplace, and he could tell the room had warmed up quite a bit, even with the numerous drafts throughout

Chapter One: The Commissioning

the cabin. He laid his head back, trying to settle his mind from the evening's events.

He had come to this place for a reason—to remove himself from the other side. But now, here she was, a woman he did not know, but who knew him and knew where he lived. It was an unsettling feeling, not simply because of the woman discovering him, but because of what she represented.

He picked up the journal and held it against his chest, exhaling slowly. He had seen this scene play out over and over again in his mind, as the Creator had Promised. He had been waiting, and now the moment was here. A Promise made, long ago, now come to pass.

The Irin. This child was to be the Irin, the one to reveal the Darkness once and for all.

But the Watcher who told him of the Promise also reminded him of the Dark Legend, the twisted version of the Creator's Promise, altered to fit their evil purpose. They too, wanted the child. And he was tasked with the protection of him. This is why she came to him.

The storm outside continued to rage mercilessly. No doubt they would find him and the child, even hidden in Creation. He had to prepare.

It was the beginning of a very long end.

Just before he closed his eyes again, he thought he caught a glance out the dusty four-paned window over the bed of three figures standing on the edge of the field. Blaming his eyes for deceiving him, he closed them in an attempt to rest his sore body from carrying the woman.

****

Just inside of the tree line, about three hundred meters from the little glowing cabin, two young men and a young woman stood side by side in the windy torrent. They were all three dressed in similar fashion: silver fitted robes that stiffly belled outward where the fabric touched the earth. There was black trim outlining their cuffs and

Chapter One: The Commissioning

collars, and they looked very calm standing there in the Darkness. If one looked long enough, they seemed to blend in with the trees entirely. As the bright light from the cabin began to fade into a dull glow, the three curious Watchers scanned the trees and the field surrounding the cabin, and every so often peered at the storm raging above them.

The older, taller of the two men then held up his hand and immediately the others turned toward him.

"I think we have served our purpose here tonight," he said with a soft but commanding voice.

"But Hagan, I don't think we should leave just yet. I do not feel that this is over," the young woman said, careful not to sound disrespectful.

She was stern in her face, with piercing eyes and soft but thin lips. She was beautiful in her own way, a match of strength with most men but still delicate in her appearance and movements.

Hagan smiled. "I am glad for your opinion, Bian. I could never argue with the feelings of a woman. They have saved my life too often. We can stay until morning."

"Hagan, Magister, do you really think it is necessary to wait that long?" the younger man said with a tone a little more challenging than his female counterpart.

"Marcus, you know we are first and foremost to honor our agreement to look after the child," Hagan responded, offering a stern but gentle criticism of his younger shadow.

"I just don't see how we are going to be of any service to the child if he is already in the care of the dweller," Marcus quickly retorted.

"I cannot understand how you could talk about the child as if the woman did not even risk her life to save him in the first place," Bian said with a flash of frustration, turning her head back to the cabin so quickly that her braids wrapped around her neck.

"Remember, both of you, that we must be watchful. The Metim are much more formidable these days," Hagan said calmly, careful not to remove his gaze from the little cabin. "Even though we are no

Chapter One: The Commissioning

longer allied with the Descendants, Nuriel has asked that we watch the boy, as he will become the Irin, the revealer of the Darkness."

The sound of Marcus removing his sword from its sheath cut Hagan's sentence short. All three focused on the sky now, as if they too had felt or heard something was out of place.

"It is strong," the young Bian breathed as she stood motionless, one arm held out in front of the other as if poised for battle. Hagan did not speak, but merely lifted his hands above his head and held them there, palms facing the sky. "They are here. We must call on the others to aid us."

"No! We can take them! I feel it!" whispered the young warrior harshly, looking at his teacher's outstretched arms.

Hagan sighed heavily, glancing over at the young brash student, then lowered his arms.

At that moment there appeared cylindrical shapes of greenish-white light falling to the earth in heaps, much like illuminated sand being dropped from the sky. There were ten of them that Bian counted, and immediately she knew Hagan's instincts had been correct, and Marcus's had been wrong. Ten was too many for the three of them.

All at once the three broke into a rush toward the fallen heaps of light, moving faster than a normal person would be able to, and in a moment they had reached their targets. A fierce battle had begun for the little child who lay peacefully in his makeshift crib, who was unaware of any of the events happening outside of his snug new home. Flashes of green-white streaks of light mixed with blue light flashed fiercely in the corner of the field as all in the cabin slept peacefully.

****

Arazel's black robes billowed in the warm breeze as he made his way up the stone steps and into the gleaming white castle. Spectacular ivory chandeliers hung from the ceiling and sprayed brilliant white

Chapter One: The Commissioning

light around the interior in an obvious display of opulence. As he crossed the threshold of the massive structure, instantly his robes transformed from black into spotless white silk-laden fabric.

Two lavishly dressed guards in pure white robes greeted Arazel with their brilliant green eyes, bowing as he passed. Although beautiful, they were not harmless, as both carried gleaming staffs that pulsed with the same green of their eyes. Arazel made no acknowledgment of them, but only hurried into the great corridors of the castle toward the interior.

As he entered, a medium-sized man with soft glassy eyes rose from his ornately decorated throne in the center of the lavish hall, his thin white robe exposing the pearl-colored skin of his chest. His perfectly sculpted body and silky long brown hair moved gracefully as he walked with his silver scepter to the edge of the platform, gazing at Arazel as he took his place among the others in the hall.

To the left of Arazel stood a large man, nearly as beautiful as the one standing in front of the throne, but he had a look of horror upon his face as he stood between two robed guards who held his wrists fast with an iron grip. His eyes blazing silent anguish, the prisoner looked to the robed man on the platform between the two ornate white columns, but he did not speak. Kachash strode silently from one end of the platform to the other, never once taking his eyes off of Arazel, and never looking at the restrained man in front of him. After a few moments of silence, the man stepped down from the platform and glided toward the man in restraints, stopping short of his captor and turning his gaze from Arazel to the prisoner who was breathing heavily.

"You have failed for the last time, Samak," Kachash said calmly. "You have had fourteen years to find the stone and bring it to me, and you were not able to perform this simple task."

"Lord Kachash, allow me to redeem myself. There were three of the most formidable Sons of Light that night and we were caught off guard—"

Chapter One: The Commissioning

"YOU DARE MAKE EXCUSES TO ME?" Kachash hissed, his eyes suddenly blazing a brilliant green.

Samak looked to the floor.

"I am at your mercy, Sar—"

Kachash's eyes faded suddenly into a glassy stare once again.

"Yes, yes, you are, aren't you...," he said dreamily. "What shall we do with an incapable leader of Metim that begs for mercy? Who chooses not himself to pass into Creation, but sends ten pathetic souls into battle for him? What shall we do with a mixed-blood drek who has been rendered useless?"

No one spoke, and the hall was silent again.

"We have mercy here, do we not?" Kachash held his arms out to the servants and guards watching the scene. "Are we not a race of mercy? Who shows forgiveness when forgiveness is not due? Yes ... we are merciful, loving beings of the Darkness."

He then turned and walked back toward the platform.

"You may go, Samak, most powerful leader of Metim."

Samak's eyes lit up at the words of his master. The guards to the right and left removed the restraints and stepped away from the freed prisoner, who rubbed his wrists and looked around cautiously. Then he turned toward the platform, taking a step forward, and falling to his knees.

"Sar, lord, allow me another chance to complete my task. I know I can—," but his words were cut off as the robed man turned silently, stretching out his hand with incredible speed, a stream of electric smoke shooting from his fingertips toward the man on his knees. In an instant, Samak was enveloped in the cloud, his screams muffled by the dense crushing weight of the Darkness around him.

Nothing but a pile of ashes remained on the floor of the hall when the Darkness dissipated. Kachash turned calmly to the side of the room where two very human-looking people dressed in rags stood cowering behind one of the pure white columns.

"Please clean my hall," he hissed at his servants as he wiped his

Chapter One: The Commissioning

hands calmly on a towel that was brought to him, as though he had just finished up eating a messy dinner.

"Now, Ebed, Arazel, my servant, come forth for your calling." Kachash swung around on his heels, his sheer white robe swirling as he turned.

Arazel stepped bravely forward, paying no mind to the piles of ashes being scooped into buckets. He lowered his hood and bent low to bow to Kachash, who quickly stepped forward and pulled him to his feet.

"Arazel, you must not bow to me. You know I am only a servant as well. Now rise."

Arazel stood to his feet and looked Kachash directly in his glassy eyes. They were shallow, hollow eyes, callous with indifference, but blazing with deep hatred.

"Do you still have the Light within you?" Kachash hissed.

"Yes, Sar Lord, the miserable Light has not yet left me … but it will not be soon enough when it does," Arazel stood his ground.

Kachash cursed and spat behind him.

Arazel leveled his gaze.

"I will serve you well," he said resolutely.

"Then, Arazel, your calling is to complete the task that Samak could not," he whispered eerily, his perfect lips glistening as he spoke. "The Prophecy of the Darkness speaks of a child—born to a Watcher of the Creator. This child will have in his possession the great Stone of the Watchers. It is said he will become the future of the Darkness, and servant of the Dark One when he arises. Since Samak was unable to retrieve the Stone from the boy, it has now become your primary task."

"Shall I bring the child to you as well, Lord Kachash, second to the Dark One?"

Kachash's rehearsed smile turned into a blank, emotionless stare as he gazed at the beautiful gleaming white hall surrounding them.

"No. He will be entering his fifteenth year of the sun, and he will be resistant to the Darkness."

Chapter One: The Commissioning

"Sar Lord, who is this child to the Darkness?" Arazel spoke carefully.

Kachash smiled darkly. "He is the child spoken of in the Dark prophecies who will lead us to victory over the Light. He will draw all Darkness into Creation, and we will destroy all who resist ..." he paused, looking suddenly to the large glowing sun symbol on the gleaming white wall. "HE WILL UNITE US TO DESTROY THE LIGHT!" he screamed suddenly, his voice like screeching nails on a chalkboard throughout the hall.

Kachash looked down at his clenched fist, then an eerie smile crept over his face.

"You are the only one who can travel the gates, with your cursed Light that corrodes your body, so therefore you must prove yourself to the Dark One." He paused, taking a moment to gaze into the sky, his eyes ablaze. "This boy ... he will become our redeemer. You must show him the power of the Darkness, for he is the key to end our suffering."

"I have submitted to the Darkness, lord, but I retain the feeble Light for just such a purpose to serve the Dark One."

Kachash smiled, his beautiful lips suddenly gentle and calm in a strange turn of demeanor.

"The curse the Dark One placed over the land before his exile has begun to erode, my fellow servant Arazel. I have employed another like you who has embraced the Darkness within Lior. He will keep us hidden a little while longer, but time is short before we will be exposed. The Watcher Stone in the boy's possession will allow us to become strong once more."

"I will ensure my pace is quick, my lord."

Kachash scowled as one of the servants coughed as he picked up the dust from the remains of Samak.

"The boy will come to us, of that I know."

"Sar, lord, what is the boy's name?"

"The one they call Samuel," the robed man hissed, then laid his hand upon Arazel's bald head. "Now rise, son of Darkness, former

🌲🌲 Chapter One: The Commissioning

Watcher, and slay all those who come against you. May your calling bring victory among the forces of Darkness. The Dark One calls you to his service!"
Suddenly the room grew dark and the columns, the guards, and the servants disappeared from sight. A swirling black cloud encompassed Arazel, and soon a great deep desire began to well up from within, and he could feel the renewed power of the Darkness taking over his body.

Chapter Two
A Secret Club

It was the middle of September but it was already beginning to get cooler in the Upper Peninsula of Michigan. The summer-burnt leaves were showing signs of early color on the trees, and already those living near the tiny town's center were purchasing rakes and lawn bags from the small hardware store in anticipation of an especially leafy fall.

The quaint streets of White Pine had been quiet for nearly a month as those of school age were forced back into the grips of math worksheets and history tests. The anxiety of a new school year was quickly fading into the humdrum of changing classes, and from the corridors of White Pine High School came the sound of slamming lockers, jocks trying to impress gaggles of teenage girls with their new abs acquired over the summer, and excited talk of the weekend's homecoming football game and dance that followed.

Outside of the school building, however, three young figures who were unconcerned with the football season or homecoming dances huddled in the corner of a large dark cavern just outside of town, the light from an old hurricane lamp casting an eerie glow on their faces.

Chapter Two: A Secret Club

The larger of the three youths, a boy, was listening as the two girls talked in a hushed, excited tone. Laying open next to him was a book—a small, leather-wrapped journal that seemed to consume his attention more than the conversation.

"Are you sure that's what you saw?" the girl with the shoulder-length dark hair, named Lillia, questioned fiercely.

"I'm pretty sure it was the same symbol ..." Emma, the girl with strawberry-red hair answered. "He drew it on his notebook in geography. Speaking of which, are you sure we are covered from class?"

"Yeah, I told Mr. Banner we needed to get some photos for the yearbook of the parade preparations early," said Lillia.

"I know it's kinda mean, but I love how clueless that man is," Emma responded, her hair gleaming in the reflective light of the arch behind her.

Lillia ignored her.

"This is not like ones we have had in the past. We aren't talking about some mindless bonehead who wandered too close ..." Then she paused with a critical huff before gesturing toward the darkest part of the cave. "... I mean, this kid hasn't a clue about us and yet he draws the Watcher wing? Could he be a Descendant of the Light?"

"Maybe," the pudgy boy called Gus said quietly. "But it is not for us to decide that."

"There hasn't been a Descendant found in Creation for nearly a century," Lillia echoed, "It's going to take convincing in Lior."

"There's no denying what he drew ... it couldn't be a coincidence could it?" Emma challenged, causing both girls to look over at the boy, who was scribbling quick notes and then scanning the pages lazily in the dim light provided by the lanterns.

"Well," he sighed heavily, "I think you are right about it not being a coincidence, but I believe the real question is, What should we do about it?"

Emma shrugged. "I don't think *we* can do anything, not having gone through mentoring yet. But I *do* think we need to tell the other members."

Chapter Two: A Secret Club

"You mean your mom and dad," Lillia snorted.

"I am not a baby. I just mean since my dad is in charge of this circle, we need to tell him."

Lillia snorted again.

Gus shifted his weight on the rock uncomfortably.

"I will talk with Miss Karpatch. And we should all keep an eye on him ..."

For a moment, the three figures sat in silence. They agreed the other members must know, but if they were correct about the boy, something must be done.

Emma spoke slowly, softly.

"I think ... we go to Samuel Forrester and ask why he drew it."

Lillia lifted an eyebrow quizzically.

"Why would we want to talk to him about it? It's not like we can kidnap him, force him to talk, and then walk away like nothing ever happened."

"True," Gus admitted, "but maybe we can get him to talk ... willingly."

"How are we supposed to do that?" Lillia looked disgusted.

Emma glanced at the large white arch structure in the cavern that gave off a dim but obvious glow.

"We invite him to Lior," she said.

For a moment the room grew silent as they absorbed her words. The only sound was the soft whine of the breeze humming past the cavern entrance.

"You know they won't go for that."

"Who says? They have brought people in before."

Lillia snickered.

"Yes, but they weren't pathetic weasels like him. They had developed skills already."

"I just—have a feeling about him, that's all. The others will understand that," Emma said resolutely.

"And what if he says no?" Gus leaned his large shoulders against the rock behind him, the scraping of his shoe reverberating loudly off the walls of the still cavern.

Chapter Two: A Secret Club

Emma sighed and picked up her backpack. "Don't worry. He won't."

****

At five feet nine inches, wearing particularly ordinary blue jeans and a black t-shirt that his grandfather had bought him, Sam Forrester was rather normal-sized for a boy his age, which made him neither horrible nor spectacular at sports, but he never cared to play anyway. He was more of the type to enjoy a historical novel on a cold evening while sipping a caramel latte, in fact. An interesting book and some good music were what inspired him, but he wasn't inspired much anymore these days.

To be quite honest, he was stubborn and independent, keeping only a few select friends—mostly quiet friends like himself, fantastical outcasts that were often forgotten as lonely introverts, rarely noticed in the shadows of the places they frequented.

It was a day he did not remember, but was plagued by nonetheless. One late evening, while coming home from a conference at the university, his father Daniel drifted left in the pouring rain and hit a tree head on. Both he and his mother Samantha were dead upon impact.

Sam was only five when it happened, and since then, he was placed in various foster homes until he came to live with the Pattons.

So he found refuge in various books, fantastical worlds that would help him find solace from his memories. Bookstores were like hiding places from the harsh world outside as well as an escape from the past—a place to get lost in a world of bravery and chivalry, where, unlike the real world, good always outshines evil. Until he was forced downstairs to finish his Latin tutoring.

But here, in this new place, Sam was even more an outcast, alone—a stranger in a foreign land. No longer did he have piano lessons at noon every day in the formal living room, nor did he come home to the smell of dinner being prepared by Estella, or to his mother's friends coaxing her through a second bottle of wine.

Chapter Two: A Secret Club

He used to steal a bite of dinner before Estella could see him and barricade himself upstairs in his room away from the cackles of the drunken women downstairs.

Now he was stuck in a little nothing town somewhere in northern Michigan, a slave in a backward school where the biggest event of the week was a tractor pull on Thursdays. There was no greater feeling of being alone than to be sent away once again to live with an aging grandfather whom he had never met.

They had packed his things one day while Sam was at school and were waiting in the car with drawn faces when he walked up the long driveway of the large brick home. They drove him downtown to the train station in silence, and handing him four hundred dollars, told him he was going to stay in White Pine with his only living grandfather, Amos Forrester.

Instead of asking why, Sam clammed up, as if already expecting it. He had a feeling this day would come, given his outwardly obvious distaste for them. They became his third set of ex-foster parents because of one reason or another, but with the Pattons he had spent the longest time. While he could never seem to live up to their standards, he had grown accustomed to them, as he thought they had with him. They were not the best of parents, but they had cared for his physical needs.

His foster father Phillip Patton was a state senator, and never really talked much with him, especially about politics, since they often disagreed. This day was no exception. Instead of wishing Sam well, he handed him his suitcase on the train platform, refusing to look him in the eye or say anything at all for that matter, other than to clear his throat loudly.

Silvia, his foster mother, showed no emotion that day. She just pursed her lips and dug through her handbag for lipstick, gobbing it on like icing on cake. Usually she was quite expressive and always had something to say, but on that day she acted like he had never existed.

Silvia had thick hips and big hair, and hadn't worked a day in her life. She spent most mornings in front of the mirror putting on makeup and tousling her hair to make sure no new grey roots

Chapter Two: A Secret Club

showed, then went shopping for a new purse and out to lunch at the country club with her other big-haired friends. She often smelled of liquor when she returned, and Sam had often wondered if she was ever truly sober.

Silvia was overly critical and had a violent side that came out every so often, where something said or done not quite right would cause her to go into a fit, throwing anything she could get her hands on. When he was younger, Sam tried his best to calm her down in the middle of a rant, but he and the Senator eventually learned to just duck out of the room until her fit reduced into uncontrollable sobs.

It wasn't that Sam wasn't grateful she raised him; it was only that she seemed bipolar at times. One minute she praised him for everything, the next minute she talked about how he would never amount to anything. He overheard her one day saying that he was going to become just a "bum pushing a grocery cart." He figured it boiled down to something missing in either her marriage or her life, perhaps a lack of purpose, or maybe she didn't know much about parenting. Whatever it was, most days Sam didn't want anything to do with her.

Phillip rarely stood up for himself when she went on one of her rampages. Apparently he had learned from past attempts. Sam guessed it was from exhaustion rather than fear. He wasn't particularly mean or violent, although Sam could see the possibility for both. At forty-nine, Phillip was a tall and beefy man, and never dressed in anything other than a black suit. He chose to spend his time working away from home, many nights choosing to stay at the office in Lansing, no doubt to avoid his wife and her cackling friends. When he was at home, he was buried in a newspaper or locking himself in his office for hours on end.

Sam remembered glancing back at them standing in the station as they watched him leave. He said nothing—just did his best to stare at the train seat ahead of him. For a moment, he thought he could see Silvia reach a hand up to wipe a tear away, but he was too far away from the station platform to tell. Either way, it didn't matter now ...

Chapter Two: A Secret Club 🌲🌲

whoever or whatever they were to him was no more. It was time to move on.

A new life in a backward town.

****

Sam slunk down in his chair in an attempt to avoid the teacher's line of sight. He sat nervously, fidgeting—waiting for his chance. From the back row, he could not see the teacher and she could not see him, especially in the dark classroom.

Sam looked around him at the other students in the class—some were intent on the epically boring *The Building of the Mackinac Bridge*, some were trying their best in the dark to squint their way through another vampire book, and the entirety of row four was passing notes to each other, giggling like junior high girls around some new guy from Iron Mountain. Most of the class, however, was sound asleep at their desks, thanks to the teacher's inobservance and the lack of light. The school's famous bully, Timothy Becker (otherwise known as "Bush" because of his curly blondish-brown hair that extended outward to form an uncanny likeness to shrubbery), was hanging half out of his chair with a string of drool that was well on its way to forming a puddle on the floor. Sam could see it glistening from the light of the projector screen. It was enough to make anyone's stomach turn.

Satisfied no one could see him, Sam slipped out of his chair and began to slink toward the half-open door of the classroom. For a moment, the girl in the second row seemed to notice the movement and glanced back, causing him to stop suddenly for a moment. She was the girl that almost always had her fire-red hair pulled back in a ponytail, and she was very pretty. Sam only knew her name, Emma, and she always seemed to be hanging around the chubby curly-headed boy that everyone called "Grimace" behind his back.

He was almost halfway to the door before he remembered his backpack and book at his desk. Cursing himself for his forgetfulness,

Chapter Two: A Secret Club

Sam snuck back to the desk in the dark and snatched up his backpack and his *Geography and Culture* textbook, and again headed for the door. Still the red-haired girl watched him, but made no attempt to announce his escape.

Unknown to him, however, Sam's backpack strap had somehow become lodged in the legs of his desk during class, and as he slunk toward the door once more, the desk attempted to follow him, making a hideous screeching noise across the unwaxed tile floor. Sam tried to free the strap by tugging his backpack from side to side, but with every tug, the desk screeched even more loudly. SCREECH! the desk went, and Sam's heart began to pound.

SCREE! Sam pulled again, trying to dislodge his backpack from its captor. Sam glanced over at the teacher's desk, but she was engrossed with the video and did not seem to notice him. Other than Emma, who was now tensing her neck and shoulders with each irritating screech, no one else figured out what was going on. He knew his window of opportunity would soon be closing, and his chances of getting caught were increasing with every horrible scrape of the desk.

Instead of trying to fiddle with where the strap was attached to the desk in the dark, Sam decided he would give one last tug before giving up the whole idea of skipping out early. He breathed deeply to slow down his racing heart, and then gave one great yank on the strap in a desperate effort to loosen it.

SCREEEEEECH! went the leashed desk across the floor.

The noise was so loud that Bush, the puddle of drool now at his feet, woke suddenly and pitched forward, taking his desk with him. His fall created a sudden domino effect, forcing the thin, well-dressed girl in front of him to jump suddenly out of her chair, which also startled two more sleeping boys, making one of them spill his books all over the floor. Jenny (Sam had heard her name because everyone was afraid of her), who sat in front of the two sleeping boys and was hit in the back by a falling book, stood and became instantly furious—demanding to know who created the nightmare that interrupted the video.

The ninth-grade geography teacher, Miss Karpatch, snapped

Chapter Two: A Secret Club

out of her educational coma and hurried over to a light switch near the door to turn on the lights. Sam, who was still holding onto his leashed backpack, could not move in time before the flustered teacher caught the edge of his shoe and pitched head over onto the floor. She screamed as she went down, sounding much like the desk on the tile floor.

Sam quickly slinked back to his desk in the dark while Miss Karpatch stood and gathered herself from the fall and flicked on the lights.

Her face was beet red, and she was taking on the ominous signs of a nuclear meltdown. She had great patience, that woman did, but even she had her limits. The only other time Sam had seen her lose her temper was when she had caught Bush pushing around one of the new kids from Iron Mountain the first week of school. She had grabbed Bush by a clump of hair and dragged him down to the school office. He was given a week suspension, but rumor had it that Miss Karpatch had given the principal an earful when he tried to tell her she couldn't physically handle the students.

But Sam wasn't particularly worried about Miss Karpatch or the consequences; this wasn't the first time he had skipped. He was a professional skipper at his old school, and worst he had ever had to endure was detention once for an hour on Thursday. No, Sam was more worried about Bush, and what medieval method of torture he would use on him later for interrupting his nap during class.

Bush wasn't an ordinary boy, but a bully with the worst kind of chip on his shoulder. Most of the older teachers had pretty much given up on him, and there was a rumor that he had singlehandedly driven two of the newer teachers out of teaching for good with his classroom demeanor.

For some reason, Bush seemed to take an interest in Sam. Maybe it was that Sam was new, or that he kept to himself and didn't talk much. Whatever it was, he was Bush's target most weekdays when class let out—pushing him into the lockers demanding money and sneaking in a few punches if Sam didn't have any.

One day Bush discovered Sam alone in the locker room after gym

Chapter Two: A Secret Club

class. Bush called him "pretty boy" and then he shoved his nose to the locker room floor when Sam called him an "overgrown hillbilly" under his breath. With Sam's nose bloodied, Bush then pushed him into the showers and turned on the cold water.

Telling on him would have been useless—it would most certainly draw attention to the problem even more, leading to more beatings and ruthless taunting. Teachers and administrators seemed clueless or had their hands tied, unable to intervene from fear of lawsuits. Staying under the radar seemed like a better idea, but he had blown that now. Not only was Miss Karpatch about to explode, but now Bush was being laughed at for the small pond he had dribbled onto the floor.

Miss Karpatch surveyed the destruction around the room. She centered her gaze finally on Sam and found the target of her meltdown.

"Sam," she withheld her rage. "See me in the hallway," she paused again, "now." Her voice squeaked a bit.

And then, as if the whole thing were planned, the bell rang and the whole class exploded into the normal chaos of changing classes. The only one lingering behind was Bush, who finally made his way over to Sam with an "it's open season on Sam" look on his face.

Finally, the only ones in the room were Sam, Miss Karpatch, and the Mackinaw Bridge, which was still being constructed on the screen.

"Sit," Miss Karpatch insisted after motioning Sam over to her desk. She didn't wait for him, but just sort of plopped down in her chair and began to rub her knuckles on her temples. Sam thought he heard her whisper something under her breath.

"I'm sorry," Sam half whispered. "It won't happen again."

Miss Karpatch looked up, forcing a smile to her lips. Her long brown hair had dropped out of its bun and was falling into her face.

"Sam, your grades are slipping, and it's the beginning of the year. You are failing geography, and your general lack of consideration for the rules is going to get you in serious trouble …" she said bluntly. "But that's not what ticks me off the most. You have such unrealized talent, and yet you don't seem to care."

Chapter Two: A Secret Club

"I'm not sure what you mean." Sam didn't look up, but he could tell she was looking at him.

"You show an aptitude for history—for academics in general, and yet you blow it off like it's not even important." Her voice squeaked again as she threw her hands up, saying, "You show such potential—"

"Yeah I know. Don't remind me," Sam cut her off.

The frustrated teacher bit her lip.

"I am going to recommend a two week suspension to the administration—"

"Oh come on! You can't be serious! I was just trying to get out and get some fresh air! I was going to come right back in—"

"Give it up Sam," she breathed. "You were skipping again."

Sam said nothing. He just scowled at the young teacher sitting across from him. She gazed deeper into his eyes, which forced him to look away.

"You really need to focus on what's at hand, Sam, and …" she sighed as her expression changed, "you know you can always talk to me about what happened with your parents."

"*Foster* parents. And don't talk about them like you know them. You read my file and now you think you know me? You have no right—"

"Do you think I am afraid of your threats?" she leveled her gaze. "Come on, Sam. At some point you have to talk to someone. You can't just live a lonely existence because you're ticked off at the world."

Sam reflected to himself. Lonely? Ticked off at the world? What would she possibly know about that? He was really tired of people trying to get him to talk. He was not crazy, or in need of someone to "talk" to. Save it for the psychos that needed it … the ones with real issues.

Even still, they had no idea what it was like not to know your real parents—and to know that your fake parents dumped you on someone else because they were more concerned with traveling than raising a kid. Miss Karpatch was just another one of them, someone who pretends to care but all they want is to make themselves feel better by asking. Come to think of it, maybe she did know something

Chapter Two: A Secret Club

about being alone. She was single. Perhaps she scared all eligible men off with her obsessive digging.

He didn't say anything more to her, only picked up his backpack and stiffly walked out of the room, certain that he could feel her eyes on him. Skipping the next class would be a breeze. Mr. Adrian spent the whole time showing videos and rarely took attendance. It was as if God was actually giving him a reason to skip class.

"Sam," she called quietly after him. "I am here if you change your mind. Everyone needs a friend … or a few …"

"Go grade some papers or something," Sam said under his breath, but not really caring whether she heard him or not.

As if fate was laughing at him, Sam found Bush waiting for him after school on the path that Sam took back to his grandfather's house. Luckily, Bush hadn't seen him yet and Sam was able to skirt around the main path out of sight of the bully. He knew the delay was only temporary—not only did he have the frame of an elephant but he had a memory like one too.

That night, after his chores around the cabin and a quiet dinner of beef stew and biscuits, Sam mouthed an inaudible goodnight to his grandfather and slipped into his room to read.

He pulled on his flannel pajama pants and a t-shirt and slunk down in the pillows of the log bed. The room was small, but it was especially warm from being adjacent to the fireplace, and strangely enough, he had even come to like the bearskin rug and rocking chair in the corner. It was as if he lived in a ski lodge, complete with snowshoes nailed to the wall.

Snatching up his third book in the series *War Walking*, he half-heartedly turned the pages, still distracted from the encounter with Miss Karpatch. It was just skipping class … it wasn't like he called in a bomb threat or something. He knew of others in class who were outright cheating, smoking weed in the woods behind school … but yet, she seemed to have picked him out for special attention.

The next day started the weekend, and it couldn't come soon enough. As Sam drifted off to sleep, he did what he did best—buried all of the problems from the week: Bush, Miss Karpatch, his foster

Chapter Two: A Secret Club

parents, the odd people of White Pine—and let his mind drift away.

He stared at the dark cloud that spread throughout the sky and valley surrounding him. It was thick like soup, and he could hear it whispering something at him, it's mouth only a moving mass of smoke-like lips. It seemed to be speaking something to him, but it was inaudible.

Then it spoke again.

Malak Eben, the voice whispered.

Then, suddenly, he was running from the cloud and through the Darkness, the cold wind chilling him to the bone. There was a flash, and a bright white light covered him as he lay in the cold weeds. He could see a dark stone arch against the black horizon, and dark fluid shapes were amassing within its interior. A cloaked person thrust something into the leg of the arch, a stone that glowed brightly of four colors. Suddenly the shapes began pouring out of the entrance and gathering above him. He could not move, he could not speak—all he could do was stare at the dark figures as they swirled closer …

Malak Eben …

****

"Sam! SAM!"

Sam opened his eyes to see his grandfather Amos standing over him. He was still in his red flannel pajama bottoms and white t-shirt, and his neatly combed white hair had the ruffled look that only a pillow could create. The remains of the fire were glowing softly from the living room, but Sam could not feel its heat. He was still cold from the vividness of the dream.

"You were dreaming again," Amos put a hand on his forehead. "You were *screaming*."

"No—I—I'm not sure what it was about," Sam lied, rubbing the grogginess from his eyes. But he did know the dream. In fact, this was the third time he had woken up this way since moving to White Pine.

"Sam," Amos said, stopping to clear his throat. His voice was low and hushed. "I want you to know …" then he stopped, choosing not

Chapter Two: A Secret Club

to finish the sentence. "I will make you some tea. A cup or two always chases away the night demons." And he turned and left the room.

Soon the fire in the little living room was blazing again and the teapot began a low whistle. Sam accepted his cup of tea and sat as close to the fire as he could. The steam rose from the white mug thickly, and he tasted the strong liquid carefully while he stared at the crackling fire. It was good tea, as sweet and nearly as strong as the coffee Amos made, and he could feel the tension leaving him with every sip.

Amos sat down in the old creaking rocking chair next to him and sipped his tea silently while he rocked. Except for his white hair, Amos looked too young to be a grandfather. He was strong, and his face showed little signs of wrinkling or aging in the firelight.

Since his arrival, Sam and his grandfather hadn't really talked much, and when they did, it was about the weather, chores, or what was for dinner. Amos was rarely much more than quiet at best, but one could tell he wasn't weak by his voice. When he spoke, Sam thought the whole cabin rumbled just a bit. He wasn't mean, but he did seem to be concerned with where and when Sam went. Sam was rarely allowed out of the cabin after dark, and when he was, it was to get firewood or close the barn door.

When he had arrived at the station in White Pine, Amos was standing on the platform of the tiny station, much like the scene when his foster parents had left him. He wasn't told what Amos looked like, but it didn't matter because he recognized him right away. He was average height but dark from the sun, and he was carrying a bag, which he handed to Sam when he walked down the steps of the train car.

"You will be needing some different clothes," he had said awkwardly. In the bag his grandfather gave him oddly while still at the station, Sam found two new pairs of blue jeans and three t-shirts—blue, green, and black. Also in the bag were two dark blue flannel shirts with thick inner linings, and a blue sweatshirt. "These will keep you until winter starts."

For as long as he could remember, Sam had only worn jeans

Chapter Two: A Secret Club

outside the house twice in his life—once when he volunteered at a horse ranch, and another time when his friend let him borrow a pair when he stayed over. His foster mother did not believe in jeans, and Sam was made to wear khakis or a suit wherever he went. School had a uniform as well, so when he wasn't in pajamas, he was always dressed up.

Halfway through the second cup of tea, Sam felt his eyelids getting heavy, so he decided to head off to bed once again. He thanked his grandfather for the tea and slipped back into his room and under the covers. He planned to explore the path he had spotted behind Orvil's country store the next day. It would be a good chance to get out and explore ... something he hadn't done much of since he arrived.

The last thing he remembered before falling asleep was the crackling fire and Bush's face as he toppled to the ground into a puddle of his own drool ...

The next morning, Sam threw a few things into his backpack and headed out the door. He would clean out the barn and finish the other chores his grandfather wanted him to do after he got back. Today, he just needed to get out and get away from everything. Even back in Grand Rapids, he found the woods to be a place where he found peace and tranquility, from his parents and from life in general.

He walked to the edge of town where the sign ORVIL'S COUNTRY STORE dwarfed the tiny wood-sided building. The once-thriving gas depot and grocery stop was now quickly becoming an aging artifact of White Pine. Sam guessed it was because of the newer Iggy's Grocery down the street, luring town dwellers with its lower prices and promise of better selection.

Often he saw Mrs. Orvil knitting on the front porch of her storefront, peering at townspeople as they passed by. Not wanting to be a target of her gossip, Sam cut off into the woods a little early to catch the trail behind the store. Since many of the trees in the area were mostly made of dense white pines, they were incredibly difficult to walk through. Fortunately, Sam had planned ahead and found a break in the trees earlier in the week that he could use as a shortcut.

He veered off into the shortcut and immediately found the main

🌲🌲 Chapter Two: A Secret Club

trail just as the sun was creeping above the clouds that laid like a blanket over the horizon. The wind blew softly, forcing an occasional whisper through the pine branches. It was cool enough to require another layer, and he was glad he brought the flannel that Amos had given him.

He walked for what seemed like an hour before the trail ended in a particularly dense wall of brush. Looking to the sides, the brush wall continued as far as he could see in either direction without a break. He wasn't going to let it stop him, so Sam cinched up his backpack, took a deep breath, and pushed through the foliage, using his arm to cover his face as he walked. He could feel the brittle leaves poking at his neck and the stiff branches tugging at his clothing as he pushed through. He trudged for what seemed like twenty or so steps before the brush finally began to thin out.

Then it happened. Before he could stop himself, the ground beneath him disappeared and his body pitched forward into nothingness.

The moment his eyes opened was the same moment he felt a tug from his backpack that had suddenly caught his falling body and jerked him backward. The rock below his feet crumbled, and Sam flailed his arm backward in a desperate attempt to grab hold of something solid—and it did. He clung to the branch and pulled himself backward to level ground.

Once sure he was far enough away from the edge, he laid his head back and looked up at the sky, feeling his heart pounding loudly and his lungs racing shallow, quick breaths. His backpack dangled from its strap wedged into a crook in the tree above him.

What the heck just happened? his mind churned, but he already knew the answer. He had just about walked over the side of a cliff. The same strap that had given him so much grief the day before had now saved his life. It was a thought that made him shudder.

When his breathing slowed, he stood to his feet and, whispering a word of thanks to the backpack gods, untangled it from the tree. Then, feeling the unnerving unbalanced feeling of standing too close

Chapter Two: A Secret Club

to an edge, Sam sat once again to look at the scene around him.

The cliff was more like a canyon, or a smaller gorge, with a snake-like stream that flowed through its interior. There were cliffs on both sides, nearly a hundred feet high where he stood. Hawks circled lazily above him, looking for mice or the occasional careless rabbit.

Now that his heart was returning to a normal pace, he could hear the turbulent stream below as it rushed through the middle of the gorge. Downstream, the water gathered into a deeper pool at the end of the rapids where the tips of car-sized boulders poked through the surface, leaving the bulk of the rock submerged like a massive iceberg.

The more Sam looked around, the more he noticed how different the canyon looked from the rest of the forest. Here, the pines looked older and larger, having an almost ancient feel to them, and thick trunks touting branches that curved and twisted into craggy fists, and one in particular looking like an old witch uncurling her hands to release a spell.

Just to the right of him, Sam noticed a ledge about halfway down the rock face where an old-looking pine hung its weeping branches over the water below. He was sure the opening in the cliff was enclosed on all three sides, but he couldn't see far enough to see how deep it went. Either way, it looked strangely like someone created it, not like a natural force of the elements.

What was that strange indentation on the wall of the opening? Sam squinted through the shaky lenses of his binoculars to try and make out the image. It was rather small, but definitely out of place from the rest of the surrounding stone. Aside from its embossed outline, the colors were slightly different, and it seemed to reflect a bit of gloss in the morning sunlight. He took out a pencil and notebook from his backpack and he drew what he saw without taking his eyes off the curious indentation.

When he looked down, he was shocked at the image he drew. It looked vaguely like the same strange symbol from his dream—the same wing-like symbol he had been drawing since the school year started.

Chapter Two: A Secret Club

Then suddenly, from somewhere close behind him, a branch snapped, startling him so badly he jerked his hand, which sent his pencil tumbling over the side of the cliff to the rocks below.

"Hello Samuel," said an instantly familiar voice.

Sam spun around to see Emma, the pretty girl from geography, standing not more than ten feet away from him. He peered open-mouthed at her.

Emma Sterling was the daughter of the president of the White Pine Copper Trust, and granddaughter to the founder of White Pine Copper Mining Company before it went out of business, but not before leaving the Sterling family with a good chunk of the remaining assets—and everyone knew it. She just didn't flaunt it like most wealthy families did.

Emma sat in front of Sam in class, but never said a word to him until now. Not even "hello" in the hallway. Sam had caught her smiling at him on occasion, and had wondered at first if she had a crush on him, but more likely it was that she was just silently laughing at his awkwardness.

"Nice weather today, isn't it?" she said, but Sam was looking at her faded jeans with a hole in the right knee.

"How did you come up on me like that?" Sam said suddenly, his voice shaking a bit.

"You looked deep in thought," she retorted quickly. Then, matching Sam's threatening tone, she said, "These woods are for anyone who wants to walk through them."

"How did you find me?" He stared at her, wondering how she got through the dense pines so quietly.

"I followed you," she mimicked Sam's expression. "You know, if you are trying to lose the world, you may want to look behind you once in a while to see if someone is following."

"I just thought—well I just came out here to see where the path—"

"Hold your horses, Samuel. I am not here to take your alone time from you. I only want to talk to you for a minute," she said, and

Chapter Two: A Secret Club

flopped on the pine floor next to him. "Pretty neat place," she said, scooting suddenly closer.

"Yeah, I thought so." Sam felt his heart beating again.

She looked at him suddenly, as if concerned.

"Do you like White Pine?" she said. "We haven't had someone new in my grade since the mines closed …"

"Uh, yeah, it's great here," he lied. "Doesn't your dad own the Sterling mines?"

She snorted.

"Yeah, I supposed he does, although, much good it does if there isn't any copper in them…"

He knew that about White Pine. You could see the evidence of the once upcoming town all around—new subdivisions filled with empty houses, a half-built pharmacy now only a skeleton of steel and masonry, and a brand new elementary school building that lacked general upkeep as chin-high weeds licked its brick exterior.

It was a new ghost town, of sorts, a remnant of its former glory days when the mines produced so much copper that the statue of Julian Lawrence in the town square was eventually plated in it. It didn't seem to bother the residents much, however, as they always seemed to have a smile on their face as they went about their daily business.

"So what does your family do now?"

Emma looked at him strangely.

"Well, my father does … research for the government … and my mom, well, she is one of the best cooks you will ever meet."

"Is that an invitation to dinner?" he joked awkwardly.

"Of course it is! You will have the best chicken pot pie and biscuits ever … I promise."

He glanced at her quickly, her curls falling over part of her face so that it was concealed from him. Was she flirting with him? No. He was too plain for her. She looked like the type that would have a football jock's arm draped around her shoulders. But why did she follow him here? It seemed a little strange—perhaps even dangerous to show up in the middle of the woods with a new guy from a different town.

🌲🌲 Chapter Two: A Secret Club

"I want you to join our group," she said suddenly, as if she had just pried open his brain and pulled out his thoughts.

"A group?" Sam said. "Like a club or something?"

She scooted closer to him again, her tan boots scraping on the rock. "Well, sort of. It's more than that though." Her voice was low and dramatic. Sam wondered if this was all a big joke and he was the victim.

"You have to tell me more than that," he rolled his eyes playfully.

"I can't—that is until you agree to join us. Then you can meet everyone else."

"Who's in this club of yours?"

"Can't tell you that either," she sighed. "Once you say yes, I can tell you more."

"Aren't we a little old to be having secret clubs?" he chided. "I gave that up when I was ten."

"Suit yourself," she said quickly, then got to her feet suddenly. "This is an invitation-only secret club, Samuel."

Sam watched her as she turned away, her red hair swishing with her stride. Instantly, something made him wish he hadn't been so short.

"Wait, don't go," he called out suddenly, surprised with his own words.

She turned on her heels and walked back, a smile on her face.

"I knew you were too curious to ignore it," she said.

Something told him her dramatic exit was part of her plan.

"So what *can* you tell me about this secret club?" he pressed.

"You like history, right?" She seemed pleased now that he was paying attention.

"I suppose. What does tha—"

"Let me finish and I will tell you," she huffed.

"Now ... before I was interrupted ... the 'club' is kind of like an ancient secret organization, just on a somewhat larger scale." Her eyes glowed like turquoise-colored diamonds in the sun.

"You mean like the Masons?" he asked, rather uninterested.

Emma rolled her eyes playfully.

34

Chapter Two: A Secret Club

"No. Not really," she said. "More like—well … there really is no comparison."

What kind of group was she talking about? Was it some sort of cult? Either way, curiosity began to well up within him. He had always been one to dive in head first and suffer consequences later. Sometimes it paid off to investigate, and sometimes it got him in trouble. But he would play coy.

"I will sleep on it," he said mechanically.

She stood to leave once again, but turned and looked squarely at him, all humor gone from her eyes.

"Samuel, you must understand … if you choose to join us, it's not a small commitment—it's something that stays with you for life."

And then she turned and marched into the deepening sun.

He squinted into the light, certain he had just dreamed the whole conversation with Emma Sterling. She had popped into one of his daydreams and flipped her auburn red hair into his face so that he could smell strawberries. Then she had disappeared. He had been in White Pine too long without civilized contact. He would likely start talking to himself any day now.

Did she really say "for life"? What kind of a club—or whatever it was—didn't allow its members to leave? Cults, maybe. Maybe a drug operation, or the mob. No wait, maybe a resurrected sect of the Knights of Camelot … and they were going to dub him Sir Samuel of White Pine.

The strange thing, however, was that they wanted him. What was it that they wanted? His good looks? Nope, that was a stretch. His love for legend and fantasy? Maybe, but there were dozens more like him. His grades were mediocre at best, although he knew he was personally capable of much higher. Perhaps the club had had trouble keeping participants in the past from sheer boredom. Maybe they chose him out of a lack of options.

He looked around at his place of solitude, away from prying eyes or judgmental voices. It wasn't the City, but it had its own sort of hidden peace and beauty about it, minus the double-chocolate lattes from Kava House, that is.

🌲🌲 Chapter Two: A Secret Club

He was still unsure how Emma had followed him so easily, and it gave him an uneasy feeling. She must have been waiting pretty early in the morning to catch him leaving. It wasn't so out of place, however, because ever since arriving in White Pine, he had felt as though he was being watched everywhere he went. He understood being the newest one in town, but even now, prying eyes would make the hairs stand up on the back of his neck.

Just last week it had been at Iggy's. He couldn't see who since they ducked out of the store before he could catch a glance, but they had followed him from aisle to aisle as he shopped for some necessities Amos had asked him to pick up. Either way, there were weird people in this strange town, and he wanted no part of it. It was the main reason he had rushed through his grandfather's chores every Saturday and disappeared into the woods—to leave people behind. This spot in the woods was the most serene he had found yet ... and the most dangerous. The gorge was indeed very beautiful, that is, when it wasn't luring its admirers off the edge of a cliff.

Chapter Three
Timothy Becker

The following day was Sunday, and Sam knew that Amos was going to make him go to church again. It wasn't that he disliked going, it was just that this church did not seem to understand the meaning of time, hunger, and boredom. That, and the only other time he had been to church was Easter Sunday with Phillip's mother, Wanita Forrester, who, just before she died, thought it best to see him converted immediately.

She had showed up in her boat-like Lincoln when he was seven, pushed her son Phillip out of the way and barged up to Sam's room, forcing him out of bed and into one of his nicer sport jackets.

The service went for hours, it seemed, and the whole time Wanita pinched the underside of his arm whenever he moved just the slightest.

The thing that bothered him the most, however, was that on the way out of the sanctuary, Wanita whispered something to one of the deacons, who promptly whisked Sam to a little room where he told him how God was going to punish him for his sins by putting him in a giant lake of fire filled with screaming people wishing they could

Chapter Three: Timothy Becker

have chosen more wisely. Sam couldn't lie, it did scare him, but more from the church's wrath than God's. For nearly a year following, he had nightmares that resembled a Botticelli painting he had studied in Medieval Art at his old school. Since that day, he hadn't been back to church until moving to White Pine.

Walking out on the front porch, Sam saw his grandfather's old red truck backing out of the barn, a cloud of dust chugging along with it. It was quite the antique, no doubt from the early sixties, except for the amateur paint job, which stopped at the rust-colored hood. He wondered if Amos only took Big Red out on Sundays, with the possible exception of especially large snowstorms, for which he typically dug out an old snowmobile buried in the dusty barn.

Since the church building was on the other side of town, they had to drive instead of walk. The only other time Amos used a vehicle was when he needed groceries or supplies from town, and that wasn't but once every other week or so.

The church was a large converted brick mansion that, when entering, looked like you were going into a haunted house. He knew little of the place—that it had been passed down through multiple generations by a wealthy lord from somewhere in Europe to the first mayor of White Pine, who eventually passed it on to the church.

When they pulled up to the large brick home-converted-church, Sam immediately spotted Emma talking with a thick boy with spiky blond hair. He peered at the two talking intensely, guessing the boy was the geeky kid from his sixth period English class named Gus.

Sam didn't know him personally, but he knew that he was only nicknamed 'Gus,' by everyone except for the black-haired girl who called him 'Grimace,' but his real name was Constantine, named after his Great Grandfather Harper Constantine Ablesworth, one of the founders of White Pine. Gus's father, Colonel James Ablesworth, was now the City Council Chair.

Sam had seen on numerous occasions the Colonel stop by the cabin and talk politics with his grandfather out on the porch. It was an odd friendship even for the small town residents of White Pine—but Sam could tell they enjoyed each other's company.

Chapter Three: Timothy Becker

As Sam climbed the enormous steps to the church, he looked over to where Gus and Emma had been, but they were nowhere to be seen. It was then that he felt someone slip something into his back pocket and thought he saw a flash of red disappear into the crowd of churchgoers as they milled about in the lobby.

He reached into his back pocket and pulled out a small slip of paper tightly folded.

Chivler's 5:30 Friday it read.

Chivler's was the old bookstore where the old kook owner stared at Sam every time he walked past. It must be the first meeting Emma was hinting to. That is, if he was interested.

The truth was that he still wasn't too sure he wanted to be a part of it, whatever "it" was. He had never really committed to anything for life before, and that's the way he liked it. And to date, life hadn't really committed anything to him either.

He sat in the padded seat, and for a moment he watched everyone around him. Emma and the chunky boy were nowhere to be seen, but there were also quite a few people standing in the room still talking, shaking hands, and laughing at each other's jokes.

As the service began in what used to be the mansion's old sitting room, the minister stood at the podium, a huge stone fireplace behind him. Sam could tell today was going to be different than the other services he had attended here, not that he had attended many. There was no bearded guy with a guitar leading worship, no special music, and no long-winded prayers as normal.

Instead, the thin, aging pastor slowly raised his hands outward, which all members interpreted as the instruction to quiet down and take their seats. When the building was silent, he bowed his head slightly, closing his eyes, and reached out again toward the congregation.

Sam, who had seen this before, bowed his head with the others in unison, expecting the long-winded weekly prayer for "hope" and "new life" for the citizens of White Pine and the surrounding communities, and for the "safety and empowering" of those missionaries around the world. He had never truly prayed before, but rather listened to

Chapter Three: Timothy Becker

others as they prayed, using strange phrases like "hedge of protection" and "spirit poured upon us" in their conversations with God. And sometimes, when the prayers were extra long, his mind would drift away to another quest in Middle Earth, where he would fight dragons and fierce creatures of evil with the other warriors. It was a good distraction—one that could keep him entertained for hours.

But this time, Pastor Jefferies' prayer was short. No one made a sound while he prayed. The only noise was the deep breathing in and out of the congregants in the room, and the occasional mutter of agreement with the minister's words.

"As we gather today, a special day of thanks and honor to God ..." the Pastor began, his voice cutting through the congregation, who seemed too deep into their own prayers to hear him, "... we must remember that we are a community that is dedicated to the service of the Lord, and in Him, we can find strength. If we remain faithful, we may be called his servants, a blessed position in His kingdom.

"This day—is a day of remembrance," he continued, "for who you are and what you have done for us, Lord. We commune together today, knowing that our responsibility is to serve you and our neighbors in need, to live as a community and not for ourselves. We know our time here on Earth in short, Father, but we ask for the ability to fight the good fight of faith, taking on those spiritual enemies that are against us, that deceive us, and that cheat us out of our joy here in your Creation. Give us strength, Lord, we ask in your name, and let us enjoy this celebration. In your name, Amen."

Somehow, Pastor Jefferies' prayer stirred Sam down deep. It wasn't enough to make him come forward and get on his knees like so many had before during the altar calls at the end of the service, but for the first time, he felt some spiritual connection inside him, and he didn't know how to respond.

The whole congregation stood and began talking again, and some immediately began filing out into the mansion's old dining room, where Sam could hear the distinctive sound of plates and glasses clinking together.

Sam was tempted momentarily to go and track down Emma, but

Chapter Three: Timothy Becker

then his grandfather grabbed him by the shoulders and pulled him over to where a few people he didn't know, and one he did know, were talking quietly. Among them were Miss Karpatch and the mayor of White Pine.

"Sam, I would like you to meet Mr. Phillis, the mayor of White Pine," Amos said, holding his hand out toward the man Sam had seen on a few occasions sitting on the front porch with his grandfather, much like the Colonel did, drinking coffee and talking in hushed tones.

Coffee was the beverage of choice around White Pine, much to Sam's delight. He loved coffee, like most of the town, although they didn't seem to care much for the high-charged espresso drinks like he did. Either way, there was a steaming pot on every porch in the morning, in every church service he had been to, and at every football game every Friday night.

"Yes, sir, I have seen you before at my house. You like your coffee with plenty of cream and sugar." Sam held out his hand to meet the meaty hands of the large man in the black suit and dark red collared shirt. His long black hair was as dark as the suit he wore, and his tapered beard showed signs of just being trimmed that morning.

When Mr. Phillis came to visit Amos, he was almost always dressed the same, which made the meeting so much more peculiar, since Amos was almost always in a flannel and jeans. They had never included Sam in their conversations, and Sam had never formally met the mayor face to face. But today, he seemed genuinely interested in meeting Sam.

"Observant, aren't you?" the mayor said gruffly, but a smile crept to the corner of his mouth. "I suppose you will join us one of these evenings?"

Sam didn't really care to have coffee with the mayor, but he nodded anyway. Perhaps he would be able to find out what was so secretive about their conversations.

Miss Karpatch seemed content enough to leave him alone today, which suited Sam just fine. She only shook his hand and then made her way to the numerous small tables in the dining room.

Chapter Three: Timothy Becker

Sam followed his grandfather to one of the tables near the large oak cabinets filled with ornate china. One of the women immediately brought them a huge basket of bread and butter and filled their glasses with iced tea. Sam had never actually been in the dining room before, and he was surprised that it fit everyone from the service comfortably. Overhead, delicate glass chandeliers twinkled softly as more congregants filed in and sat down, each one talking and laughing happily.

"Today is a day of communion," his grandfather leaned over and said quietly to him.

Soon the women brought out huge dishes of food—meatloaf, baked and mashed potatoes, corn, salads, and more bread than Sam had ever seen. The smell hit his nose before the food even touched the table, and immediately his mouth began to water.

It wasn't that Amos wasn't a good cook; it was just that he hadn't had a meal quite like this in forever. It was a feast fit for a king, and the woman who set the huge bowl of potatoes in front of him with a genuine smile made him feel like he was one.

As they ate, Sam began to feel more at ease while people laughed and talked about the crazy Northern weather and the Festival of Northern Lights the following weekend. He listened to the legends that floated around the table.

"...remnants of the great spiritual battle before the great flood..." an older balding man Sam knew as Abraham gestured animatedly. Sam tried not to stare at his oversized thin-wire glasses that looked ready to pitch forward off his nose. "The borealis are a reminder of the spiritual battle that rages on even today. Angels wielding their great swords against the forces of Darkness ... demons, and all those that seek to oppose the Creator who made them."

"Is that why we have the Festival?" a young boy with tousled blond hair asked as he looked up from his mountainous portion of mashed potatoes.

The bald man smiled.

Chapter Three: Timothy Becker

"It is, yes. We celebrate the fact that we have spiritual forces that continue to fight for Creation—for humanity."

Sam listened as other old men chimed in and defended their stories of great warriors of "Light" fighting the Lords of Darkness right there in White Pine, leaving behind ancient relics that have yet to be found.

*Warriors of Light…Demons of the Dark…*he thought as he thumbed the slip of paper that had been slipped into his pocket. *Crazy old men and their stories.*

That was the other thing he had come to realize about White Pine. It was a deeply spiritual place, unlike anywhere he had ever been. He couldn't put his finger on it, but it was strange that this little backward mining town was the only place he knew of that celebrated the Festival of Light.

The town already showed signs of preparation for the big event. It was strange, such a small town going to so much trouble, but it would be some excitement to break up the otherwise dull day-to-day of White Pine.

The town offered virtually nothing for the visitor, except perhaps for the festival once a year. For Sam, after schoolwork and chores, his typical routine involved holing up in his room to avoid the strange townspeople. A cup of coffee and a good fantasy book were much more normal company.

If he decided to go, he would be meeting Emma right around the time the festival started. Perhaps that was the plan … a merciful attempt to get him to come out of his shell and join the rest of the community. They were on a mission of intervention, and he was their humanitarian project.

When his grandfather wasn't looking, he pulled the slip of paper out and read it once again. Chivler's. There would be plenty of people there, he assumed, in the middle of Main Street, partaking in the festival activities. If they were going to kidnap him and force him into a cult, it would be difficult to do so in the middle of a throng of people.

Chapter Three: Timothy Becker

He chuckled to himself. The thought of Emma and Gus trying to stuff him into a van was amusing. They would force-feed him until he was plump like the large boy, then they would roast him over a fire while they sprinkled him with paprika.

A cult? There was no way Emma and Gus were capable of doing such a thing ... at least not alone.

After the communion dinner and another silent ride home in the old pickup, Sam got to work on his paper. He wondered why his history teacher, Mr. Wilson, was requiring an essay so early in the year, but he wasn't going to protest. He was always good with essays, and it happened to be his favorite subject anyway.

Amos was nowhere to be found; he seemed to know that Sam needed to be alone to finish homework. As he worked on his essay, he rubbed his overfilled stomach, thinking of the hospitality of the ladies at church. He had eaten entirely too many potatoes and buttered rolls, and it was unlikely he would be hungry at all for dinner. But just in case, the ladies from church sent him and Amos home with plenty of leftovers.

It was strange that a church would eat so lavishly for their communion, like a family sitting down to dinner. Communion at Wanita's church was cold and rigid, much like the feeling the congregants gave you the minute you walked through the doors. Wanita wouldn't let him take communion that day anyway, as she sternly explained it was for those that were "right with God"—not for foolish boys with foolish notions.

It was that same judgmental feeling he received every day living with Sylvia, so he was not at all intimidated. She was the master at manipulation and guilt, and it drove him to despise her more as the years dragged on.

But Amos's church was different. They were never pushy or judgmental that he could tell. They always smiled and welcomed him, even if he never cared to sing the songs or listen to the sermons.

He still didn't understand their church lingo, and the prayer before communion was no exception. It was like they had their own ancient language—like reading from an Elvish scroll or something.

Chapter Three: Timothy Becker

Some words were just downright ridiculous ... what in the world did "consecrated" mean?

But the words meant something to the preacher and to the congregants ... including his grandfather Amos. It was something they believed in passionately, a faith in someone or something they had never seen before ... and that was foreign to him.

****

As Sam sleepily waded through the crowded halls of the tiny high school the following afternoon, he found Bush waiting for him at Sam's locker. His locker door was standing open and the bully's size eleven shoe was digging at the binding of a now-destroyed geography book on the floor. It didn't take a genius to know that the book came from Sam's locker, the bent door obviously having been pried open.

This time there were no escape routes to avert the clueless bully, so Sam did something he had never done before. He casually set his books down on the floor and prepared to fight. There was no more running now. He would have to face Bush head on, right here in the hallway, in the middle of the school.

Bloodthirsty students were already gathering as if they had been waiting for this fight since Sam had first stepped foot in the school. A semi-circle quickly formed, closing up the chance for a quick escape. It was just him and Bush, the dimwitted jock-wannabe, and he was out for blood.

"Missed ya on Friday, pretty boy," he sneered at Sam as he leaned heavily against the lockers.

"I bet you did, Bush," Sam said dangerously. "I went looking for you to say I was sorry for knocking you over in your own drool, but there was no smell of butt anywhere to be found."

Bush's face flushed beet red as a few laughs and giggles went through the crowd of students. Sam knew he had done it now.

"That's it, punk. I have had it with you being here," he snorted angrily. "You city trash all think you are better than us, and I'm here to tell you that it's me who runs this place."

Chapter Three: Timothy Becker

"Funny, I figured you were the 'cleanup' type, since your dad runs the trash route."

More laughs ran through the crowd.

"You're going to pay for that, pretty boy."

Sam had run out of things to say, and he could see that Bush was done talking anyway as the bully's fist started to clench up. This was the moment he had been waiting for since school started. It was inevitable, so he balled up his own fist as he had practiced in his room so many times before that moment.

He knew there was only a short window between the element of surprise and getting a hook to the face, so at that moment, Sam decided to take his chance, swinging as hard as he could right at Bush's pig-like nose.

He put everything he had into that punch. From the moment he sent it flying, the room and all inhabitants disappeared from sight. Only he and the bushy boy remained in an epic slow-motion battle of reflexes. He could see where his punch was going to hit, a flabby spot on the side of Bush's peach fuzz cheek, and he could anticipate his target reeling backward from the force of the blow, then lying on the floor in complete shock. Sam would have won his respect, and that of the rest of the school.

But as most hopeful visions go, it would not turn out that way.

The punch did go where it was supposed to, but the surprised bully was too quick and managed to fall backward enough to miss the brunt of the throw. Sam nearly fell into him from the force of his own punch, but Bush merely shoved him backward into the lockers. As Sam fell, the oversized boy was instantly on top of him, throwing punch after punch until he was satisfied with the blood that covered his entire face. Those who were laughing now cheered and hooted at every blow.

Finally, as the bell rang for class, the bushy-haired brute stopped his pummeling, scooped up his torn books for class and waved at the savage crowd on his way to the Language Arts room.

Sam looked up at the ceiling, afraid to move for fear of seeing the damage. He felt the dull pain on the back of his head from the force

Chapter Three: Timothy Becker

of the blows against the tile floor and the trickle of blood making its way down his earlobe.

He just wanted to close his eyes and beam himself back to Grand Rapids and Kava House for a latte—maybe sneak into a matinee with his best friends Joel and Dalton, or maybe even church with Bruce's mother—anything to get away from this backwards school and their barbaric ways.

****

As Sam lay motionless on the floor, he began to wonder if anyone was going to stop and check to see if he was alive or if he would be left alone to bleed to death. It would be a likely end—alone, having just made the decision to meet Emma and find out what her club was all about.

His question of help was answered by a muffled scuffle of feet near his head, and then someone stroking his head softly.

"Looks like you got it pretty bad there pretty boy," a voice said quietly in his ear. Sam didn't respond, nor could he see who was talking to him, partially from the smeared blood dripping in his eyes. He only knew it was a girl.

She and two other people helped him to his feet, and while he wasn't sure exactly what happened next, he heard loud murmuring from some of the teachers in the hallway rushing to his side. The girl let go of him, but another hand helped lead him down the hallway to the nurse's station.

"It doesn't appear to be too deep of a cut ... and his nose doesn't seem to be broken," the portly nurse proclaimed from inside the tiny clinic.

Miss Karpatch, who had helped Sam into the room, now stood beside him, looking him over as if she were peering through a microscope. "I think you are right," she said strangely.

"But you must look into who started this mess," the nurse said, suddenly angry. "This is going to end up with one of these students getting a concussion—or worse."

Chapter Three: Timothy Becker

"What happened, Sam?" Miss Karpatch turned her attention to him, at which point Principal Curtis suddenly walked into the room stiffly, peering over the scene from his thin black-rimmed glasses.

"I don't think it matters what happened, Sarah," the balding administrator proclaimed as if answering her question for him. Then he pretended to dig for something important in his pocket. "He started a fight, and now he's reaping the consequences."

"Oh spare the tough talk, Tom. Look at him. Which one do you think was defending himself?"

Principal Curtis hoisted himself up to full height.

"We have zero tolerance in this school, Sarah, and both of them will serve a suspension, so it really doesn't matter, does it?"

"Yes it does, Tom. You know that zero tolerance thing is just a bureaucratic ploy. A bunch of suits sitting around making up tough-sounding rules. We can't expect these kids to go around defenseless."

Principal Curtis shrugged as he wiped his glasses with his napkin. "Well ... we have no way of telling who started it, so it is what it is." Then he turned toward the door, placing his glasses back up on his nose, and walked briskly out of the room.

Sam could tell that both the nurse and Miss Karpatch were fuming as they all watched him walk out of the clinic. He was glad someone was on his side.

"Don't worry about him," Miss Karpatch said quietly. Her voice showed compassion. "I will take care of the suspension, and you can forget what I said about reporting you. Just make sure you at least try to diffuse the situation next time instead of making it worse."

Then she patted him on the shoulder and turned to walk out the door, but stopped momentarily.

"Sam, bullies are kind of like politicians in a way—the more their egos are fed the less violent they become."

"Thanks," he told her through the blood dripping down his nose.

Fortunately, the nurse let Sam stay in the room until after the last period of the day. She dabbed the small cut above his eye and applied a bandage to stop the bleeding, then gave him an ice pack for the large bump on the back of his head. He promised her he

Chapter Three: Timothy Becker

would go to the doctor to get checked out, but the moment he was out the door he tossed away the note she had given him to give to his grandfather. He could take care of himself.

Chapter Four
wollemia nobilia

Sam watched the soft amber and yellow festival lights glow over the treetops as he walked toward downtown White Pine. Even after five o'clock, the fall sun still bore down on the streets. It was going to be an unusually hot, muggy evening, and the fuzzy ring around the sun promised of rain in the near future.

He hadn't been much of anywhere since the Bush incident—partially to avoid him, and partially because he didn't care to see anyone else. If it had been up to him, he would have barricaded himself up in his room for the rest of the school year, not out of fear, but anger—not toward anyone in particular. Maybe he could try independent study, or even an online school.

It was only curiosity that drew him out tonight, and the promise of finding out what the "club" was all about. Or perhaps it was partly to see Emma once again.

Thankfully, Bush had been suspended from school for two weeks, and thanks to Miss Karpatch, Sam was only on probation. Even better, since Sam was not the only one bullied by Bush in the

Chapter Four: wollemia nobilia

school, no one else really missed his cotton-head walking through the corridors either. Sam even noticed he commanded a little more respect for the incident. Not that he cared much for the attention, but nearly everyone in his classes would greet him when he walked in. Apparently he was the only one to stand up to Bush in quite a while.

But tonight being the kickoff to a large week-long festival of White Pine, cotton-head was certain to be there, strutting his elephant-sized haunches through the middle of Main Street. There was no telling what would happen if he caught Sam at the festival, and there was no amount of deep-fried cheesecake that would pacify him.

Sam knew he may end the night stuffed in a trashcan with another blood plastering, but he was going to brave it anyway.

He let the slip of paper fall through his fingers back to the confines of his pocket. He was almost there. Time to figure out what this was about …

As he approached town, Sam glanced behind him at the skyline. A line of clouds was beginning to thicken into giant chocolate marshmallow-like puffs just over the horizon as the sun dipped behind the trees. The massive front seemed to extend on forever like a huge advancing army, and Sam wondered if the evening was going to be cut short due to weather.

Crossing Main Street, he entered the throng of people that made up the festival goers. He was amazed at how many people were packed into the narrow streets, standing in lines for rides, eating from the numerous food vendors that laced the street, and playing carnival games.

Folk and Bluegrass music played loudly from the stage in the center of Main Street, and there was even a small Ferris wheel in front of Carter's Hardware Store.

He was stunned. What was once just a few old brick buildings and a marble bank in the center of town the day before was now a thriving center of lights, music, and nightlife.

He walked past the street vendors who were cooking furiously on their grills, and the smell of grilled steak and deep-fried goodies

Chapter Four: wollemia nobilia

filled his nostrils, reminding his protesting stomach he hadn't eaten dinner yet.

He watched the pastry vendors wrapping up as many meat pies as they could in foil, but still lines seemed like they were growing outside the little tents and booths.

I should have brought some money, he thought, doing his best to hold back the hunger pains.

Sam stared at all of the shops lining Main Street selling shoes, jewelry, and homemade pottery. He hadn't noticed until now, but most of the vendors and shopkeepers were dressed in old, colorfully stitched clothing, as though they were handmade from the renaissance era. The outfits seemed to mimic the general mood of the entire festival, with many of the younger festival-goers dressed the same way but not quite as authentic—wearing faux leather boots and colorful robes that billowed as they dragged their parents from attraction to attraction. To Sam, it looked like the beginnings of a medieval circus.

Mr. Partich stood at a little table outside his wood carvings shop, *Partrich's Collectibles*, in a red and green quilted shirt, tweed pants and a multi-colored hat, and old lady Cataran of Odds and Ends Antique Store was peddling a table of strange rusted metal statues wearing what looked like a long quilt-like dress made with every color and pattern of the rainbow.

The inside of Chivler's looked dark from the window, but at second glance, Sam caught a glimpse of two older men arguing at the front register. As he approached the glass storefront, the old man in front of the counter snatched his hood over his head and rushed out the front door, looking very determined to leave without being seen.

As he pushed past Sam, he thought he recognized the man from around town—of what he could see of him under the hood. He watched the man disappear down the street away from town, careful to avoid groups of people as they made their way toward the festival.

It's five-fifteen, I'm still early. He glanced at the sterling silver watch his foster mother Sylvia had given him. Normally, his foster mother only gave gifts that somehow made her look good as well, and the

Chapter Four: wollemia nobilia

watch was no exception. But this watch, for some reason, Sam had become attached to since leaving the City. Perhaps it was because it was one of the last mementos to remind him of where he came from. Even if his life growing up wasn't that happy, it was still considered home, and Sylvia was the only mother he knew.

There was no sign of Emma or the old store owner behind the counter as he entered the dimly lit building. If she or whoever else from the "secret" group was in there, they were waiting for him. If he was going to find out what it was all about, the time was now.

****

Chivler's was an old, dusty bookshop that Sam was surprised was still around, given the size of the once-thriving town. The only time he had been in the store was with Amos to donate some books, but even then it had given him the creeps from the moment he walked in the door.

The store owner, Fenton Chivler, was most likely in his seventies, but was still spry for an old man. He had a long, bushy mustache that extended downward to his mouth, and small spectacles that hung on the tip of his abnormally large nose.

The store hadn't changed much in the few months that Sam had been in White Pine, and with the exception of the small display with copies of the semi-latest best sellers, the store was full of old dusty books. There were stacks of every type of book lining the walls and throughout the middle of the store, and from what Sam could see, they were titles of which most people weren't aware.

He wandered down the aisle labeled Ancient History, looking at the titles in various languages, the smell of old pages and dust making him fight back a monstrous sneeze.

The old wood floor creaked and groaned as Sam walked carefully toward the center of the aisle, his eyes drifting to the old bookshelves themselves. Carved on the front of the ornate shelf was a flying creature clutching what looked like a snake with a bird's head in its

🌲🌲 Chapter Four: wollemia nobilia

claws. The creature looked as though it were about to eat its prey. Another carving held a creature that looked somewhat human, but then again birdlike as well, with its wings spread out to its sides as if embracing whomever walked through the aisles.

Sam walked through the tight rows of two-story shelves that extended almost to the ceiling, glancing at the strange worn titles as he passed. *Curse of Leviathan* was one that caught his eye, and he paused briefly to run his fingers over the embossed serpent on the binding.

"One can bring harm to himself by holding sneezes back, m' lad," said a voice directly behind and to the left of him. It startled Sam so badly that it made him swallow another sneeze entirely.

"How may I aid you, good sir? Or were you just aiming to spew mucus on my antiquated collection of medieval writings?"

The old man stepped out from the shelves carrying an oversized brown hardcover book covered with dust and wearing a dark tweed sport jacket and light colored khakis that looked as dusty as the shelves around them.

Did I just step into sixteenth century England? Sam chuckled to himself.

"I—ah, well, I was just looking around," Sam tried to act like he was browsing the vast bookcases casually.

"Is there anything in particular that I can help you find?" Chivler said. His gray hair and mustache made him resemble a slightly less insane Albert Einstein.

Truthfully, this was the first time that Sam had actually met Chivler, having only seen him from afar, but his personality fit perfectly with Sam's perceptions.

Glancing quickly at his watch, he noticed the time was nearing 5:30, but there were no signs Emma had even entered the store yet. Perhaps she and the chunky boy were going to pop out of an old trap door somewhere and drag him to the basement. Maybe Chivler was involved in it and was distracting him until the right moment.

"Uh—actually, sir, I was wondering if you had any books about this area … maybe something older, like a historical reference?" he said at last, thinking quickly about a book report that was due in Mr.

Chapter Four: wollemia nobilia

Wilson's class the Tuesday following the week of the Light Festival.

Chivler turned and set the huge dusty volume down on an old wooden chair behind him.

"Hmmm …" he stroked his mustache, which after a moment curved into a modest smile. "I may have something that would suit your needs," and he motioned for Sam to follow him.

Chivler led the way halfway down the middle aisle of the stacks, turning back every so often to make sure Sam was following. As they moved deeper into the store, again he felt another sneeze coming on. Sam plugged his nose and swallowed.

"Let it out, lad. We don't want to have an accident right here in the middle of the aisle," he laughed oddly, making Sam cringe a bit. *He has good hearing for an old guy*, he thought.

Suddenly, the shopkeeper halted in front of a section of particularly large books, and shielding his eyes from the yellowish lanterns above him, seemed to take abnormally long to search for a specific title.

"Ah!" he exclaimed. "Go get me the ladder, lad."

Sam obeyed, and soon Chivler was huffing up the wooden rungs, stopping every other rung to catch his breath. When he was near the top, he immediately pulled out a small soft cover book curiously hidden between the large hard covers. With the book came a cloud of dust that descended upon Sam, sending him into an uncontrolled sneezing fit at the foot of the ladder, which was only quelled when the dust began to settle and the bookkeeper was down the ladder once again.

"Here it is, here it is." The old man handed Sam the dust-covered book. It was dark red leather and had a soft binding, making it look more like a journal than a book.

"You would be right if you were thinking this isn't a book." The shopkeeper seemed to hear his thoughts again. "This would be a historical account of White Pine and its development," he said.

Sam flipped through the fragile pages carefully. The paper was brittle and discolored, obviously printed many years ago. There were

Chapter Four: wollemia nobilia

diagrams, handwritten notes, and strange blots throughout, as if the author wasn't careful with his ink. Why would Chivler entrust him with such a treasure? Regardless of the contents, it was no doubt rare and very valuable.

"How old is it?" Sam asked, noticing that some of the pages from the middle of the journal had been carefully removed. He thumbed the remnants of the missing pages, noting the almost perfect incision in the paper. Someone didn't want those pages to be seen.

"I cannot give you an exact date, I am afraid," the shopkeeper frowned. "What I can tell you is that I know it was written sometime after the town was established in eighteen sixty-two—before a fire destroyed the town, killing many of the townspeople."

"How much is the book, sir?" Sam asked. He had no money on him then, but he still had a few hundred dollars that was left over from what Phillip and Sylvia had given him.

The bookkeeper looked sideways at Sam.

"It is priceless, m' lad, and to sell it would be an act of dishonor to this town ... considering its historical value."

He wondered what Chivler's intention was—did he want him to take the book or just look at it?

Chivler leveled his eyes, his voice lower and showing urgency as he motioned toward the door.

"Take it boy. You are a man of history, are you not? Return it when you are finished. Now I have things to do, lad, so why don't you go meet up with your friends?"

Friends? What friends? Who was he talking about? Sam glanced toward the door, then back at Chivler. This was beginning to become a wild goose chase. Where was Emma?

"Thank you sir," Sam said frowning, carefully putting the book in his backpack and hurrying toward the door. Then he stopped and turned back toward the bookkeeper.

"How did you know my friends were waiting for me?"

The old bookkeeper smiled, his thick mustache only allowing his bottom teeth to show.

"I suppose there could be another reason three powdered sugar-

Chapter Four: wollemia nobilia

covered young people would be peering in the window at you, but something tells me otherwise..."

Sam turned to see Emma, Gus Ablesworth, and a girl of Asian descent holding an array of fried foods and juggling drinks outside of the front window. Emma's eyes lit up when Sam looked at her.

"Those look healthy," Sam smirked as he joined them on the sidewalk. The air seemed more humid than it did earlier, making him wish he had chosen the t-shirt over the long-sleeves.

"What makes you think that?" she mimicked his sarcasm and handed him a pastry. "These babies are absolutely nutritious—no fat or cholesterol, only vitamins. Plus, I know you are hungry. I could hear your stomach rumbling from outside the window."

"Well thanks," he said, taking a big bite of the warm pie. White Pine was known for some of the best pastries in the North, and had won many county bakery contests over the years. Some people said that the secret ingredient was the copper that still ran through the water. Tonight, it was especially tasty, or he was exceptionally hungry.

"So, are you going to introduce us, or are we just going to watch Gus eat pie all night?" the Asian girl snickered.

Emma nearly choked on her bite. "Oh! I'm sorry! Sam, this is Gustavo Abelsworth and Lillia Farmer. Guys, this is Sam Forrester—who you—already know."

"Hi Sam, it is good to finally meet you in person," the large boy said as he stuck out his thick hand. He had short spiky brown hair and wore tan shorts with a belt and a blue polo shirt with an alligator in the right corner. He was cordial and spoke like a refined Englishman from the old world, very much like his father. He sort of reminded Sam of what Teddy Roosevelt would have looked like in his younger years.

Lillia, on the other hand, Sam could tell had an attitude to go with her black hair and dark clothing. She was light skinned and pretty, with a small doll-like nose and thin lips. When he looked at her, she merely squinted at him like he had fangs.

"Nice shiner, pretty boy," she snickered and gestured toward the remnants of the black eye that Bush had so generously given to him.

Chapter Four: wollemia nobilia

"Thanks," he said sarcastically. "I suppose you were the ones that dragged me down to the nurse?" he gestured in toward them.

Gus and Emma looked sheepishly at each other.

"I'm sorry! We got to you too late! We were watching so close but then Bush disappeared right past us in the gym and oh—I'm truly sorry!"

"Don't worry about it," Sam shook his head. But truly he was appreciative. "But thank you for helping me anyway."

Emma looked at him like she had never before—with concern, even pain in her eyes. They were mesmerizing—her turquoise eyes, like giant shining jewels against the bright festival backdrop.

So they had all been watching him. Who knew how long or when, but obviously it was important enough to them—and to the club.

"So this is the club," Sam said lightly, attempting to keep the focus off of him.

Emma only smiled, half ignoring him.

"Hey, we should check out Middle Night. I heard they are a pretty good band." Gus sipped his large plastic cup with the words "White Pine Festival" on the side.

"Bluegrass? Really? Oh, that sounds splendid!" Lillia snorted. "Why don't we grab our lawn chairs and join the eighty-somethings over by the stage?"

Gus looked confused at her sarcasm, but Emma was obviously already tired of it. "Seriously Lillia? Are you going to be like this all night? We only have a few hours before we need to be there."

"Only until seven-thirty when the geri-hicks pack up their lawn chairs and the real bands come out." She snuffed her nose at Emma.

Emma rolled her eyes in disgust, but then immediately brightened as the ring toss vendor furiously motioned them over for a once in a lifetime try for a stuffed lion.

But Sam was hoping for some more answers. Why continue to keep him in the dark? He had met them here, and now they just wanted to eat, play games and listen to bands at the festival? Was this

Chapter Four: wollemia nobilia

their way of hooking him so he couldn't say no? They must be really desperate to get people to join.

That was it. They needed friends. But it was just that—well, they didn't seem like the likely people to hang out together. All three of them had very different personalities.

After a few rounds on the Tilt-A-Wheel and the Matterhorn, he began to loosen up. It was nice to have people to pay attention to him, even if he wasn't the attention-desiring type. And after being cooped up in the house avoiding Bush all week, he needed to blow off some steam. Even if they weren't his ideal choice of friends, they were enjoyable to be around. They were very different, but they seemed to mesh together better than most friends. And they included him like he had always been a part of their group.

The ring toss game proved to be the most fun of the night. Sam had mastered the trick of the game and won everyone their choice of stuffed animal with only a handful of quarters that Emma handed him. Another stack of quarters landed so many animals they could barely carry them, and as they walked away from the confused game attendant, they nearly laughed themselves silly at his reluctance to let Sam keep playing as he nearly single-handedly cleared the booth of prizes.

Sam watched them give away their prizes to children, who lit up when they were handed raccoons, snakes, and giant stuffed bats, and he wondered how such a strange group of people could have so much fun together. Emma was beautiful, with her curly red hair and slender shape, popular with many of the football players at school. Gus was one of the group of pimple-faced science geeks that hung around after school doing extra projects over pizza and two-liters of Mountain Dew. And then there was Lillia, a sarcastic, nearly-never smiling girl who hated the world.

Where did he fit in? Of all of them, he was most like Lillia, without the black hair and deep-rooted sarcasm of course—but she seemed to have a similar mood about life. Why did they want him specifically?

Chapter Four: wollemia nobilia

He was an outcast, a nobody, an out-of-towner, or "townies" as they called them. What could he possibly contribute other than a bunch of stuffed animals?

At least they won't shove me into a locker.

"What next?" Gus dusted his hands, having just given away his last stuffed dog. He kept a large stuffed snake for himself, which he wrapped around his neck like a scarf. It made him look like a large turtle poking his head out to sniff the air.

"I think the new kid should try the Icee challenge." Lillia's black eyes resembled those of the giant bat she was carrying.

"YES!" Emma nearly screamed, jumping up and down with her raccoon on her shoulders. "Do we have time?"

Time? Time until what? What were they keeping from him?

"The what?"

"Icee challenge," Gus repeated. "It's a game to see who can drink their Icee beverage the fastest. I don't really get into all that …"

"Oh that's because you have never won!" said Emma and Lillia in unison.

"Only because you two always start before I can even pay for my Icee," Gus whined.

"Sounds like someone is making excuses," Emma smiled.

"I don't think I should … I have had quite a bit already."

"Sam, will you do it?" Emma smiled at him, her eyes wide and beautiful.

He had never backed down from a challenge. Marshmallows, cinnamon, habaneros …

"Yeah I guess—"

But before he could get the words out, Emma and Lillia had already disappeared to find the Icee stand. Gus suddenly looked at Sam and puffed out his stomach jokingly, making him look curiously like a giant marshmallow and making Sam laugh out loud.

Emma and Lillia returned a few moments later with four large Icees, one of which Lillia immediately shoved into Sam's hand.

"The rules are—" Gus started, but was immediately cut off by Emma.

Chapter Four: wollemia nobilia 🌲🌲

"No, you make up stupid rules," she shushed him with her hand over his mouth and glanced toward Lillia. "The rule is that you must drink your entire Icee with NO ice left over, and the loser must jump off Pike's Bridge in their underwear."

"What?" Sam asked suddenly, making the other two girls laugh at him. "I didn't know there were going to be consequences like ..."

"Ugh," Gus stuck out his tongue and looked at his Icee, no doubt wondering where he was going to fit it after three pastries and an elephant ear.

"You're not going to chicken out, are you Sammy boy?" Lillia teased.

"Nope," he said resolutely, counting on Gus's inability to eat another bite as his edge.

"Are we ready?" Emma giggled, holding the straw up to her mouth.

Sam thought quickly and took the lid off of his Icee. Lillia saw his plan and decided to take her lid off too.

"GO!" Emma said as her words quickly faded into large gulps of Icee.

Sam filled his mouth with the frozen liquid, immediately feeling his tongue go numb from the cold globs of ice, but after two big gulps, he felt he had a good head start on the other two. Lillia seemed to be not far behind him, but she struggled with brain freeze from drinking too much too fast.

Only about a minute later, Sam had nearly downed his entire Icee. He had only four or five big gulps left before he could claim his title at the Icee challenge.

"DONE!" Emma yelled just as he was swallowing his second gulp from being done. Lillia finished moments after her, leaving Sam and Gus to fight it out.

Sam glanced into his cup and picked up his pace. His head throbbed, but he gulped on, ignoring the pain. Lillia and Emma were both cheering for Gus now, maybe to see the new guy lose, or maybe because neither wanted to see Gus in his underpants.

With only a few more painful gulps until Sam finished, Gus' straw

Chapter Four: wollemia nobilia

slurped its last, and Sam was beaten. Gus elegantly crushed his Icee cup in a medieval knight victory fashion, and held it, fist shaking, into the air.

The two girls cheered for Gus and laughed at Sam's loss, and Sam could imagine the same response when he would have to strip to his undies and dive into the river. It would be humiliating to say the least.

"Emma is the reigning champ of the Icee Challenge. Oh … I can't believe I let you guys talk me into that again," Gus said, his whole body doubled over in pain.

"I think I'm going to puke," Lillia groaned as she tossed her cup in the trashcan next to the Icee booth. By then, other groups of younger teens were rushing to the booth to try the Icee Challenge, having seen Gus and the others.

"Oh suck it up you guys! Let's quick go on the Ferris wheel!" Emma nearly shouted in Sam's ear. Gus groaned as the four headed toward the giant slowly spinning wheel spewing blue, green, and orange lights into the night sky. To Sam it looked more like a glowing death trap.

The line wasn't quite as long as it was at the beginning of the night, but it still stretched around the backside of the pastry vendors and into the kid's rides. Gus immediately began talking with a tall skinny kid with a chest that curved inward about the upcoming science fair, and Emma and Lillia were quietly discussing something of which it looked like Sam was the main topic.

Sam looked at Emma and the others. If this was the extent of what he could expect from the mysterious group, he was okay with it for the time being. They were an odd bunch and there was no way to replace his friends back in the city, but he had been alone since he arrived. He enjoyed being alone, but having someone his age around again was nice too. And they were the only ones that had helped him after the incident with Bush.

"But the eye is so complex that there is absolutely no way for a single protein cell to develop into a detailed sensory organ," Gus was explaining furiously to his skinny friend.

"Let's go kid," the large sweaty Ferris wheel operator said coldly.

Chapter Four: wollemia nobilia

Before Sam realized it, the line had diminished in front of him and they were stepping up the metal steps to the wheel of death. The two girls had already climbed into the basket and were coaxing him to get in.

The operator closed the gate to the basket and the Ferris wheel began to turn quietly. The higher they went, the more Sam could see just how small White Pine really was. There was only the main street through town and a few side streets that held small neighborhoods of modest houses. The curiously old buildings and small shops that made up Main Street Square were really the only civilization for miles around. It was as though someone picked up a rural town from the eighteen hundreds in England and plopped it in the middle of the Northern Michigan wilderness. Quaint, but primitive.

The lights ended almost immediately following the s-shaped road through the town square, with only a few lights dotting the landscape from the small cattle farms and rural cabins. Sam strained to see his grandfather's cabin in the trees, but it was too well buried in the hills that led to the larger Porcupine Mountains.

The rest of White Pine was surrounded by the thick, dense pine forest that led into what seemed like a never-ending darkness of trees. There were no cities or town lights in the distance that he could see, and he was pretty sure they were the only civilization for miles around.

****

Sam could see the clear sky end abruptly at the line of clouds he saw earlier. It was larger now, and huge thunderheads were developing along the front, stretching as far as Sam could see in both directions. Judging from how far it had moved since they got to the festival, it would be upon them in less than an hour. The others didn't seem to notice, but he had no doubt rain was on the way, and a good amount from the looks of it. Whatever they were going to show him, it had to be pretty fast.

As they reached the top of the wheel and stopped, the noises of the festival faded into a faraway murmur, and the only sounds heard

Chapter Four: wollemia nobilia

were Lillia and Emma talking softly as they peered over the side of the basket. Then the wheel began to move again, faster this time.

Around and around they went, and almost immediately Sam felt a nauseating feeling in the pit of his stomach, but not from nervousness this time. He had never really enjoyed rides that spun quickly, but with the Icee, pastry, and part of a funnel cake sloshing around in his gut, he began to regret getting on the Ferris wheel. The more times they went around, the worse it got. Judging from the purplish color of Gus's face, he wasn't enjoying it either.

When he thought he couldn't stand it any longer, the spinning wheel finally stopped to let them off. The two girls bounced out of the basket as though the junk food hadn't affected them at all, but Gus immediately thrust his head between his knees and sported a flush, white face.

Sam helped Gus to his feet, and out of instinct, Gus headed for the trashcan. Almost immediately, Gus threw his head over the side of the large trash barrel and upchucked a large purple pile of regurgitated Icee. His face was as purple as the mess in the barrel, and seeing it made Sam suddenly queasy, forcing him to take turns with Gus throwing up over the side.

"A little too much fun tonight, eh?" Lillia chuckled when the heaving slowed, making Emma burst out in full laughter.

"Poor guys! You must have weak stomachs!" Emma snorted through her laughing.

"Anyone up for another Icee?" Lillia kidded. "I think there's a new flavor over by the scrambler."

This sent Emma into a laughing fit that made even Lillia smile through her dark eye shadow.

"Funny," both Sam and Gus echoed in the barrel between dry heaves.

"Hey, I bet you could scoop up some of that and analyze it in your science club—" Lillia stopped, and her smile faded. "Did you guys just hear thunder?"

Indeed Sam heard the low rumble, and no doubt Gus did too, as it was amplified in the barrel.

Chapter Four: wollemia nobilia 🌲🌲

In the distance above the trees, there was a dim flash of lightning that followed. The smile on the two girls' faces faded into a look of concern.

Another flash illuminated the tops of the trees across the field from town, followed by a low rumble of thunder. Other festival goers must have also noticed it because the lines around the rides began to empty quickly.

"We should probably think about heading over there now." Emma was staring at the quickly approaching storm.

Sam lifted his head up from the rim of the barrel to look at the front. It had grown significantly larger since they had been on the Ferris wheel. It was moving quickly.

"Yep, it's nearly time anyway. We better get moving," Lillia looked at her watch.

Here comes the big reveal. They want me to become their newest study buddy, Sam thought between the nauseating waves washing over him.

"Okay, give me just a minute." Gus lifted his head just enough to speak.

Lightning lit up the field in the distance, and a long, low rumble followed a half a minute later. It was going to be a doozy of a storm.

Sam felt a cool breeze begin to blow softly on his face, a nice feeling in comparison to the moist, stale air of the night, especially after throwing up multiple times into the trashcan.

"Gus, we need to go now," Emma urged.

Gus didn't move.

****

They helped Gus get upright and half carried him past the parking lot to the woods closest to town. Sam wasn't sure where they were going, but he knew the pathway connected with the same path he explored behind Orvil's store. It was where Emma had followed him only a week earlier.

Cars were emptying out of the parking lot now in droves, and a

Chapter Four: wollemia nobilia

long string of lights could be seen as the festival goers headed out of town to try to outrun the rain.

The festival was nearly empty now, with carnival operators and vendors frantically trying to cover up their rides and wares as the storm rolled in angrily. For a moment, Sam looked back and watched the lights from the rides turn off one by one, silently wishing the festival would have lasted just a little longer.

As they reached the woods, Emma and Lillia stopped suddenly just inside the blowing trees, looking in both directions with concern. Then, as if they appeared right from the trees themselves, eight figures materialized out of the darkness.

Instantly there was a blue flash of light, and a weak but brilliant blue iridescent bubble formed awkwardly over Lillia, Gus, and Sam. Emma held her hand out strangely as if shielding her eyes from the unknown persons in front of her, the blue bubble connecting to her palm.

Sam watched the glowing blue bubble around Lillia ebb and flow as if it were a wave rolling in from the sea. It was beautiful—the brightest blue he had ever seen. He looked over to Emma, who was now struggling to hold her hand up, the wave of blue encasing her as well. And then, just as quickly as the flash began, it ended, and they were in darkness once again.

"Dad! Mom!" Emma breathed suddenly in the darkness. "Oh! I didn't know it was you! I am so sorry!"

"Emma! You know better than to use that here!" A short thin woman with shoulder length curled hair emerged from the dark with a scowl on her face. She was an exact replica of Emma, just years older and with a few distinguished wrinkles around her eyes.

"Samuel, how are you?" she turned instantly to him and took his hands in hers.

"I'm good, Mrs. Sterling," he said mechanically, unable to take his eyes off of Emma's hands.

"You must be so confused by now," she continued to hold his hands. "I am so sorry sweet boy! You know these things, they just have to be so secretive. But don't you worry, we will look after

Chapter Four: wollemia nobilia

you—Emma? You make sure and keep close to Sam. It can get a bit overwhelming to take in all at once."

Then she turned suddenly and dug though a large handbag, producing a black rain jacket about Sam's size.

"Here, this should do you nicely."

The others followed suit, each donning their own jackets in anticipation of the impending rain.

Sam instantly felt comfortable with Mrs. Sterling. She reminded him of the mom he never really had. Nurturing and loving—nothing like Sylvia.

"Jack Sterling," an averaged sized man with glasses smiled and stuck his hand out to Sam. He reminded him of a history professor in a university, complete with a tweed sports jacket and drivers cap. "And I see my wife Cindy has already taken you under her wing."

"Uh, yes sir. Nice to meet you."

Then Gus and a larger, more portly version of him came waddling up in the darkness.

"This is my father, Colonel James Abelsworth," Gus offered.

"How te' do, lad?" the rotund man stuck out his puffy hand to Sam. Large, but broad shouldered, the Colonel wore a navy uniform and spectacles that made him look like a librarian for the British navy. It was a strange sight, but still he seemed to fit the look as a stately military man.

The Colonel then held his beefy hand out toward an incredibly skinny woman with tight curls below her hat, dressed in fur from head to toe. "This is my wife Violet, lad."

It was then that Sam noticed the Colonel's leather bracelet beneath his cuff with a curious flat stone embedded into it that almost had a glowing blue quality to it. Looking around briefly at the others, he noticed Mr. and Mrs. Sterling had one too, and the Colonel's wife as well, although it was hidden amongst the many other gold and diamond-studded jewelry on her arm.

Sam put his hand out to her, but she had quickly discovered something wrong with her ruby leather purse, acting like she didn't see his gesture. "James, you must go and find my lipstick in the car,"

Chapter Four: wollemia nobilia

she commanded her husband, who immediately began digging for his car keys in his watch pocket.

"I simply don't understand why we must be out here in these dirty woods with a boy we don't even know," she muttered quietly, but it was loud enough for Sam to hear.

"On the ground in front of you," Sam said suddenly, spotting the shiny metal tube in the pine needles reflecting the light from the moon.

The furry woman's eyes lit up upon seeing the case, motioning for her husband to pick it up for her. Then she took a step forward and hugged Sam awkwardly with her bony arms.

"Oh my! I am overcome with gratitude! You are just a little Ferdinand Magellan, aren't you?" she chuckled like a screeching cat.

Emma shrugged as she turned away, and even in the dark Sam could tell Lillia was laughing silently.

Mr. Sterling cleared his throat and looked at the dark thundercloud that was nearly upon them.

"Ladies and gents, I believe we cannot wait any longer for—" but he was cut short by a young woman and a short thin balding man who had silently joined the party.

"Ah, Harper and Sarah. Good. We were beginning to worry."

Sam strained to see who the woman was in the darkness. She was medium height, thin, and moved with animation as she talked. Something about her made him think of Miss Karpatch.

"Good evening, everyone—Sam—sorry I am late," the flustered woman said, a flash of lightning illuminating her face eerily.

Miss Karpatch? What was she doing here?

Instantly Sam began second-guessing this little "club" of Emma's. She had certainly left plenty of details out—like the fact that parents and nosy geography teachers were involved. Perhaps he was to be the subject of some ridiculous intervention of sorts. He had seen plenty of those on the plethora of reality TV shows that seemed to invade the cable airwaves.

The strangest part was that it seemed the group was prepared for an extended hike through the woods, as all had large backpacks

Chapter Four: wollemia nobilia

stuffed to the point of exploding—with the exception of the four extra packs propped on the tree behind Mr. Sterling.

Where were they going? And when were they planning on telling him? Or his Grandfather Amos?

"Well then," the Colonel boomed happily as he stuck his large hand in his blazer pocket and retrieved a pipe. "It looks like you brought the weather with you!"

Miss Karpatch cinched up her canvas pack tighter to her chest, then turned toward Mr. Sterling.

"Yes, Jack, I would really like to get there before that—" she pointed to the thundercloud now descending upon them, "gets here."

Emma's father looked at the sky with concern.

"Yes, yes, gang, let's head 'em up and move 'em out. Say your goodbyes everyone."

Gus hugged his parents, then picked up one of the extra packs, slinging it on his back. Both Lillia and Emma did the same.

As the rest of the group said goodbye to the Abelsworth's, Sam pulled Emma aside.

"Where are you going?" his lips not whispering as quietly as he had hoped.

"Not just me," she said mysteriously, the wind now beginning to softly toss her strawberry red hair as the storm approached. "You are coming too."

He was stunned. Did they really expect him to drop everything and go on a backpacking trip in the middle of the night? In what looked to be a rather ominous storm?

What were they thinking?

"Uh, I don't think my grandfather would allow ..."

Emma leveled her gaze.

"It's now or never, Samuel. Time to choose. They won't wait."

This is crazy. No one in their right mind would wander off into the forest with a bunch of people they didn't know—with the promise of being part of a "club." Yet, as crazy as it was, there was something different about them, about her. The strange blue light that seemed to jump from her hands was evidence enough of that.

Chapter Four: wollemia nobilia

The truth was that he was now more curious than ever. He did worry that Amos would be upset for him leaving, but he wasn't going to miss the chance to find out what this was all about. Amos would have to deal with it, just like he had to deal with Sam when his parents dumped him off on him.

As another flash of lightning came dangerously close to the field across from the festival grounds, Sam made his decision. Amos could wait. He would follow them to find the truth, even in the middle of a lightning storm.

Just to be courteous, however, he left a message for his grandfather with Gus's father (who had urgent business to attend to in White Pine and couldn't go with the group) not to worry about him.

As the storm bore down on White Pine, Sam snatched the pack from the outstretched hand of Lillia and followed Gus and Emma into to the deep black of the woods. Where they were going would remain a mystery, but he would find out soon enough.

****

"That's cranky Cooley," Lillia said snidely to Sam under her breath as they walked briskly, pointing to the odd man leading the group through the trees. "He's a bit on the 'don't-turn-your-back-weird' side."

"Lil', cut it out," Emma scowled quietly at her from behind Sam. "His name is Harper Cooley."

"Oh yeah, sorry, he's a real role model if you're looking to become a number-one creeper," Lillia chuckled, her voice thick with sarcasm.

"Lillia!" Emma scolded. "You promised you would try harder."

"Look. This guy shows up from the old group. Says he's the Chief Seer, investigating White Pine. Then he doesn't speak to any of us for weeks? Sorry, Emma, he's a bit too strange for me to ignore."

"He is the Chief Seer! Daddy knows him!" Emma protested.

"Yeah, well I know the Metim but you don't see me trusting them," Lillia huffed under her breath.

"Whatever," Emma threw her hands up, exasperated.

Chapter Four: wollemia nobilia 🌲🌲

What in the world were they talking about? Sam shook his head. Seer? Metim?

He looked at the man they called Cooley. He looked slightly familiar. Had he seen him before? Was he the man that stormed out of Chivler's just before Sam arrived?

They owed him some answers, and he wasn't going another step until he got some.

"Uh, I'm a little unclear as to where we are going. I mean, we had fun tonight, but walking into the middle of nowhere in a storm and then this blue-light-Avengers-thing and strange names you keep saying are weirding me out."

Allowing Lillia to go on ahead of her, Emma dropped back beside him and pulled a small copper lantern out of her backpack, which immediately bathed the path in front of them in the same blue glow that had sprung from her hands earlier.

"Look, I'm not supposed to say anything yet. All I can tell you is that we aren't who you think we are," she drew close to him and whispered.

"Are you witches ... or ... part of a cult?" He couldn't find the words.

"No, certainly not a cult. More like ... protectors," she looked strangely at him.

Sam looked at the pines bristling above him in the wind of the impending storm. For some reason, the strangeness he had felt since moving to White Pine began to make more sense. Protectors, people that watched out for the town. Maybe the reason he had felt as though everyone was watching him was because they were.

"Are you not human?" he asked, the words feeling strange leaving his mouth.

She smiled and took his hand for a brief moment, sending chills up his spine, making the wind whipping through the pines even more cold. But he wasn't going to complain.

"Something like that," she said smiling, hurrying them along the thin path to catch the others who were already lost in the darkness ahead.

🌲🌲 Chapter Four: wollemia nobilia

As they slipped back in line with the others, Emma let go of his hand and concentrated on holding the lantern in front of her, as the others in the group had already retrieved theirs from their packs. Sam asked no more questions, only followed the blue light of the lanterns in front of him silently. There would be plenty of time for questions later, he hoped, when they were out of the storm and the wind had quieted down to allow conversation.

As suddenly as it started, the wind instantly stopped. An odd quiet persisted, with only an occasional low growl of thunder in the distance. The only indication the storm was still there was the silent flashes of light above them that grew dangerously close together.

The storm was not yet over, but was instead gearing up for the main event. From the concerned looks on the blue-lit faces of the others ahead, they thought the same. Wherever they were going, they would need to find shelter soon.

Sam then spotted a scraggly tree to the side of the path looking much like the one he saw before nearly falling over the cliff into the gorge. A closer observation made him realize they were indeed on the same path he had taken only a week prior.

Moments later, with the thick wall of brush in front of them, Mr. Sterling led the caravan quickly to a sharp right that followed the length of the thicket. Almost immediately the path descended into the ground—an optical illusion that wasn't visible to anyone unless they were right on top of it. Even in broad daylight, Sam didn't see it, and he had been only feet away.

The path continued downward into the earth until there were sandstone rock walls that seemed to merge together the deeper they went. What little moonlight was peeking through the darkening clouds above them was now lost completely. The only light they had was the rapid strobe of the lightning all around them and the eerie blue lanterns to guide their way.

Then the path took a sharp right turn and continued to descend. On a quick thought, Sam closed the gap between him and Emma so he didn't accidentally walk off another unknown ledge or into a rock in the path.

Chapter Four: wollemia nobilia

Finally the way leveled out and a small opening lay ahead of them. Directly in front of them was a large weeping pine that hung over the water.

It took him a moment, but then he recognized it as the same tree he saw only the Saturday before, nestled in the side of the cliff. *Well I guess that answers how you get to it.*

The opening led them to a large ledge that was cradled into the wall of the canyon, about the size of the living room of the cabin. It looked completely shielded from almost every view, except for the very spot where the gorge nearly claimed his life. No doubt there were few that knew of this spot.

He stared at the strange tree, seeing the large ball-like clumps of needles that dotted the loose-hanging branches.

"It's a wollemia nobilia ... or more commonly known as the Wollemi Pine," Gus said above the wind in the glow of the blue lantern. "It's one of the oldest and most rare trees in existence, dating back to the time of the Antediluvian Period."

"I haven't seen any like it around here." Sam walked to the tree, feeling the bead-like bumps on the trunk.

"It is native to Australia, but there are sightings on occasion from other places around the world. It's one of the reasons I believe the dinosaurs were eliminated from the earth. They were the biggest carriers of plant seeds ... and disease."

Then, out of the corner of his eye, Sam spotted the symbol on the rock near the tree that he had seen the week before, the same symbol of the wing he had seen from his dream. Before he could reach out and touch it, however, the storm finally unleashed its fury on the visitors of the gorge.

****

As if mother nature had lost her patience, the storm suddenly immersed them in a sea of raging wind and rain. Thunder and lightning held nothing back, booming deep within the walls of the

Chapter Four: wollemia nobilia

gorge, the blinding flashes striking the forest angrily above them. They were safer where they were, but this was also not a storm to be reckoned with. Dead branches from the more dry pines fell around them, almost immediately followed by large grape-sized balls of ice falling from the sky. Even though it was somewhat protected, the tiny ledge was still prey to the dangerous barrage.

"Let's move, everybody!" Mr. Sterling called out from the back of the ledge, near a small overhang on the rock.

No one protested or lingered at his words. Emma, Gus, and Lillia made their way to the back of the ledge where the others were, and Sam followed quickly behind them in the blizzard-like rain and hail. He wasn't quite sure where they were going to take refuge in such a small space, but he followed anyway.

As they reached the back of the ledge and the overhang, the others disappeared suddenly into the rock wall, as if inside the stone itself. First Mrs. Sterling, then Miss Karpatch and Cooley, then Lillia, Gus, and Emma.

As the wind whipped the Wollemi tree violently behind him, he stepped up to the wall under the tiny overhang. He reached his hand out to grasp the cold rock in front of him, but as his hand moved forward, it only felt darkness.

He inched his body forward, one cautious step at a time, until he was sure his next would be into solid rock. But as he moved, he was only met with more cool air.

Stepping back once again, he was able to see the illusion so blatantly hidden in front of him. Like the path that descended down to the ledge, this too was invisible to someone who wasn't privy to the disguise.

Suddenly a hand reached out of the darkness and grabbed him, pulling him into the coolness of the opening. Emma drew his face only inches from hers to look at him in the dim light of the ledge.

"Look at you. You're already soaked! I thought you might be smarter than to stand out in the middle of a storm!" she fussed, her

Chapter Four: wollemia nobilia

hair showing rapid signs of frizzing from the humidity in the air.

Sam mouthed the word "sorry" casually, but his voice was silenced by the sight of the massive structure standing before him in the middle of the cavern.

****

This can't be real, he thought. *Dreams aren't real like this.*

The two-story arch-shaped structure was the same as in his dream, with the exception of the color. It was white—almost iridescent in color, reflecting colorful expressions of light that bounced from the inner walls of the cavern, which too were made of the same iridescent stone.

It was an incredible sight, and he felt instantly drawn to it, unable to take his eyes off of it. He held his hands out to it, feeling the soft light radiate around and through him. It was warm, not like warming your hands over a fire, but a deep warmth, almost like embracing warmth itself. The closer he came, the more the feeling intensified. It was a sudden feeling of peace—almost as if he was always meant for this moment, meant for the arch. It filled an emptiness inside that he could not ignore.

Suddenly Gus was at his side.

"Look familiar?"

Sam nodded slowly. It was the same structure, as magnificent and captivating as the one from his dream, and yet drastically different. The one burned into his mind from the sleepless nights was black as the night sky, and certainly didn't retain the same euphoric warmth this one did. It was cold and lifeless, inspiring instant fear upon first glance.

But the shapes of the two arches were identical. And this one was real.

What was truly strange, however, was that the brilliant structure gave him a sense of familiarity, of longing for somewhere—or

Chapter Four: wollemia nobilia

someone—that he knew before. It was a strange but settling feeling, as if he was right where he needed to be at that moment.

"Beautiful, isn't it?"

They watched the soft glow of the arch dance around the cavern. As each vibrant beam bounced off the walls around them, there seemed to be a moving, living quality to it, almost as if the light was breathing.

"Yes … it is," he said finally, unable to find the words that would truly describe its allure.

Mr. Sterling made his way over to them.

"It doesn't matter how many times I see the arch, I am always awed by its elegance," he said, putting a hand on Sam's shoulder. "I'm sure you have plenty of questions, and we will answer all of them, I promise you. But right now we need to get moving. Can you be patient?"

Sam nodded compliantly, and Mr. Sterling smacked him lightly on the back and turned to address the rest of the group.

"Excellent. Now if I could ask the adults to take positions at the arch."

Miss Karpatch, Mrs. Sterling, Cooley, and Mr. Sterling began to assemble at the feet of the brilliant structure. The four youths watched as they reached out in unison, each taking hold of the iridescent leg in from of them.

Immediately, a silvery blue stream of light begin to snake down the arch, moving slowly and with personality, as if aware of its purpose.

Sam's mind raced. There was no ability to account for what he saw before him. It was all so confusing, and it felt like a dream—but very much unlike the one that woke him nearly every night.

The streams of light reached the cavern floor and spread across the center of the arch, unifying into a flowing river until it covered the floor beneath them.

Slowly the entire arch began to throb as though it was breathing rhythmically. A roaring breeze moved suddenly throughout the cave,

Chapter Four: wollemia nobilia

nearly knocking Sam to the dusty floor, but not before Emma grabbed his hand to keep him on his feet.

When he tried to shield his eyes from the increasing light radiating before him, her hand held fast, and she pulled him close to her, leaning over until her lips were millimeters from his ear.

"Don't be afraid, Sam. I am right next to you."

Mr. Sterling, Cooley, and Miss Karpatch motioned for the others to approach the arch. Even above the roaring wind in the cave, a quiet, still presence hung over the scene. The arch pulsed so intensely now that it looked as though it would explode.

"We walk together, right?" Emma winked at him.

His mind raced as they inched toward the light. At any moment, he was sure he would wake up to a steaming cup of tea from Amos, but still the dream endured. He held Emma's hand so tightly that he feared crushing it with his sweaty palm.

The warm light hit his feet first. It was soothing, and he welcomed it with his eyes closed. A sudden calm rushed over his body once again, and then he couldn't feel Emma's hand—only the warmth from the light.

Dizziness overcame him, and for a moment he thought he was rolling down a large hill, gaining speed with every rotation. But soon the spinning turned into an ocean of light, where wave after wave crashed through him. It was warm, and it soothed him to the soul. It was as if he was wrapped in a warm blanket on a cold day, without a care in the world.

His feet felt like they were encased in stone, but as he looked down, he watched his feet moving. He had no idea where he was going, but Emma and the others were no longer with him. He only continued to walk, soaking up the warm light.

Then, as suddenly as it had engulfed him, the light was gone. The wind and noise of the cavern had stopped. He was alone in the silence, his body still reeling from the enchanting light.

Chapter Four: wollemia nobilia

****

It was then that Sam realized that his eyes were still closed. He opened them carefully, unsure of what they would show him. Slowly the cold met him, and the light and the warmth raced from his body as if they were released suddenly by their cold captor.

His eyes adjusted to the scene around him, and he listened for anything that would tell him he wasn't alone. The faint smell of pine filled the air around him, and he breathed it in deeply. Icy air filled his lungs and he expelled it quickly, realizing suddenly the depth of the frigid temperature where he stood.

In front of him, his vision began to reveal the shape of a colorless tree, then another. The wind and the rain from the storm were gone, and no voices from the group could be heard anywhere. He wished again for the warmth of the light, but there was no summoning it back. He was alone in the darkness.

As his eyes adjusted, the trees around him showed the triangular outlines of pines, much like the ones in White Pine. But these were larger, and much taller. There were no recognizable signs that he was back in White Pine. He only knew he was in the forest.

Where was everybody? Why would they leave him alone like this?

Seeing the outline of a toppled log in front of him, he carefully picked his way through the darkness and sat on the rotting tree to wait for the others. He could barely make out the small white patches that could only be snow … where was he? It was September in Upper Michigan, wasn't it?

Suddenly, behind him he heard a noise—like the soft crunch of pine needles.

A chill instantly went up his spine at the sound, but when he strained to hear it again, he could only hear the occasional wind through the needles of the trees and the hot throbbing of his temple.

Crunch. There it was again. He was hoping the first noise was his imagination, but this one proved he was wrong.

Crunch. Crunch.

Chapter Four: wollemia nobilia

Whatever it was, it was behind him, and it was big.

Crunch.

Sam readied himself to move fast. His mind raced instantly to wolves. He was told by his grandfather about the potential dangers of getting caught in the woods alone with a pack. If he was going to have to outrun them, he was going to have to be smart about it, maybe climb a tree quickly.

Move fast through the trees, find one that is easy to climb, get up it as fast as possible.

Seeing the outline of a fallen branch to his left, he snatched it up silently and held it stiffly like a sword in front of him, facing the unknown noise in the trees.

CRUNCH.

He decided he would make the first move on it, not allowing it to get the jump on him. *Surprise it before it surprises me.*

Whatever it was, it was getting dangerously near.

He gripped the branch tightly as he waited for something to appear in the trees. A shadow, a figure of something—anything. *Wait. What was that?* Something green was moving toward him. *Are they eyes?*

"SAM!" he heard in the distance suddenly behind him, making him nearly topple over onto his makeshift sword. It was Emma.

"Over here!" Sam hollered, refusing to take his eyes off the trees in front of him.

"He's over here—I found him!"

The footsteps stopped as Emma came rushing through the trees, her blue lantern piercing through the darkness.

"Sam! Are you okay?" Emma rushed to him, her eyes drawn immediately to the stick in his hand. "What happened? Did you see something?"

"No, I didn't ... but I heard ..." he stopped. "I'm not sure what it was ..."

"Sam! Dear boy! Are you alright?" a concerned Mrs. Sterling came huffing out of the dark trees. Mr. Sterling was right behind her, holding another odd blue lantern.

Chapter Four: wollemia nobilia

"He must have let go right at the turn," Mrs. Sterling huffed as she looked him over with concern.

Soon the others emerged to join the commotion, and where he was completely alone before, now he was surrounded by concerned blue faces, each doting on him to ensure he was indeed all right.

Emma whispered something to her father, and suddenly Mr. Sterling was instantly at Sam's side.

"What is it boy? Is there something out there?"

Although reluctant to do so, Sam pointed at the trees where he heard the noise. Mr. Sterling glanced to the spot where he had pointed into the darkness, then turned his attention back toward Sam, drawing him close to him.

"If you did see something, Sam," he said quietly with concern thick in his words, "I need to know right now."

As he looked once again toward the woods where he saw the green eyes, a shiver crawled up his spine. It was so close, like it could have attacked him at any time. Those eyes ... did he make them up? Was it all part of the grand illusion he was experiencing? Perhaps he was still dreaming, and his body refused to allow him to know it.

"No, nothing. Just footsteps in the woods," he lied.

Mr. Sterling scowled and put his finger out in front of him, using it to draw silently in the air. Immediately trailing his finger was a gleaming blue fire that spelled out the letters as he wrote them, similar to the blue that shone out of the lanterns. Then with a swipe of his hand, he snatched the gleaming words out of the air and packed them into a bright, glowing orb. He tossed it gently into the air. The orb rose slowly above them until it reached the treetops where it hovered only briefly and then streaked away into the night sky.

"Poor boy! You must be freezing! Let's get you inside. The cabin is just over the rise," said Mrs. Sterling, who had slipped another jacket on Sam's shoulders without his knowledge, and who now took hold of his arm and turned to demand a lantern from her husband, to which he complied instantaneously.

"Jack, I'm taking the kids to the cabin for a bit of coffee and to

Chapter Four: wollemia nobilia

get them properly dressed," she announced with unease in her voice. "Let's go, all."

"What was that?" Sam mimicked to Gus the writing in the air that Mr. Sterling had done only moments prior. Mr. Sterling, Miss Karpatch, and Cooley had stayed behind, no doubt to investigate the possibility of an intruder in the trees, even though Sam didn't allude to it.

"It's the way we communicate through long distances. Kind of like a telegram with light," Gus huffed as he struggled to keep up with Mrs. Sterling's quickened pace. "Called a Lightscribe. It's really pretty neat. Each person has a unique Light signature that we are able to use to personalize each message, and only that person will be able to retrieve it."

"Like a coded email. Do you know what he was writing?" Sam pressed as they weaved their way through the silent trees.

"Most likely something about our arrival. It is standard procedure that when anyone enters or exits through a gate to alert of safe travel. These gates," Gus motioned behind him, "are great ambush sites, not to mention Mr. Sterling is on the Council, and Mr. Cooley is head Seer, so there are most likely high profile targets traveling through. We are taught to travel the gates cautiously."

Sam had more to ask, but he could tell Gus was not likely to talk. He, like the others, seemed to be giving information to Sam on a need to know basis only. Somehow Emma had known enough about him, however, that she believed he would choose to go with them. But the light—the gate, traveling through to another place, was incredible. It was almost too much to conceive, and his mind raced to make up answers in the void of their secrecy.

He had to know what they were and where they were. And why bring him? It was strange—and they weren't telling him. But he would not demand more information now. He was too cold. His mind kept returning to the coffee Mrs. Sterling had promised. He would press for more information later.

They wound up a gentle rise in the trail by the light of the dim

Chapter Four: wollemia nobilia

blue lanterns, which reflected eerily around the large pine branches above them. Here and there Sam could see small patches of snow around the faint trail, cast blue whenever the group passed near them. Sam judged by how heavy he was breathing that they were at a much higher elevation than White Pine. There was no doubt now that passing through the arch brought them many miles away in a few moments.

Just over the rise the trees opened up into a small clearing, and a modest cabin overlooking a narrow but quickly moving river appeared in the moonlight. It was dark, and from the piling snow around its exterior, it looked as though it hadn't seen inhabitants in a while.

Mrs. Sterling stopped just inside the trees of the clearing and held up her hands for the others to stop behind her. In the silent darkness, she lifted her hands up toward the cabin, palms outstretched into the cold air. Suddenly there was a blue light much like the one in the lantern that began to glow in the cabin's window near the entrance.

She paused for a moment, then Mrs. Sterling marched the group forward across the small clearing and up the wooden steps of the cabin's front porch. To the left of the porch stood a structure that looked like a shed on stilts, with the silhouette of a small narrow boat leaning against its side.

Mrs. Sterling seemed unconcerned any longer with any danger that may have been present from the trees, and she opened the thick wood door to the cabin and shooed Emma, Sam, Gus, and Lillia inside.

Immediately, the three girls set about starting a fire in the old cast iron stove in the small kitchen and making some strong coffee.

Gus and Sam were charged with getting a fire going in the living room fireplace. After finding the small wood pile outside on the porch of the cabin, they soon had a blazing fire going that almost immediately warmed the cold little living room up to a tolerable temperature.

Soon Emma brought Gus and Sam a cup of coffee and sat down to warm her hands by the stone hearth. The cabin was almost identical to his grandfather's place—small, but very open feeling due

Chapter Four: wollemia nobilia

to the vaulted ceilings and large windows. It was strange, though—the whole cabin took on a curious familiarity.

His intention had been to ask a few questions when they had stopped for the evening, but after feeling the effects of a very long day beginning to sink in, he chose instead to join the others in watching the flames crawl around the logs in the fireplace and sipping his coffee in silence.

"Don't be up too late, you all," Mrs. Sterling warned as she headed back to the kitchen, a steaming cup of coffee in her own hands. "We have quite a trek tomorrow, and you know how your father travels."

It feels so much later than when we left the festival, Sam thought.

"It must be nearly midnight," Gus echoed his thoughts.

"Actually, it's midnight right on the dot," Emma added. "We took quite a bit of time finding Sammy boy here."

"Thanks a lot, Columbus," Lillia chided with a grin on her face as she poked her head above the book she was reading.

Emma chuckled and set her coffee cup down to help her mother get the beds ready for the night. There were log bunks in the living room, a couch, and a rather comfortable looking chair, but other than that there was very little floor space. Where would they sleep?

Even with Cooley, Miss Karpatch, and Mr. Sterling still out in the night, the cabin was still rather crowded. But it was cozy. And no one seemed to mind.

Suddenly Lillia slammed her book shut, creating a large plume of dust from its pages.

"Well, that does it for me. I'm headed in for the night," she said in her usual satirical way.

"Oh, take these blankets up with you," Mrs. Sterling hurried over and handed Lillia a stack of blankets from a large chest at the end of one of the bunk bed beds.

"Lillia, I will help you. I'm ready to pack it in as well." Gus set his cup of coffee down and got up to help Lillia with the blankets.

Mrs. Sterling reached just above her head and grabbed hold of a handle with a string and pulled down a hidden set of stairs that led to a dark, unknown space above them.

83

🌲🌲 Chapter Four: wollemia nobilia

"Sam, when you have warmed up those skinny bones, you can take one of the bunks upstairs," she said cheerfully, spreading out a comforter on one of the bunks near the fireplace.

At her words, Sam felt the warm heaviness of exhaustion. Maybe it was the fire, or the leftover feeling of upchucking blue Icee into the trash bin—either way he was truly tired. Traveling to strange new worlds was tiring. If they were to travel further tomorrow, he would need to get some rest.

"I think I am ready too." He stood, looking around for a place to set his empty coffee cup. "Where should I—"

"Here, give that to me. You just get upstairs to bed." Mrs. Sterling snatched the cup from his hand.

"Uh—thank you Mrs. Sterling."

"Oh dear boy, you are welcome," she said with such a smile on her face that he thought her face was going to split wide open. Then she snatched him up in her arms suddenly. "Oh you poor boy, you must be so confused. Do get some sleep and we will talk it over in the morning during breakfast, alright?"

Sam allowed himself a pause in her arms, feeling strangely safe and comfortable. She smelled of lavender and fresh linen, much like his maid Estella did back home. Estella would pull him aside and squeeze him around the neck on occasion, and mutter phrases like *que lindo niño mio* softly in his ear. She came to be the only person he really trusted, and he looked forward to those squeezes, especially when Sylvia was in one of her moods.

Not that he would think of Mrs. Sterling as a maid, but that she was a genuine person who seemed to care for his well-being, and it was nice.

"Yes ma'am, I will," he yawned sleepily.

He climbed the steps behind Emma, who was carrying a rather large bundle of extra fluffy-looking pillows with fresh smelling sheets.

The loft was simple, but nice and inviting. There were two small armchairs in the corners, each with its own side table and little lamp in the shape of a log cabin. One wall of the room was made into a bookshelf and was filled corner to corner with books of all sizes and

Chapter Four: wollemia nobilia

kinds. There was no bathroom inside the cabin, so he assumed the little shed outside served that purpose. One glimpse out the little loft window into the cold darkness made him glad he took care of that earlier in the evening.

On the floor was a large brown and red area rug with an intricately woven winged creature of sorts. Lillia sat there, cross-legged with a book in her hand, intently reading in the dim light of a candle. Gus was changing into his pajamas in the closet that was closest to his and Sam's beds, conveniently out of sight of the girls' bunks and the center of the room. Sam hadn't brought anything to change into except for his hooded sweatshirt, but then again he hadn't had a whole lot of time to prepare either.

"Sam, you take that bunk over there by Gus," Emma pointed toward the small bunk underneath the loft window.

He silently made the little bed with the sheets that Mrs. Sterling had given him, then tugged off his shoes and rubbed his heel. Out popped a rock from the cavern where the arch was held. He held it in his hand, examining its sandy exterior, wondering how a rock could have gotten into his boot.

This must be a dream, he thought, staring at the rock. *One large, inescapable, incredibly vivid dream. One of those dreams where the feelings of danger and confusion are so real, and even the rocks in your shoes hurt.*

"Hello there!" Sam heard Mrs. Sterling say from downstairs.

"Hello there!" A muffled reply was heard outside the large wooden door.

Mrs. Sterling creaked open the door and Mr. Sterling, Miss Karpatch, and Harper Cooley entered the small cabin living room. Immediately, Cooley began demanding coffee, to which Mrs. Sterling must have complied because he could hear the clanking of cups and saucers on the stove.

Emma immediately bounded down the steps to her father. She embraced him on the steps as if her father had been gone for months.

Feeling a twinge of jealousy, he fought to push it out of his mind like too many times before. He knew the feeling all too well—wishing the other kid's parents could be your own, and the hole in your heart

Chapter Four: wollemia nobilia

that just didn't disappear. But over the years he had learned to control it. He had learned how to fight his emotions, and push back the anger. He was good at it.

"Hello up there!" Mr. Sterling smiled up at him. "You gave us a bit of a scare Sam!" he said, his eyes glowing through his black-rimmed glasses.

"Sorry about that," Sam said sheepishly, stepping into sight of the stairs below.

"It's not your fault. You will get the hang of it." He paused to kiss Emma goodnight and then shooed her upstairs, his curly sandy hair glowing in the firelight.

"Sam, I was wondering if I could have a word with you for a moment?" he turned suddenly from his cup of coffee.

Panic suddenly overtook him. Did he do or say something wrong? Was it about Emma?

Without responding, he walked down the steps and followed Mr. Sterling outside, noticing the long glances that Miss Karpatch and Cooley gave him as he slunk past them. Once the door was shut, Mr. Sterling motioned for Sam to sit in one of the rocking chairs on the porch as he eased himself into another.

Even in the colder air, Sam felt warm. He stared at the black line of thick pines just beyond the boundary of the cabin property, thinking about what could be waiting in the darkness of this strange place. The nearly full moon shone brightly above them, making the small river that cut directly through the property glisten with each ripple and crest over the deeply submerged rocks. It was just barely passable by boat, but judging by the overgrown foliage creeping up around the canoe, it hadn't been traversed in quite awhile.

"How are you doing with all of this, Sam?" Mr. Sterling asked him as he sipped his coffee. The smell wafted over to Sam, who suddenly wished he had another cup.

"Good, I guess," he answered quickly, but really, there was no way to tell how he was at that moment.

Mr. Sterling smiled.

"I know better than that. Let me see if I can get this right—first

Chapter Four: wollemia nobilia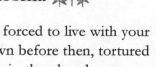

you were shipped to a backwoods town and forced to live with your grandfather, whom you had never truly known before then, tortured incessantly by a no-good yokel with bushy hair, then lured to a cave and told you have entered another world," he paused and smiled casually. "I would say that most people wouldn't be fine with that."

He nailed it right on the head, Sam thought.

"Yeah, I guess it's a little much all at once."

"Sam, you will see and understand everything in due time," he sighed. "I know it's frustrating, but we feel it best if you learned about us and this place little by little."

Sam curled his eyebrows in defiance.

"I don't understand. I just wish I could know more about this place—and whatever this group ... is."

"Yes, yes, I do know what you are going through. But I need you to be patient—to accept what you do not quite understand yet. This place," he pointed with his coffee cup at the cold dark scene in front of him, "is where I—well we—believe you belong."

Sam didn't answer, only nodded in the darkness. Something about Mr. Sterling's words felt right, even though everything inside him just wanted to scream out as loud as he could. *Belong here? Where even in the world is here?*

"Sam, there is something else I wanted to talk to you about."

Sam froze. Here it is. The talk about Emma and how he should keep his hands off ...

Mr. Sterling took a deep breath.

"Sam, you are going to be faced with challenges here you never anticipated. Challenges, such as, well, whatever you struggle with will be amplified here tremendously." He sipped his coffee again. "I know you were thrown into this without really being asked, but there are things here ... that will try and take advantage of your weaknesses."

"I noticed," Sam sputtered without thinking, his mind racing to the unknown noise in the woods.

"Sam, I need to know what really happened out there," Mr. Sterling said sternly as he leaned forward on the chair, making it creak loudly in the darkness.

Chapter Four: wollemia nobilia

Sam considered holding back once more, but then concluded there was no other way but to tell him the truth.

"Please know I only have this group's—and your best interests at heart."

"I uh ... well, I think there was something out there," he stammered, the words sounding strange coming out of his mouth. "Something maybe with ... well ... green eyes."

Mr. Sterling leaned back in his chair and began to rock slowly, staring off into the night silently. For a moment, Sam wondered if he said something wrong. Maybe it was only part of the effects from the arch—delusions that came with the intense light. But he knew that was unlikely, and judging from Mr. Sterling's expression, it was significant enough for him to be concerned with.

"Mr. Sterling, what is this place?" he decided to avoid the topic of the green eyes for the moment.

Mr. Sterling sighed, staring into the thick black night.

"I suppose it could be considered a different world, except that wouldn't be entirely accurate," he stopped, still focused on the dark tree line in front of him. "Sam, what do you know about the spiritual world?"

"Uh—like good versus evil?" Sam guessed.

"Yes, in a way," Mr. Sterling nodded. "Here, however, our evil has substance, and a name. Its name is Sevel. It is pure emptiness, absolute Darkness, void of Light and morality—and it is very powerful."

"I have always thought that kind of stuff to be a myth," Sam paused. "And—"

"And?"

"... a religious crutch. Like the hero that shows up and saves everyone ... except that he never does."

Mr. Sterling laughed, and Sam looked cross-eyed at him.

"Emma told me you were an intelligent boy. I guess she was right," he smiled at him. "But you know, believing in a hero requires faith, and so does not believing."

"I'm not sure I am following," Sam admitted.

Chapter Four: wollemia nobilia

He sipped his coffee more slowly.

"Your understanding will come in due time, Sam. It will just require a little realignment of faith on your part, but it is ultimately your choice."

Sam's face grew warm again.

"I hope to understand, sir. I just wish I could really see what is happening. It all seems so surreal, almost like a cruel joke someone plays on you."

Mr. Sterling chuckled.

"Thank you for that, Sam. It takes me back to my first time in this place."

"When did you find out about here, sir?"

"My father showed me when I was thirteen—the age of understanding," he paused. "He brought me out here to this cabin, in fact. I, too, was on a need-to-know basis."

"Where did you go from here?" Sam pressed for information, eager to hear the story.

He chuckled once again, and Sam knew that he had pushed him as far as he was going to go tonight.

"Then on to Lior City, where we are going tomorrow," Mr. Sterling said with finality.

Lior City? Where was that? Even though his knowledge of world cities was extensive, that one was unfamiliar.

"Now, Sam," he patted Sam's knee, "off to bed with you. We have a long walk tomorrow."

Sam stood and walked toward the door, knowing that Mr. Sterling wasn't going to discuss any more detail with him. His place was finding out on a need-to-know basis.

"Sam," Mr. Sterling called after him as his hand touched the cold metal latch of the cabin door. "Be careful with my daughter. She means a lot to me," he said smiling.

Sam nodded and closed the door behind him, his reply choked in the surprise of Mr. Sterling's parting words.

When he reached the loft, the others were in their bunks reading by the dim light of the table lamps. He silently went to his own bunk

Chapter Four: wollemia nobilia

and found a package waiting for him. It was wrapped in brown paper and tied with a simple white piece of string.

Glancing around the room, he looked to see if anyone would give away who had given him the package. No one even so much as glanced up from their reading.

He untied the string and opened the thick brown paper carefully. Inside were a new pair of satin blue pinstripe pajamas and a pair of leather house shoes with flannel linings.

Sam slipped into the closet in the corner and changed into his new nightclothes and house shoes. They fit perfectly.

Stepping back out into the room, he noticed suddenly that everyone was gone. He was alone.

Then from the stairs below he heard what sounded like whispers. Instinctively, he snuck to the stairwell to listen to the hushed conversation.

When he reached the top of the stairs, however, he was suddenly met with a howl of cheers and claps from the living room below as the entire cabin stood watching him.

For a moment he stood completely stunned, but at their beckoning, he was forced out of hiding and down the stairs to the group. He was immediately greeted with more whoops and cheers from everyone as they surrounded him, hugging and patting him on the back.

Mrs. Sterling then emerged with a huge strawberry frosted cake and a pitcher of tea, which drew more whoops and calls.

"Eat up, everyone! This is a special day!" she called, handing out plates of cake as quickly as she could.

"Oh, very nice!" Emma whistled at his new pajamas. "I think the satin blue goes with your eyes!"

Lillia looked at her in disgust, but then smiled smugly at him.

"While I don't share her pathetic romanticism, the threads do look pretty great."

Gus patted him on the back awkwardly.

"We all wanted to let you know how glad we are that you are here with us."

Chapter Four: wollemia nobilia

"Welcome to the family, Sam," Mrs. Sterling hugged him, smiling ear to ear and handing him a huge piece of cake with extra frosting.

Then without warning, fat tears welled up in the corners of his eyes, and no matter how hard he tried, he couldn't stop them from flowing. For the first time in a long time, he felt really welcomed somewhere.

Miss Karpatch hadn't spoken much to him since he saw her at the arch, but now she smiled and put an arm around him, her long ponytail nearly landing in his frosting.

"Sam, you need to know how much we all care for you."

Sam looked at his teacher. Part of him wanted still to be angry with her for constantly invading his personal life, but somehow he knew there was more to her worrying than just his grades and home life. She was only trying to understand him.

A stiff hand was suddenly on his shoulder.

"We are all grateful you were able to join us," Harper Cooley said queerly, then turned quickly to refill his coffee from the pot.

Sam enjoyed the company of his new family around him and the strawberry cake that seemed to appear from nowhere. At some point during his second piece of cake, someone turned on the little radio in the corner. Lively music that simulated a cross between classical and folk erupted into the cabin, and suddenly Mr. and Mrs. Sterling, Lillia, and Miss Karpatch were all out in the middle of the living room, dancing and taking bites of strawberry cake whenever they could.

Before he could stop her, Emma had dragged Sam out into middle of the group and all but forced him to dance with her. They danced until Sam felt as though he was going to pass out from exhaustion. Emma laughed at him for his lack of rhythm and stepping on her toes while they danced, but Sam didn't care.

While they danced, at some point he began to laugh at Emma's poking fun of his dancing, and couldn't stop, which made Emma laugh even more. They laughed and danced, holding each other up for support so they didn't fall into Gus and Lillia and Cooley and Miss Karpatch dancing. Then he whispered to Emma to look at Cooley's

Chapter Four: wollemia nobilia

face, solemn and determined, but it didn't help his dancing. He was worse than Sam. This set Emma off on another laughing spree, one from which she wasn't going to recover very easily.

Suddenly, Emma had a hold of his arm and before he knew it, she had whisked him out the front door and pressed her lips to his.

She kissed him softly, making his senses flood wildly throughout his body. Tingles rushed to the surface of his skin, and he stiffened, unable to move in her grasp.

Then she pushed him away and began laughing once again, but Sam couldn't laugh. He could only stare at her, his lips still burning hotly from the surprise kiss.

She dragged him back indoors, and they danced again until Mrs. Sterling finally shooed everyone to bed, which was well after one o'clock in the morning.

Sam snuggled comfortably under his covers and stole a glance at Emma, who seemed not even to notice he was looking at her. But even in the darkness of the loft in the cabin, he could see that she was smiling, and that was all that he needed before drifting off to the best sleep he had in year.

Chapter Five
Jester's Pass

"Yes. I'm positive. One was seen in the storm that just hit White Pine."

Downstairs, Mr. Sterling's muffled voice was heard.

Sam heard them before his eyes opened, and when they finally did, he could tell it was still dark.

The men were talking in excited tones, and although they were trying to contain their voices, Sam heard them loud and clear.

"How is that possible? How could they have gotten through the gate?" Cooley whined.

"My guess is that it was the same as the incident fifteen years ago … a former Watcher of the Light let them through."

"That was circumstantial. No one proved it."

"And yet it happened. How else could the Storm Lord get through the gate? We know there are those loyal to the Darkness in Creation, but the Dark Watchers? How can fallen get through?"

"Maybe with a spell, or perhaps the gate had a hiccup or something," Cooley smacked his lips angrily. "But we don't know

Chapter Five: Jester's Pass

for sure it was Sar Serhah that caused the one in White Pine. The monitoring tower still shows all three Lords locked up."

"True, but how can we explain the storm? Its signature from the PO office suggests—" Mr. Sterling attempted to keep Cooley under control. "

"Either way, I don't think it's substantial enough to report to the Council or the Chancellor. They will require proof, and we can't give that to them."

"I agree," Mr. Sterling said softly, then lowered his voice so low that Sam strained to hear from his bunk. "But it is unusual, all this activity—first Sam's encounter and now this. We must be on our guard—and find proof if we can."

Mr. Sterling must have heard Emma come down the stairs because he immediately began speaking in his normal volume. Sam hadn't even noticed her slip past him in the dark because he was so intent on the conversation below.

"Hi honey. How did you sleep?"

Emma kissed her father and murmured something incoherent, but then, only a few moments later, she could be heard happily reciting wakeup songs with her mother in the kitchen.

Last night, she had kissed him. He touched his finger to his lips to recall the feeling of hers against his. Still lying in the dark, another chill went up his spine that resembled the one from the previous night. It was soft, delicate, and unlike anything he had ever felt before. It was, in fact, his first and only kiss.

The smell of coffee and bacon frying permeating upstairs woke him from his daydream. Gus was already dressing and Lillia was already gone, her bunk neatly made.

After they were ready, he and Gus went downstairs for breakfast, which consisted of a very large bowl of eggs and another of fried potatoes, a pile of bacon, biscuits with jam, and milk. Sam wondered how the groceries had made it to the cabin. Perhaps one of their magical blue lanterns had brought them here.

Mr. Sterling waited until everyone had taken a seat before he

Chapter Five: Jester's Pass

himself sat at the large table, which took up nearly the entire first floor of the small cabin.

"Let us give thanks for our abundant blessing," Mr. Sterling announced, and folded his hands. Sam followed the rest of the table and closed his eyes.

"Our Lord and Creator, please bless this food. We thank you for its nourishment, and for protecting us here. We are grateful for our newest member, and we ask that you would guide him in his steps as he searches for answers," Mr. Sterling paused, "and Lord, please guide us today as we travel. In your name, Lord, amen."

Sam felt his face grow warm when he opened his eyes. He hadn't prayed much before, and he had never been talked about during a prayer in a group. Something inside him made him angry when he thought about these things, and he couldn't explain it. It just made him angry.

Although he didn't usually eat much for breakfast on normal days, today he felt ravenous and had three eggs, multiple pieces of bacon, two biscuits, and two large helpings of potatoes. Gus, Lillia, and Emma must have felt the same because they ate nearly as much as he did.

Mrs. Sterling seemed pleased with the amount they were eating and offered more to all of them, but no one could eat another bite. However, when she offered to refill coffee cups, they held their cups up eagerly.

After a few minutes of conversation and sipping coffee, Mr. Sterling cleared his throat to get their attention. Instinctively, everyone at the table quieted and looked toward him.

"First of all, I would like to thank my wife Cindy for a wonderful breakfast."

Cheers and thank yous rang around the table to Mrs. Sterling, who promptly blushed and waved them off.

"Now, our plan for the day." He pulled a map from his tweed sport coat and laid it on the table. "We will be heading to Lior City by way of Jester's Pass, then through the Lior Forest."

Chapter Five: Jester's Pass

There were surprised glances from the around the table.

"Why aren't we taking the Lightway in Warm Springs?" Emma asked disappointedly. "This is the first year we can all use it!"

Mr. Sterling sighed, "It's been having problems."

Grunts and groans rippled through the group.

"For the hundredth time," Lillia rolled her eyes.

"Now, don't complain. This will give Sam a good chance to see the area."

"And we all could use the exercise anyway," Miss Karpatch offered cheerfully.

"There's one more thing," Mr. Sterling said over the chatter. "Fenton Chivler is missing."

A hush fell silently over the group. Lillia looked the most disturbed.

"Since when?"

"Last night during the storm," Cooley answered. "However, it could be that he is simply taking a vacation."

Sam looked around the table and saw the looks of concern on Emma's and Mrs. Sterling's faces. Lillia looked as though she was going to punch whoever was responsible.

"Mr. Cooley is correct," Mr. Sterling attempted to take a lighter tone to calm the group. "We aren't certain of his whereabouts yet, but let's not get ahead of ourselves."

"He was taken. There's no way Chivler would just leave for vacation," Lillia said quickly, ignoring Mr. Sterling's request.

Mr. Sterling sighed and shook his head. "I may need to report back to the Council if they request, so we will need to make our sightseeing time short."

"If there are no dark spots out there," Lillia said under her breath.

"There most certainly are not," Cooley said defiantly. "The Seers would know immediately."

Lillia lifted one eyebrow in disbelief.

"Then how do you explain all of the sightings? Or the reports of residual Darkness in the City?" she ventured with the slightest tone of disrespect.

Chapter Five: Jester's Pass

"Rumors. None are true," Cooley leveled his eyes toward his younger counterpart. "You are mistaken."

No one dared challenge Cooley, though not out of fear, but impatience. Mr. Sterling had held his peace, but Sam could tell he wasn't entirely sure where he stood on the issue by the expression on his face. But like the rest of the group, he wisely stayed silent.

He himself wished to hear the argument further, since he had no knowledge of the "Darkness" Lillia was talking about. But getting information on either could prove to be difficult, especially if there were conflicting opinions.

As Mr. Sterling outlined their path to both cities on the map in front of them, Sam followed along on the old document but didn't recognize any of the land features or names of cities. They didn't sound like any of the names he had ever heard before. He was truly in a foreign place.

"Okay everyone, let's pack up and head out," Mr. Sterling announced once breakfast was cleaned up, looking toward his wife, who nodded as she put away last dish in the tiny kitchen and stooped to pick up a backpack to lay it on the table.

"Samuel, I have packed a few things for you in this backpack that you will be needing." Mrs. Sterling handed him a canvas pack, which seemed lighter than it looked. "All your essentials are there. Toiletries, pants and shirts, socks and undies—"

Emma overheard her mother and giggled at the word undies, to which Sam promptly blushed.

Mr. Sterling stepped in with a scowl on his face to rescue Sam.

"Oh dear, let's not embarrass the boy this early—"

But Mrs. Sterling held a hand up at her husband gently.

"And your journal."

"Journal?" Sam questioned, looking at the blue leather softbound poking out of the top of the pack.

"Oh my dear boy, have you never kept a journal?" she prodded.

"No, ma'am, I haven't. I suppose I never did because life seemed to change so much that it didn't make much sense."

Chapter Five: Jester's Pass

"That's exactly why you need to start keeping one, Sammy boy," Lillia interjected with a smirk on her face.

"Well then, Lillia's right. You must start keeping one." Mrs. Sterling smiled and patted him on the shoulder. "It is very important. Just write about anything you think of throughout the day that has significance. This one is blue, like your eyes."

"Thank you Mrs. Sterling." Sam looked curiously at the leather book, which looked a bit like the one Mr. Chivler gave him, only newer.

"Are we going to hang out here all day, or are we going to get to Lior before everything closes?" Mr. Sterling said with a scowl on his face as he swung open the large cabin door.

As if everyone were on cue, the whole lot stood and headed for the door, laughing and talking excitedly about the journey. Sam stood also and took a deep breath, then swung his new backpack over his shoulder and followed quietly.

Mr. Sterling led them across the bridge over the small river and onto the narrow path through the musky smelling pines. He walked so fast that Sam had trouble keeping up, but eventually found the pace and fell in behind Lillia.

The path seemed to wind endlessly through the trees, and after only a short time, the excited talk began to die down until there was only the sound of the soft wind blowing past them as they walked.

The terrain was much hillier than it was in White Pine, and there were occasions on the trail where the trees opened up and they could see a glimpse of the mountainous terrain in front of them. Slowly, the doubt of whether or not he was still in Michigan began to ebb away, and he gave into the awe of his surroundings.

To pass the time as they walked, Emma slowed to talk to him, and they recalled the previous night's celebration and laughed at Sam's dancing. He was enjoying their talk so much that he didn't even realize that they had been walking uphill for nearly twenty minutes, and that he was struggling to catch his breath and talk at the same time. Every so often Lillia turned and looked at them with an annoyed expression, but Sam had learned to ignore her, as her expressions were not rare.

Chapter Five: Jester's Pass

After a few more minutes of strenuous trudging, the train of travelers stopped suddenly, forcing unwary Sam into the back of Lillia.

"Hey, would you look where you are going?" she sneered.

"Sorry," Sam smiled and rolled his eyes, at which Emma laughed and winked at him.

"We are at the top!" Emma said suddenly, grabbing Sam's hand and pushing past the others in line to the front.

She pulled him to where the trees opened up into a wide panoramic vista of the valley below, where her father was already admiring the view. The sight took Sam's breath away.

"Welcome to Jester's Pass," Mr. Sterling said as he stood on a rock outcropping near the edge of the cliff. "It is the highest point of the trail. That over there," he pointed in the distance to a clump of small buildings wrapping itself around a mountain, "is Warm Springs."

"The best place ever," Emma sighed happily.

"Yes, yes, and we will go there soon enough," he smiled at his daughter.

Sam was stunned. He was definitely not in Michigan anymore. Snow-capped mountains laced the horizon beyond the valley, and thick pines blanketed the valley far below them. The jagged peaks surrounded the valley in every direction but one, which led to a vast forest, then to open plains. Far beyond the plains was the faint blue outline of an ocean.

"This is Lior," Mr. Sterling made a sweeping motion with his hand. "It means—the Land of Light. And that," he pointed toward the ocean, "is the way to Lior City."

The places, the names, the landscape—it was all new, but grasping it was another story. Where were they? Was it another planet? Another part of Earth that was hidden from society?

"Lior is a land created for us, the People of Light, The *Descendants of Light*," Mr. Sterling said, as though anticipating Sam's question.

All at once it him Sam. He knew who they were.

"You mean the angels. You're Descendants of them."

Mr. Sterling nodded.

99

Chapter Five: Jester's Pass

"But why here?"

"When the earth was created, it fell into Darkness for a period of time. We, the People of Light, needed another place to go. Our gifts and abilities did not match with the mortality of humanity. So Lior was created for us. It is an in-between land of sorts, until the Creator returns and reunites us."

"So we are in another dimension," Sam frowned.

"You could say that," Mr. Sterling nodded. "But think of it more as two places that exist side by side, and each has a purpose."

Sam stared at the majestic valley below him, enjoying the cool mountain breeze that brushed past him. It was beautiful, but Mr. Sterling's words were not resonating with him. Beautiful or not, he was still in an alien world.

It was frustrating to know that he had lived so ignorantly his whole life ... as so many others on Earth still did.

"So we are just blind to what is really out there? Every day, people walk around without a clue that there is another world—and one glimpse could change their perspective in so many things, like whether or not there is a God?"

Mr. Sterling thought for a moment and smiled, his eyes glowing with empathy.

"Faith in what cannot be seen is essential to having the freedom to choose whether or not to believe in something," he said finally.

It was then that Sam squinted and noticed what looked like large green kites floating strangely around the valley. They were huge—nearly the size of small airplanes, and blended into the trees that crawled up the mountainsides. Their long slender tails seemed to slither through the air like a snake through the water.

"Those are Northropi," Gus pointed toward the closest as he squinted and attempted to adjust his glasses. "Largest flying reptiles in existence. Herbivores, and harmless ... well, unless they land on you," he chuckled.

"A dinosaur?" Sam was exasperated as he watched the green monster slip through the sky. "You can't be serious."

Just then, a Northropi drifted gracefully just below the outlook

Chapter Five: Jester's Pass

where they stood, making everyone in the group crowd the ledge to watch it.

With the head of an oversized brachiosaur, the Northropi moved like a thin blimp, its green shiny skin like it had just taken a dip in the lake. The wingspan was even wider than his grandfather's cabin, and with the creature's size, Sam wondered how it flew at all.

He remembered hearing about the larger of the Pterosaur's remains being found in Mexico, but here was a living, breathing example. How could there be living dinosaurs here?

"They like to hug the mountains because there is more of a breeze," Gus added.

Sam was dizzy from the sight. It was all too much—traveling to another world ... dinosaurs.

"It seems impossible."

"Yes. It makes you question the laws of physics. It did me," Gus said. "From what I can tell, their wings are balanced so incredibly perfectly that they are able to create their own updraft under their wings."

"No, I mean, dinosaurs—they are extinct. Something killed them off."

Gus nodded.

"On Earth, yes. But here, they are still alive and well."

Sam was frustrated. They weren't getting it. People had been living with the idea that dinosaurs had been dead for millions of years—those that believed in evolution, anyway. One step through the Light gate would destroy all that science and history had been built upon.

"Then why allow Earth to live in the dark?"

Mr. Sterling laughed.

"Truly!" he said, taking out a few pieces of jerky and handing them to Sam and Gus. "I remember when I came to Lior for the first time. There were so many perceptions about what I knew that changed so suddenly. I stayed in bed for nearly a whole day not eating. And even then, it was only after meeting Cindy that I began really to believe what I saw. But I tell you, Samuel, people on Earth are not in the dark. They are only misguided. Even if we were to bring them

Chapter Five: Jester's Pass

here, they would swear the dinosaurs weren't there. There is nothing we can do with a closed mind."

"That is why we don't invite anyone here that is much older than you are," Miss Karpatch had snuck up on them. "Adults have a hard time adjusting."

"And because we were born in Creation, we weren't allowed to come to Lior until we were thirteen," Emma offered, the slightest disappointment in her voice.

Mr. Sterling swept a hand out toward the valley.

"The Northropi are only one part of that perception you must change. This is the last valley they inhabit. The Darkness drove them from the others long ago."

The Darkness? Why did they keep talking about it like it had a mind of its own? "Is that what I saw last night? The Darkness?"

Mr. Sterling gazed off into the valley below. The breeze from the mountains seemed to be warming as the sun was now high in the sky. For a moment, Sam felt the slightest bit of fear as the uncomfortable pause grew to a long silence. Although he knew Mr. Sterling would eventually answer him, he couldn't help but notice the reluctance to give him complete information.

"Although there are still remnants of Darkness here in Lior, we haven't had any incidents with Dark Forces in almost fifty years, thank the Creator."

Lillia, who had rejoined the group from her perch of solitude, showed obvious signs of irritation with Mr. Sterling's response.

"What about Boggle's report from his Darkness anomaly detector?"

Upon her words, Cooley seemed to appear out of nowhere, looking anxious to hear the next response. Mr. Sterling looked around, and seeing he had an audience, stood to address the eavesdropping group.

"As the Director, I can assure you the Protector's Office takes every report seriously, but no residual traces of Darkness were found upon investigation. We assumed it was a problem with the device,"

Chapter Five: Jester's Pass

he said carefully, which didn't sit well with Lillia, who rolled her eyes at his words.

Mr. Sterling continued.

"We are safer than we ever have been in Lior. The Seers have assured us of that." He glanced appreciatively at Cooley. "Now, I believe the time has come that we must get moving. We have a lot of ground to cover today. Shall we?"

****

Lillia caught up to Sam when they were nearing the bottom of Jester's Pass. It had taken nearly two hours to reach the bottom, partially because of the dangerous path that wound down the mountain, and partially because of Gus's fear of heights. Every so often they would stop to give him a breather, and to talk him out of retreating to a wider portion of the path where he would back himself up against the cliff and refuse to move. They still had a considerable amount of walking to do, but already Sam's feet were groaning at him.

"A long time ago the Darkness had no power anywhere in Lior. It stayed in hiding, cowering from the Light," Lillia said beneath her breath as the others attempted to coax Gus around a large rock that half-blocked the perilous path. "But nowadays, whatever the Council believes or doesn't, it is out there, and I think it is stronger than it used to be. If it is spreading, we are in deep trouble."

"How does it spread?" Sam probed, thinking of a cool mist moving silently along the surface of a lake.

Lillia was silent for a moment. Then she turned to look at one of the last glimpses of the Northropi before the group descended below the tree line of the pass toward the valley floor.

"Choices—the choices of men, and of those that live here. It thrives on evil acts. The more bad people choose to do, the more the Darkness grows. It gives power to the Dark Forces. The Dark Watchers and their Lords, and the Metim that follow them."

Sam said nothing, but something told him that what she said

Chapter Five: Jester's Pass

made some sense. If they truly believed that the Darkness wasn't growing, then they hadn't been outside of White Pine recently. The world was a dangerous, angry place.

"But you don't know for sure?"

Lillia hugged the wall on a particularly thin spot on the path, then waited for Sam to follow. Emma had joined the group trying to convince Gus to move, but with little luck. No doubt it was going to take significantly longer to get him to cross the spot Lillia and Sam just did.

"Boggle told me. He believes that information is being held back about the Darkness in Lior. He thinks it's growing, and either the Council is purposefully denying it, or is too ignorant to see it," she whispered furiously. "Boggle said those devices he made were almost foolproof. But the Council never wants to hear what Boggle says."

Before he could ask who Boggle was, however, Gus had somehow mustered up the courage to open his eyes and face his fear, and the group was on the move again. At the halfway mark, Miss Karpatch made sure to point out that the temperature had risen nearly ten degrees since first descending into the valley, which immediately started a string of useless facts and information from an already talkative Gus, who loved to talk loudly when he was not afraid.

It was nearly lunchtime when the group reached the bottom of the pass. Mr. Sterling called for a break near a small stream that seemed to flow straight from the rock next to the path where some brush and small trees easily concealed it.

As they ate, they all took turns drinking from the small spring and filling their canteens. The water was cold and refreshing, and Sam drank long and deep from the bubbling spring. Mrs. Sterling handed him a sandwich—roast beef. Not his favorite, but filling nonetheless after a long hike. According to Mr. Sterling, they still had much of their journey ahead of them, and sunset would be upon them in only six hours.

"Eat quickly, group," Mr. Sterling said with urgency, but still smiling, "if we are to make it to the City by nightfall, of course."

"Here, try this." Miss Karpatch handed him a napkin wrapped up

Chapter Five: Jester's Pass

in a ball as the rest of the group finished up their lunch and repacked their backpacks.

He opened the napkin and without hesitating, took a bite of the green spongy ball, which tasted very much like a cupcake straight from the oven. Chocolate, but there was another flavor—something he couldn't explain, almost like chocolate, and perhaps coconut but not as strong. It was deliciously moist, one of the best cakes he had tasted.

"It's made from an ancient root, the Colacree."

"It's good," Sam said, still feeling a bit strange that only last week his history teacher was rubbing her temples and calling him lazy, but now he was eating root cake with her in a strange land.

"Sam," she started as she unwrapped another cake ball. "I am sorry for the way people treated you in White Pine. I tried to make you feel as welcome as I could."

He felt a little warmth in his cheeks when she mentioned how people treated him. He did feel like he was an outcast at times. That was, whenever he wasn't face down on the hallway floor with Bush bloodying his face. But outcast? He could understand that. He always prided himself on his ability to handle such labels.

"It's okay, Miss Karpatch. Really," he answered, but more out of the desire to end the conversation than to console her.

Miss Karpatch sighed.

"In Lior, please call me Sarah."

Sam poked at an oversized bug with a stick and finished off the rest of the cake ball, his muffled words barely heard as the moist dessert filled up most of his mouth.

"Sure Miss Karpatch," he smiled awkwardly at her.

They packed up their lunch remains and headed back down the trail toward the dense forest that led out of the valley. As they walked, Sam thought he caught glimpses of the huge Northropi gliding through the air in the distance, but they were good at blending into the scenery behind them.

As they traversed the winding trail through the dense pines, wildlife began to appear more frequently now. Some animals he was

Chapter Five: Jester's Pass

used to—squirrels, deer, and the occasional bright yellow finch— and a few he wasn't—oversized woodland birds, giant green and silver dragonflies that swooped around their heads curiously, and even a Rhynio insect, thought to be one of the oldest extinct insects known in the scientific world.

He looked over at Gus, who was puffing his way through thick undergrowth that had begun to snake over the path, and thought about a short break to chew on some jerky Mrs. Sterling tucked into his pack, but he knew nothing was going to stop Mr. Sterling's goal of reaching the City by nightfall. It was a long trek yet, but doable if they didn't stop for unnecessary breaks.

Suddenly ahead of them, a yellow lizard-like creature the size of a small fox with a curious domed head paused to size them up as a possible meal. At the sight of Gus's looming frame, he decided against it and scurried quickly into the dense underbrush to the right of the trail.

"That one is a Lotio," Emma whispered while pointing to the bit of yellow that poked out from an extra thorny bush. "He's an extinct lizard. Don't worry, he's more scared of us, but I still wouldn't go sneaking up on him."

Then, immediately ahead of them, there was a loud crashing in the brush that sounded like a bulldozer plowing through the trees, but as soon as it started, the noise was deadly silent.

"Everyone get hidden and be quiet!" Mr. Sterling turned and hushed the group frantically before ducking into a small clump of brush to the side of the trail.

Before Sam realized it, Emma had pulled him off to the side of the trail and was busy searching for a suitable place to hide. But they obviously didn't move fast enough, for out of the trees ahead stepped a large grey and tan lizard with teeth the size of spearheads and skin that glistened as though he had just been through a creek. As its gleaming tangerine eyes surveyed its surroundings, it calmly purred as though a cat would, but in predatory fashion.

Chapter Five: Jester's Pass

Turning its sleek head to and fro, for a moment it spotted movement near Sam and Emma and charged suddenly within five feet of where they stood, glaring at the two immobile shapes in front of him.

"D-don't M-move," Emma hissed through her teeth.

Sam obeyed. Not only was he terrified of the agile monster in front of him, but also his foot was caught securely in the exposed roots of a scraggly tree next to him. For a moment he remembered his backpack stuck in the chair in Miss Karpatch's classroom and cursed the untimely irony under his breath.

The creature eyed them both, turning his gaze upon Sam, as if waiting for a move, and then Emma. He clawed the ground with his gigantic feet as if to elicit some response from either of them, then seeing none, turned and quickly disappeared through the trees.

"That," Emma's heart galloped as she clutched Sam's shoulder, "was a Sarse."

"A what?" Sam was still trying to free his foot and figure out what had just happened.

"Are you two alright?" Mrs. Sterling looked panicked as she rushed to their side, closely followed by Gus, Lillia, Miss Karpatch, and Cooley.

"Oh man, I thought you were goners," Lillia shook her head.

Mrs. Sterling grabbed her daughter and looked her all around as if searching for invisible wounds, while Mr. Sterling had pulled out his binoculars and was scanning the trees for any sign of the creature's return.

"We're fine, mom, really. It just scared us, that's all," Emma finally succeeded in controlling her breathing.

"That was a young Allosaurus. We call them Sarse's, but very rare in this area nonetheless. You and Emma were lucky," Gus patted Sam on the back.

"Allosaurus?" Sam had finally freed his stuck foot. "Now I know I am dreaming."

Chapter Five: Jester's Pass

"It's not even that unthinkable, if you consider how young the Earth is," Miss Karpatch added. "Lucky for you two, Sarses are pretty thick skulled."

"Doesn't matter what or where it came from if it is going to have you for dinner," Mrs. Sterling huffed.

"That was a close call," Mr. Sterling turned from his guard. "I have never come across a Sarse this close to Warm Springs before. They must be migrating for some reason. We need to be on our guard always, and close together as a group from now on."

"Agreed," Mrs. Sterling pronounced resolutely. "I want adults in front and back of the line, and you kids in the middle." She snapped her fingers sharply and pointed in front of her.

No one argued with her request, and instead picked up their packs and began to file in line back on the trail.

"Welcome to the neighborhood, newb," Lillia snickered as she brushed past.

They walked a while before seeing the first sign of water, which was good timing since their canteens were nearly dry. He could tell the rest of the group was beginning to worry about getting lost as the afternoon waned, but Mr. Sterling seemed confident he knew where they were.

A beautiful waterfall emerged as they rounded one of the more dense portions of the forest, and Sam was once again stunned by how beautiful Lior was.

"We need to keep up the pace, gang," said Mr. Sterling as they filled their canteens in the icy cold mountain water. Sam had already noticed the change in pace after the encounter with the Sarse dinosaur, as most of the group had.

"How long until we get there, Daddy?" Emma dropped a rather large looking rock out of her boot.

"Oh, I'd say we have a few miles left—maybe a few hours at most," said Mr. Sterling as he surveyed the forest around him.

Sam was hiding an uneasy feeling, like he figured most were, but it was rather obvious by the look on her face that Mrs. Sterling was upset that the children had been put in danger in the forest.

Chapter Five: Jester's Pass

They walked on in silence until they saw the forest begin to thin out into long grassy slopes and meadows of wild blue and yellow flowers. It was there that the trees allowed a view of the full majesty of the snow caps surrounding them. They were higher than Sam had ever seen, including the Rockies. Massive cliff faces boasted their sheer elegance within the valley depths, and for a moment, Sam thought he could see the shadows of the Northropi as they glided gracefully on the upward winds. It was a truly humbling sight to behold.

As he admired the scenery behind them, however, Emma slid up next to him and thrust her hand into his, sending another icy but pleasant chill down his neck. She grasped his hand tightly and spun him around to see the meadows descend into the forested valley where it crashed into the shores of a large body of water.

"That over there," she pointed toward an open space in the valley forest, "is the City of Lior."

Chapter Six
Lior City

In front of them lay the tiny outline of a city perched neatly on the coast of a picturesque sea, whose waves were rolling in perfect patterned surf for miles in either direction. The mountains and the forest behind them and the valley in front of them was an incredible sight to behold. The sun was just beginning to set before them, sending brilliant beams of light to the City spires that rose skyward in an almost holy glow. The group of travelers stood quietly in awe of the beauty for several moments, almost disappointed that they would have to leave such a moment. It was almost as if the most beautiful scenes on Earth were all placed together into one perfect scene.

But something else drew them—the sights and sounds of a city on the verge of a great celebration. Even from a distance, the sound was easily heard but not distinguishable, except for a loudspeaker that could almost be comprehended every so often as the voice rang out through the hills.

Exhausted from the many miles they had already traveled, they trudged on through the tall grass toward the City in the waning light, wondering if the tiny buildings in the distance were ever going to

Chapter Six: Lior City

get closer. The muffled sounds from the loudspeaker died out as a grassy knoll now separated them from the City. As they walked, the grass emerged into a rather large wheat field where there were neat pathways cut through, like the corn mazes back in White Pine.

Mrs. Sterling perked up the more they distanced themselves from the forest, relieved that the danger was behind them.

"We'd better hurry if we are going to catch the opening ceremony!" she said, glancing toward the sun as it dipped beneath the watery grave of the sea.

Mr. Sterling too seemed happy to be rid of the forest as his pace became more brisk through the maze the closer they got to the City gates, which were now visible in the distance. As Sam struggled to keep up with him, he glanced at the iridescent spires gleaming like massive blue stalagmites rising out of a cavern floor. They seemed to complement the magnificence of the City perfectly.

"It's often called the City of Illumination," Mr. Sterling said, refusing to slow his pace, "partly because of its natural beauty—as you can see—but also because of its ability to dispel Darkness."

"Darkness hates Light," Sam muttered, remembering seeing it in a book he had read the previous summer.

The city entrance stood largely before them, with four smaller spires lining a great stairway leading upward through the City walls. Larger-than-average Wollemi trees stood as grand living guards along the length of the massive walls to either side of the steps, making it difficult to see the edges of the City. The walls rose nearly a hundred feet into the air, and protruding from the exterior were winged creatures carved into the light-colored stone.

At the top of the stairs was a great iron gate illuminated by the glowing spires, where two robed men with hoods stood solemnly, watching as people entered the City. Mrs. Sterling hurried them through the last bit of wheat and toward the stairs, urging the rest of the group to stay close.

There were families surrounding the stairway to the City, with children eager to get inside and attempting to prod their parents along before their turn. All of them wore robes of various colors

Chapter Six: Lior City

like the adults they accompanied, but the closer he looked he noticed only the adults wore a thick leather armband that glowed blue under their robes. It was then that Sam noticed Mr. and Mrs. Sterling, Miss Karpatch, and Cooley's bands under their deep red robes glow blue like the others, a small stone embedded in the armband barely peeking out from Mrs. Sterling's robe. The light from the stones seemed to intensify the closer to the City they came.

As they waited, Sam also began to notice differences in the people around them. Although they all dressed similar, some were of Asian descent and wore uniquely-patterned headbands over their long braids and handmade leather shoes, while others were shorter and darker-skinned with black hair and deep brown eyes. Still others had the appearance of refined fishermen with chiseled Slavic faces, each carrying a long dagger on the outside of his or her robe and smelling a bit like seawater.

"They are from different regions of Lior," Miss Karpatch whispered as they neared the midpoint of the line to enter the gates. "That family—" she pointed to the light-haired family behind them with a tall boy who wore his dagger awkwardly, "is from Telok, the lake country. And they—" she gestured discreetly toward a family with two younger boys and an olive-skinned girl who was eyeing her mother's purple stone on her armband, "are from the mountains of Nais."

"What about them?" Sam was curious about the shy dark-skinned family with an older daughter who was finishing the braids on her younger sister. She reminded Sam of what Pocahontas would look like in a green robe.

"Themane. The forest region. A strong, but very quiet people," she said, almost before he could ask. "But even though different, they are all people like us."

He wanted to probe her for more answers, but the line moved quickly as the robed guards hurried families through the gates. Emma squirmed her way back to where Sam was and grabbed his hand just as the group made it to the checkpoint.

"What do I do?" he said, suddenly nervous.

Chapter Six: Lior City

"Nothing. They will just want to see that you are with us," she said, pulling him closer to her.

"What are they checking for?" he asked as the guards surveyed Mr. Sterling up and down in an almost mechanical motion.

"Traces of Darkness. They are Seers, trained to make sure Metim, or dark creatures, don't get into the City. But don't worry, they can only see everything you've ever done . . ." she smacked him and smiled when he looked horrified at her words.

"Don't worry, newb. If Em' can forgive you, they certainly can." Lillia turned around to level her eyes at Sam, having obviously heard their conversation.

Emma was next in line and stood between the two guards, keeping her body perfectly still as they walked around her, looking her up and down. She stood facing straight forward, hands at her side while they probed her with their hooded eyes.

Suddenly above them there was a flash and a rushing noise, like that of a powerful gust of wind.

Sam looked up in time to see the remnants of the blue light streaking through the night sky.

The brief distraction caused him to forget momentarily where he was, and when he realized it, the guards were facing him and Emma was calling his name loudly beyond the gate.

"Move it Sam! They won't wait on you!" she yelled.

He moved into position quickly and suddenly felt a warm rush come over him, much like when crossing through the gate from White Pine. He froze as the guards moved around him, the warmth intensifying as they drew closer to him, searching him up and down with their hidden eyes, like they were peering into his soul. Around and around they circled him, like vultures waiting for his last breath to be taken. It seemed like they probed him forever, but then they backed away slowly, the warm feeling disappearing as they concentrated their efforts on the dark-haired boy from the lake country behind him.

"Kinda weird, the first time," Emma said as they walked inside the gate.

Just inside the gate were two more hooded guards, but with

Chapter Six: Lior City

swords strapped at each of their sides. They paid no attention to Sam or Emma, but carefully watched the happenings at the gate entrance with the Seers. Above them, the blue trail of light was just beginning to fade from the sky.

"Was that the Lightway that just went over us?" Sam remembered them discussing it at the cabin.

She nodded.

"Yep. Last minute Council member or Protector, I suppose. For most everyone else it is shut down during the Light Festival, but certain government officials are allowed to use it any time."

They climbed the second set of stone steps between massive pillars of white stone that formed the entrance foyer of the City. Seeing the interesting markings on the pillar, Sam reached out suddenly and brushed the intricate markings with his fingers, matching every stroke. Arches with three legs and winged creatures made patterns up the side of the pillar. His eyes followed them as they curved upward to where they formed a massive arch above their heads.

One in particular caught his eye above him—a simple shape, almost like a wing, hovering over the creatures as though a parent protected their young.

"It's called an *Irin*, I think." Emma watched his gaze. "The Watcher wing."

Sam suddenly knew the symbol from the cavern back in White Pine. The one he had been drawing from the moment he arrived in the tiny northern town.

"The wing has always meant something of significance to the Descendants," Emma said as she traced the patterns with her own fingers carefully. Then, seeing Sam's confused look, she only smiled and pulled him away from the pillars and up the stairs to rejoin the others.

****

Main Street was bustling with every kind of vendor one could imagine. There were sugared doughnut carts, meat and vegetable

Chapter Six: Lior City

pastry trays, two story chocolate drizzle contraptions for cake pops and exotic fruit sticks, beverage carts with all sorts of herbed teas and colorful fruit juices, carts with giant cheese sticks and smoked meats, and even candy carts with flower suckers and glowing dragon candies the size of your hand, not to mention the coffee carts, whose fresh roasted flavors were the first smells that hit Sam's nostrils.

They maneuvered through the stone streets around crowds of festival goers, buying large-topped festival hats, spiral glowing balloons and bracelets, and shining silver jewelry.

Sam was so entranced by the interesting shops of strange items for sale and delicious looking breads and cakes that he hardly noticed the huge white building in front of them, magnificently standing above the thousands of people gathered around its exterior.

In the center of the building stood one of the enormous spires of brilliant luminescent rock that glowed in the darkening night sky above it. Inside the stone structure was the most magnificent display of light flowing and swirling in different colors. It reminded Sam of the enchanting brilliance of the arch back in the cavern, except that it glowed with white, green, purple, and red. He wasn't the only one staring at the spectacle, as hundreds of others began to herd toward the edge of the building as if the spire was signaling the beginning of something.

"That's the City Center!" Emma had to shout over the cheering and people around her. "The Council is about to send up the Watcher signal!"

In an effort to keep up with the group, Emma pulled Sam past a group of people who were crowding in from the street, eager to get as close as they could to the stage that had been set up in front of the ornate building. Sam and Emma, however, were not going to the stage, but heading for the cabins immediately to get showered and changed as Mrs. Sterling had carefully instructed them before entering the City.

"The more we dawdle the more we miss!" she had told them cheerfully.

The City Center had four entrances aside from the main entrance,

Chapter Six: Lior City

each containing large ornate domed halls on four equally-spaced sides around the circular center of the building, with each hall displaying their respective colors in fine etched glass windows, and each bearing a different creature carved into the stone along the hall.

Gus, doing his best to keep up, attempted to tell them of the history of the building—its purpose of bringing all of Lior together.

"It's meant," he puffed, "to withstand any force in Lior—or Earth!" he told them.

It took them a while to circle to the Center, and as they passed the green hall's square of the forest people in Themane, they watched vendors selling lighted green hats to show support of their hall, as well as many natural goods like leather and wood products, small bow and arrow sets, and beads and knitted items.

When they reached the red hall of Thalo, it too, was packed with vendors and shops selling their hall's lighted red hats, as well as fresh grilled seafood and potatoes, mugs of birch beer, fresh roasted coffees, and hundreds of glowing suckers of every flavor.

With a hint of salt water already drifting about, the red hall square was almost as though they had stepped into a small coastal village, much like Boothbay Harbor in Maine where his foster family vacationed every other year, except here there wasn't a half-sloshed big-haired woman arguing over a designer purse in one of the quaint shops. But it wasn't too hard to imagine his foster mother stumbling out of one of the entrances, her peacock colored dress and makeup glistening in the late harbor sun.

The street gradually inclined as they passed the shops and vendors, and at the end of the street, lighted cobblestone paths disappeared in various directions. Mr. Sterling veered right, just past the small wooden fruit stand in front of the yellow brick Middle Eastern-style Makolet's Foods, to one of the pathways that snaked through the trees until they were enveloped in the thick pines.

Moments later, with the sounds of the City faded to a muffle behind them, the woods finally opened up to a perfect view of the ocean, and before them, eight large cabins stood perched high above the water in a half-moon shape. The centerpiece of the cabin lot

Chapter Six: Lior City

was a white stone pavilion, open to the breeze, a glowing fire already burning happily in its hearth.

A calm breeze of salt and mist touched Sam's face as he followed the group toward the outermost cabin, reminding him suddenly of his one and only trip to Florida. He had loved the ocean instantly, spending most evenings on the beach to get away from his parents, his feet buried in the cool sand while the waves crashed on the shoreline. The smell and sound—the feel of the ocean—it calmed him.

As they walked toward the cabins, a large flash of light filled the sky behind the weary group, illuminating the trees where the pathway to the City led. The flash formed into an image of a winged creature, whose light burned steadily in the darkness above. From the City they heard the hushed sound of cheering in unison at the sight in the sky, and for a few moments Sam and the others watched it as it branded the muted blackness behind it.

****

The cabin was large but cozy, more ornately-decorated than the cabin near the gate, but still offering the feeling of being home—though White Pine was a very long way away. Immediately a fire was started and was soon beginning to creep up the fragrant logs.

Mrs. Sterling immediately set to work divvying up responsibilities so as not to miss any more of the celebrations in town.

"Sam, your room is upstairs with Gus. Gus, I know you will want to stay with us, since your family is on watch back in White Pine. Emma, can you make up Lillia's bed for her?" She shooed the girls upstairs and handed Sam some bed sheets and a soft down comforter. "There you are. Fresh linens that'll keep you warm. I would make the bed for you, but some things a young man can do himself, am I right?" she smiled.

"Yes. Thank you Mrs. Sterling," he said.

Though they were weary from travel, the excitement of the opening ceremony of the festival made them hurry to freshen up and change clothes, and each followed Mrs. Sterling's orders with urgency.

Chapter Six: Lior City

Following Gus up the stairs, Sam was happy to see a large room and a fireplace of their own, and making his bed was quick and painless in the cedar log bed. They had their own bathroom and shower as well, lighted by a single blue lantern, the same as in the bedroom. They changed as quickly as they could, but already people had begun gathering in the living room below, ready for the hike back into town.

"Let's go people!" Miss Karpatch barked as she burst through the door, wearing a large blinking red hat on her head and a red robe with silver cuffs and hems. "We have to get to the Center before the parade!"

As more of the group massed in front of the fireplace, Sam began to realize he was the only one not wearing a robe.

"Sam, did mom give you a robe?" Emma huffed as she emerged from one of the rooms downstairs, fiddling with a beret on her hair.

"Um—"

"Oh dear, I forgot!" Mrs. Sterling came flowing into the living room in her own robe. "Oh dear, I am so sorry Sam! We will have to get you one in town!"

"I didn't know we needed—" he started.

Mr. Sterling came whistling into the room and winked at Sam. "Darling, don't smother the boy. He will be fine until tomorrow."

Lillia snickered from the back of the room where she had already pulled a book from the wall-length bookshelf. Her hair and makeup matched the mood she was in.

"But he will be out of place!" Mrs. Sterling looked stricken.

"It's okay, Mrs. Sterling, really."

"Nonsense! I know a perfect place we can stop off before the parade." She grabbed Sam by the arm. "We can still make it if we hurry!"

Mr. Sterling shrugged as Mrs. Sterling pulled Sam out the door and down the cobble path, through the trees and into the street in front of the red hall's entrance. There, a small shop with a brick face

Chapter Six: Lior City

and aging overhang had hardly any of the pomp and decorations of the other stores. The bell above the door jingled as Mrs. Sterling hurried into the shop, and immediately a hunched, tiny old man emerged from the doorway behind the counter.

"Ah! Camisera Sterling! My beautiful girl! You are a sight for sore eyes!" the old man said.

"Uncle. How are you doing? Are you sleeping well?" Mrs. Sterling let go of Sam's arm to hug the tiny man.

"Eh, you know, here and there. But you didn't come back to Lior to ask about my sleeping habits, now did you? What can I do for you Camisera? Oh! I see here you have brought me a stowaway!" The old man looked Sam up and down from his spectacles crouched low on his nose.

"Samuel, meet my dear uncle Osan. He's the finest robe tailor in all of Lior," she said hurriedly as she scanned the racks of robes in the cluttered store.

"This young man must need a robe for the festivities," said the old man as he continued to look Sam over like a prized ham.

"Yes, Uncle, and we're in quite a hurry," Mrs. Sterling cut him off but smiled gently at him, proceeding then to bury herself in a rack of robes.

"She won't find you a robe over there," Osan winked at Sam. "I moved the men's robes to the front of the store."

Then he motioned for Sam to follow him toward a small rack of dark red robes, almost identical to every other robe in the store, and fumbled in the material for a moment.

"Ah, this will do," he said as he produced a robe and prodded Sam to try it on. Sam obeyed and slipped the soft material on his shoulders. It fit perfectly.

"Still got the touch, Uncle," Mrs. Sterling said after abandoning her search in the women's robes. "How does it fit, Samuel? Any pull in the arms?"

"Very well I think," Sam said, admiring the smooth touch of the

Chapter Six: Lior City

sleeves. It was hard to think that the robes were any different than each other, but at closer glance, he began to notice tiny variations in the material—some thicker than others, some shiny like silk while others were like burlap, and all had either red or silver sleeves.

"Young man, there is no think. Either it fits or it does not," Osan peered at him once again.

"It fits very well. I like it," Sam responded.

"Good. It's yours," Osan said with a wave of his bony hand.

"Thank you Sir," Sam said quickly, admiring the robe in the mirror at the front of the shop.

"Uncle, you can't keep business going if you keep giving your merchandise away," Mrs. Sterling said.

"Do not argue, Camisera. It is my store, I will do as I please with my robes," he said defiantly, pushing his glasses high on his nose.

Then he studied Sam for a moment.

"You're not from Lior, are you?" he questioned quietly, and then frowned at Mrs. Sterling. "I see why you are in a hurry."

"Yes, Uncle, but we believe he is one of us," she said in a hushed tone.

"Well." Osan put his hand out and snatched Sam up by the shoulders. "Then you best call me Uncle," he said, slapping Sam squarely on the back.

"Yes—Sir, and thank you for the robe," Sam choked out.

Seeing that she had lost the argument about paying for the robe, Mrs. Sterling kissed her uncle on the cheek before marching Sam out into the crowded street where Emma and Gus had already bought blinking red hats and were sipping iced berry tea through glowing red straws.

Following Mr. Sterling, the group maneuvered through the crowd toward the City Center where masses of families were already gathering on both sides of Main Street in front of the main entrance. They found a place next to a vendor who was stirring a large wooden handle into a huge cast iron pot of colorful popcorn, the smell reaching Sam's nose almost immediately, reminding him how hungry he was.

Chapter Six: Lior City

But before he could get rid of the hollow feeling in his stomach, Emma shoved a bag of multi-colored popcorn and a frozen mug of tea in his hands.

"It's just to hold us over until the banquet!" Emma said loudly over the crowd that was quickly gathering in around them.

Sam didn't have time to answer her because suddenly there was a loud "BOOM" from the direction of the building's front entrance, and all lights in the City blinked off, which immediately quieted the crowd and left the street in utter darkness.

The blackout was only temporary, because the massive doors with a raised carving of a great winged creature opened, and a blinding white light flooded Main Street.

Out of the entrance stepped an iridescent blue dragon, glittering with a silver and white breastplate and brilliant lights of all four halls' colors attached to its wings. Around its neck was a stunning silver collar with blue lights that beamed like glowing spires into the night sky, and a chain that led to a man in a shining blue robe, walking confidently with the huge creature that towered over him.

There were gasps and hushed awes as the beautiful animal obediently walked beside its Master Keeper, who carefully guided the dragon down Main Street.

At first the crowd continued in silence, struck at the magnificence of the great lizard, its legs and arms showing years of power and strength. But then, as their sense of immediate fear seemed to subside, a lone cheer quickly morphed into a full-fledged roar, into which Sam, Gus, and Emma joined.

The Keeper walked the animal to the beginning of Main Street before halting and turning to the audience, who hushed to almost complete silence once again.

"TODAY MARKS YEAR FOUR THOUSAND FOUR HUNDRED FOURTEEN OF THE LIOR LIGHT FESTIVAL!" he said so loudly that Sam had to cover his ears, as did many of the others around him.

Suddenly, at a gentle tug of the chain, the great dragon lifted his

Chapter Six: Lior City

head and spewed a stream of fire into the night sky, the searing heat blanketing the crowd in a few moments of warmth.

Again the crowd roared with approval, watching the Keeper and his trained fire-breather thunder down the street, calling the opening of the festival and belching fire.

Then a small group of people emerged huddled tightly in a circle, their faces hidden from the crowd, the hems of their robes glowing bright red against the dimly lit street. They moved together fluidly, as if one person, their red-tipped robes creating a kaleidoscopic effect.

Suddenly out of the circle shot an acrobat high into the air, latching onto an unknown force and twirling around it before another joined him, mimicking his movements. The glowing red robes disbanded into patterned movements of dance, each using their partner to propel them high into the air, creating a mystifying effect with red light.

"That's our hall! The red flyers! Aren't they great?" Emma said loudly to Sam.

"Yeah, they are!" Sam hollered back, not taking his eyes off the scene.

It was an awesome sight as each hall presented their own glowing team of acrobats, stilt walkers, and elaborate costumes of various creatures thought to be extinct or fictional back in the world Sam knew.

The word "great" couldn't even begin to describe what he was seeing in front of him. The lights, colors, and flying acrobatics were otherworldly. Only a dream of something really great could have compared to this.

The world he knew. He still fought with the reality of it all—there just couldn't be another world like Lior. No dragons have ever existed, and dinosaurs were extinct. No person has ever been able to travel by light beams before, and no one has ever conjured light into a form of any kind that he knew. His recent experiences in Lior defied all that was sensible. Any reasonable person would keep trying to pinch himself back into reality.

Chapter Six: Lior City

Sam wondered if maybe it was a really vivid dream. Or maybe he was in a coma. Did he get in a car wreck, and was he hanging on the edge of death and life? Or could he have fallen off the cliff and didn't know it? Or maybe Bush had punched him one too many times.

****

"I need some air," Sam said in Emma's ear as they watched a nearly life-size paper version of the dragon, complete with fire-breathing nostrils, wind down the street.

"Come with me," she pulled him out of the crowd and led him around the City Center to the red hall in the rear, where a guard with a silver beard immediately stopped them before they could slip through a side door. He was dressed in a red robe with silver collars and sleeves, and wore a metal pin of a tree with many branches. In front of him he held a very large sword with red engravings on the handle.

"There's no one allowed in the hall until after the ceremony..." he stopped when he recognized Emma.

"Munchkin! When did you get back in town?" the tall guard said as he reached out with an especially large hand and gave her a rub on the top of the head.

"Hi Achiam!" she beamed at him, at which point he nabbed her for a big bear hug.

"Not quite as young as you used to be, are you?" he said, reaching down to fix her tangled hair. "I suppose we all get older. And who might this be?"

"This is Sam. He's my..." she stopped.

"Friend," Sam answered quickly as Emma turned an especially dark shade of pink.

"Oh, I see," Achiam smiled largely. "I suppose you would like to show Sam here the balcony?"

"Yes—if it won't cause any trouble." Emma attempted to regain her composure.

Chapter Six: Lior City

"Of course not, especially for a munchkin and her—friend," he said, smiling even more.

The guard lifted his sword and shoved the blade deep in a small opening in the door frame, then turned it slightly till a large click unlocked the large metal door of the hall. Achiam followed them into the small, dimly lit but ornately decorated room.

"Don't forget the feast, you two," he said and turned around once again to face the doorway, removing his sword from the opening and placing it in front of him.

"Thank you!" Emma called behind her as she led Sam to the stairwell. "He's my father's friend. My father actually was the one to recommend Achiam to guard the hall."

"He's big, that's for sure."

Emma laughed.

"I've seen him take out three people at once in a Protector competition."

She led him up the fourth flight of stairs and down a long, marble hallway, decorated with red vases and lavish drapes, until they arrived at a set of large glass doors opening up to a stone balcony that overlooked the entrance to Main Street. The crowd was cheering loudly as the purple acrobats emerged from the winged doors. At the end of the street stood the large arch that rose above the great iron gate into Lior, where they had seen the winged creatures etched on the columns.

Emma must have seen the scowl on his face because she snuggled up to his shoulder on the railing of the balcony. She was good at that—getting to the point of what was wrong so she could coax it out into the open.

"How are you doing with all this?"

The truth was that he wasn't okay with all of it. Up until now, he was content with thinking there was no concept of good and evil in life—you are born, some get lucky with good circumstances, and some get handed the short end of the stick. He believed he was somewhere in between.

Chapter Six: Lior City

"I'm just having trouble believing in all this, that's all."

She didn't seem surprised at his words. "You mean you are having trouble believing that we are half-angel and half-human," she said carefully, looking deep into his eyes. "We call the angels the Watchers, since they have always been the protectors of people."

Watchers. The first beings ever created, servants of God himself.

"So you are the children of Watchers? Meaning that the angels must have come to Creation and ..."

Emma smiled.

"Exactly. But that wasn't the Creator's plan. Those choices are why evil exists in both worlds today."

Sam listened to the crowd roar once again, the glowing lights of the regions waving like a field of wheat in the wind.

"So since you are half Watchers, it gives you magical powers with Light?"

"It's a gift. The Creator gives us the gift of Light Manipulation."

"But the Dark Forces have powers too."

"Yes," she told him. "They have learned to *force* the Light into obeying them. It is not our way, however. We believe it is a gift, and so we treat it with respect and honor."

"The Dark One has power too, doesn't he? Why does the Creator allow that?"

"Samuel, the Creator offers the gift to any Descendant, but some choose to use it for their own purposes," she paused as the chanting of the crowd grew loud as the parade drew to a close. "He uses it regardless of how it was intended."

"And the Creator just *allows* it?" Sam pressed.

"Choices, Sam. Remember? He allows the freedom for all to choose."

Watchers were angels that followed the Creator, and Dark Watchers were those that followed their own path. Both can manipulate the Light, but each in their own way. It was the spiritual battle he always knew existed but refused his concrete mind to accept. It was just like the world he knew on Earth—ruthless dictators and benevolent

Chapter Six: Lior City

governments, heroes of philanthropy and mass murderers, the good versus evil. It was the same, but then again, it was all so different.

"I must be dead ... caught in some sort of limbo between heaven and hell," he said jokingly, but silently pinching himself to see if he would wake up.

Emma laughed.

"No, Lior is very much alive. We—are alive. We are just in another dimension of the Creator's realm. It's wonderful, isn't it?"

"Have you—seen Him? The Creator?" he hesitated to ask for fear of compounding his already spinning mind, but chose to anyway.

"No," she said smiling. "Long ago our ancestors did. But every time we use the Light, Descendants feel Him in us. Soon, I think you can feel Him too."

"God. You feel God in you." The words left an obvious skeptical feeling in the air, but even he couldn't deny what he had seen since yesterday.

"Yes. The Creator is God."

There was no God. Science had proven that. He was a fictitious creature man made up to give himself hope, and now the people of Lior were also caught up in it, and even they couldn't see it. God was a crutch for people who needed relief from pain and suffering. Plus, there were too many holes in the theory of an all-powerful being controlling the universe.

But he had seen so much already that challenged all reason. He had learned to comply with the unreasonable, and to open his mind to what he saw. Perhaps even he needed to allow the impossible to penetrate him.

****

The parade had ended and Emma led him down another hallway and a main stairwell that led to the hall, where people were already being led into the lavishly-decorated room.

The inside of the hall was even larger than it seemed from the outside, and even more ornate than its exterior, with carved columns

Chapter Six: Lior City

and finely-detailed creatures with wings spread and sitting atop. It was decorated in different shades of red curtains lining the stained glass windows, with candelabras of silver staggered on the walls. Spectacular glittering chandeliers hung from the ceiling over the many tables where the people of Thalo were now being seated.

Emma spotted her parents and the others from the cabin circle right away as they filed in, and she led Sam to a long table near the center of the hall, which boasted huge lighted fountains of sparkling punch and tea, tables of various meats and cheeses, artfully arranged fruits and vegetables, and an entire table just for unique kinds of bread.

Around the outer edges of the hall were similar tables of finger foods and juice fountains, which many had already discovered and were filling plates.

"I can't believe how many people fit in here," Sam said loudly as he and Emma rejoined with Gus and Lillia at their cabin's table, which was as full of pomp and fanciful decorations as the others in the hall. Gus, who was eagerly looking at the long tables of food, bumped past Sam on his way to the mountain of cheeses.

The hall didn't seem crowded, but the noise reached concert levels as people laughed and talked while they searched for their seats and circled the tables of appetizers. Sam sat with the rest of the group near the middle of the table, with Miss Karpatch and Lillia on either side of him, and Cooley finding a spot next to his History teacher. Gus, when he returned with his plate full, and Emma sat opposite them, with Mr. and Mrs. Sterling next to them. Mr. Sterling seemed engaged in a deep conversation with the man next to him, whom Sam recognized immediately as the man he saw from afar carrying firewood into the pavilion at their circle of cabins.

There were others at the table too, about twenty in all, that Sam didn't recognize. All seemed to know each other well, however, and laughed and chatted as they sat down with plates of cheese and bread. But before he could lean over and ask Emma who they were, Mr. Sterling stood at his wife's beckoning and held a glass of bubbling liquid in the air.

Chapter Six: Lior City

"Friends, it has been a long time since our last reunion," he said loudly over the noise of the hall. "I am grateful to be back in your presence once again, and I am glad to be back in Lior, as I am sure all of you are."

"Indeed!" some said as they also stood, raising their glasses to meet his.

"We have a new member of our cabin circle that I would like you to meet."

Sam froze. He was unaware that there was going to be any sort of introduction.

"Sam, would you kindly stand?" Mr. Sterling raised his arm toward him. "This young man has joined us from the far reaches of Thalo, and thanks be to the Creator that he has now rejoined his family." He paused, raising his glass. "As a once lost member of our family, we are thankful now that he is found."

While Sam was confused by Mr. Sterling's words, by instinct he raised his cup of sparkling juice that Emma set in front of him gingerly and smiled at those who smiled at him. It was then that he noticed the girl sitting opposite him at the other end of the table.

She had long silky brown hair and blue eyes, which seemed to sparkle along with the glass she was holding up. She smiled immediately when Sam glanced, her lips showing a bright shade of natural red.

Sam quickly turned and sat, but watched her out of the corner of his eye. She was beautiful, elegant in every way from her soft physical features to the way she poised herself at the table. She was laughing and joking with another younger girl at the table, every so often glancing discretely in his direction.

He caught himself staring at her more than once and forced himself to look toward the cart that was now passing the table, large bottles of dark red liquid being placed at each end.

"Sam," Miss Karpatch put her hand on his shoulder, snapping him suddenly out of his gaze. "Emma has been trying to get your attention."

He turned toward Emma, whose face was now as red as her hair.

Chapter Six: Lior City

"I was trying to point out something behind you," she said snidely, "but I think you would rather know that her name is Sayvon."

Sam didn't get a chance to respond because the hall fell suddenly silent. Others were turning to watch what Emma had been trying to point out to him. Needless to say, he was rather glad for the interruption, embarrassing as it was.

There was a large shudder, and then the wall that stood at the back of the great hall began to move apart, revealing the interior of the heart of the City Center—a large semicircular amphitheater built into the floor adjoining all four halls, connecting the entirety of the building together in one massive banquet hall of diverse people sitting at similarly decorated tables with large candelabras at their centers. Each hall was decorated lavishly in their various colors and boasted similar sparkling beverage fountains and mountains of bread and cheese finger foods.

The amphitheater, which Gus explained as the central meeting place for the Council, looked as though it could hold another entire hall itself. Toward the rear of the center held one more table decorated in white and silver linens, and seated in the chairs were eight figures dressed in the robes of the various halls.

"Who are they?" Sam asked no one in particular.

"They are the members of the High Council. Two from each hall—representing the regions they come from," Miss Karpatch whispered loudly as the halls began to quiet. "Each of the halls points in a different direction, and each direction represents a different region of Lior. She pointed at two of the older men, one with shoulder length white hair and the other with silver patches on each side of an otherwise balding head, both wearing red robes like the rest of the Thalo banquet hall, but with gleaming silver cuffs to represent their position. "And those two are the two High Council members from our hall."

"Each of the four halls appoints one hundred Council members to meet in Lior to discuss issues that arise in the regions," Gus said. "but the High Council is chosen from those members to serve the Chancellor."

Chapter Six: Lior City

"And here comes the Chancellor now," Miss Karpatch gestured toward a door behind the High Council table.

Another inner door to the amphitheater opened, and a man with gray hair and beard, dressed in a silver robe with red cuffs, glided gracefully across floor to his designated chair at the High Council's table. Before he sat, he raised his hands in a simple gesture of acknowledgment, and all four halls suddenly erupted into cheers and enthusiastic clapping.

In another gesture of gratitude, the aged man opened his arms and turned to all four halls as if embracing the air. For a brief moment Sam thought he saw the Chancellor glance right at him.

Then, holding his hands out as if to embrace all who attended, the members of the High Council stood and mimicked the Chancellor's posture, their hands held out in a similar gesture.

The hall was deathly silent as a blue glow began to emerge from their palms, softly in the beginning, but then increasing in intensity. Then suddenly, from each of their palms, a thin wisp of light crept upward above the center of the table, where each stream converged into one massive display of radiance that spread throughout all four of the halls instantly.

Again the four halls erupted in cheers and clapping of hands, which lasted for nearly a minute after the light had long faded and the other three men had taken their seats. The Chancellor remained standing and held his hand up for silence, to which the halls finally obeyed. He prayed quietly, a simple prayer to the Creator who had given them life.

When the man finally sat, four more doors opened up and strings of servers dressed in their representative hall's colors pushed huge carts of food down the rows of tables in each direction. There were whole pigs, turkey, and sides of beef lusciously prepared on huge platters, and large bowls of food of every kind steaming from the carts.

Instantly a waiter was at Sam's table and offered heaping amounts of delicately prepared potatoes, vegetables, and colorful salads.

Chapter Six: Lior City

Another waiter appeared and offered an array of croissants, dinner rolls, and pastries, and still another refilled their drinks and changed out their silverware.

There were waiters and waitresses attending tables everywhere. It was amazing how many of them there were.

"Wow. This is more than I could ever eat," Sam said to Gus, who wasted no time digging in.

"Enjoy it. The feast only happens one week a year," he mumbled between bites.

"People from all four regions of Lior come for this feast," Miss Karpatch said, nibbling on a buttered beet. "It is a time of blessing, and of serving—those who serve us now will be the same ones we serve at a later feast. In essence, we all serve each other."

Sam nodded his head. He remembered how willing the people of the church had been to cook, serve, and clean up the meal after the service. Here, in Lior, people seemed the same way—helpful, caring, and non-judgmental, a far cry from the church his grandmother took him to. Immediately these people had made him feel at home—no judgment, no forced communion, only an open invitation to join them.

He glanced over at Gus, who had morphed the conversation from the feast to the regions of Lior, and something about the first crossing of the Descendants into Lior.

"No, actually, from what Mentor Varsak's publication on the *People of Light* says, the original location of the entrance of the first Descendants into Lior was in the Themane region, 'buried in a vast forest,' and was abandoned and eventually lost."

Miss Karpatch shook her finger in his direction.

"What Mentor Varsak forgets is in the earlier journals the mention of 'frozen peaks' that surrounded them. Clearly, Gus, you forget the words of our ancestors," she said playfully.

Gus paused to take a breath from his potatoes.

"I just find it hard to believe that the region of Thalo contains the gate," he shook his head.

Chapter Six: Lior City

"What gate?" Sam asked suddenly, in between bites of a turkey leg, which was better than any he had had at the Renaissance Festival back in Michigan.

Gus looked up from his plate and was already sporting a sour look on his face from the four slices of beef, two of chicken, and two extra-large helpings of mashed pumpkin he had eaten. Sam too pushed around corn on his plate as his stomach began to bloat to an uncomfortable capacity.

"The Sha'ar Gate," he groaned and held his belly as a server set down another huge piece of pork chop in front of him. "The only gate at the time said to be built by the Creator so that the first Descendants could leave Earth and come to Lior."

"The original gate," Miss Karpatch added.

Sam pushed back from the table in a show of defiance as the server attempted to set more food in front of him. "Is that like the one we came through to get here?"

Gus shook his head and took a bite of roll that was nearly twice the size of his mouth, having suddenly gotten over his inability to shove in another bite.

"No. The Sha'ar gate has not been found. Buried by the Watchers after the Great Battle because it contained too much power."

"The only gates we have now are those that were built by the Watchers for us to travel."

Miss Karpatch too put her hands up as if waving off an imaginary server who was attempting to coax her into another round of steamed vegetables.

"One in each of the regions." Gus let out a little burp, drawing an exaggerated eye-rolling from Lillia. "Four total, if you don't count the Sha'ar gate."

"What about the Darkness? Can they use the gates?"

"No. But they have tried in the past, which is why the Protector families watch the gates. Why *we* watch the gates," Gus said.

"Fortunately for Lior, life has been peaceful as of late," Miss Karpatch smiled as Gus accepted yet another roll after finishing the first and immediately began inhaling it. "In fact, there hasn't been any

Chapter Six: Lior City

known activity in any of the four regions in almost fifty years—since the destruction of the old Lior City."

"That you believe..." Lillia said quietly, to which the conversation quickly accelerated into sporting jests and lively debate about whether or not the Seer office and High Council were able to see the potential threat outside the Descendant-controlled territory.

As they talked, Sam stared at the rest of the food on his plate. He felt bad throwing away good food, but it didn't look like anyone else at the table was going to finish theirs either. Usually he kept himself in check while eating, but tonight he had been unusually hungry, and he was enjoying the atmosphere—and surprisingly, the people around him.

The intensifying debate halted suddenly as, once again, the four corners of the inner hall opened up and a stream of servers paraded in with a caravan of carts that were overflowing with the most colorful cakes, sweets, and pies Sam had ever seen.

Even though it looked as though the rest of the table was suffering from being as overfed as he was, when the cart arrived, they all stood and stared at the delectable treats like buzzards circling above.

The server placed a number of desserts on the table, many of which looked like fancy fruit cobblers, coffee and red velvet cakes, and meringue topped pies. In front of the youths she placed a vase full of assorted white and dark chocolate cake bites, a giant bowl full of chocolate and vanilla iced custard, and a large platter of berry muffins. The desserts looked so good that they momentarily forgot how full they were.

The dessert Sam tried first was a chocolate-topped meringue pie that tasted somewhat like peanut butter, but richer in texture. Then he tried a velvet cake pop, and liked it so much he went for a whole piece of the velvet cake. Gus wasted no time digging into the cobblers and cakes, while Emma and Lillia showed more restraint, daintily forking through pieces of strawberry pie with a dollop of ice cream.

Except for Gus, who seemed to have a bottomless pit for a stomach, they were stuffed to the point that they couldn't possibly take another bite. Watching Gus eat made Sam feel even more full, so

Chapter Six: Lior City

he contented himself by sipping on some strong coffee the servers had set in front of them.

As the rest of the table chatted merrily about the festivities of the Light Festival, or caught up on what had happened while each was away, Sam would glance toward the end of the table and at Sayvon every so often when Emma wasn't looking. She pretended not to notice his looks, but the smile on her face told him she didn't need to pretend.

Emma was ignoring him, but every so often he caught her staring at him, her eyes level and lips pursed into an obvious scowl. He knew she was angry for the Sayvon thing, so he tried his best not to look her way. But there was something about the girl with the soft brown hair—something intriguing—that he just couldn't get out of his mind.

First time this problem has ever come up, he thought, smirking on the inside. But truly, the feeling of having one beautiful girl pining over you was exciting enough, but two? The possibility was intoxicating.

Lillia woke up suddenly from her I'm-so-bored-I-can-hardly-stand-it expression and motioned for them to slip out of the feast. Sam was reluctant to leave the table and the momentary glances he snuck at Sayvon, but followed them anyway, just as the Chancellor began to rise and the crowd of well-fed Liorians began to quiet down.

"Friends of the Four Corners, welcome to the City Center!" the man speaking said loudly from the podium as the four slipped out of a side door that seemed to appear magically from behind a long draping curtain. Sam stopped for a moment before exiting the hall to listen to the deep, methodical voice of the Chancellor. His voice combined with a full belly would have put anyone to sleep.

"I'm not really into speeches," Lillia whispered as they walked down the now deserted street toward their path to the cabins. "They go on forever it seems, talking about the four regions and the strength of Lior and how important the Light Festival is. You know, a bunch of political crap."

Sam laughed out loud, which only egged Lillia on further.

"The Chancellor says maybe three or four short sentences about the future of Lior and Creation united, then up comes each of the

Chapter Six: Lior City

High Council—who pretty much ramble on about nothing until our ears bleed."

Gus looked suddenly shocked at her words.

"What? What do you mean?" he stuttered. "They are always talking about important things of Lior, like the current status of the Protectors and arches …"

"Yeah, yeah. We all know they just want the chance to torture us with their political bullcrap—"

"Lillia!" Emma scolded her. "Watch your language! You have been around high schoolers too much!"

"Sorry, I guess the 'Gullas have gotten to me."

"The what?" Sam asked.

Emma had marched on ahead of them, but then turned around and waved an angry finger at a very annoyed Lillia.

"Gullas are the term some ignorant people have given to the human race. It's silly and childish."

"It's from an ancient word *segullah* meaning *treasure*, but to many who do not study Ancient Text, it means 'peculiar,'" Gus added, which only made Lillia roll her eyes even more. To Lillia he said, "Just because you wish you were one doesn't mean we all do."

Sam ignored Lillia, but walked determinedly down the path. It was the first time Sam had seen Gus even the slightest bit annoyed, and he enjoyed watching him finally stand up for himself. And Lillia deserved it, although the meaning of 'peculiar' didn't really bother him.

"No offense, newbie. I didn't mean it that—" Lillia started to say, but he cut her off.

"It's fine," he told her quickly, not really caring if she apologized or not.

They strode quickly through the trees towering over the path until they reached the clearing and the smell of the salt from the ocean. There was no one to be seen in the cabin circle, but the blue lights were happily burning and giving the log buildings an inviting look.

Emma led them to the pavilion in the middle of the circle and immediately set to work building a fire in the round fireplace. Gus

Chapter Six: Lior City

took the black coffee pot from the hanging rod over the fire and filled it with water from a spigot over a small sink.

"I have found the neural stimulants in coffee to be necessary on nights like these," he said to Sam as he replaced the pot on the rod, cinched up a handful of grounds into a filter and dropped it into the pot.

Sam accepted a cup of very strong coffee from Gus as the two girls appeared with roasting sticks and a bowl full of dark purplish nuts.

"They're called Fuzers." Emma handed him a stick. "Go ahead and put it in the fire."

He obeyed, but quickly realized why the others had stopped to watch him intently. The nut began to swell up to double, triple, and then four and five times its size. Even when he pulled it from the fire, the nut still swelled so badly the skin began to strain from the pressure. Looking around, he could find no suitable place to set it, so he dropped it on the floor in front of him where it promptly exploded, sending pieces of purple foamy stuff onto his hair, his clothes, and all over his face.

Emma and Lillia burst out laughing when Sam, stunned, finally realized what had happened. Gus cackled loudly, spilling his coffee all over his robe, which only made the two girls laugh even harder, until Lillia was on the ground rolling in the purple foam.

After he composed himself, Sam chuckled along with them, but tossed a teasing angry glance toward Emma. Really, he was just glad she was over the thing with Sayvon.

"Do you eat these?" he picked up the nut that now looked like a large piece of purple popcorn.

"Try it." Emma placed a nut on her own stick and placed it just inside the flame.

Sam gingerly put the purple kernel to his lips and tasted the foamy exterior. It quickly melted in his mouth, dissolving on his tongue and leaving a soft, velvety taste. He immediately took another taste, and another, until he had eaten the whole thing.

"It's delicious," he said, looking at the bowl longingly. Even though

Chapter Six: Lior City

his stomach was still full from the banquet, the smooth-tasting nuts made the coffee taste even better.

With the salty cool air and the warmth of the fire around him, for the first time in months, Sam began to feel the tension ebb away from his shoulders. There were no papers due for class, no Bush to avoid, and he hadn't had the dream about the swirling shapes since arriving in Lior. It was nice to get away from it all.

"I'm guessing once the Light Festival is done we have to go back to real life," he said, watching Emma's Fuzer nut swell in the flames.

"Actually, these are our real homes," Emma gestured toward the cabins. "Ours, Miss Karpatch, the Abelsworth's, the Halfon's, the Calpher's, Uncle Osan, the Farmer's, and the Mirke's. But we can only stay here until the end of the Light Festival week."

"So your folks have a place here too?" He glanced toward Lillia and Gus.

"They do, but not all of us are able to come at once. Someone has to watch the gate," said Gus.

"Then, it's back to Gibson's class," Lillia said bitterly.

Gus stuck another Fuzer on the end of a stick and displayed it over the fire.

"Every year we come during this time for the Festival, and then back to our houses in White Pine until summer," he said. "We have—well our folks have—taken a calling as Protectors of the gate, and we only get to come back here when we can."

"Until next year when we start mentoring," Emma almost sang the words.

"Yep. No more class," Lillia mimicked Emma's singing sarcastically.

Gus cleared his throat.

"Technically we will still be gathering for daily study, so don't get too excited."

"What? You mean you won't be back at school next year in White Pine?" Sam was intrigued. "What about the gate—or your parents?"

"Our parents chose to protect the gate, so they will be there while we're at mentorship," Emma offered.

"The group in White Pine is in charge of gate protection for

Chapter Six: Lior City

the Thalo region that connects to the northern passage—er—North America," Gus added. "The Sterlings are in charge of gate sealing, Lillia's folks monitor Dark Watcher movements, and my folks manage the movement of Descendants in and out of the gate."

Sam yawned loudly and took another sip of his steaming cup of coffee, which obviously hadn't nearly enough caffeine to keep him awake, or to follow what they were saying.

"So let me get this straight. There are four gates, each one connects a part of the world with a region in Lior, and one is missing, but you live in Creation because your parents watch the gate. But you will come back here to live on your own for the 'Mentor-thingy' while they as alter-egos pretend to be normal citizens of a small town in northern Michigan?"

Snickering was heard around the group.

"When you put it like that, yeah, it sounds weird, but I suppose that about sums it up," Lillia smirked.

"It's our family," Emma said defensively. "But it's the way we live in Lior—in communes, or family units. Each one has their own circle they live in."

"Like an extended family unit," Sam mouthed. "What about Cooley and Miss Karpatch?"

Lillia looked at Gus arrogantly, as if he could respond to the one question she had been waiting ages to know.

Gus sighed and looked at Lillia directly.

"Miss Karpatch is in charge of historical records, and Mr. Cooley ... is the head of Seer transmission here in Lior."

"But Lillia thinks he is a fraud," Emma interrupted him, her eyes showing obvious signs of disgust in Lillia's direction.

Lillia snorted and shook her head.

"Isn't it obvious? There's no reason for him to be in White Pine! All he does is wander around the City and then disappear into the woods every day. If you ask me, I think he is watching us for the Council." Then she lowered her voice to a mumble. "And I wouldn't doubt he has something to do with Chivler missing."

Emma was suddenly angry.

Chapter Six: Lior City

"That's underhanded and completely against everything Lior stands for! Why would they send Cooley anyway? He's just a messenger, not a spy!"

"But he's still a Descendant. Can't you just see whether or not he is a fraud?" Sam hoped to interrupt them from their bickering. "I mean, you brought me here, you must have known something ..."

Gus looked at Emma quickly, who seemed to nod ever so slightly back to him, as if giving him permission to answer.

"We can't see the Darkness within someone, although Boggle tries with his inventions. But the truth is that we can never really know for sure."

Unbelievable, he thought. *They can't even tell if I'm a Descendant or not.*

"So what do they do with people from Earth?"

Gus poked at the fire with a roasting stick, answering slowly, as he understood where Sam's question was going.

"Whenever a possible Descendant has been discovered in Creat—er—Earth, the Council must follow a rigorous set of steps before admitting them into Lior. Yours might take a little longer to establish because your parents—" he stopped.

"You snuck me in," Sam was flabbergasted. Not only was he a stranger, he was a potentially uninvited one.

Gus shot a look back to Emma for help.

"Yes, that's true, but the right people believe you are a Descendant and that's all that matters," she jumped in quickly.

"But I am still not supposed to be here."

"True, but—"

"What if they find out? Will one of those Protectors with the creepy hoods come and lock me up?"

"They would never do—"

Then for some reason, in that moment, it all hit him at once. Anger suddenly welled up inside of him, and he couldn't stop it. Perhaps he had been too relaxed to remember all the needed facts that they were still keeping from him—and they weren't telling him what he needed to know. He was in an alien world with dangerous creatures—and he was *uninvited*.

Chapter Six: Lior City

"Look, I'm sorry, but I just need some answers here. I still don't understand why you have brought me to this place, and while I have had a riveting good time being here with you all, I can't help but feel I have been lied to the whole time."

Emma stood and placed herself directly in front of him, blocking his view of Gus's Fuzer nut expanding in the fire.

"Sam, you can't judge us like that yet. We haven't really done any of this without careful consideration and prayer. The Creator's Promise—"

Prayer? Seriously? That's all they had for him?

It wasn't enough.

Sam leaned back on the bench, satisfied that his rant got through to them.

Lillia lay back on her bench as well.

"Well, look at it this way, newb. At least you don't have Bush to worry about anymore."

"What'd you do, kill him?" Maybe if they could kidnap him, they were capable of much more.

Gus smiled and stuffed another Fuzer into his mouth.

"Nope, just scared him a bit."

"Yep, 'cuz no one else seemed to want to stand up to that fat lard," Lillia mumbled from the bench, but ended her words short on account of Emma's sharp look. Lillia then laughed loudly and sat up. "Scare him? Emma nearly dropped a tree on him! It was only inches from ripping one of his chubby cheeks off!"

"Yeah, but let's not tell anyone about that," Emma giggled. "Besides, a come-to-senses moment would do him good. A bully is only going to listen if he's 'seen the light.'"

As he stared into the fire, all sorts of questions filled Sam's thoughts. Emma, Gus, and the rest of them believed he was one of them. But how? Who was he? What happened to his real parents? Did the Darkness play a part in their death? They were only teachers at the university, and that was before they died in the wreck. But were they really Descendants with a calling like the others to live on Earth?

Chapter Six: Lior City

And, if that was true, was he a Descendant as well? Did he have the same Light gifts that the others did?

Grabbing another nut, Sam speared it and stuck it in the fire. These questions only made him want to know who he was and what happened to his parents even more, but he wasn't ready to ask the questions now. He needed more time to think—to take in this place, and everything he had already seen but couldn't explain.

Then, as if almost prompted by some unforeseen force, Emma scooted closer to him, putting her hand softly on his. Lillia took one look and rolled her eyes largely, which even in the darkness could be seen clearly. Sam didn't care, though. He was just glad Emma had forgotten Sayvon. Sure, Sayvon was very pretty, but he was happy right where he was ... feeling the warmth of Emma's shoulder on his. She made him feel like he was her protector with the way she snuggled up to him so tightly. He had never been in a relationship quite like with her—not like the shallow girls he met at the country club, or even the one real girlfriend he had at his old school who ended up dumping him after the first month. No, it was deeper than that. She trusted him, and she seemed determined to believe in him.

"Wish we could go to the Cedars tomorrow," Lillia announced quietly, throwing off his train of thought. "Maybe it would even help pretty-boy clear his thoughts."

Gus tipped his cup of coffee over on the bench loudly, making everyone jump from their mesmerized state.

"Sounds like fun, but I was planning to go to the library tomorrow. There's some new books out on the ancient towers of Lior ..."

"I was going to see Boggle," Lillia said.

Emma scowled and laid her head on Sam's shoulder.

"I'm sorry, I have to help Mom with Uncle Osan tomorrow."

Lillia looked disgusted with Emma's display of affection. "Newbie could always go on his own, unless he needs princess here attached at his hip at all times."

Emma shot her an angry look.

"Just because you are too—" she caught herself. "Never mind."

Chapter Six: Lior City

Gus stood and paced the fire.

"It may be therapeutic, given the circumstances. I remember many occasions I needed to get something off my mind and it was the perfect place to do so."

Emma nodded and smiled at Sam.

"This is your chance to have your alone time, Samuel. It may do you good."

Sam nodded. He wasn't going to refuse a chance to get away from people for a little while …

"There's a path just outside the City gate, right along the City wall. Follow it until you get to the coast and then take the path toward the trees. You will be in the cedars in less than a half hour," Gus told him.

"We used to go there when we practiced Light manipulation," Emma said quietly. "If you figure it out, it could help you understand yourself a bit more."

"Yeah, newb, but don't forget—we aren't supposed to be doing Light manipulation until we're in mentorship. So keep your big trap shu—"

"Really Lillia? Do you have to be so nasty?" Emma interrupted angrily.

"Just reminding ol' newb here what's at stake."

Sam was ready to try it. He needed to find out who he was, and if he could do the same things as the Descendants, it would be a big clue. He wasn't worried about getting in trouble, as Gus informed him that since he hadn't gone through mentorship, he would likely not be tracked by the Seers. But the thought of learning about his past was an exhilarating feeling.

Gus stood once again and began pacing while Emma laid her head on Sam's shoulder again, yawning loudly.

Lillia, who was tired of the lovebird display, began a perpetual round of eye rolling until she stood and stomped toward the cabin, shaking her head. Sam wondered why she was angry all the time, but instead of dwelling on the thought, he contented himself with staring into the fire, yawning and listening to Gus as he droned on to

Chapter Six: Lior City

himself about the Eben stone armbands they would all receive once mentorship was complete.

After another few minutes, Gus sat down, his eyes heavy as he attempted to hold back a yawn.

"I've been thinking," he said. "Tomorrow, I think I am going to check out the Protector's Office to see if I can find out anything more about Chivler too. While I'm not always the conspiracy theory type, for Lillia's sake, I am going to at least make a concerted inquiry."

Seeing that Emma was motionless and breathing heavy on his shoulder, Sam nodded to Gus's statement and then gently woke her.

"She would no doubt appreciate that," he said quietly.

Gus, who was mid yawn, looked at Emma, and then stood and poured a small bucket of water on the already dying coals.

"Guess we'd better head to bed too, right?"

The two boys helped Emma into the cabin and then retreated upstairs, where soft sheets and heavy comforters waited to keep them warm through the cool coastal night. After slipping into the pajamas that Mrs. Sterling had bought for him, Sam climbed into bed and stared at the ceiling. Gus wasn't far behind him, but seemed to linger a bit reading his journal in the dim light of a lantern before getting into bed. Just before he covered the lantern, however, Sam thought he saw Gus peering at him curiously from under the covers.

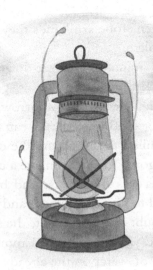

Chapter Seven
Boy With the Shadows

In the shadows inside the old building, the blackened arch loomed in front of him, glowing an eerie shade of purple as the cloaked person stood at one of its legs, holding the glowing stone in front of him. For a moment, he looked up, as if sending up a prayer, then he inserted the glowing stone into a small hole in the arch. Instantly he stepped back, as if waiting for something to happen, but there was nothing.

Then all at once, black shapes emerged through the arch, descending upon him.

"Ayet Sal," a voice whispered. "Malek Eben."

Sam awoke to an abrupt knock on the door downstairs, which silenced the sounds of the peaceful lapping of the waves on the shoreline.

"Just a minute!" Mrs. Sterling's birdlike voice could be heard through the living room to whoever was waiting outside, asking them to wait until she was dressed.

Chapter Seven: Boy With the Shadows

The others must have come in during the night after Sam, Gus, and the girls were already in bed, but they were too sound asleep to hear them arrive.

"I wonder who could be here this early during Light Festival week," Gus yawned and sat up in his bunk. "Usually this is the week we all sleep in."

Sam rolled out of bed and headed to the bathroom to brush his teeth. Light was just beginning to shine through the window of the cabin loft and drown out the pale blue light in the bathroom from the Lazuli lamp.

The dreams had returned, and they seemed to be growing more intense, more clear. He was used to them by now, but they still left him shaken for a few moments after he woke up. He splashed some water on his face to clear the sleep out of his eyes.

The sky showed a promise of a clear day, and Sam's heart leapt as he thought of the possibility of finding out more about himself. He was glad to take his mind off the dreams for a little bit. Was he really a Descendant? Could he manipulate Light like the others?

Gus had told him that as head of research, Miss Karpatch would likely be involved in searching through the records for his connection to the Descendants. If she was unable to find one, as Director for the Creation side of Lior's Protector Office, Mr. Sterling would have no choice but to inform the Council of Sam's unknown past. What the Council would do at that point was anyone's guess.

Why bring him here if they knew his past couldn't be verified? They had to have a reason, but they weren't telling him the whole truth. Why not tell him? It wasn't like he couldn't handle it … or maybe they didn't know … But one thing was for sure, at some point he figured he would have to confront Mr. Sterling to get some real answers.

Gus stumbled into the bathroom when Emma came bounding up the stairs, nearly catching both of them in their underpants. Luckily Sam had learned from the last time Emma appeared upstairs without knocking, and had folded his jeans and set them at the foot of the bed for easy access. Gus, although not quite as prepared, was able to

Chapter Seven: Boy With the Shadows

get the bathroom door closed with his foot before her head poked into the room.

"Saaaaam!" Emma said rather snidely. "You're requested downstairs." Then she curtly turned on her slippers and huffed down the steps, stopping only to throw her hair back in the most pretentious imitation she possibly could. "By *Sayvon*."

Sam's mind raced. He immediately flushed at the thought that Sayvon wanted to see him, but also because Emma seemed genuinely jealous. He wasn't intending to make her that way—he really liked Emma, and it was only for a brief moment that he thought of how beautiful Sayvon was at the feast.

Gus popped the door open and with a mouthful of toothpaste blubbered, "Girlths. Thaas why I try not ta' meth wid 'em!"

Sam couldn't help smiling both for the dripping white foam sputtering out of Gus's mouth and for thinking of what Gus's girlfriend would look like.

Descending the steps, he was met with a tall, broad shouldered man with a newly pressed red robe and shiny brown shoulder-length hair. His smile spread ear-to-ear but fit well with his chiseled features. As Sam had seen so many times before, this man looked like a politician.

"Sam, I would like you to meet Mr. Talister Calpher. He's an Elder on the High Council, a neighbor here in the circle, and a good friend of ours. We were just telling him about your first time in Lior City," Mrs. Sterling said cheerfully.

"Good to meet you, Sam. I heard some about you last night at the feast. Have you met my daughter, Sayvon?" he gestured toward the kitchen table where she and Emma were chatting over a cup of tea.

"Not formally, Sir," he managed to say, but was entranced by Sayvon's hair as it glowed bright brown in the light that was just beginning to filter through the living room window.

"Ah, I see," Talister nodded, the smile returning to his face.

"Talister and I go way back here in Lior," said Mr. Sterling, who handed him a cup of coffee and kept one for himself. "We were talking about how to best introduce you to the Council—being new

Chapter Seven: Boy With the Shadows

to Lior. We believe it would be best if you would go to an informal meeting with the Chancellor first. Talister has agreed to take you to see him, seeing as how he has a meeting already scheduled. Then later, we can present you to the Council when the time is right."

"And I could show you around the City Center afterward if you like," Sayvon said suddenly, surprising her father and leaving a horrified look on Emma's already sour face.

"Sure," he told them both, refusing to look at Emma. "What time do I need to be ready to go?"

"My meeting is immediately following coffee hour. We will meet you out front then if you like," Talister said.

Coffee hour?

"I'm sorry sir, but what time is that?"

"Oh, dear lad, I apologize! We often forget that our human counterparts live by the clock. Although it's not accurate to the minute, I would assume three o'clock would be about the time, where you come from."

"Uh, okay," Sam said dumbly.

"Good. Then after our meeting and your tour, you can be sure we will have you back before dinner!" Talister said happily.

Once they had gone and he had gulped down a quick scrambled egg and blackberry muffin breakfast, Sam hurried upstairs to shower and get ready for his solo excursion. Mrs. Sterling had somehow washed his only two sets of clothes in the last day since they arrived, and they lay neatly on the small nightstand next to his bunk, along with two new pairs of Lior-type soft cotton pants and shirts, a white pair and a brown one. For his excursion today he decided he would try the brown outfit and his new red robe to go along with it.

The outfit fit well, and he noticed right away it was designed for cooling and comfort. It was almost like wearing pajama pants and a nightshirt.

Gus had lingered downstairs at breakfast a while, much to Sam's frustration, to drink coffee and discuss the games that evening with Mr. Sterling and Cooley, so Sam couldn't pin him down for some last-minute questions about how best to try Light manipulation, but

Chapter Seven: Boy With the Shadows

with what information he had been told by Emma, it only required a bit of focus.

He thought about waiting on Gus, but instead, decided to wing it and threw together a few items in his pack for the morning outside the City. He slipped in another shirt, a knife he had found in the kitchen, a few muffins from breakfast, and his canteen. He considered matches, but finding none, settled for the small device that Gus had left on his nightstand that he used to light the fire in the pavilion.

Lillia appeared suddenly in the doorway, just as he was about to head downstairs, carrying an egg-shaped marbled blue stone in her hand.

"Here," she smirked and thrust the stone in his hand. "It was my grandma's Eben stone. It has a concentrated amount of Lazuli in it, which helps with Light manipulation. Maybe it will help you 'see' the light."

"Are we supposed to be using these now?"

"Nope," she said with a smirk. "But it's rare, and probably worth more than you are … so don't lose it."

"Thanks. I won't," he told her, certain she was for once being kind in her own way.

****

The cabin was silent when he left, which was what he had hoped. No one other than Emma, Gus, and Lillia knew he was going to the Cedars, and they had warned him to keep it that way. Part of him wished Emma were there to see him off, but she was nowhere in sight. No doubt she was still upset about Sayvon.

Walking through Lior, Sam found the red hall street buzzing with shoppers in the small shops once again. He saw robes and hats, silver rings, dragon pins and statues, and countless trinkets—some that shined silver, and others that glowed red. Doughnuts were being rolled in sugar and bagged as quickly as they were made, and there were large pitchers of every type and color of tea one could imagine.

Chapter Seven: Boy With the Shadows

He glanced down the green glowing street of the Themane region, where children were up early playing swords in the streets and flashing people with green lights they had strapped to their palms. Strange fruits and vegetables were being placed out on carts, and the strong scent of coffee wafted from nearly every block. It was different to see in the daylight, almost like a theme park that had just opened its doors to coaster-hungry patrons.

On a thought, Sam stopped by a coffee vendor who was pouring steaming black liquid into a mug from a large pitcher.

"It'll make your hair stand on end today, boy," he said, as the steam drifted up past his neatly-trimmed grey beard and into his colorful toboggan cap.

Sam accepted the mug from the vendor and sipped gingerly. It was so strong it made him cough at first, but then he tasted the smoky roast of the coffee on his tongue. He tasted it again, allowing the sweet liquid to roll around in his mouth before swallowing. It was the best coffee he had ever had.

"It's all in the brewing process, boy. It must be perfect," the short vendor smiled. "I brew the honey with the grounds—no other coffee brewer does that, you know. Coffee should be as strong as love and as sweet as honey."

Sam smirked and paid the vendor with coins made of Lazuli that Mrs. Sterling had given him, and made his way around the City Center to Main Street, past the bookstores and more vendors, and toward the City gate.

The gate guards stood stone silent as he walked through the great gate and down the stone stairway, making no movement toward him, only staring ahead into the grey mist of the morning as it hovered low over the golden fields. Immediately he turned toward the coast upon reaching the bottom of the stairs, where a small faint trail could be seen hugging the City wall all the way to the shoreline.

It was a cloudless day—warm near the shoreline, and only the soft breeze from the sea kept the sweat from building on his face. Every so often the trail disappeared and then reappeared, showing

Chapter Seven: Boy With the Shadows

only spots of wear here and there in the tall grass, but per Gus's instructions, he was confident he was on the right trail as the forest lay ahead and to the left of him.

He followed the traces of the path until it split near the end of the City wall, veering left toward the forest, which now loomed largely in front of him like a distant rain cloud draped in patches of sunlight.

After another few minutes of walking, he stopped to catch his breath for a moment, looking back to see how far he had come from the City. The wall had grown so small behind him that it nearly blended in with the horizon, and the City spires were now only gleaming white needles reaching into the sky.

Suddenly he realized that he had a choice—if he wanted to make a run for it, he could. Not that he was a prisoner, but he wasn't really an invited guest either.

He could abandon them and head into the forest, following the same path they took to get here, if he could find it. He could figure out how to use the arch, then go back to White Pine to a grandfather he barely knew …

It's not worth it. He dismissed the thought as he picked up his backpack and found the trail toward the woods again. *I need to know who I am, who my parents were … and I have no idea how to use the arch.*

Another fifteen minutes of walking brought him to the edge of the immense forest, which looked ominous even in the growing sunlight behind him. He wasn't the type to give in to his fear, so he marched out of the clearing and into the forest floor.

It wasn't long before he came upon a set of flat rocks surrounding a small fire ring and a meager stack of firewood. It was a perfect spot, tucked behind a knoll on one side and a rock overhang on the other—obviously chosen as a spot that would be concealed. If he hadn't followed the trail perfectly, he would have missed it entirely.

Sam immediately got to work lighting a small fire, even though sweat still beaded his forehead. Emma had told him the flames would calm him and allow him to think. Judging by the sun's position, he believed it was right around ten o'clock White Pine time. At Gus's suggestion to better blend in, he had taken his watch off. It seemed

Chapter Seven: Boy With the Shadows

as though everyone had clocks internally in Lior, although they didn't seem to mind being late anyway. It was certainly different than the busy pace of Earth.

It was cooler in the trees, and the fire warmed him. Carefully, he reached into his pocket he pulled out the Eben stone Lillia had given him and examined it. It was the color of a deep blue sky on a cloudless day, and smooth like a piece of glass. He ran his hands over its face, half expecting something to come to life as he touched it, but nothing happened.

He sat down on one of the flat rocks and held the stone in his hand, still half-waiting for it to do something—perhaps send warm pulses of Light through him like at the arch in the cave when they first came to Lior, but nothing happened. Closing his eyes, he attempted to blank his mind like Emma had told him. As he had so many times before when his foster mother came home a little too drunk, he blocked out all of his senses—allowing in the sounds of the forest, the smell of pine and the ocean, the feeling of Emma holding his hand …

He wasn't prepared for what happened next. Suddenly, he was drifting off the rock and floating upward toward the forest canopy. Even with his eyes closed, he could see clearly as the blackness became a blue vision of his surroundings, allowing him to see even further through the trees than he could before. The sounds of the forest became almost deafening as he continued to float toward the treetops, with every creaking of the branches as they swayed in the breeze and the birds around him sounding as though they were right next to him.

His vision became so amplified that he could see every crack in the rocks below him and the veins of the leaves many yards away from him in perfect detail. He could feel the wind as it brushed past him like the ripples of a stream, and his skin almost burned with an aching feeling of electricity.

🌲🌲 Chapter Seven: Boy With the Shadows

****

"Boy?" Sam heard suddenly from behind him, jerking him quickly back to reality. "Yor' must be looking for the Ayet Sal?"

"Uh … huh?" Sam was still in a blue stupor, wondering how he had gotten back to sitting on the rock.

He turned to find a small old woman dressed in a torn, dirty red robe, with eyes that looked like foggy yellow glass and long curly snow white hair. She was carrying a small package under her arms and a walking stick that was ornately carved on the handle.

"Ayet Sal, ther' Valley of Death—yor' looking for him aren't yeh?" She spoke with a thick and informal accent. "I be'n told tha' he's lookin' for yeh." She stared off into the trees as she spoke, with no intention of looking at him.

"No. I'm not looking for Yet Sa—whoever. I'm just here enjoying the outside," he said, rubbing his arms from the burning sensation that still coursed through him.

The old woman turned to Sam, but looked past him with her hollow distant eyes.

"Sure boy, yor mig' fight it but he will find yor no' the less."

Sam looked at the sun and was surprised to see how high in the sky it was already. How could he have been there so long already? He needed to give himself plenty of time to get back to the City to meet up with Talister and Sayvon. Besides, the craziness that was coming out of the old hoot's mouth was a little creepy. He would just politely excuse himself and be off.

"He is waitin', yeh can expect it! And he'll tell yeh where ta find what you're lookin' for."

"I'm sorry, I don't know who you are and I don't have any idea what you are talking about. My name is S—"

"Samuel. I know yor' name. Boy wit' the shadows. Be careful, boy wit' the shadows," she turned without completing her sentence and began to hobble away.

He was stunned. Watching her go, he stared open-mouthed at

Chapter Seven: Boy With the Shadows

the old woman. What was she talking about? Ayet Sal? Boy with the Shadows? Could she know something about his past?

He jumped up and hurried up behind her.

"Lady, uh—ma'am! Excuse me!" he called to her, reaching out to grab at her tattered robe. "How did you know who—"

The old woman spun around and glared directly into Sam's eyes, her eyes blazing yellow and no longer foggy. She threw her hand into the air above her and a blue light shot from her other palm, hitting Sam squarely in the chest.

Flat on his back on the sandy forest floor, Sam opened his eyes to find the old woman standing over him, palms outstretched, a pulsing blue beam of light extending from her palm to his chest.

"Who are yeh?" she said in a low gruff voice.

She looked directly at him, unlike before.

"I—I...you don't remember? My name is Sam! You just got done telling me about the Ayet Sal!" he choked out.

"Boy, I don' know who yeh are, but yeh need to neve' sneak up on an ol' woman," she barked. "An' I don' know nothin' about Ayet Sal, 'cept it's a place yeh don' wanna be."

Sam tried to move, but the beam held him securely to the ground.

"A place? You told me it was a person."

She seemed to see his evident frustration with restriction of movement and recognized that he wasn't a threat, so she released the light on his chest. The flowing light particles disappeared back into her palm and Sam was free once again.

"Boy, I think yeh need to check yer facts. There ain' no Descendant nor Watcher—Light no' Dark—that want ta' go to Ayet Sal." She eyed him curiously with her bright yellow eyes. "Yeh bes' be gettin' back, alrigh? This fores' may be property of Lior—buncha' ignoran' fools—but it's still gots' its potential fo' problems yeh want nothin' a part of."

Sam thought about pressing her for more information, but it was obvious that the dazed woman with the glassy eyes was no longer with them.

🌲🌲 Chapter Seven: Boy With the Shadows

"Yeah, thanks. Sorry if I startled yeh ... I mean you," he corrected himself quickly.

"Think nothin' of it, boy," she mumbled a little less gruffly this time. Then she turned and hobbled around a rise and a few medium-sized boulders that resembled her same hunched form.

When Sam made it back inside the City and up the path to the cabin, Emma was sitting long-ways on the bench in the pavilion reading an extra thick book. As he walked up the rise through the trees to the opening, she merely lifted her head in acknowledgment and stuck her nose back in her book.

"She's in there waiting for you," she mumbled snidely.

Chapter Eight
City Center

"Emma, I don—" Sam started to say but was stopped by the approaching form of Talister Calpher with his long brown hair and a shiny robe.

"Samuel! My boy!" Talister smiled largely and held out his hand, which was just as large as his smile. "Are you ready? Oh, maybe you'll want to clean up a bit, eh?"

"Uh, yeah, sorry about that," Sam said quietly, looking down at his dirt-crusted pant leg. He figured the rest of him looked nearly as awful.

"Not to worry, Sam. Not to worry," he continued to smile. "Plenty of time 'till we need to be there! I'll wait out here and talk to this beautiful young lady here while you get cleaned up."

Emma's face broke into a smile and she immediately began to tell him about how life had been in White Pine, while Sam headed up to the cabin. He walked as slow as he could to catch what she was saying, but couldn't make it out over the sound of the distant ocean waves.

He was concentrating so much on what they were saying that when he entered the cabin and kicked his shoes off, he didn't even

Chapter Eight: City Center

notice Sayvon, Miss Karpatch and Mrs. Sterling sipping tea at the dining table. Sayvon smiled when he finally noticed her, but then immediately went back to her conversation with the older women.

Sam said nothing, but ran upstairs to clean up. He wanted to throw on a new outfit, but Mrs. Sterling must have taken his to wash, so he splashed some water on his face and changed into the one clean shirt he had, then carefully wiped his pants down so they resembled a fresh pair. Looking around Gus's things, he spotted a little bottle of what looked like deodorant or body spray and spritzed a little under his arms.

"Sorry about that. I am ready now," he said awkwardly when he was finally downstairs putting on his shoes.

Sayvon hugged Miss Karpatch and Mrs. Sterling and then brushed teasingly past Sam on her way out the door. She was wearing a silk blue shirt that matched her eyes, while her hair was up in a wispy but purposeful braid. She walked so gracefully that Sam wondered if she could float.

"Ah! Sayvon, Sam, are we ready then?" Talister smiled at them.

"Yes, daddy, Sam just had to change … and apparently apply some gnat spray on himself." She looked him over and scowled while plugging her nose.

"Huh? I didn't know …" Sam was dumbfounded. But before he could finish his sentence, Emma broke out into an incredible sinister laugh that only Lillia would appreciate. Hearing this, both Sayvon and Mr. Calpher broke into a roar that sent three shades of pink to Sam's face.

They were laughing so hysterically that Mrs. Sterling ran out of the cabin to see what the ruckus was all about. She too burst out laughing when she heard about his misfortune with the spray, but at the same time failed horribly at trying to comfort him with her usual sympathetic nature.

When the group finally quit laughing—partly due to their inability to breathe and partly because Mr. Calpher realized their potential tardiness to the meeting—Sam was thoroughly embarrassed to

Chapter Eight: City Center

the point of sweating, and he wished instead of going to the City Center that he could just crawl under a shady rock for the rest of the afternoon.

Sayvon did her best to make Sam feel better the whole way to the City Center, but she couldn't help smiling every time she saw a group of gnats swirling in the sunlight.

As they came up to the massive doors of the red hall entrance, Mr. Calpher strolled through the smaller entrance to the right without so much as a look from the entrance guard. Sam and Sayvon followed him through another door into a long hallway that led to a set of ornate stairs and yet another door.

Sayvon stopped short of the entrance and turned to Sam.

"In the common room past this door is where I will wait for you."

Then she smiled softly and turned to follow her father through the door.

Inside the common room were huge ornate columns leading upward to massive sculptures of silver dragons emerging from the stained glass ceiling. Along the outer edges were twice than life-size statues of winged creatures and warriors—all who seemed to be looking upward toward the ceiling's rotunda and a three-dimensional cutout of what looked like a tree that was engulfed in flames.

There were two smaller wooden doors and one larger one near the far end of the common room, each carved with a perfect embossing of a flaming tree. The larger of the three, however, included a warrior kneeling before the tree in flames, the man's head buried in his hands.

Sayvon left them and wandered over to one of the many benches that were inset along the walls in the common room, while Talister led Sam through the smaller door on the left and up another set of stairs where still another ornately carved door stood with a similar image on its face. Two guards nodded slightly and opened the door as Talister held out his hand, where he displayed his leather armband with a deep blue stone marbled with faint black rippling throughout its exterior. For one moment, Sam thought he saw the blue glow, then disappear.

Chapter Eight: City Center

The guards held large staffs that glowed instantly blue when Talister and Sam approached, covering the archway to the Chancellor's office in light.

As they walked through the light, one of the guards held out a hand suddenly and stopped them before they could pass through the door frame.

"I'm sorry sirs, but I must ask you to step back while we search you," said the younger guard in a commanding tone, staring intently at the light in front of them, which had slowly begun to cloud with an inky smoke-like substance in the corner. It was subtle, and for a moment, Sam wondered if Talister even noticed it.

The older guard grabbed the younger's arm and pointed at the silver cuffs on Talister's robe, whispering something furiously in his ear. After a moment, the guards turned to them and nodded for them to pass. Talister nodded back, the entire time his smile never left his lips.

They walked in through the small doorway to an expansive, sunlit room with glass windows looking out to the dome-shaped rotunda of the City Center. Around the office stood four evenly spaced pillars that curved inward to meet at the top, forming an arch with its center hovering directly above the Chancellor's desk. Thin, blue wisps of light made their way up the arch legs until they met at the top and disappeared into the ceiling above.

The Chancellor met them immediately at the door, his white and silver robe gleaming in the rays of sun that were pouring through the glass.

"Talister, Talister, it is good to see you again. How was your trip to the Outer Edge?"

Talister stepped forward and put his hand on the Chancellor's shoulder, smiling largely.

"It was wonderful, Chancellor," he said, smiling largely. "Many good days of rest. And how are dealings with the Tanniym? Any progress?"

Chapter Eight: City Center

The Chancellor frowned and motioned toward two large leather chairs facing a long, dark wood desk.

"Unfortunately no," he said sadly as he sat opposite them. "The Tanniym are extremely stubborn, and still skeptical that we are going to turn against them once again I am afraid."

"Oh to have the free spirit of a Dragon Keeper," Talister smiled.

"Yes, yes, if only we could leave the pressures of political life behind and live life in the freedom of the mountains. But that is not why we are here today—to discuss Lior diplomacy, are we?" the Chancellor eyed Sam.

"No we are not," Talister reached out and put his hand on Sam's arm. "This is Samuel Forrester, Chancellor Almeous. He has come to us from White Pine."

"It is good to meet you, Samuel," said the Chancellor. "I fear you slipped out too early at the feast for me to introduce myself."

"I am sorry, sir—Chancellor," Sam corrected himself. "I didn't realize …"

"Not to worry, boy, not to worry. I am just glad to finally meet you," he said genuinely.

The Chancellor did not take his eyes off Sam at first, but then turned to look at Talister.

"And how did Samuel come to us, then?"

At that moment, Sam wondered why Mr. Sterling didn't take Sam to the meeting himself. He, too, was important in Lior, and as the head of the Protector group in White Pine, he would have more information than Talister did. And this seemed like a pretty important thing, seeing as how Mr. Sterling was the one that brought him here in the first place.

"Jack Sterling accompanied him through the Northern Gate. He would have been here for this meeting, however he had some business at the Protector's Office to tend to."

The Chancellor did not look away from Sam, which made him feel like he was back in White Pine with every eye watching him. But

159

Chapter Eight: City Center

he knew now that it was mostly Emma, Gus, and Lillia that he saw peering behind the shelves at Iggy's, or following him up Main Street after he had ducked out of school a few minutes early. They had watched him ever since arriving in White Pine. It had certainly had its element of creepiness to it.

The Chancellor picked up a parchment from his desk and scanned it briefly.

"So how certain is he?" the Chancellor finally looked away. "There hasn't been one found in Creation in many years."

"Jack is pretty certain."

"I see, I see," the Chancellor frowned suddenly.

"How many of the Council and Protectors know he is here?"

"There are twenty-two of us that are aware."

The Chancellor smiled, and then purposefully changed the subject as if he had already said too much.

"And what of this that you heard in the forest the night you came through the gate?" he said suddenly, taking Sam off guard.

"I'm sorry sir?"

"The night you came to Lior … you heard a noise in the trees. You said it was right in front of you."

"Uh, yes, that's true, but I didn't see it," Sam stammered. "It could have been an animal or something."

The Chancellor peered at Sam once again, then looked at Talister and shook his head.

"Given the presence of the gate shield, I fear that is impossible."

"I have already tasked the Protector's Office to investigate. It is possible that perhaps the Lazuli shield generator was malfunctioning," Talister offered.

"Yes, yes," the Chancellor waved his hand at Talister, then turned toward the window, frowning as he did. "But we will need to find out more about his background, and I am uncertain how the High Council will respond to his being here." Then he smiled compassionately at Sam, "Forgive me for discussing this as though you are not here."

"I count on a bit of a tussle with the Telok and the Nais halls,"

Chapter Eight: City Center

Talister said. "But if you will let me, Chancellor, I could talk with them first."

"Yes, yes, you have a good rapport with the members. They will listen to you," the Chancellor nodded. "But let's see what the Research Office comes up with first."

Then the Chancellor strode to the window, gazing at the lazy blue light rising up the spire on the other side of the rotunda.

"The long standing rule in Lior has been never to allow a human entrance into the City without evidence of their ancestry." He turned and leveled his amber eyes at Sam, causing the age lines on his face to wrinkle just a bit more. "Samuel, you must understand that your background is of utmost secrecy in this matter. We cannot reveal anything until we know for certain."

Sam swallowed hard. Suddenly he was the center of a potential conspiracy for all of Lior. He was a liability, in fact. One that jeopardized the secrecy of all Descendants.

Suddenly, a small orb of blue light appeared in the window of the office and drifted through the glass to where the Chancellor stood. At its sight, the Chancellor reached out and put his palm to the orb until it unfurled itself into words. Quickly, the Chancellor stood in front of the message, blocking any chance that Sam had of seeing its contents.

Gravely, the Chancellor turned and faced them once again, having wiped the message away with his hand so that it became pieces and specks of light before it blinked and disappeared.

"Can I count on you to be silent, lad?"

"Yes, sir. I will," he said automatically.

The Chancellor smiled a moment, lightening his tone.

"Sam, don't mistake me. There are reasons I believe that you should be here too. We just need to approach this carefully."

Talister stood and motioned for Sam to stand as well.

"We will take good care of Sam, Chancellor Almeous. You can be certain of it," he said.

"Good, good. And before we part, Talister, do you have something for me from your most recent trip?"

Chapter Eight: City Center

Talister held out his hand, and Sam watched a small blue orb emerge from it, floating gently over to the Chancellor, where he carefully reached out and scooped it into the pocket of his robe.

"The latest report from the detectors."

Once the orb was safely hidden, the Chancellor held out his arms and smiled, reminding Sam strangely of Talister.

"Please give my regards to Jack, and thank him for bringing this matter to me. Now if you will excuse me, I must prepare for the Council meeting."

The Chancellor shook their hands before seeing them to the door. Even for an older man with strong features, he looked tired. Something was definitely causing him a lot of grief.

Talister led Sam past the guards and back down the stairwell to the common room. Before stepping through the door, however, he stopped Sam with a hand on his shoulder.

"The Chancellor is right, Sam ma' boy. I think it best you not share any of this with anyone except those closest to you. The less people who know the better."

Sam nodded silently. His group already knew, but did he mean his grandfather? Or others in the circle? He wondered if any of it had ties to what he saw in the forest that night. It seemed to trouble Mr. Sterling, and now the Chancellor. Could he have been just meters away from a Metim or some Dark creature? It was a sobering thought, and he had seen neither of them.

Talister seemed to wait for him to confirm his vow of silence, but hearing none, seemed to accept the nod as sufficient that Sam understood.

"Now then, I believe Sayvon is waiting for us," he said.

They walked back out into the common room where he was surprised to see it filled with people of different ages and races, whisking from group to group in their region's robes, laughing and visiting with one another. The larger wooden door was open and people were filing into the amphitheater in the heart of the City Center.

Chapter Eight: City Center

Talister waved to his daughter, who was tucked away on a bench reading.

"I will leave you in the capable hands of my daughter now, ma' boy. The dreary work of politics calls."

When he was safely enveloped in a group of robed politicians, Sayvon took Sam's hand and smiled long into his eyes.

"Are you ready to see some of the City Center?" she held up a set of peculiar looking keys for him to see.

Sam could feel his face getting hot as she squeezed his hand.

"Sure, let's go."

She grinned and led them to a small door around the corner of the common room.

"I don't suppose you hate politics as much as I do?" she said. "Both my father and grandfather have been in politics nearly their entire lives. What do your father and mother do?"

"My foster parents? Phillip is a Senator, and Sylvia—well, uh— she just embarrasses him," Sam said jokingly, but quickly changed his tone at her questioning look. "But I suppose she just helps him with some of his fundraisers and political parties. You know."

Sayvon removed her shoes to silence the clicking that echoed behind them. "Yes, I know all too well, I am sad to say."

He followed her down a wide stone staircase and into a smaller but well-furnished room. The ornate decorations and luxuriously draped curtains reminded him of the day when Phillip took Sam and his foster mother, Sylvia, to the Capitol to meet the governor. He laughed to himself—not because it was funny, but out of spite as Sylvia had made a fool of herself stumbling about the room and putting her arm around various senators and representatives. That wasn't the worst of it, and all Phillip could do was watch.

"Not too fond of your parents, I see," Sayvon said sadly. "What does your ... foster mother do to embarrass you?"

Sam sighed. He knew he had spoken too quickly about Sylvia. Maybe she would just feel sorry enough to drop it.

"We were at a dinner party once, but my foster mother had a little

Chapter Eight: City Center

too much to drink that night and ended up throwing up on another Senator's wife's shoe during dessert."

"Wow, that really happened?" She forced back a smile.

He decided not to hold back from her. It was, after all, only the people he had lived with for the last fifteen years without any indication that he was anything more to them than a charity case or a tax deduction. His contempt ran deeper for them the older he got.

"If you knew my parents, you wouldn't have been surprised."

She stopped suddenly and turned on her heels to face him directly, staring deep into his eyes the same way Emma did. For a moment he felt almost uncomfortable.

"That's too bad, Sam. Everyone should have parents who care about them."

He thought about what she said, but only after she had turned away from looking at him. For some reason he just couldn't seem to muster up words when she (or any girl for that matter) was face to face with him. It was almost as if he was frozen in time—a slave to her words.

What she was saying about his parents—or any family for that matter—was true. Perhaps they did care about him and just couldn't show it. Perhaps they didn't know how.

He had felt it his entire life though, like something wasn't a fit. Perhaps it was that he wasn't a flesh and blood Forrester, or perhaps they were just too caught up in their power-hungry politics to care about raising a child, but either way, the deep, caring, passionate emotion that was easily read on any real parent's face was not evident in his home.

It was confirmed the day he finally convinced Sylvia to take him to the park. He was six years old, and he remembered every detail—how he dug in the sandbox for the first time in his life. He remembered watching another mother who had taken her shoes off and was helping her son to bury her feet in the sand. He then glanced over to his own foster mother, who sipped cognac from a bottle she had kept in her purse, passing it discretely to her other big-haired friend whom she had forced to join her. Neither of them paid him

Chapter Eight: City Center

any mind. He could have walked off into traffic and no one would have noticed.

Since that day, the jealously grew inside of him, and gradually took him over. The Sterlings were the complete opposite of Sylvia and Phillip. They were loving and attentive.

Since arriving in Lior, he had occasionally thought about them as his own parents—and he would be "Sam Sterling." But there was no use fantasizing about such things. Besides, it would have made Emma his sister.

Sayvon led them through the smaller common room until they came to a small plain door with the words RESTRICTED etched on a small plaque on the wall. She fumbled through her set of keys until she found the one she wanted, then held it up to the brass door handle, where a small beam of light shot from the tip and unlocked the door with a loud click.

Inside was a large round room that domed at the top. The center of the room was empty, except for a thin trickle of blue light that passed lazily up through the floor to the ceiling.

"What is this place?" Sam asked her in the dim light.

"It's a sanctuary for Seers," she whispered, "for those with the gifts to see things that are happening."

"Like prophets."

"Well, no, actually. Seers can only see events as they take place," she whispered. "There hasn't been a prophet in Lior for a very long time."

There seemed to be no one in the room at first, but then they saw a small man with a long white beard hobbling over to the center of the room, where he closed his eyes and held his feeble hands out to the light in front of him in silence.

Sam watched the man as he stood unmovable in the center of the room for nearly a minute. Then he began mouthing something passionately as the light passed between his fingers, pulsating and quickly intensifying.

"What is he doing?"

She pulled him suddenly out of the room into the corridor once

Chapter Eight: City Center

again to escape the now blinding light. Then she held her finger up to her lips, whispering, "He sees something that is of importance to record."

Sam was mesmerized by the light that spilled out into the corridor. The idea of seeing visions as they occurred was fascinating, even if completely unrealistic.

"Well, here they watch a few different things—parts of the forest, the regions, and some of Creation. Anything that contains a certain intensity of Darkness in it, they record, but," she tossed her hair to one side, and the strong scent of lilacs brushed past his nose, "there haven't been any major incidents since the Old City fell."

He thought about what the Chancellor said about what he saw in the forest that night. Wouldn't they see that happen? He knew Talister didn't want him discussing it, but he was tempted to confide in Sayvon.

"So can they see people on Earth?"

Sayvon smiled, leading them away from the Seer chamber for fear of disturbing those inside.

"Sort of, yes. They help the Protector's office watch traffic through the gates to make sure the Dark Forces don't—"

"Attack Descendants, yeah, I heard," he answered her quickly.

She sighed and stopped in the middle of the corridor, which was now significantly darker with the Seer chamber nearly out of sight.

"Sam, you don't have to believe me if you don't want to. I only brought you here so you could see."

"I'm sorry, I didn't mean—" he started, feeling suddenly sorry for having offended her. "I have just spent my whole life believing none of this existed, that's all. Now it's all here, and it's just so … crazy."

Sayvon smiled and nodded.

"It's okay, I get it. I couldn't expect you just to walk into all this believing everything right away."

She coaxed him down another set of stone steps to a balcony that overlooked a large rectangular room with numerous steel weapons lacing the walls. Large wooden columns spaced evenly throughout

Chapter Eight: City Center

the room sported large chunks missing from the beams, an obvious sign of swordplay.

"This was the main training room for the Sons of Light before they moved out of the City," she said. "They are the best of the best with their gifts, the warriors of our people that fight when the Protectors are overwhelmed."

Even though it was empty and no one was training, the room was still impressive. He wondered what it would look like in full training mode.

"You will see them tonight," she said brightly, her hair gleaming from the sunlight flooding into the room. "The newest members are being inducted."

"At the Light games," Sam added.

"Yes. And my father will be conducting the ceremony, since he was once one of them," she said proudly, pulling him once again from his trance into a darkened hallway.

After unlocking the next entrance, Sayvon braced herself against the wall to reveal a door that was thicker than Sam had ever seen, and it took both of them several tries to prop it open. As they did, a loud hissing could be heard as pressurized air escaped the interior. Immediately, a blinding blue beam poured into the corridor, forcing them both to shield their eyes until they had adjusted to the brightness.

Past the door, at the bottom of a stone stairwell lay a monstrous cavern filled with a pool of gleaming blue liquid, which seemed to move and ebb as though something rippled just beneath the surface. A continual stream of the liquid was slowly drifting upward like a lazy stream toward the cavern ceiling, casting reflections of light around the room on the walls like a million candles of brilliant blue light. Shielding his eyes, Sam watched the liquid light disappear into the cavern ceiling, where it no doubt supplied all of the City Center with its life.

"Lapiz Laz—" he stopped, forgetting the word, even though Gus had said it a hundred times.

"Lazuli," she corrected him.

Chapter Eight: City Center

They walked to the edge of the pool where the blue liquid suddenly bubbled furiously before bursting into pockets of light, then joined the stream that floated toward the ceiling above.

"It's the source for the entire city. See the rocks over there?" She pointed to the other side of the pool where massive boulders held deep veins of shining blue rock. "After the Descendants' first city burned, the old Lior City, we weren't sure if we would ever find another source. But then they found this place. It was nearly twice the size of the pool in the old City."

She led him around the edge of the pool where it gave way to a peninsula of marbled blue stone, walking onto the narrow ledge until it nearly surround them. The light was so incredible, so intense, and yet it still calmed him. He was instantly transported back to the night when they crossed through the gate into Lior—the warm feeling of the light as it seemed to enter his very soul. The light made him feel alive, like someone was reaching inside him and manipulating his every sense.

"SAM!" she yanked suddenly on his arm. "Don't touch it!"

He looked down in front of him where he was kneeled at the edge of the pool, his hand outstretched toward the blue light. He had no idea how he got there.

She pulled him back up to her.

"You can't touch it," she said, panting heavily. "It's too high of light concentration. It would send any Descendant into shock."

She led him up the stairs from the pool of Lazuli and down the long corridor into the smaller common room overlooking the old Sons of Light training hall, to a small bench where she forced him to sit for a while to allow the effects of the Lazuli to wear off.

The feeling was strange, wonderful and warm, like the moment he walked through the arch …

But there was another feeling that was evident, deep down and subtle, along with the exhilaration from the Lazuli. It was an odd feeling, and not a pleasant one. Almost like the feeling one received when experiencing pain.

Chapter Eight: City Center

"Watch this," she winked suddenly and strode to a blue circle etched into the floor of the common room. Then, putting her hands to her sides, she closed her eyes. Suddenly, the circle sprang to life, and blue liquid illuminated upward to the ceiling from the floor, creating a stunning tube of Lazuli light. Then Sayvon herself shot upward from the circle and disappeared into the ceiling above, leaving no trace of herself or the cylindrical light that carried her.

Looking around the room, he noticed six other circles dotting the marble floor that were completely unnoticeable when they first entered. Each had a similar circle in the ceiling directly above them.

Now alone, he wondered if he should follow her and attempt to use the tube. He figured he had been unsuccessful in the woods attempting to manipulate the light, but he couldn't be sure because of the old woman's interruption.

Centering himself in one of the circles, he closed his eyes as she did and waited for something to happen.

Suddenly, the hole in the ceiling burst into a bright blue glow and the light met the floor with a cylindrical splash. Sayvon descended gracefully through the middle of the tube, her hands at her side and her eyes still closed.

"How did you do that?" Sam rushed to her side when the light finally flickered and disappeared from around her form.

"It's a Lightway of sorts," she said, stepping out of the circle and stroking her hair. "One of the inventors here in Lior created it after getting tired of going up and down all the stairs."

"Like the light thing that beamed into Lior when we came into the City," Sam said, which drew an instant confused look from Sayvon.

"That's strange," she said suddenly.

"You've never traveled the Lightway?"

"No, its just that no one would have traveled the Lightway during the Festival," she scrunched her nose, then smiled again quickly. "Never mind."

Sam still found himself staring at the now lifeless circles as if they would magically start glowing again, but they remained quiet.

Chapter Eight: City Center

"You have nothing like light travel in Creation, do you?"

"No, not really. Just escalators and elevators. Nothing like this," he told her. "Pretty boring, right?"

"No!" her eyes grew suddenly wide. "Creation is wonderful! There are airplanes, and novels, and ice cream. It's like a fairy tale adventure, from all the books I've read anyway."

"You would be the first to think that," he joked. "Don't forget to add famine and disease to that list."

She squinted at him queerly as if trying to determine whether or not he was making fun of her. To be fair, he was being a bit sarcastic. Perhaps being around Lillia brought it out in him.

"Well I still think it's pretty great."

Sam watched her silky brown hair turn the slightest bit blue as an extra large stream of light snaked up the wall.

"You haven't been to Creation, well, Earth, have you?" he asked, hoping he wouldn't offend her more by prying.

She seemed truly discouraged with the question.

"No. I haven't. My father won't let me."

"Oh, well, it's not that much to see any—"

"He says I am too young, and Earth is too dangerous for Descendants. It's really ridiculous I think. We have way more harmful things here than they do," she huffed.

"You really want to go, don't you?"

"Yes. And I wish someone would have the courage to take me. I'm not afraid."

"Well, like I said. It's not much to see."

"I'm just tired of being treated like a child. I know I'm still underage, but I know many who go all the time."

Why did she want to see Earth so badly? What was so interesting?

"Well, I would rather be here," he said.

She looked discouraged again.

"That's what everyone says."

"It's not all that great, really."

170

Chapter Eight: City Center

Sayvon sighed deeply, then put a hand on his arm, sending momentary shivers up his back.

"Sorry to complain. That wasn't what I wanted to show you. I saved the best for last. Come with me."

She led him out of the common room and up a set of stairs, and another, and yet still another and another until it seemed like they had reached the roof of the City Center.

After climbing a final set of smaller stairs and reaching another carved wooden door, Sam realized that indeed they had reached the top of the City Center, as only the spires could be seen outside the small stairwell window.

Sayvon inserted the largest key into the hidden hole of the tower. Through the stone arches surrounding it's interior, the tower overlooked nearly all of Lior City, including the City Center and all four halls. The forest from where they came and the forest near the sea where Sam had met the old lady was in front of them, and today, a dull mist hung over both. The sun was just beginning to dip lower in the sky, signaling that day was on its last few hours.

Inside the tower also was a room set into the floor, much like the amphitheater, where nine simple chairs formed a semicircle in the round room with a small pedestal in the center. A curious looking holographic screen emerged from the pedestal as soon as the two entered the circle.

"What is this place?" Sam said as he sat carefully in one of the chairs after Sayvon nodded that he could do so.

"It's the monitoring tower for all of Lior," she said, leaning in and speaking with a lower tone. "If it weren't the day of the Council meeting or of the ceremony tonight, I wouldn't be able to show you."

"This you will want to see," she redirected. From her pocket she withdrew her set of keys and pointed one of the longer keys at the pedestal screen. Immediately it sprang to life, spraying eerie images throughout it like tiny holograms moving about the air.

Sayvon pointed the key at one of the holograms and it immediately

Chapter Eight: City Center

enlarged before them. From what little he could see of the image, it was a cave, dark and silent with the exception of a small flickering light in the corner. Eerily, a dark figure passed in front of the light and seemed to glance momentarily toward the two young people watching the hologram.

Then, as if suddenly aware they were being watched, three disturbing images in the cavern came alive, manifesting themselves into dark, hollow forms.

"Who—?" Sam watched, fascinated as each of the forms seemed to writhe in agony as if bound in pain with imaginary chains.

"Who—are they?"

"This is a prison reserved for the four First Lords of the Dark," she said quietly, and for a moment, Sam wondered if the images could hear them.

"They are the most dangerous of the Dark Watchers, and the original fallen Watchers."

She pointed at one figure that stood shorter than the others while he twisted and turned painfully as if being tortured.

"That one is Yaren, Lord of Fear. He has forced and coerced many Descendants into becoming Metim simply by terrorizing them."

"What about that one?" Sam peered at the tall, hooded figure that seemed to take on the distinct appearance of an especially dark thundercloud. His form did not seem to mind the pain as he clawed at the cavern wall, but almost seemed to enjoy it in an eerie way.

"Sar Sehrah, the Storm Lord. He is the most powerful one of the three."

The Storm Lord ... He remembered the conversation between Cooley and Mr. Sterling when they first arrived in Lior. From what he could hear from eavesdropping on the two, Mr. Sterling had concerns that the storm in White Pine the day they left could have been caused by the Dark Lord in front of him.

But how could he if he was locked up here?

Sam was very interested in the next one, as the image was one of a beautiful woman. For some reason, even though she was filthy, and her eyes resembled only hollow empty pits, she was appealing.

Chapter Eight: City Center

Something about her was really intriguing. She drew you to her—even though it was only a holographic image, buried deep within the darkness of the cave, she was beautiful.

"And that one?"

"That's Taurs, Lord of Seduction. She was known to have seduced her way into men's hearts—and was the one who let the Metim into the Old City before they destroyed it."

The Old City—the Descendants' first city to serve as government for the regions of Lior. Gus has spoken about it before. Many Descendants of Light who lived in the City died because of an invasion of the Dark Forces. It was the last time the Watchers intervened, destroying the invading Dark Forces, but at a very high cost. Since then, the Watchers have not been seen.

Sam searched the images, looking for the fourth that Sayvon mentioned.

"Wait—you said that there were four Dark Lords. Where's the fourth?"

Sayvon frowned grimly.

"He's not there because he was never caught after the destruction of the Old City. His name is Kachash, the Lord of Deception. He has been in hiding for almost—uh—fifty of your years now. But most think he is dead."

Incredible. Sam thought. *Fallen angels, right here in front of him.*

"But Kachash isn't near as powerful as the Dark One, Nasikh. He is the original Dark Lord before Creation, before Lior."

Satan. She's talking about the legendary evil one. Even Sam knew who that was.

"What does he look like?" Sam wanted to know, his mind instantly racing back to the night in the forest when he first stepped through the arch. He didn't see it, but the thought that maybe it could be him …

"No one knows. Some say he looks like a hideous monster with sharp teeth and horns that can tear someone in half, but others say he looks just like us."

"Like people in Lior? So he could be in the City?"

Chapter Eight: City Center

Sayvon laughed for the first time that Sam had ever heard. But then she turned deadly serious.

"No, there is no way. After the Old City was destroyed, the Council put in a detection system that works on Lazuli light, and that's when they also commissioned the Protectors Office to monitor the City. They are on guard from sun up to sun down."

Sam remembered the guard at the front gate, and walking into the Chancellor's office with Talister. This must be the detection system to which she was referring.

His mind went back to the guard stopping them momentarily, seeing something in the light that didn't add up. Did he see something hidden inside him?

Sam pushed the thought out of his mind and stared at the eerie images once again. Sayvon held her key up once again and instantly the scene of the figures in the prison retracted into the hologram, where there were four other images in the montage waiting to be viewed. They were all void of figures, and all appeared to contain an arch in different places.

"Where are those places?" Sam asked, his eyes centering on the one in the woods that looked similar to the one he came through.

"Those are the arches in Lior, four of them total. I believe that one," she pointed at the one surrounded by familiar pine trees, "is the one you came through."

He stared at the lifeless arch, where only a patch of sunlight shown on one of its legs. It seemed like only yesterday that he knew nothing of arches, or of a spirit world like Lior.

"What about the Metim? Can they use the arches?" he asked without considering the answer.

She brushed her hair back and stood as the late afternoon sun began to pour into the tower.

"No, they can't. Once the Light leaves them they are unable to manipulate the Light any longer."

He stood with her, accepting her incredibly soft hand in his, watching the rays of sunlight inch their way up the interior wall with

Chapter Eight: City Center

incredible patience. Light—it was free to roam as it pleased, shining as it wills, a slave of no one.

"Unless they were forced."

"Yes. Unless they were forced, or chose to follow the Metim when they were still within the Light. But that is nearly impossible."

"Nearly."

Cheering sounds from around the City echoed suddenly into the tower's stone walls. Sam stalled as Sayvon attempted to lead them toward the monitoring tower door.

"Has it ever happened? Have the Metim ever gotten through an arch?"

She stopped suddenly and turned suddenly to look at him, completely ignoring his question. Instead she gazed intently into his eyes, not allowing him to avert his gaze.

"Sam, are you and Emma … exclusive?" The cheering in the background intensified, but she refused to let him be distracted.

The question stopped him cold. He didn't know. Emma was sure not happy to have him be with Sayvon, that was obvious, but whether or not they were dating exclusively was still a mystery. Neither of them had really talked about it, and he hadn't really thought about it until this point. If it were true, she would be the only girlfriend he had had since Jenny Hampton in the fourth grade. Saint Mary's Parish and School may have been the best education in the area, but it didn't allow much for a social life.

"I don't think so," he started to say, but was immediately silenced by her lips pressing to his.

For a moment, the act sent a chill up his spine as his lips quivered, but it quickly faded into an uncomfortable feeling of guilt. Something didn't feel right about her kiss, and she knew it too in the same instant as she pushed away suddenly.

An awkward silence hung in the air on the stairwell for nearly a minute as the two stared confused at one another. There was something different about her, but he couldn't explain it if he tried. It was almost as if he already knew her—had known her his entire life.

Chapter Eight: City Center

"I'm sorry, we'd better go," she said quietly, fumbling with the Light keys on the ring she had slipped on her wrist. "You are late for dinner."

"Sayvon, I don't know what—" he started, but couldn't finish the words for lack of finding them.

"It was so foolish. I suppose I was trying to be wild and crazy like your women in Creation—"

He smiled and took her hand in his, immediately understanding what she must be feeling, torn between two worlds. No doubt the same lure was what drew the Watchers to Creation in the first place.

"You don't need to be crazy for me to like you," he said genuinely.

"It doesn't matter," she tried to play it off, but smiled still the same at his compassionate words. "We can talk about it later. Mrs. Sterling doesn't like it when her guests are late for dinner."

Chapter Nine
Games and Dark Dreams

They walked back to Thalo's Main Street in silence. The sun was just beginning to show signs of red and orange over the roof of the cabin as they made their way up the pathway. Stopping suddenly, Sayvon grabbed his hand and squeezed comfortingly as if to tell him she enjoyed being with him. He squeezed back, knowing it would not be the end of their conversation. Whatever they had felt when she had kissed him, it required more thought, and more figuring out. It was yet another mystery in a long line of mysteries since entering Lior.

Emma had not left her spot in the pavilion, but when Sam and Sayvon emerged from the trees, she immediately got up and walked toward the cabin, refusing to look behind her. Mrs. Sterling smiled as Sam came through the cabin door after saying goodbye to Sayvon and slipped into his seat at the table, where everyone else except Mr. Sterling had already taken their seats and were waiting on him. In the middle of the table was a large festive vase full of flowers and glowing red dragon figurines.

"Now, as soon as the Mister arrives, I believe we can eat," Mrs.

🌲🌲 Chapter Nine: Games and Dark Dreams

Sterling said as she set a large steaming pot of coffee on the table. When she set it down, Emma stood from where Sam had taken the seat next to her to move across the table to another chair.

"Guess she is still mad at you," Gus whispered from the only other occupied chair next to Sam.

"Yeah, I suppose," he said.

At that moment, Mr. Sterling burst through the door wearing a large red hat and carrying a newspaper titled "The Watcher." The headlines were visible enough for Sam to realize that it had to be the main newspaper for the whole of Lior.

"Let the games begin!" he hollered with his hands outstretched, causing cheers from everyone in the room.

"What do you think the odds are for the Thalo hall this year, Jack?" Miss Karpatch said as Mr. Sterling plopped in his seat at the head of the table.

"Not good, I am afraid," he said sadly. "This year they have a rookie who hasn't seen but two games in his whole career, and has never started in a tournament."

Mrs. Sterling set a large plate of roast duck and potatoes on the table.

"Now if we don't eat then we won't be able to see any of it, will we?" she huffed loudly.

Mr. Sterling stood and stretched out his hand to Cooley on one side and Mrs. Sterling on the other.

"She's right, of course." He cleared his throat. "Let's bow and thank our Creator for the harvest."

All at the table closed their eyes, with the exception of Emma, who glanced briefly at Sam before closing her own. Sam was sure he saw hurt in her eyes.

"Our Lord and Creator, we ask that you accept our thanks for this bountiful harvest. We deserve nothing less than to be wiped from your memory, but instead you have favored us from your mighty hand. It is with great honor and humbleness that we accept your blessings," he paused, "and if you will be with those participating in the games

Chapter Nine: Games and Dark Dreams

tonight and the rest of this week, we ask for their protection and safety. We ask these things as Descendants of your Kingdom."

After eating a heaping plate of tender duck meat, potatoes, and two large pieces of bread, and drinking nearly three glasses of a purplish looking tea that had the flavor of herbs and grapes, Sam excused himself at Mrs. Sterling's shooing and followed Gus upstairs to change clothes as everyone else hurried to get out the door for the start of the games.

The stadium was tucked behind the City Center, nearly on the edge of a tall cliff overlooking the sea, and as they walked through the throngs of other halls cheering and making their way to the field, the sun finally made its exit below the horizon. The stadium was packed to the brim, and by the time they reached their seats, the moon had peeked itself from behind its hidden location in the blackened forest, blanketing the whole city with a soft glow like a lone light in a dark universe.

There were thousands of seats lining the huge wood beams that made up the rows, and the group followed Cooley to a front row spot right in the center of the field.

Suddenly, high above them a bright blue firework exploded, signaling the game start was near, illuminating the black liquid expanse for a moment.

"What ocean is that?" Sam pointed at the blackness in front of where Emma had surprisingly pulled him into a seat next to her.

She looked into his eyes calculatingly.

"We call it the Sea of Yarey."

"Yarey," he repeated.

"It means fear, from the ancient language Descendants used to use."

"It looks pretty scary," he said jokingly.

For the first time that day a subtle smile formed in the corner of her lips. She may not be completely over his spending time with Sayvon, but at least she was on speaking terms with him now.

She punched him in the arm suddenly, causing him to reel back

Chapter Nine: Games and Dark Dreams

and knock over a lighted cup of iced tea all over the woman sitting behind them.

He apologized to the woman repeatedly and flagged down another vendor in the next row while Emma laughed herself to the floor of the row at his clumsiness.

Sam slumped back down in the seat when the whole ordeal had ended, the woman choosing to move to the seat beside her to avoid his "uncontrollable movements." She sipped her tea and glared in his direction every so often. Emma punched him again, softer this time, but then mimicked his outburst by flinging her hands wildly into the air behind her, and then she broke out into another fit of laughter. He was certainly glad to see her smile again, even at his expense, and even if it did feel like she was taking out her frustrations about Sayvon on his arm.

The stadium filled up quickly with spectators as the opening ceremony began with light-bearing acrobats from all four halls shooting each other high into the air and dangling from tall poles held by incredibly strong acrobats below.

Spectators were instantly on their feet as the band moved onto the field, playing the chorus of each of the representative halls, with each colored section of the crescent shaped stadium cheering more loudly as their lighted hats bobbed and moved in a waving pattern to the music.

Then, as the band bowed and ended their round of choruses, suddenly it seemed that everyone had found their seats and were quieting down. Acrobats pranced quickly off the field following the small band, at which point the lights in the stadium dimmed and a small man wearing a white robe emerged from the far end of the stadium, a blue spotlight hovering curiously above him as he walked.

Once he arrived at the very center of the stadium, he held his hands outstretched until there was an eerie silence throughout the air. No one spoke, and the only sound was the occasional creak of a stadium bench and the soft rolling of the waves in the darkness.

"Who's that?"

"Shhhh!" Emma punched his arm sharply. "Be quiet!"

Chapter Nine: Games and Dark Dreams

"I'm sorry I—" Sam started.

"Welcome!" his voice boomed through the stadium, drowning out any noise from the sea, "to the games of Lior!" He threw his hands in the air once again to the deafening sound of cannon booms behind him and sprays of blue light shooting high into the air around the stadium.

At first Sam didn't notice Emma holding his hand because of the eruption of the stadium around him, but when the cheering simmered into a lull once again, he felt the pressure of Emma's soft hand squeezing his rather tightly. He squeezed back, hoping she would see it as his apology for Sayvon.

Hooded white figures suddenly ran onto the field carrying a long white carpet, which they immediately rolled out in front of the man in the white robe, who only watched as he continued to hold his hands out above him.

Gus opened a large bag of popped Fuzer nuts and a box of dark brown egg-shaped candies rather loudly, at which point Mrs. Sterling leaned forward from behind them and shushed him.

"That's Mentor Aron," Gus whispered as he pointed toward the field. "He's the master Mentor for the School of the Shining One. He conducts the ceremony for the new recruits into the Sons of Light."

With the crowd still silent, the man turned toward the end of the field, and white lighting instantly shot from his outstretched hand and illuminated a candelabra standing at the end of the carpet where the hooded figures had placed it. Then he turned, and another bolt of lighting shot from his other hand and lit the candelabra on the other side.

Turning toward the audience with his arms still outstretched, he bellowed, "Let us welcome the newest Sons into the service of Lior!"

Bright spheres of light on each side of the Mentor dropped from out of the sky and splashed onto the field, and suddenly eight hooded figures were visible in the blinding blue light.

People cheered so loudly that Gus's next commentary on the happenings was impossible to understand. Instead, Sam chose to join in with the elated crowd and clapped as loud as he could. It was an

Chapter Nine: Games and Dark Dreams

amazing sight, even though the light that blinded the field from the Son's appearance still left blind spots in his vision.

With the audience finally settling down after yet another round of whistles and cheers from the emotional crowd, the eight figures removed their hoods and knelt before the Mentor. Once again, Mentor Aron stretched out his hands and spoke as if his voice was broadcast through a loudspeaker.

"These Descendants are called by the Creator for the purpose of defending Lior! We welcome them into the family of the Sons of Light!"

Again the stadium erupted into cheers, and couldn't be quieted for several more moments.

"Never has there been a greater calling, or a greater challenge than the one that has been accepted by the Sons. We ask our Mighty Creator for protection upon them, and upon the land of Lior as they fight the forces of Darkness!"

He then turned and faced the first hooded individual, and bowed deeply before him, bringing himself lower than the figure next to him. Then he moved onto the next one, and the next, until he had bowed before all of the figures on the field. When he was finished, he stood and returned to the center of the carpet once more, at which point all of the recruits dropped to their knees in a humble bow, each in one motion. Again, silence echoed loudly throughout the stadium.

"As the Creator has permitted me, it is now my distinct honor to call these Descendants ... Sons of Light! Rise and be acknowledged!"

Everyone in the stadium was once again on their feet, and the cheering couldn't be stifled this time. The newly appointed Sons huddled around their Mentor, hugging and holding each other until the acrobats rolled up the carpet and began setting up for the game.

"So those guys—the *Sons* ... help the Protector's Office defend the City?" Sam leaned over to Gus who was polishing off a second bag of Fuzer nuts.

"Actually," he crunched away, "they are sent around Lior making sure the Metim stay within their boundaries. But they do aid the PO when they need extra help."

Chapter Nine: Games and Dark Dreams

"If they don't?" Sam persisted.

"Don't what?" he looked cross-eyed suddenly.

"Stay within their boundaries," Sam repeated.

"Then they destroy them," he said cheerfully, shoving another purple handful of nuts into his mouth and peering at the now empty field. "But it hasn't been necessary for quite some time now."

Suddenly, the field came alive with players wearing green on the left side of the field and purple on the right. Teammates on both sides were tossing baseball-sized lighted blue balls with short leather slings with efficient speed.

Emma, who had taken on the noble job of teaching him all about Kolar Ball, had now seemed to forget any memory of his day with Sayvon and was snuggled up to his arm once again. Sam felt a bit strange with Mrs. Sterling just behind them watching every move they made, but he knew Emma and her intentions, and she had obviously earned the trust of her parents because they made no move to stop her.

"There are two goals spaced out in the field on each team's side, and one main goal for each. And see those?" she narrated as the balls of light whizzed about the field like shooting stars, each one leaving a trail of light behind it. "Each team has three lighted Kiols that they try to throw in the other team's goals. There's seven Kiols total."

Suddenly a player produced and swung a larger gold ball in his sling, slinging it to a teammate with precise skill. Emma grabbed his arm and pointed excitedly.

"And that ball over there makes seven. It's the Kolar Ball. It is worth double points!"

Suddenly, all balls ceased movement and players lined up in straight lines in front of their team's goals. The stadium grew steadily silent with only the occasional hoot from unknown parts of the stands. Gus, who had put down his giant mug of tea and bag of Fuzers, was the first to stand as a lone voice boomed from somewhere above them for all Descendants to stand as they prayed.

The stadium clanged to their feet in unison and became instantly silent once again.

Chapter Nine: Games and Dark Dreams

Barukh atah Adonai, Eloheinu, melekh ha'olam. Oseh ma'asei v'reishit!

Blessed are you, Lord, our Creator, sovereign of the universe who does the work of Creation! Keep us and our paths straight, and bind us to your tassels as we seek to honor your purpose!

"The prayer in the ancient tongue," Emma said once the prayer ended and the stadium returned to their seats. As soon as she said it, suddenly a huge bright ball of blue light streaked center field and unfolded before them into a series of huge gleaming letters. It read:

Welcome all Descendants to the Games!
Tonight's games will be Nais against
Themane, and Telok against Thalo!
Purple and Green, take the field!

Then the lighted words dissolved into a huge gleaming circle, looking very much like a sun setting across the stadium. The game clock circle pulsated and began its trek across the night sky as a horn blast signaled the start of the game.

There were whizzing lights suddenly on the field, with players running every direction catching and throwing Kiols. The gold Kolar Ball could only be seen every so often as the teams attempted strategy plays to end the match quickly. After a while of getting dizzy watching the lights flash around the field, Sam began to see a rhythm to the madness and was able to keep up with the plays and even cheer when a team scored a goal.

"We want the green hall to win, because then we will see them in the final game," Emma said in between sips of Sam's tea. "Oh I just can't stand how they act after they beat us like last year! So—so—*happy* that they beat us!"

Chapter Nine: Games and Dark Dreams

With only seconds left in the third match, the green hall players scored their tenth point to beat the purple hall ten to five. The green hall had won all three matches without much effort. The purple players walked solemnly off the field as the giant gleaming numbers showed the final scores above them.

"Here they come!" Emma shouted suddenly, and the entire red section jumped to their feet.

The players jogged out onto the field amidst deafening cheers from the blue and red spectators.

"Descendants, please welcome the halls of Telok and Thalo!" The words rolled across the field as the teams tossed a few light balls to each other.

As the sunset timer ticked it's last few moments away before the game, the players took their positions. Then the horn lights began to fly as players sprang into action, lighted balls flying everywhere. The red hall scored in the leftmost target in the first few seconds of the game, but then didn't score again for the entire match. The taller blue team player with a large letter "S" on his back dominated the field, catching the red player's balls every time they would get close to scoring. Another shorter blue player would constantly throw the gold-lighted ball at the red's right target, causing the red players to focus most of their attention on defending their most important goal.

With the score of the first match being one to ten, the second match went nearly as badly, but the red hall was able to catch on to their strategy mid-game and won ten to eight.

The final match was a struggle for both teams, the red hall and blue hall players whizzing balls to each other in trick plays and fake throws. Suddenly, the slender rookie player named Pattok, with the sandy-colored hair, caught three balls in a row and scored in the left target.

The crowd chanted "Rookie! Rookie!" as the red hall pulled ahead of the blue hall halfway through the match, and Sam, Gus, and Emma stood to their feet with the crowd, chanting alongside.

By the three-quarter time mark, the rookie had scored three more

Chapter Nine: Games and Dark Dreams

goals, and the plumper but agile bald player named Taris scored two as well, making the game eight to seven in favor of the red hall.

After another two scores by the blue hall in rapid succession, the extremely tall and bony white-haired coach for the red hall called a time out. He stood over the players like a giant skeleton in a red robe, pounding his fist into his hand animatedly as he yelled.

As if a fire had been lit beneath him, the rookie was instantly all over the field when the glowing sun-clock started, snatching lighted balls from the air and returning them with incredible speed.

"Rookie! Rookie!" the crowd continued to shout, everyone now on their feet.

The blue players tried their best to keep up with the throws, but eventually they were overwhelmed, and two balls were rocketed into their left and right targets. The crowd roared as the red players collided into each other, the words "Thalo hall has defeated Telok hall 10–9" scrolling across the field.

"Rookie! Rookie!"

The red team hoisted the young player onto their shoulders and carried him off the field as numerous red and green lights streaked into the dark sky, signaling the winners of the night.

"It means tomorrow night we have an even tougher game with Themane," Emma said as they exited the stadium amid hoots and whistles from the winning teams.

"So you aren't still mad at me?" Sam asked suddenly, unaware where the question came from. He would have been smarter to let it go, but then he had never been very good with girls.

She ignored his question, and instead babbled on about each of the hall's origins.

"Sorry, I should probably have told you what the halls were earlier, but each one is named in the old language for the different regions of Lior.

"The blue hall, Telok, means 'land of the ancient.' They are from the Northern lake region. Themane, the green hall, means 'land of sorrow,' but I really don't know why they call them that—it's a perfectly beautiful place in the Southern forest region. Nais is the

Chapter Nine: Games and Dark Dreams

purple hall, named after the cloud people in the Eastern mountain range, much too cold for most people to stand but they seem to make it just fine. And then there's Thalo, our region, which includes Lior City, named after the 'land of skulls,' a truly dreadful name.

"Are you even listening to me?" she stopped suddenly in front of a coffee vendor who was filling mugs as quickly as possible as more of the exited crowd lined up for a caffeinated nightcap.

"Yes, I uh—"

"Never mind. You'll hear all about it from Gus anyway."

Sam breathed a sigh of relief as they passed the City Center where they waited for Gus, Lillia, and the rest of the group to catch up. She obviously had gotten over being too-mad-to-even-look-at-him angry and had moved on to the burying-it-under-chit-chat phase.

"So why these particular colors? Do they have some significance?" Sam gazed at the stained windows that glowed in the halls of the City Center with almost living colors, a deep contrast with the darkness that now held the City.

"Why would I know that?" she said contemptuously, the sudden flare of anger revealing that the issue with Sayvon was not completely dead.

"Never mind. I know that each region chose a different part of Lior because they disagreed with each other after one of the wars," she continued.

"So Thalo was not always together with the other halls?"

"No. In fact, the halls disagree a lot. But the games and the yearly feast help us remember we are together—now don't try and ask if I'm mad. I'm fine now that Sayvon's not batting her prissy little eyes at you anymore."

Gus and Lillia caught up with them about the time they were entering the pathway to the cabin, and Sam was glad for the extra company. He even enjoyed Lillia's snide comments about the other halls and players at the game for a change. As they walked, the smell of sea air drowned out the smell of doughnuts and skewers of meat being sold on the red hall street.

Chapter Nine: Games and Dark Dreams

"I could use another beef stick or two," Gus mumbled as he huffed up the pathway.

"No you couldn't," Lillia said under her breath but loud enough for all of them to hear.

"Lillia, really?" Emma lashed out suddenly, but was met with an animated eye-rolling back from Lillia.

"Sorry Gus," she said quietly, but then mumbled under her breath, "that you can't control yourself."

Emma turned on her heels and stood directly in front of Lillia, her eyes blazing. "Lillia, that is enough!"

While Gus was unquestionably hurt by her words, he seemed more focused on getting them to the fire pit in the pavilion, as he no doubt had some news of his research earlier in the day.

Mr. Sterling, Mrs. Sterling, Cooley, and Miss Karpatch emerged from the woods still hooting and wearing their red hats.

"Don't be out too late you four! I'm not waiting on you for breakfast!" Mrs. Sterling shook her large red glowing foam finger in the air as she and Mr. Sterling mounted the stairs to the cabin while the four teens found their way to the fire pit.

"We won't, mum!" Emma said obediently.

Gus coaxed everyone to take a seat while Lillia poked at the ashes, which still showed some life in the glowing coals from the previous evening's Fuzer roast.

"I was hoping to have a little time before bed to tell you what I found out today," he started. "Although I'm not thoroughly ready to commit to any of the Lior legends, I did find a little information that may shed some light on Chivler's disappearance," Gus said with the slightest bit of nervousness in his voice, while the others stared confused at his connections. "I was reading in the library and luckily overheard one of the Protectors quietly discussing the break-in at Chivler's Books."

Suddenly all eyes were on Gus.

"So I sat at one of the tables near them so I could hear what they

Chapter Nine: Games and Dark Dreams

were saying." Gus took a large breath. "Apparently whoever broke into the store was looking for something—a journal."

"A journal? What for?" Lillia wiped her eyes casually.

"Apparently it belonged to a man who founded White Pine—a man name Julian Lawrence."

"Isn't that—oh! Chivler's Bookstore!" Emma had wrapped herself up in her deep red knitted sweater with "THALO" stitched on the front and was trying to shift her chair away from the evening breeze off the ocean. "Wasn't it the first building of White Pine?"

"It was. Julian was a banker, and when the copper mining began to take off a few years earlier, he sought to become the central bank for all of the Northern Midwest and Canada mines in operation. The building was to be the main branch for the entire region."

"So?" Lillia pronounced.

"It seems that Julian, ever since moving to White Pine and building the Bookst—uh—bank, started having dreams and visions about arches."

"He was a Descendant?" Emma's eyes grew to saucers.

"Yep. But the dreams—they were, well, a little different. It seems that Julian was having dreams about a specific arch. A Dark arch, in fact—complete with visions of dark creatures who would enter and exit it freely."

Both girls were suddenly on the edge of the bench, precisely in front of Gus to catch his every word.

"Like, as in *the* Dark Legend?" Emma stammered. "The theory of the Dark arch?"

"I would assume so," Gus replied. "I read somewhere that many in Lior believed he was one of the ancient prophets. His journal is said to contain many secrets."

"But that's impossible. Descendants have dreams about the white arches—never the dark one we've only heard about in stories," Lillia said.

Suddenly, a wave of panic engulfed Sam, and his almost nightly

Chapter Nine: Games and Dark Dreams

dreams about the black arch rushed back to him in clear, full detail, as if he could reach out and touch it. His face grew hot, even in the cool night air. His dream had not only featured a Dark arch, but he was a part of the dream. The voices of the others suddenly morphed into a blubbering mess of noise, and he could no longer understand them.

****

"Sam! What is it?" Emma was instantly at his side.

Sam hadn't realized it, but he was now slumped over on the bench and feeling quite faint. The coals from the leftover fire blurred in front of him and all sounds around him became only muffled noises.

"Sam!" rang Emma's voice rang, which was beginning to sound clearer.

He struggled to sit up. Immediately his mind went to the Dark arch once again, and wooziness nearly took him over once again. Instead of giving in, he grabbed Lillia's arm, who had jumped off the bench mumbling that she needed to find a doctor.

"Don't—" his words slurred, but he forced himself to form the words as his head pounded like a giant hammer inside his skull. "Just—don't. I … I'm fine."

"No you're not, weirdo. You just fainted," Lillia attempted to retrieve her arm.

"Don't! I'm fine!" Sam said sternly, his senses finally returning fully.

"Fine. Your funeral."

Sam couldn't keep it to himself any longer. As he rubbed his temple, he held his hand up as if to quiet them again. Lillia reluctantly sat down on the bench, looking queerly at him from the other side of the fire pit. "I had—uh—dreams about an arch too."

"We already know that," Emma said gently. "Every potential Descendant of the Light does."

What Sam told them next was something he had been keeping bottled up inside for quite a while now. He knew others had dreams like his own, but there was a difference in how they had reacted as

Chapter Nine: Games and Dark Dreams

opposed to him. The waking up in the middle of the night screaming in a pool of his own sweat, heart beating so fast he couldn't possibly count his own pulse, had driven him nearly insane the past few months. Those around him did not seem to share the same sense of gripping fear he did. Since coming to Lior, he had suspicions his dreams were not normal, not like the wonderful feeling of being in front of the beautiful, pulsing white light of the arch in White Pine as it transported them to a different world. The fear terrorized him, tortured his mind in the night, leaving him cold and senseless to the world around him. Now was the time to tell them the truth.

"But in my dreams, the arch is always *dark*," Sam told them.

Chapter Ten
Old Lady Wrenge

Emma gaped at him open-mouthed.

"What? Why haven't you told us this before?"

Sam felt light-headed once again.

"You never asked."

"So you just thought everyone went around having dreams about Dark arches?!" Lillia joined in with Emma's astonishment.

"I—uh—didn't really know," he stammered. "It's not like you told me much of anything."

"Does that mean he is cursed with Darkness?" Emma sputtered, refusing even to look in Sam's direction.

He remembered the guard stopping him and Talister just before entering the Chancellor's office. *Could I have been the one to set off the alarm? Did the old lady in the forest know something about me and that's why she called me 'boy with the shadows'?*

Gus stood and began pacing in front of the fire pit silently, and no one said much of anything for several minutes as they processed Sam's announcement. It was Lillia who noticed Gus's unwillingness to engage in the conversation.

Chapter Ten: Old Lady Wrenge

"Did you know about this?" she glared in his direction as he paced.

Gus stopped, looking quietly into the night air beyond the pavilion toward the City. He obviously had been holding back on some information that would bring light to the situation.

"Yes. I mean ..."

"Spill it, Grimace," Lillia chided him.

"I had an idea, yes," he breathed loudly. "He talks in his sleep ... and his demeanor in the mornings following his dreams wasn't quite one that would suggest his dreams were of the blissful nature like ours were."

Neither girl responded to this, only continued to stare at Gus with concern as if he had the answers for why Sam had been dreaming in this manner.

"It's not like I can help it," Sam said angrily as they continued to act like he wasn't hearing everything they were saying about him.

"No one is saying it is your fault." Emma put her hand on his knee gingerly. "We will just have to figure this out, right Gus?"

"Right. I—"

Gus was cut off suddenly by Lillia, who had gasped loudly, making Emma nearly drop her coffee.

"It *is* the Dark arch theory again, isn't it?"

"The what?"

Gus nodded.

"The Dark arch theory comes from the Dark Legend, the proclaimed Prophecy by the Dark Lords about the future of Lior."

Oh great, Sam thought. *Dark arch theories? Dark Lords? What have I gotten myself into?*

Gus continued, "The Creator, when He formed the Earth, made sure that man would have a written code to live by, and a promise of His destruction of evil in the world. We call them the scrolls of the Creator, you call them the—"

"Bible. I know."

Gus nodded again.

"But there isn't much written about the future of Lior, and what

Chapter Ten: Old Lady Wrenge

will happen to Descendants when the Creator returns. For that, we rely on theories and hypotheses from our researchers, which often are debated because there isn't much to back them up."

"He's not an idiot, Gus," Lillia snorted. "Just tell him about the Dark Legend."

Gus sighed, as if regaining his train of thought.

"The Dark Legend is taken from the only promise we believe we have ever received from the Creator Himself about Lior, spoken down throughout the ages, called the Prophecy of the Shadow."

"How is a dark legend taken from a promise by the Creator?"

"Good question." Gus nodded. "No one knows where or how the actual Promise was given. It was said to have been heard by only a few throughout the centuries. Some time after it was given, we believe the Dark Lords took it as their own, twisting it to suit their own needs."

"So they are using the Creator's words to come up with their own prophecy," Sam understood.

"Yes."

Suddenly Lillia dug through her pack, pulling out her journal and opening its worn pages.

"Why don't we just read it instead?" she said snidely.

She traced her finger down the page of the journal until she found what she was looking for, then began reading:

> *In that day all of Lior will moan as the shadow is cast upon the lands. From the mortal world will come the last prophet, third to be called, who will seek the hidden gate to release the Dark One from his bonds. He will call unto himself the Darkness, and the shadow will be revealed. It is then the time is near.*

"That was Boggle's translation," Lillia added when she was finished. "He worked on trying to preserve the original Prophecy as best as he could from the regions."

The whole thing sounded strange and confusing to Sam.

"Why is the Promise called the Prophecy of the Shadow?"

Chapter Ten: Old Lady Wrenge

"Researchers say it's some sort of curse that would look like a shadow, I suppose ... but I would have to look into it. My knowledge on the Prophecy is rather lacking," Gus admitted.

Lillia laughed for the first time that night, even though it was obvious she was laughing at Gus's expense.

"That's a first, you not knowing much about something."

This wasn't anything new. Nearly every culture in the world had some sort of prophecy, legend, or set of stories to help them cope with not understanding the end of all things. It wasn't the legend that scared him, rather the fact that he was having dreams about it.

"Why would the Dark Lords want to believe in all this?"

Emma threw up her hands.

"Because they're a bunch of frauds, that's why. Which is why the legend is nonsense—"

"So tell me why nearly half the Descendants in the regions and nearly a third of the Council is starting to believe there might be some truth to the Dark Legend? Are you really that naive to think no one else thinks the same way you do?" Lillia interrupted angrily, her momentary rage shutting Emma up for the moment.

"Regardless of who believes what, the legend been taken more seriously in Lior now than ever before, especially by those on the Council," Gus said solemnly.

"Why do the Dark Lords want this Prophecy to happen?" Sam thought it best to direct his questions to Gus since the girls were obviously becoming emotional about the ordeal.

Gus sighed as though heavy in thought.

"For obvious reasons, they want nothing more than to release the Dark One from his prison. But more than that, some say the Dark Lords believe the third prophet to be sent will end up leading their dark army against the Creator."

Sam chuckled.

"You actually believe this?"

The other three did not answer, but chose rather to listen as the sea seemed to pound the shoreline as the night breeze began to pick up.

Chapter Ten: Old Lady Wrenge

Everything inside Sam wanted to believe that there was a rational explanation for his dreams—maybe lack of sleep or stress from school ... but the truth was, nothing would justify the coincidences that were present now that he had heard about the Prophecy and the Dark Legend. He would not be able to let this one go.

"Doesn't seem to me like the Promise the Creator made is a very good one," he ventured.

Emma stood suddenly to warm her hands close to the coals.

"It's the Creator's Promise. How could it be bad?"

"It sounds like the Dark One will win."

All three sets of eyes peered at him, as though he had just stabbed each of them in the heart.

"That's not true," Emma was the most offended.

"He's right, 'Em, the Promise has always been tough for Liorians to accept. On first glance, it just doesn't sound like it ends well for us," Gus started to see Sam's perspective, "and there have been many theories about the Prophecy. Maybe it was corrupted, maybe there's more to it, or maybe the whole thing is a lie. Either way, it just doesn't seem to fit our narrative as Descendants and followers of the Creator."

"But it has been passed down for ages," Emma argued quietly.

"No one is saying it is wrong, 'Em. We are just trying to figure this whole thing out, that's all."

Emma snatched up her backpack, setting her half-empty cup on the table behind her.

"I think I've heard enough. I'm going to bed."

Gus stood also.

"I agree. We are jumping to some pretty crazy conclusions anyway."

But before they headed back to the cabin, Sam held back once more, the others stopping also to find out why he lagged behind.

"So this guy Julian, would he be the first prophet then?"

Gus's eyes looked yellow in the moonlight.

"It is possible," he said slowly. "If what I heard was correct."

Chapter Ten: Old Lady Wrenge

"Well then, fortunately if that is true, I would only be the second one." Sam scoffed at his own words. "If Julian is the first."

They didn't answer him, but as Sam and the others walked to the cabin, the Sterlings's front door suddenly opened, and out stepped a rather rushed Mr. Sterling, throwing his robe over him hastily and hurrying down the steps.

Without so much as a word, he broke into a trot and sped past them, a look of worry and determination on his face. The four watched him silently, and even Emma, who wanted to call out to him, knew she wouldn't get an answer, so she chose instead to turn to her friends with a look of *What just happened?* across her face.

"There seriously can't be another meeting this late at night. That would make it the third time this week!" Lillia sputtered as she threw her jacket over her shoulders to fend off the chill in the air.

"Yeah, I heard daddy talking about old Miss Wrenge to one of the other Council members," Emma said. "Apparently she's been causing some trouble at the PO again."

"Ayet Sal," the old woman had said in the forest.

An impulsive thought flashed into Sam's mind.

"Let's go and find out."

****

While Emma protested, the rest of them had convinced her it was indeed important enough to find out what was happening that would draw out the PO on a dark evening in the middle of the light festival. That, and the fact that Sam had just told them he was experiencing dreams that could be connected to a legend of the end of Lior could have given credence as well.

The four hurried through the salty cool air toward town, keeping to the path as best as possible and traveling by moonlight to keep them somewhat hidden. When they reached town, it was almost as if they had stepped into a ghost town. Only an hour prior the streets had been filled with vendors looking for last minute Kolar

Chapter Ten: Old Lady Wrenge

fans to sell their overpriced goods to, but now there were no carts with glowing hats or mugs, and all shops had closed up for the night. The soft blue lazuli lights lining Main Street were the only life present, except for a small group of cloaked individuals circling an old hunchbacked woman near the front gate of the City.

They appeared to be in a defensive posture surrounding her, but strangely she seemed unafraid. The four kept to the shadows and moved quietly down the street toward the huddle until they were as close as possible to hear the altercation. They huddled behind a pastry cart outside of a jewelry shop just as the woman began to raise her voice toward the Protectors who surrounded her.

"See ye all who live under the Light! You are deceived! The Dark'ness is nigh to your doorstep and you do nothing!"

"Ma'am, you must understand, we must see to it that our city is protected and find out how you were able to enter the City without …" a Protector sounding much like Jack Sterling attempted to say, but was immediately interrupted by the old lady, who was growing ever impatient with those who stood before her.

Suddenly, Sam knew who the old woman was. He had met her in the forest, where she had nearly blasted him with a bolt through the chest. She had the same disconnected look as she did when she first interrupted him. While her accent was still audible, she sounded different, almost as though someone was speaking through her. Needless to say, seeing her made Sam shudder.

"I know her. I saw her in the forest today," Sam said, forgetting how his voice carried between the buildings.

"Shush!" Emma covered his mouth, obviously not hearing the words he had said.

"You must listen! Lior is in danger! The curse will soon be revealed and the dark gate will be opened!"

"Ma'am, I'm going to have to ask you—"

The woman took a step forward, which prompted an immediate response from the circle of Protectors, who assumed defensive

Chapter Ten: Old Lady Wrenge

postures, holding their palms outstretched toward the woman.

"Do not come any closer!" Mr. Sterling raised his voice to match the woman's.

The woman stopped, but seemed unafraid of those that threatened her. Then she looked directly toward the very spot where the four were hidden and smiled.

"He's waiting for you, *boy*," she said strangely. Then she raised her hands hastily to the night above her and with a flash of blue light, was suddenly gone.

****

Back at the cabin, the four friends quickly slipped into the warm living room and parted ways to discuss the matter in the morning. Mr. Sterling and the other Protectors were instructed to search the area following old lady Wrenge's disappearance, so they would have been discovered had they stayed any longer.

Clearly shaken from the ordeal, the two girls swore never to do such a thing again if they were given the chance, but on their way back, they did admit it was something they needed to bring up to Mr. Sterling ... in the morning.

"Ayet Sal," that old woman in the forest had said. Sam laid in bed trying to shut down his mind without success. Where did he hear it before?

Ayet Sal. Malek Eben. They were phrases he remembered. Were they from his dreams?

Sam rolled over in his bed, trying to re-situate himself into a more comfortable position, but it was no use. His brain was in high gear, and there was no way he was going to sleep anytime soon.

He peeked over at Gus, who was snoring soundly. *Must be nice.*

Looking at the dark pine ceiling above him, he opened his mouth and let a small prayer slip out above him.

"Creator—God, whoever you are, can you tell me what is happening to me? Why do I see these things?"

Chapter Ten: Old Lady Wrenge

Silence was his only answer.

"Who am I? A Descendant? Why am I here? If you are real, please show me what to do."

Nothing.

Sam laid in the silence, talking himself out of believing there was someone who would actually respond. Gus's snoring was becoming more rhythmic. Perhaps he could fall asleep if he pretended it was the soft lapping of the ocean on the beach.

Just as he was about to give up, outside the window a soft blue light glowed dimly at first, then grew steadily brighter as it neared the second floor of the cabin where Gus and Sam were.

The small blue orb pulsated outside the window, then passed through the glass and into the room. The light circled the room once, then floated toward Sam, who lay perfectly still under the covers away from the cool air.

He recognized it as the same kind of Lazuli orb that he had seen Mr. Sterling send into the night when first arriving in Lior, and again in the Chancellor's office.

Heart racing, Sam reached out and touched the orb, which now hovered directly in front of him. It unfolded into a message that scrolled softly across his hand:

Please join me behind the cabins. Jack. It read.

Then it faded away into the dim light of the room.

Without hesitation, he slipped out of his bed, and keeping an eye on Gus, slipped his shoes on. The stairs creaked as he tried his best to descend them without noise, and when he reached the cabin door, he paused to listen for signs of anyone stirring from their rooms.

Hearing nothing, he slipped out the front door and carefully made his way to the back of the cabin. Gentle waves lapped the shoreline of the Yarey as he peered in the moonlight for the messenger of the orb of light.

Suddenly, the form of a man was behind him, and he spun to see a cloaked Mr. Sterling standing in the shadows of the pines that extended to the west of the cabin circle. He motioned for Sam to join him beneath the branches of one of the larger of the trees.

Chapter Ten: Old Lady Wrenge

"I apologize for the clandestine nature of this meeting, Sam," Mr. Sterling said quietly. "It turns out there are some things we need to discuss outside the prying ears of many."

Did he know they had watched them earlier with Miss Wrenge?

"I figured that sir," Sam said instinctively.

Mr. Sterling nodded, his face showing obvious signs of exhaustion.

"Sam, I would like first of all to apologize for bringing you to Lior under pretense of better circumstance," he said. "We did not tell you the whole truth."

"I know that Sir."

Mr. Sterling sighed.

"The Chancellor is concerned about your presence in Lior. Your background is, well, uncertain."

"So the Research Office can't tell if I am a true Descendant of the Light."

Mr. Sterling nodded.

"Regardless of what we believe, or know …" he paused as if he knew something Sam did not, but thought it better not to share, then continued. "It presents a bad situation for the laws of Lior, which protects humans from coming too close to the spiritual realm."

"So send me home, sir."

"It's not quite that easy." He peered around the two of them, as if looking for eavesdroppers. Finding none, he continued. "Once someone has been to Lior from Creation, the Council must trust that individual to keep silent on what they have seen. It is part of the oath of every Descendant of the Light."

He dared not ask what would happen to him if he was found not to have the gift. "Why *did* you bring me here then?"

Mr. Sterling smiled.

"There are a few of us that truly believe you have the gift of Light. If we didn't believe it so strongly, we wouldn't have taken the chance."

"I understand, but what now? Won't the Council find out I am here?"

"They already know. I informed them today."

Chapter Ten: Old Lady Wrenge

Sam's heart beat faster. Strangely, he wasn't angry with Mr. Sterling, but he did feel a bit like they were taking a huge risk on him. What if he let them down?

"How do I find out if I am truly a Descendant?"

Mr. Sterling put a hand on his shoulder and scowled.

"I will be working with the Office of Research to help determine your lineage. I am certain we can trace your mother, but your father—" he paused, his greying hair reflecting in the moonlight. "There is much yet to learn."

Sam's heart began beating quickly again at the mention of his parents. Mr. Sterling had information on them, but judging from his expression, it wasn't the time to tell him. When would the time be?

"There's more." Mr. Sterling's eyes blazed in the fluorescent moonlight.

"The Council doesn't like that I am here." It was the obvious guess.

"They are divided—over the current vitality of the Darkness," he ignored Sam's statement. "There are many who believe that the Dark Forces are uniting once again in hopes of seeing the return of the Dark One."

"The Dark Legend."

Mr. Sterling cleared his throat quietly, but did not answer him right away. Why was everyone avoiding telling him anything? Like he couldn't handle the answers?

"A small group of us believe a great deception has fallen over Lior, and over the City. A curse, so to speak."

So the fact that there could be spies in Lior was not out of the question. He thought of Emma, and her faith in the system. *How blind they were.*

"If we do not expose this curse, we could be very vulnerable to attack, which is something this city cannot afford again."

"I understand."

"Sam, there are a few of us that believe there is an Eben stone that exists that is said to have great power over the Darkness—called the *Malek Eben*—the Watcher Stone."

Chapter Ten: Old Lady Wrenge

There it was again. The phrase. *Malek Eben*. So it meant Watcher Stone.

"Long ago in the old city of Lior, many artifacts were kept that were said to contain great power of various purposes. Most were collected safely in the moments before the old city was destroyed, but the Watcher Stone went missing. It was considered destroyed or taken by the Dark Watchers."

"Was it?" Sam asked. "Taken by them, I mean."

"Good question. Actually, we have recently discovered that at the time of the invasion of the City, the Stone had been moved to a different area in the City. An inventor named Jerma Bogglenose was going to study it, but was never able to."

"You think it's still there?"

"It's possible. The Office of Research said everything in the old city had been destroyed, but something tells me otherwise ... then again, I could be wrong and the Dark Forces have had it all along."

"You want me to go find it." Sam stared at the man before him.

"I would not ask if it wasn't truly necessary."

He couldn't be serious.

"Why not talk to the Sons of Light or get the PO to go?"

Mr. Sterling sighed heavily, as if reluctant to reveal any more information.

"There are some of us in the Protector's Office and in the Council that suspect there are some among us who have turned to the Darkness, and they may have infiltrated some of the highest positions in the City."

"But why—"

Mr. Sterling held up his hand for Sam to be patient.

"We are being watched, all of us. As Descendants with our own Eben stones," he slipped his cloak back to reveal his bracelet and Lazuli stone, which glowed softly the same color as the moon, "we risk losing the element of surprise if we are to find those spies among us. But to the Seers and other Lior departments, those your age are—well—invisible until you go through Mentorship. For this reason, I am unfortunately unable to aid you in preparing for your journey,

Chapter Ten: Old Lady Wrenge

should you choose to go. But I believe Gus will be very helpful in your endeavors."

"Sir, can't you just take off the Eben stone so they couldn't track you?"

Mr. Sterling passed his hand over the stone softly, making the Eben stone glow brightly for a moment. "Our Eben's are a wonderful gift from the Creator, and we are bound by the laws of Light to wear them. It is something you will understand when you go through Mentorship yourself."

Strangely, Sam understood. It was more than a bracelet with a stone, it was part of who they were. Perhaps the same was true with the Watcher Stone.

"How will the Stone help Lior?" He asked.

"The Watcher Stone is said to have many gifts, one of which being that we believe it can reveal the Darkness from great distances, even if it is being purposefully hidden."

"Why would the Dark Watchers want the Stone?"

Mr. Sterling lifted his head to the breeze that was suddenly upon them.

"Some Dark Watchers also believe the Stone will somehow unite the Darkness, but no one is quite sure why they believe that."

"So it depends on which side finds it first," Sam said bluntly.

Mr. Sterling nodded.

"If the research around the Prophecy is true—which I am believing more and more that it may be—the Stone could have the power to show the Council the need for . . ."

Mr. Sterling paused, as if he had already said too much.

"Well, never mind that."

Sam remembered the Chancellor's office and the Light alarm going off when he and Talister Calpher stepped through it. Could Talister be part of the ones fallen to the Darkness and now a spy? Or could Sam have set off the alarms because of his dreams?

"I just don't understand why you want me to go."

Mr. Sterling sighed.

"I trust your judgment. And—as much as it pains me to let my

Chapter Ten: Old Lady Wrenge

daughter and her friends be put in harm's way, I believe it would be necessary for them to go with you."

Mr. Sterling rubbed his eyes, looking longingly toward the cabin as if he couldn't wait to get in and get some much needed rest.

"Without you, the others will not go. I know my daughter, and even if I asked her, she would not believe me," he said quietly. "Sam, you may not see it now, but there are some who believe you are special to Lior's future."

Suddenly, Sam understood why he was being asked. Not only could Sam and the others get away without being tracked because they hadn't gone through mentorship, but also Mr. Sterling was indirectly saying that it would be best if he were out of the City while the Council decided his fate ...

Sam gazed off into the moonlight that was casting rays over the seemingly boundless sea.

"Mr. Sterling, is there something wrong with me?"

Mr. Sterling glanced briefly at the same cascade of light Sam gazed at, but then turned to face Sam directly.

"I assume you mean because of your dreams," he said with compassion. "No, my boy, that is not the case."

"How did you—"

"Gus told me."

Mr. Sterling, in a genuine gesture, then put his arms around him. While hugs were not normal to him, Sam let it happen. He trusted this man for some reason—his family, what he stood for.

"Whatever dreams you are having are part of the Creator's plan. I believe that with all my heart. What that purpose may be is still unknown," he smiled. "But that conversation is for another day. We must get in and get some rest. You will need to leave for the old city as soon as possible."

Sam stared at Mr. Sterling as part of a shadow of the trees beside them covered half of his body. It was a strange sight, half of his body visible from the light of the moon, but the other half doused by the shadow, showing no detail of that part of the man before him. It was a perfect symbol of what Sam believed Mr. Sterling was telling him

Chapter Ten: Old Lady Wrenge

was happening to Lior. If there truly was a curse that covered the Descendants from seeing the Darkness before them, they would be totally unprepared for what the Dark Lords had in mind.

"I'll do it, Mr. Sterling," he said finally. "I'll go to the old city."

Chapter Eleven
Office of Research

"No. No way!" Emma jumped up and began pacing the nearly lifeless fire pit at the pavilion the next morning after Sam told them what Mr. Sterling had told him.

"He just wants us to go to the old city alone? Why would daddy ever do such a thing? Doesn't he know we haven't even gone through mentoring? And there's *Darkness* surrounding the City—"

"Right. No way daddy would send his little angel out."

"Shut up Lil! You're just mad because your parents aren't here!" she spouted angrily.

It was the first time Sam had ever really heard Emma be nasty with her words.

"This isn't helping," Gus offered. "Didn't Mr. Sterling ask us to go?"

"He said Lior is in danger," Sam said quietly. He wasn't quite ready to tell them his thoughts about the Council.

"I heard you. I just don't—"

"Believe me?" Sam finished her sentence.

Chapter Eleven: Office of Research

"No! That's not it at all," Emma huffed. "It's just strange, that's all."

Emma paced the fire pit even faster, the coals showing only the occasional wisp of smoke from the previous evening's fire.

"The Watcher Stone ... it's ridiculous," she spat. "There's no evidence that it's still in the old city."

"Your father believes it is," Sam said gently, at which point Emma softened, but the scowl did not leave her face.

"I can't believe he would ask us to do such a thing."

Lillia, who looked elated with the prospect of adventure, turned to Gus, who had been thumbing through his journal

"How dangerous of a trip will this be?"

Gus did not look up from his journal.

"The Darkness surrounding the old city is residual. While it is significant, it is also fifty years old and does not have the power it once did."

"That's stupid," Emma threw up her hands. "It's still *Darkness*, Gus."

Gus nodded.

"But contained. I think our biggest danger will come from any Dark creatures or Metim still residing in that area, of which there haven't been any reports lately."

"Whatever, Gus. Of anybody I would have thought you to be the reasonable one."

Gus nodded grimly.

"I can't deny that it there would be some risks."

There was no fire in the pit, but Lillia stuck her hands out as if expecting the imaginary flame to warm her hands.

"I'm up for it," she said suddenly.

For a few moments, no one spoke as they digested Lillia's decision. She was certainly the most reckless of the bunch, but now the rest had a decision to make.

"Has anyone thought about how we would get to the old city?" Gus broke the silence. "I hate to say it, but the terrain between

Chapter Eleven: Office of Research

here and there is quite perilous. It would take weeks with the best equipment under the best conditions."

"Boggle would know how to get us there," Lillia said quickly.

Jerma Bogglenose. Sam remembered his conversation with Mr. Sterling the night before.

After another few minutes of arguing the craziness of the task they were given, Emma and Gus began to come around to the idea, even though Emma still planned to talk with her father about the whole ordeal.

"Gus?" Emma said quietly. "Do you really think this is a good idea?"

Gus sighed, finally looking up from his journal.

"Your father believes it, Em'."

The words struck Emma silent. Her father, a man she desperately trusted, was now asking for their help. All for a Stone that may or may not be there.

She stood and paced the fire, looking deep into each of their eyes. For her, this would be more than just a little leap of faith; it would be a monumental one. Everything she had been taught since she was young about being safe was now being tossed out the window. Her parents were allowing her to go into an unknown situation in a dangerous place, with three others her age, none of them proficient with the gifts.

But they had always reminded her there could be a day when she would have to make some really tough decisions on her own, apart from her parents' guiding. It was a difficult transition for her to accept, but one she knew she needed to do.

"We will need to do some serious research about the City, and the Stone if we go. Boggle and the Library are good places to start," Gus told them while Emma paced.

"I can't believe I am even considering this," Emma plopped back on the bench, "and what for? For a Stone that may or may not help Lior?"

Lillia smiled.

Chapter Eleven: Office of Research

"Come off it Em'. It's about time you had some adventure in your life."

She sat silently for a few moments, and the others were perfectly willing to let her work it out in her mind, perhaps because they too were considering the consequences of such a journey. But there was one thing none of them could deny. Mr. Sterling had asked them to go.

"When do we leave?" Emma said, finally, drawing nervous chuckles from the group.

****

Heeding Mr. Sterling's warning about leaving quickly, Gus, Emma, and Sam immediately went to the library to see if they could dig up any more information about the old city and its secrets, and Lillia went to see Bogglenose, the old inventor they had all been talking about.

They knew they couldn't talk about it, and they would likely not be getting help in preparing to go, but it was exhilarating nonetheless, and even Emma began to show signs of being excited. But it was still going to be up to them to make arrangements, including planning for all provisions they would need for their journey.

That morning, Mrs. Sterling had left in a hurry to go see her Uncle Osan at the robe shop, but promised to have chicken and dumplings ready for dinner that night, while Mr. Sterling and Cooley went back to the Protector's Office. Miss Karpatch announced that she would take a walk down the path by the shoreline.

Before Miss Karpatch left, however, she had pulled the four youths aside and asked them to keep her informed about what they found. Already she seemed to know what they had been asked to do, but didn't seem privy to all that Mr. Sterling had told them.

"While I cannot be a part of your plans directly, I can still help you figure this out. You might be surprised to know that I can provide some needed assistance where you might not expect," she told them,

Chapter Eleven: Office of Research

to which all of them agreed to keep her apprised of anything.

At the Lior library, which stood nearly fifteen stories high and had large stained glass windows flooding light in from the sun and the blue glowing spires of the City, Sam, Emma, and Gus searched for anything that could represent more information about the Watcher Stone, old Lior City, or of the dreams Sam had been having.

He felt it necessary to recount the details of his dreams to Gus to aid them in their research, although it wasn't the least bit pleasant. He had enjoyed a few nights' break from them, but he could still see them vividly as if the dark figures were still hovering above him and the cold wind licked at his face. Even now walking through the tall stacks of books, the eeriness of the whole thing gave him chills up his neck.

But he had learned to block out the feeling most times, and he focused on looking through the dusty old books in front of him. Each book was labeled with three letters and a number sequence, just like the Dewey Decimal System in White Pine.

I suppose some things are the same no matter where you are, he thought.

"Can I help you with something?" a smaller old lady with spectacles and bright silver hair appeared behind him suddenly, sounding very suspicious.

"Uh, no thank you. I was just looking around for—well the history of Old Lior for uh—a personal project," he fibbed.

"Oh! Well then!" she suddenly changed her tone. "We have plenty to choose from, however, you are not even close to being in the right area. Why don't you follow me?"

He shrugged at Emma as she peered at him through the shelves, watching him follow the woman.

"There are hundreds of books on just the history of the City, from the four occupied territories of Lior until the first Chancellor was chosen."

"Uh, well, I was looking for more of an overview of the City."

She nodded approvingly and led him over one more row to a long shelf of neatly stacked tubes.

"If you are looking for layouts of the City, these scrolls will have

Chapter Eleven: Office of Research

to do." She immediately picked out one of the tubes and handed it to Sam. "You may check them out for five days, but be aware, they are expensive to replace."

Sam thanked her and hurried back over to where Gus was nose deep in a thick book with yellowish pages, and Emma was gazing at the light creeping up the spires outside the window.

"What is that?" she asked when he plopped down beside her.

"Layouts of the old city," he said proudly.

Her face lit up.

"Gus! Look at what Sam has!"

"Perfect," he said as he thumbed through the rolled up pages, which looked like they were newer copies of the originals. "I wasn't turning up much over here."

"Yeah, I think you pretty much covered every book in here too," Emma rolled her eyes playfully.

They checked out the scroll at the front desk with the smiling lady with the enlarged spectacles and headed out toward Bogglenose's.

After passing the stadium where busy preparations were being made for the games that evening, and after stopping twice for a meat stick and a bag of candied marshmallows for Gus, they passed through a clump of trees and climbed up a long, steep path toward an old iron gate buried deep in the brush.

Sliding around a small hole where the brush met the gate, the three continued on the overgrown path until they reached a large rock ledge looking over the sea. Half buried and partly perched on the ledge stood a somewhat dilapidated old building with hastily built sections clinging to the main structure high up the rock face.

"Who lives here? Frankenstein?" Sam snorted when they rounded the last tree and got a clear view of the place.

"Hey I read that book!" Gus said. "It was a classic with elements of the romantic era and was considered one of the first science fiction stories."

Emma flashed a look at him immediately that made Gus trail off into silence. She rapped on the old metal door and waited until they heard high pitched but inaudible yelling from inside the building.

Chapter Eleven: Office of Research 🌲🌲

Then there was a huge crash, and the door opened slowly to reveal a very light-skinned older man with long, wavy, unkempt graying hair that looked like it had had a run-in with a light socket. Around his neck he wore a contraption that was emitting a very bright blue light, and he wore dark oversized goggles, which made his eyes appear bug-like.

"I told you to leave me alone!" he slammed the door suddenly, and then after a few moments of rather loud commotion inside, a tiny holographic blue image suddenly popped out of the wall next to them.

"Wha—?" the image of the man turned around suddenly behind him, arguing with an unknown subject in the background.

"Ah! I should've known!" the little blue image of the clumsy inventor said from the wall. "Lillia told me it was you three at the door," he snorted loudly. "Well come in already! You don't need to knock!"

"It's locked, Bogglenose," Emma rolled her eyes at the now blank wall. The sound of nervous fumbling with the latch could be heard behind the door.

"Oh yes! I forgot. Silly me," said the bug-eyed inventor now standing in full form before them. "I have been having some unwanted visits from the ODA lately. They claim my place is unsightly! What would give those ignorant bureaucrats that idea? Ridiculous I tell you!"

"I can't imagine," Emma snickered as he finally got the door unblocked from the pile of junk on the inside and let them in.

"Who's the ODA?" Sam whispered to Gus as they followed Emma through the door and past the piles of strange-looking mechanical parts and abandoned inventions that were designed for who-knew-what.

"Office of Descendant Affairs. Not quite the PO, but they also receive reports from the Seer Chamber regarding internal activities in Lior City," he whispered back. "Never been much of a fan myself."

Immediately upon entering Sam realized why Lillia liked it here

Chapter Eleven: Office of Research

so much. There were flashing, mystical lights coming from strange machines everywhere in the huge, cluttered room—moving parts with robotic arms, contraptions that buzzed on the tables and even some that whizzed silently through the air about the room.

Lillia was draped over a hammock with a pair of strange looking gloves on, tiny blue images projecting from her fingertips that danced and moved while she wiggled her fingers. She nodded nonchalantly as Gus, Emma, and Sam made their way through the buzzing workshop.

Sam glanced to the tables of whirring and buzzing objects, noticing one small urn that burped a concentrated smoke-like blue light that drifted lazily upward, dispersing itself slowly throughout the room.

"It's a Lazuli diffuser," Gus held his hand in the next puff of light. "It turns Lazuli into a gas to dissipate throughout the room. It is supposed to make everything that uses light more powerful ... but I think it just makes him crazy."

Sam caught a glance of a lighted medium-sized box with a slowly spinning dial on the front. Then, the sides and the top of the box began to collapse inward, and suddenly the box morphed into a perfect circle, it's exterior glowing a faint blue.

"A device that transfigures based on what shape first enters the person's mind closest to it," Bogglenose said gleefully as he clumsily twisted and adjusted the lenses of his goggles while peering out the window in front of him. "There is so much you can do with light!" the inventor shouted. "Capture it and shape it into whatever you choose! Hold it in your hand like putty! People don't get it, no! They are too closed-minded, those buffoons. They wouldn't understand progress if it smacked 'em in the face!"

"Yeah, but why would a person need a thing that changes shape?" Sam stared out the window at the imaginary thing that captured Boggle's attention.

"It works!" Bogglenose squawked so loud that the little shape-changing box suddenly melted into a puddle on the counter. "Look through here boy. Oh—I didn't realize there was a new member to

Chapter Eleven: Office of Research

your group. What's your name? Never mind! It doesn't matter. Here look through these." He shoved the goggles into Sam's arms.

Sam put the goggles on his head and peered out the window. At first, nothing appeared but the shoreline below. Then, to the left of the pathway to Bogglenose's cliff house, he noticed a thin wisp of black smoke lazily drifting up from the ground and being swept into the breeze over the cliff to the sea.

"I see smoke."

Bogglenose punched him square in the arm.

"See that? Now take the glasses off."

Sam obeyed.

"I don't see it now," he said. "That rock is in the way I think."

"Exactly! That's a long-range Darkness detector, that is!" He punched him in the arm again. "What did you say your name was again? Oh, wait! Don't tell me. I am going to try—to—use my light foreteller." He fumbled around the long counter for a small device he slipped inside of his ear. "Your name is…L-A-S…TEA?"

"Um, no. It's Sam," he said.

Bogglenose crinkled his nose and dug in his ear for the device. "Trash! I knew this thing wasn't worth a pile of duck squat." He tossed the device on the counter.

Gus cleared his throat loudly from where he and Lillia lounged on the hammock as buzzing contraptions circled around them.

"Bogglenose, we are looking for a way to get to another place in Lior rather quickly, and perhaps without being seen," he said before the old inventor's attention was diverted elsewhere.

The man twirled his increasingly frazzled hair, looking very thoughtful.

"I don't know if I can help you there, that is, unless you have access to my Lightway. The PO took away my key after I tried to retrieve my invention when they wouldn't let me use it, those controlling Poppincorks! Can you believe it? Not even able to use my own invention!"

Emma leaned over to Sam.

Chapter Eleven: Office of Research

"Bogglenose used to work for the Council, making inventions. Some say they canned him because he almost killed the Chancellor when one of his prototypes exploded."

"Of course I don't have the resources here to make another Lightway, nor do I have the coordinates to be able to line them up," Bogglenose shrugged.

"It's okay, Boggle," Emma hopped off the hammock with Lillia. "We would appreciate if you didn't let anyone know we were planning to go somewhere, please."

Bogglenose snorted.

"Those pompous monarchs? Not a chance! Oh! I do have something you can take with you when you go." He dug around in one of the larger armoires lining the wall, then produced a small box.

"What is it, Boggle?" Lillia was suddenly interested, popping off of her hammock to get a better look.

"Watch," he said, opening the box and pulling out a small silver disc.

He rubbed the center of the disc and held it in front of him. Suddenly, the disc glowed bright blue and grew to the size of a small surfboard, right in front of them. Boggle dropped the disc and it immediately began floating above the floor, blue Lazuli light holding it up in mid-air.

"I call it, affectionately, a Lightboard!" he said giddily. "Hop on this little gem and you will be—how does the human say—surfing? Yes, land surfing wherever and whenever you want."

Emma whistled low.

"Wow, you have been working while we were away."

"You would be correct, Miss Sterling. Got five of them. You can take these four." He pressed the center of the floating surfboard and it immediately returned to its original shape. "They aren't easy to learn, but once you do, no one will catch you! Except of course for the quicker of the leviathan species who tend to rip apart their prey starting at the throa—"

"Thanks, Boggle," Emma said quickly.

Boggle smiled awkwardly.

Chapter Eleven: Office of Research

"I don't suppose you could tell me where you will be going?" he said.

"The old city," Emma said quietly, quickly regretting telling him from the looks she received from the others.

"Whoa. I suppose everyone has to meet the Creator sometime," Boggle snorted, making Emma squeak and cover her mouth. Then he turned and fumbled underneath his countertop, tossing boxes and objects onto the already littered floor. "Here, take these too." He handed Gus a velvet satchel and snorted once again. "Just press and hold the button, and throw. Best not to be too close when it goes off!"

"Do you have any information about the Watcher Stone, Boggle?" Gus ventured.

For the first time since arriving at his shop, Boggle's face grew solemn as he took a seat on his swivel stool.

"Yes, yes, it is a curious artifact," he said. "Created by the Watchers themselves to keep the Darkness from hiding …"

All four listened intently, Gus writing down notes in his journal.

"It was found by some researchers deep in a cavern long ago, and it was thought that a child prophet led them to it, believe it or not! But the Stone is said to have properties embedded by the Creator himself, designed to be a sign of His eventual return! Imagine! But …" he stood once again and walked toward the window, "it is also said that it will be a time of great danger for Lior. Suffering, sadness, a time of division. The Darkness will be most powerful during that time."

"The Last Battle," Gus whispered.

"Didn't you study the Stone, Boggle?" Lillia asked.

"Never got a chance to!" he said loudly. "Was supposed to be transferred to my lab but—"

"Your lab in the old city?" Emma interrupted. "Where is that?"

"The library, of course, which is highly secured, of course!" Boggle snorted suddenly. "My assistant Jules kept all the records of my most valuable research, Oh! Poor Jules! Shame that he didn't make it out of the City! Wish he was still here to help me now! Such a good boy …"

Chapter Eleven: Office of Research

"So you can't get us into your old lab?" Sam was careful not to offend the old inventor.

He shook his head sadly.

"I'm afraid I don't remember the codes ... all of which were changed suddenly to ensure security as we fled the City ... oh what a horrible day that was!"

Instead of pursuing Boggle's aging memories of the day of the invasion, the four thought it best to leave it be for now, and they weren't even sure they could count on the information he gave them to be accurate anyway.

Boggle made sure to give them a few more odds and ends for their trip, then he shooed them out the door as he was certain the ODA would be stopping by once again.

They thanked him and headed out the door, having acquired some helpful gear but still not answering the question of how to get to old Lior City, or his old lab.

"Wow, he's ... quite a guy," Sam said as they squeezed around the iron gate of Boggle's property after saying goodbye to the unconventional inventor.

"There's nothing wrong with him. He may be socially backward, but he's brilliant," Lillia said defensively.

"I wasn't saying anything," Sam said defensively. "He's great."

****

Instead of heading back toward the cabin, Gus suddenly made a turn toward the City Center in town.

"I think I have the answer to our problem on how to get to the old city," he said, drawing quizzical looks from the others.

They followed Gus past the Thalo hall and into the City Center's Main Street entrance. When the guards let them pass, Sam discovered that they must have entered the Center's administrative offices, which looked curiously like a small eighteenth century gaslight town with it's quaint porches dotting the interior of the vaulted lobby.

Gus led them past a number of offices with large picture windows

Chapter Eleven: Office of Research

down the cobblestone street, where he abruptly turned into one of the small shops that said "Office Of Research" on the plaque on the door. Inside, there were large tables with scrolls, strange looking artifacts, and many dusty books that littered them. Standing over the tables were robed individuals who glanced up briefly at the sight of the four teens and then went back to their work.

"Do my eyes deceive me?" A plump, older woman with deep blue eyes came rushing to the door. "Gus? Lillia? Emma? How are you?" she said, ruffling Gus's hair and pinching Emma's cheeks.

"Good, Mrs. Yarns. How are you?" Gus said in a muffled voice as she pulled him into her extra-large chest and squeezed him tightly until his cheeks flushed bright red.

"Oh you all just grow so quickly. Oh dear heavens! Good thing the Mr. isn't here. He's having an especially hard time with the garden this year, and you three were his best workers! He'd have you out picking parsnips if he saw you—" she stopped. "Ooooh, and who's this handsome boy you dragged in?"

"His name is Sam, Mrs. Yarns. He's ... new to the City," Emma said carefully.

"Well well, I hope you are enjoying your time here. Are you here long?"

"Yes ma'am, I hope so," he said.

"Well that's good news!" She clapped her hands around Sam's cheeks and squeezed until he thought there was no more blood left in them.

"Sarah's in the back. Why don't you grab some homemade root cakes I brought in and come on back and visit?"

"We can't stay long, Mrs. Yarns. We are heading back to the cabin soon," Gus attempted to say but was ignored, a large plate of round cakes being shoved in his face.

"Nonsense. You can stay for a bit. There's teacups in the fourth cupboard on your way back." She then turned and motioned something at a young man with jet-black hair who was trying desperately to get her attention.

They obeyed, grabbing a few cakes from the plate Gus was

Chapter Eleven: Office of Research

holding as they walked into the back room. Miss Karpatch was bent over, her face inches from an old map. Her face lit up when she saw them. Mrs. Yarns returned with four chairs and a teapot, which she used to fill their cups.

"I knew you would figure it out." Miss Karpatch turned and pulled off her glasses, putting them into her robe pocket.

Mrs. Yarns closed the door to the front room, throwing a kiss to them as she slipped out, then warned in a muffled voice in the next room to the staff members that the "Chief Researcher" must not be disturbed for the next few moments.

Sam, Emma, and Lillia were still clueless as to what it was they were supposed to figure out, and that Gus apparently already had, so after digging into more root cake and tea, they waited for Gus to fill them in.

"I remembered that you had special access to use the Lightway for your research projects," Gus said finally with a grin, which was met with immediate sighs of realization from the other three.

"As Chief Researcher, I am the only one with unlimited access in Lior," she smiled at them. "And thanks to Cooley when he oversaw the department, he made sure there were no restrictions on Lightway travel, and very few that monitor us."

"But we are leaving Lior and may be heading near Metim-infested areas," Emma reminded them.

"True, but I have spent the last few days plotting out a course that should avoid the worst areas."

Emma still looked concerned.

"Miss Karpatch, you would really help us do something like this? Isn't it kind of, well, devious?" she said.

"I have been planning this with your father, Emma. In fact, there are a few of us who have pulled quite a few strings to make sure this was possible."

Lillia half-laughed.

"You seriously already knew we would go, didn't you?"

Miss Karpatch nodded.

"I *am* a researcher, you know."

Chapter Eleven: Office of Research

Emma looked bewildered.

"Wow. You are good, Miss Karpatch."

She smiled.

"If only I was as good at teaching as I am at research."

"I think you are a good teacher," Sam said awkwardly, surprised at his own words.

Miss Karpatch raised a surprised eyebrow at him, then smiled.

"Well then, let's get you to old Lior City."

After finishing their tea and cakes, Miss Karpatch let her staff know she was going to be out for a few moments. She led the group up to the fifth floor of the building, where she used a light key to open a thick metal door, then led them up a long set of circular steps. At the top, they stepped into a tower room much like the one where Sayvon took Sam, except this one had a large cannon-looking device taking up most of its interior. The device pointed a long telescoping barrel out of the other side toward the forest.

"It's the most complicated of the Lightbases to operate," Miss Karpatch said when they were assembled inside the tower. "I am assuming that none of you will have to use this alone, but better to learn it now than be sorry later."

"How does it work?" Sam asked.

"Well, the Lightway isn't just like jumping in and pressing a button. You have to put a key into the Lightbase and use the correct coordinates, but I am assuming you three," she pointed at Emma, Gus, and Lillia, "have done this before."

"Actually, none of us have," Emma answered for all of them. "The Lightway at Jester's Pass is always broken, it seems."

Sam reached his hand out and thought he could feel a slight hum coming from the metal tube in front of them. Suddenly, a small light began to glow in a circular glass globe on the top of the Lightbase. Sam quickly put his hand down and stepped back.

"That's strange," Miss Karpatch placed her hand on the glowing globe. "There are no incoming waves. I wonder if this one is acting up?" she said.

"Might be a Light spike," Gus offered.

Chapter Eleven: Office of Research

While Miss Karpatch examined the base, Sam looked out the window at the forest in front of them, and behind them, the mountains. It was spectacular, like all of Lior was. It reminded him of what he used to daydream about when his foster parents were boozing it up at a snobby political party. Even though they weren't truly his parents, it still hurt to see them so wrapped up in themselves. He even remembered the day he vowed he would never touch alcohol because of what it reminded him of.

"I can't figure out why it started up. Let's hope it doesn't quit on us before you go," Miss Karpatch scowled.

"Dad says there have been some problems with the Lightway system lately. He's not sure why, but he said one guy from the mountain regions of Nais ended up in a wave that got stuck for two hours."

"They are temperamental on occasion, but I must say, it is one of Boggle's better inventions," Miss Karpatch said laughingly. "Anyway, I had these made for each of you."

She handed them each a necklace made of leather with a small blue stone embedded in the band.

"It will help concentrate the Light in the Lightway so it will flow easier. It's not an Eben, but it has Lazuli in it."

All four immediately put on the necklaces, tucking the stones under their shirts. Sam immediately felt the warmth creep into his body as the Lazuli touched his chest.

"Now, let's learn how to use this properly," Miss Karpatch instantly resumed her teacher role. "Just in case you are separated, you all need to know how to dial up where you are meeting."

"We couldn't just dial in Lior City?" Emma wondered.

"It's protected with a failsafe mode. It is pretty complicated to dial in Lior City, so instead, if there is a problem, we will meet in Warm Springs."

Emma's face lit up.

"I love that place! So many quaint shops and they have the best parties."

Miss Karpatch walked over to the large metal structure, holding

Chapter Eleven: Office of Research

her key up to a glass opening in the base, which immediately began to bring the Lightway to life.

The device began to hum softly, and the glass globe on top turned from a dark, smoky color to a milky but bright blue.

"I will provide each of you with a key to operate it. Don't lose it. I am responsible for returning them." She then turned a large dial on the side of the base seven clicks counterclockwise, then one clockwise. "Seventy-one are the coordinates for the tower on top of Mount Halpa, where your first stop will be. Warm Springs is seventy-three. Lior City is seventy-two."

As the dial clicked in place, the globe on top of the Lightway changed from a cloudy blue to a solid blue.

"When you dial in the coordinates, the globe will change to the color of pure Lazuli. That is how you know you are locked into the base at the other side," she told them.

"Seventy-one through seventy-three. Got it," Gus said.

Lillia tapped lightly on the metal tube as it hummed happily.

"Not to be the downer here, but how do we plan to get back if we are separated?"

"Good question," Miss Karpatch offered. "I have included the instructions you will need for the trip in this envelope." She handed Gus a small envelope sealed with the official Office of Research stamp on the crease. "But for now, we need to get back downstairs before anyone wonders what we are up to. Does anyone have any questions?"

As they assured her they did not, Miss Karpatch looked out the window toward the stadium, briefly catching Sam looking at her, so she winked at him.

"You will want to leave tonight, during the games. Your parents may know you are going, but neither the Council nor the Elders may know you are gone."

When she had powered down the base station with her key, they carefully left down the stairwell and out the main door to the street.

"You will want to get here as soon as the games start," she told

Chapter Eleven: Office of Research

them. "Gus, Lillia, Emma, pack like we did for our overnight hikes. Now, I will see you all soon."

She turned and walked back into the City Center main entrance, leaving the four to themselves. Although they weren't showing it, Sam could tell the others were beginning to feel the slightest bit of nerves as the seriousness of the journey became a reality.

"I can't believe mom and dad are letting me do this," Emma said once they had set off for the cabin. "I mean, they would have never allowed this before. They barely let me stay out in the pavilion after dark without them there."

"I have to admit, it is a little strange," Gus confessed.

Emma scowled.

"I mean, I know Uncle Osan isn't doing very well with his store, and daddy having to be at the PO office means there's something important going on, but I just don't understand why they would let us go."

"Whatever. It happened," Lillia said. "Let's just make sure we help newb pack correctly so he doesn't screw things up before we get there."

****

It was an amazing feeling to know what they were about to do. An adventure to an ancient city surrounded by Darkness, perhaps encountering the Metim. They trusted Miss Karpatch to get them there, but still the whole idea was a bit nerve-racking. None of them were proficient enough with Light gifts to defend themselves, and Sam knew nothing. Regardless, they kept cheerful and positive as they followed the path to the circle of cabins, taking turns reminding each other what necessities they would need to pack.

Expecting the cabin to be empty as everyone had business to attend to, they were surprised when they walked through the door to find dinner on the table and Mrs. Sterling buzzing around in the kitchen.

Chapter Eleven: Office of Research

"Sit down everyone, sit down. The rest of the group should be here in a few minutes," she said cheerfully.

Emma was clearly troubled by her mother's cheery attitude in light of her knowing she was to depart that night into the dark parts of the forest in Lior, but she decided not to press the issue after seeing a very obvious wink from her mother.

Miss Karpatch arrived soon after they did, and without any indication of what they had discussed. She sat down and began picking at the freshly made biscuits on the table.

As Emma helped her mother finish filling glasses with tea, Mr. Sterling walked through the door with Cooley, both looking uneasy. Taking the head of the table, he waited until everyone was seated and took the hands of those on either side of him, then motioned for all of them to do the same.

Sam took Lillia's and Emma's hands and bowed his head instinctively.

"Our Lord and Creator," Mr. Sterling began rather solemnly. "We ask for a blessing on this food that has been given to us. We petition now for safety on the ceremony and games tonight, and that you would keep us all safe from harm—that you would guide us with your Light. We ask these things as Descendants of your Kingdom."

No one spoke or lifted their heads when Mr. Sterling finished. Instead they continued in whispers with their eyes closed for several minutes.

It wasn't until he heard the sound of plates and cups moving about that Sam realized he was the only one still praying. He looked up to find Emma smiling at him and still holding his hand.

Mrs. Sterling snatched his bowl and ladled in a generous portion of soup, although it looked more like a creamy white broth. Still smiling, Emma reached across the table with a huge biscuit and plopped one on his plate.

"I am sure you have had chicken and dumplings before dear?" Mrs. Sterling said to Sam as she ladled some broth into Emma's bowl.

"Yes ma'am, I have. My foster dad's family was from Texas."

Chapter Eleven: Office of Research

"Good. You need to eat plenty for the games tonight. Big night," she winked at him.

He nodded and took a bite of the dumplings, which were truly amazing. Soft, plump, and flavorful, they were definitely a rival dish to his grandmother's.

"How are things at the PO dear?" Mrs. Sterling tried to sound chipper, although it was obvious she knew he wasn't feeling that way.

Mr. Sterling looked at his wife, then rose slowly, waving off a biscuit from his daughter.

"Friends," he said quietly, his head still slightly bowed. "I received word from the Protector's Office that Fenton Chivler was found today. He's in pretty bad shape."

Silverware ceased clinking, and suddenly there was a hushed murmur of surprised whispers around the table while Mr. Sterling sat back down, staring at his bowl of dumplings.

"Is he okay?" Emma asked.

"We don't know yet. He has been transported to the healers in Themane. We'll know more later."

More hushed whispers emitted from around the table. Some speculated that it could have been an accident, but others discussed the break-in and his disappearance, taking the position that the events were related.

Sam remembered Mr. Chivler and his bookstore, and the old leather book he had given him. He hadn't had much of a chance to look it over, but it still took up space in his backpack. Again he wondered why Chivler would want him to have it.

"What happened? Who did it?" Miss Karpatch was the first to break the silence and speak aloud.

"We don't know yet. I can't go into details, but it looks like the place was ransacked."

"What about my mom and dad? And Mr. and Mrs. Abelsworth? Is everyone else okay?" Lilla asked, her face flush.

"They are fine, I assure you, and they are still looking into the matter. Whoever did it must have known their schedule—and Chivler's."

Chapter Eleven: Office of Research

"Was there evidence from Lior?" Emma sounded as though she was afraid to hear the answer. "I know the ... Metim ... aren't supposed to be able to enter Creation."

"We have only scratched the surface, but it may be just a local looking for an easy place to pick off some extra money." He continued, "I will be heading back with Cooley to finish the investigation."

"I agree. It wasn't Metim," Miss Karpatch said calmly. "The arches are too protected after the fall of the old city."

Mr. Sterling looked as though he would ignore the comment, then sighed heavily as if looking for appropriate words not to divulge too much information.

"We are pretty sure it was a local resident. Evidence points that direction."

The rest of dinner was eaten with only a few words spoken, mainly concerned with Chivler or what the PO was going to do about the situation. Sam noticed Mrs. Sterling glancing at her daughter a few times with a look of concern on her face, but she said nothing about their upcoming travel.

When dinner was over, the four youths helped Mrs. Sterling clear the table and then headed upstairs to pack their things quietly. Before Sam and Gus made it to the stairs, however, Mr. Sterling pulled them aside after sending Cooley back to the PO office without him.

"This is going to be no easy task, boys," he said solemnly. "But I think you need to know why we agreed to let you all go alone."

He glanced around him and then lowered his voice to just above a whisper.

"We are pretty sure whoever hurt Chivler is not just looking for money. The PO office has a suspect, but I can't divulge any names. The problem is that—among the other things we discussed—the suspect's name has to be kept a secret while we investigate. That means no changes in our schedule that would help them to recognize we are on to them." He took a breath and continued, "If you are not able to find the information on the Stone or the Stone itself, then you'll need to get back here as soon as you can."

Chapter Eleven: Office of Research

"Have they found out anything about my background, Mr. Sterling?" Sam asked candidly.

Mr. Sterling put a hand on his shoulder.

"Not yet. But the Council isn't going to be worried about your presence here just yet."

"If they don't find anything?"

"The next option would be to try and prove your affinity to the Light by showing them you can—"

"Manipulate Light like the rest of you."

Mr. Sterling nodded.

"It's not a guarantee, but it will help. The area around old Lior City has one of the largest and oldest Lazuli pools—which, I am told, gave many different levels of Light abilities. I am confident that you will find one."

Gus nodded.

"Yes, we have a few maps of the area."

Mr. Sterling again lowered his voice, drawing the two boys even closer to him to ensure no others were overhearing.

"But there is another thing you need to know." He stopped and looked around him before proceeding. "The day we investigated Chivler's after the break-in, we discovered something we think he left as a clue for us to find him. In his log book of checked out items, he had you, Sam, listed."

Sam's face suddenly grew warm.

"Yeah, I got a book from him about White Pine for a paper I had to do."

Mr. Sterling sighed.

"I see. Well, a few of us are concerned that Chivler's disappearance was not linked to a local resident, like we led on earlier this evening."

"You think it could be Metim?" Gus's eyes widened.

"It may seem impossible, but I think there are Dark Lords still actively finding ways through the gates. I'm not sure how, but—"

"Unreal," Gus whistled silently.

Mr. Sterling nodded.

"We aren't sure what they were looking for in Chivler's, but you

Chapter Eleven: Office of Research

interacted with Chivler right before he was kidnapped. You must be on guard wherever you go."

Gus and Sam both nodded, but the last part seemed like it was directed at Sam. Why would he have to be so careful? Just because his name was in the book, did that mean he was a target?

Then Mr. Sterling dug into his tweed jacket pocket and produced a small white stone.

"Here. If you get into trouble, you only need to rub this and help will come," he said, dropping it into Gus's hand. "Do not lose this, and promise me that you will only use it in an extreme emergency."

Gus nodded.

"Yes sir."

After Mr. Sterling left, Gus helped Sam pack for their trip to old Lior City. He wasn't quite sure why he needed to pack two pounds of coffee, but he complied with every item Gus tossed at him, stuffing it into his pack.

"How long will we be there?" Sam asked while he stowed away two changes of clothes, soap, and a bedroll.

"Two, three days, maybe," he shrugged. "I have never been there, so I don't have much of a guess at this point."

"And you didn't have much time to research it," Sam joked.

As they walked down the steps to see the girls already waiting for them, a flustered Mrs. Sterling hurried into the room with a rather large knitted bag in her hands. "For later tonight when you get hungry," she told them. Then with a slight scowl on her face, she gathered them all together and hugged them tightly.

"You must know I would never let you all go without us if there was another choice," she said, her voice cracking. "But I will leave you in the Creator's capable hands."

Then she shooed them out the door, likely because she was near sobbing. Emma was instantly a wreck when they were out of sight of the cabin, and it took both Lillia and Sam to help her put one foot in front of the other until they reached the center of town.

Chapter Twelve
The Lightway

Miss Karpatch was waiting for them at the main entrance to the City Center when they arrived, a look of concern but determination on her face.

"We are in luck. The place is deserted," she told them, then motioned for the four youths to follow her through the smaller but equally solid door next to the main entrance door.

They huffed up the long circular steps of the tower, Sam silently cursing Gus for the unnecessary items he made him pack. But then looking at the size of the girls' packs, he decided to be happy with his own.

When they reached the top, much to their relief, Miss Karpatch called for a five-minute breather. Emma dragged Sam out onto the tower balcony overlooking the City and the vast Tarum Forest. The sun was just beginning to set on the horizon, and behind them they could smell the breeze of the ocean and hear the loud roar of the beginning of the Kolar games.

"I'm scared," Emma said quietly, grasping his hand.

He squeezed back.

Chapter Twelve: The Lightway 🌲🌲

"Me too."

As the rest of the group came out to join them on the balcony, Miss Karpatch looked thoughtfully at the mountains to the left of them.

"The first wave will put you straight into the tower on Mount Halpa. The second will be the tricky one," she said.

"What do you mean?" Gus asked, dropping his backpack on the floor to cool down in the evening breeze.

Miss Karpatch chuckled slightly.

"Well, the Old Lior tower was disabled on the other end to ensure no Dark creatures would ever use it. You were going to have to walk from Mount Halpa, but I think I have figured out a way to use the Lightway and get you close."

Gus's eyes widened.

"We are going to *skim*?"

"Yes, but don't be worried. I have done it quite a few times—too many to keep count. I found a large pool enhanced with Lazuli not far from the entrance to Old Lior you can skim into safely."

Emma's face suddenly lost all color.

"Are you sure about this? I heard jumping off a wave halfway through can be seriously dangerous!"

"There are risks, yes. But I am certain I have calculated correctly," she assured them. "We don't have a lot of time."

"I'm up for it," Lillia said nonchalantly.

"Me too," Sam chuckled nervously.

Miss Karpatch smiled and picked up Emma's pack for her, seeing that her emotions were about to get the best of her.

"Let's get moving then. Time's wastin'."

She led them inside the tower, and after using her Light key to power up the Lightway, she turned the dial for the correct coordinates—first, seven turns counter-clockwise, then two turns back clockwise. The light above the large metal tube began to turn a cloudy blue, then green.

Suddenly, the Lightbase began moving slowly on its axis with a low rumble, clicking seven clicks toward the left, then two toward the

Chapter Twelve: The Lightway

right. When it was in place, a brilliant green glow replaced the dull green in the globe, and the hum of the machine gained in strength until it was vibrating the floor of the tower.

"It's time!" Miss Karpatch motioned toward Gus, who reluctantly climbed into the sliding door on the side, clutching his backpack tightly to his chest. "You will want to lay back slightly! And don't shift a lot while in the wave!" she said loudly, to which Gus nodded nervously, his face white as a sheet.

Then Miss Karpatch closed the door, and when Gus was in position, she waved to him and pushed a large silver button on the side of the tube.

The Lightway instantly shot bright blue out of its mouth like a great flash of a camera, piercing the evening air with a beam stretching far past the forest and up into the mountains.

Gus was there and then he wasn't, and was nowhere to be seen in the stream of light between Lior City and the Light tower beyond. Sam knew his heart wasn't the only one racing as he looked over to Emma who, panting heavily with her hands on her knees, was nearly as white as Gus was just before he left.

Then as sudden as the beam had dispersed from the Lightway, it blinked out, leaving a whining hum to resonate off the tower's interior.

"Successful wave. Who's next?" she said cheerfully.

Judging from the terrified looks in their eyes, neither of the girls was ready to be the next guinea pig in Boggle's contraption, so Sam volunteered to get it over with.

"This thing isn't going to turn me into a piece of toast, is it?" he chuckled as he picked up his backpack and headed toward the opening in the tube.

"It's as safe as getting married," Miss Karpatch winked at him.

He climbed into the humming metal barrel facing into the clouds and the mountains distantly in front of him, feeling oddly like a bullet in a rifle. He slipped easily into the seat of the tube, which looked as though it was made to eject the person once the wave began. Swinging

Chapter Twelve: The Lightway

his backpack around in front of him, he waited, heart pounding, for Miss Karpatch to push the button.

In front of him was the end of the tube and the open sky, now deep with the color of the oncoming night. The mountains were barely visible, but their outline could still mostly be seen, the white of the snow-covered peaks contrasting against the darkened sky.

His pulse quickened even further as Miss Karpatch shut the door and smiled at him through the glass. He was about to be shot out of a cannon like a circus performer. Although he put full trust in his history teacher, he couldn't help but think of the worst of possibilities.

As the hum of the Lightway steadily increased, for the first time in his life, Sam wished he knew how to pray.

Suddenly, a brilliant blue flash engulfed his entire body, and the metal tube was gone. Instead, he was sailing hundreds of feet above the treetops in a cylinder of pulsing translucent light. He was moving fast, but not so fast that he couldn't make out the outlines of the forest floor below, or feel the cool air rushing past him. It was an amazing, dreamlike experience—silent and exhilarating.

In less than the time it took him to brush his teeth, Sam was rapidly approaching a tower on top of the mountain, its outline standing out black against the snow surrounding it.

Below him, the forest changed to steep inclines and rock faces, then to all snow, the occasional tree still poking out among the frozen white.

He watched the as the tower grew larger in front of him, then burst into bright blue as the second wave from the Mount Halpa tower rushed out to slow down the first. There was a sudden shudder, then the wave slowed quickly, forcing Sam to clutch tighter to his backpack from the momentum. Seconds later, the light wave drifted him into the elongated tube of the Lightbase, his body finally coming to a gentle stop opposite the way he left.

The door to the base was suddenly flung open, a plump boy with fogged glasses there to greet him.

"Best thing you've ever done, just admit it!" he said excitedly, nearly pulling Sam out of the base.

Chapter Twelve: The Lightway

He couldn't deny—it was a spectacular experience that left his hands shaking and his brain swimming, and as he stepped out of the base, it took a few moments for his eyes to adjust to his surroundings. Blinking, he realized it was identical to the tower in Lior, except for one thing—it was cold.

Sam's eyes adjusted just in time to see Gus gnawing into a huge turkey leg, a steaming cup of coffee at his side.

"Is there a restaurant here or something?" Sam asked, still rubbing his eyes, and glad the tower room was rather dark.

"Sort of. Rather it's the caretaker that runs the tower. He's got quite a bit of turkey down there if you're hungry," Gus said between mouthfuls.

"Just some coffee, maybe."

Sam headed toward the little window that was puffing out clouds of steam. He saw a small girl tugging on the apron of a heavy-set, middle-aged woman, who was fluffing a large bowl of rice with a fork. She turned at the sight of Sam in the window and shooed the little girl toward the window. The girl scowled at her mother's request but then stomped over to the window.

"Would yeh like somethin' from the kitchen?" she spoke in an annoyed mouse-like voice.

Sam couldn't help but stare at her, at her dingy looking clothes, neat but plain brown hair and fiery blue eyes.

"Uh, sure. Coffee please," he requested.

Without a word, she turned and took down a large mug from the cupboard and filled it from a large kettle from the small fireplace in the kitchen.

He accepted the cup and thanked her, but she didn't acknowledge his thanks.

"Who are they?" Sam asked Gus after wandering over to a small table that he had occupied next to a roaring fireplace.

"Natori. Outsiders," he said. "They are technically Descendants, but with less of the Light gifts than Descendants have."

Sam looked back at the girl who was twirling her apron around her finger behind her mother.

Chapter Twelve: The Lightway

"Do some live in Lior City?"

"A few. Most of them deny the ancestry, but some still want to be Descendants of Light."

"Why can't they be?" Sam pressed Gus while sipping the strong coffee.

Gus put down the turkey leg, hearing the sound of the Lightbase beginning to hum.

"There are some areas of Lior that want more pure Light ancestry—those that have full Light abilities," he said, standing, "but some don't have full gifts, if any at all. They lost the Descendant blood through continuous marriage with humans long ago."

"What about them?" Sam asked, glancing toward the woman and the little girl who were wiping off gleaming white dishes. They looked like everyone else in Lior, but then again, so did everyone else in White Pine. He wondered why having more human blood in them made them so undesirable.

Gus stood as the humming of the base increased—no doubt indicating another traveler was about to arrive.

"They work for the Lior government, but would rather stay out of public life."

There was another flash of light that instantaneously illuminated the otherwise dark tower, and a beam of light shot from the barrel of the Lightbase to meet with the oncoming wave.

When the Lightbase stopped humming, an open-mouthed wide-eyed Emma stepped from the tube and immediately clung to Sam for support.

"That ... was ... incredible!" she squealed through her quivering lips.

They led her over to the little table, and Sam handed her his coffee cup, which was now beginning to cool down.

"I've n-never done anything like that before—I have always imagined it, but I never thought it would be like this," she said, accepting the coffee.

"We know," he smiled at her.

A few minutes later, Lillia arrived through the Lightway looking

Chapter Twelve: The Lightway

very unlike her normal moody self. She was smiling from ear to ear and stumbled out of the base, falling flat on the floor in a laughing fit.

"Guess she enjoyed it too," Gus smirked.

While they looked over Miss Karpatch's instructions, Lillia, Sam, and Gus drank coffee and huddled around the fireplace to warm up. Emma, on the other hand, immediately welcomed herself into the kitchen area and was exchanging recipes for root cakes and cream pies.

"She always does this," Lillia answered Sam without so much as a questioning glance from him toward the kitchen.

"She is not shy, that's for sure," Gus wrinkled his nose and stared down at his empty coffee cup. "I remember once my father told me that when she was younger, she walked into a Council meeting with Mr. Sterling and told them all they needed to quit arguing and start being better friends."

Sam laughed. It was so like her to be that bold. Even though he had only known her a short time, it seemed like longer. She was the complete opposite from him—outgoing, emotional, and trusting. He was reserved, cold, and trusted no one. It was amazing she liked him at all.

As they studied the instructions, a small folded paper dropped out from between the maps.

> *I am sorry there are no instructions on how to return back to Lior. For reasons I cannot say, you must use what you have to find your way home. Please know I have confidence in all of you, and I know you will find what you are looking for. Do not fear, for it is your greatest enemy. Fear is your greatest weakness. Don't let it consume you. Others will use it against you. You must trust one another, though even they may fail you. Remember—the road to knowledge is only found in the Creator.*
> *Sarah*

****

Chapter Twelve: The Lightway

"Are you kidding? We can't just take the Lightway back to the City?" Emma nearly shouted as she read the note for the first time.

"I think the recipe swapping has melted your brain," Lillia said sharply, thrusting the note back into Gus's hands. "You don't remember her telling us we can't get back to the City through the Lightway?"

"If I would have known, I wouldn't have asked!" Emma tried her best to control herself, but was losing the battle.

"She told us it has failsafe codes," Sam told them.

Emma snatched the note from Gus, walked over to the table and sat down, reading it over and over.

"How are we supposed to get back?" she said, nearing tears. "What is happening in Lior?"

"What do you think, Em?" Lillia said quickly. "It's not like it can always be perfect, you know."

"We know the Council has spies," Gus said. "Mr. Sterling all but told us that. I think Miss Karpatch didn't tell us because she wanted us to have the best chance of keeping it quiet."

"We should go back," Emma said, unsure of herself suddenly.

"Run to the problem. Great idea, Em'."

Emma scowled, her face showing instant anger.

"Well, at least I have *someone* to trust."

At these words, Lillia retreated to her dormant self and stared out of the tower window, obviously done with giving her input into the conversation. Sam wished he could join her.

Then, the little girl from the kitchen walked out into the tower room holding a large bundle of napkin-wrapped items and handed them to Emma.

"This is for your journey," she said, then turned on her heels and ran back into the kitchen.

Emma stood open-mouthed, torn between her anger and the generosity of the little girl. She dropped her backpack to the floor and stuffed the bundle into her pack, then plopped down at the table with Gus and looked over the note with him.

"It says that we will have to program the Lightway to cut the wave

Chapter Twelve: The Lightway

off halfway through the transfer," she said, suddenly having changed her tone. "The Light from the Lazuli pool will connect with the wave and slow our descent ... if we do it right."

Without another word, the three friends seemed to understand what had happened. Emma had changed her mind because the little girl had given her permission to go. It was, in essence, the Creator giving her permission as well. Her faith in the journey as well as in their ability to complete the task had been renewed by a simple gift from an Outsider.

"Right," Gus looked sideways at Emma, unsure of how to proceed. "The note said we will have to engage the secondary override system on the base here before we go."

Below Miss Karpatch's note, the instructions and the coordinates were laid out in detail. They would be cut off of the wave just over the Pool of Garis—and according to Gus, would experience a bit of turbulence near the end of the wave. Once they exited Mount Halpa tower, they would sail directly over the pool, which, having its own source of Lazuli light, would help them descend from the wave to jump into the pool below. The last part of the note she had starred and traced over a few more times for emphasis. It read:

> *Fear is your greatest weakness. Don't let it consume you. Others will use it against you. You must trust one another, though even they may fail you.*

Emma stood.

"We can do this," she said suddenly, confidently. Then reaching out her hand toward Lillia, said, "I'm sorry. It was wrong of me to say that."

Lillia took Emma's hand and, with a strange turn of mood, smiled at her.

"No worries, Em'."

Gus stood and walked over to the base, holding the note out in front of him.

Chapter Twelve: The Lightway

"I agree. We can do this. The directions aren't as difficult as I thought," he said, oblivious to both Emma's and Lillia's exaggerated eye-rolling.

"I'm just glad we don't have to sit through another Kolar game," Lillia said. "They can make you incredibly dizzy."

Their spirits lifted in the room even though it was getting colder in the tower as night progressed. The woman wandered out of the kitchen to stoke the fire in the main tower room, and while Gus and Sam poured over the directions in the note, Emma and Lillia helped her bring in wood. The girls also repacked all of the backpacks with special waterproof linings Miss Karpatch had them take while back in the City.

In a short time, Gus was sure he had figured out the coordinates. Sam was confident in his abilities, having seen him at work in the library memorizing full passages of text within a book and then moving on to the next, but the thought of going into unknown and potentially dangerous territory without any weapons or ability to defend himself left him uneasy. He knew Emma and Lillia could produce a little Light because of their secret practicing, but he didn't know how well. Gus still had trouble producing the Light, having mastered the concept of how to do it properly, but he hadn't been successful in actually using the gift.

Sam personally had only fired a gun once with Phillip's brother Arthur, and it was under duress. Not that he was afraid of them, but Uncle Arthur wasn't the best—or safest—teacher to be learning from. He insisted that his finger was to be kept on the trigger at all times in order to "get the feel of it," which ended up with Arthur almost shooting his own foot off while trying to help Sam steady his gun. Luckily, the bullet missed within inches and only sprayed dirt up into his eyes.

"Was there anything about how to defend ourselves in that note?" he asked Gus as he finished up the base preparation.

"I didn't see any," Gus responded, adding sudden concern to his already perplexed face.

Chapter Twelve: The Lightway

"How does she expect us to defend ourselves out there? I mean, aren't there a few things—people or animals—that we should worry about?"

Gus's eyes searched the night toward where the newly positioned Lightbase was pointing.

"There are quite a few things we should be worried about out there—but the Metim, hopefully, will not be one of them. There hasn't been Metim out there for—"

"Fifty years, I heard," Sam cut him off. "But what about Mr. Sterling talking about the Metim on the move again? And Chivler being taken? Shouldn't we be a little worried?"

Gus didn't take his eyes off the dark valley in front of him.

"I suppose. To tell you the truth, I am not sure what to think at this point. Lior has always been a safe place to me."

"Don't worry, I will take care of them with these," Emma pointed to her flexed arms.

"Ha. We would just toss *you* off to them. They would give the princess back before the day was over," Lillia joked.

Emma snorted.

"Thanks. I suppose I can't count on you to back me up," she retorted.

Both girls had their backpacks slung over their shoulders and were wearing knitted hats that Sam didn't notice before.

"Aren't they pretty?" Emma said after seeing that he had noticed them. "The little girl made them."

Sam nodded. It was convenient too. The note, the food, and the hats—everything seemed like it had been set up in their favor. He hoped their trust had not been misplaced.

Something, however, was prying at him as they prepared to leave. He was thinking suddenly about the Creator they all talked about, and Lior. None of this was a coincidence, and he was now certain it wasn't a dream. It was real, and he had been stuck in a realm of disbelief for too long. He felt a pulling deep within himself, but it all seemed to pull toward something. Perhaps, maybe, this Creator was the God that he had never been looking for but knew he needed.

Chapter Twelve: The Lightway

Despite Gus and Emma's protests, Sam convinced them to play Dove-Count-Six—a game of Emma's to determine who would ride first in the Lightway—and he was chosen to go first, with Emma second.

Sam climbed into the chamber once again and settled himself with his backpack the best he could into the tube. Miss Karpatch had warned them to lay back even more when skimming, so he obeyed. He was unsure what would happen if he didn't, but he didn't want to find out.

The hum of the base began to grow louder and Sam looked out into the night air. He wasn't facing the distant glowing spires of the City anymore, only thick darkness and the unknown. He clutched his pack, waiting for the immense light pulse. With a quick glance out the small glass window, he saw the three friends huddled together watching him with anticipation.

With an enormous flash, the Lightway sprung to life once again and sent Sam out into the night. He leaned back uncomfortably, but knew that it would be just over three minutes of travel time before he would drop out of the wave into the pool. He felt the cool mountain air rush past him, stinging his face with its chill. The night spread out in front of him like a blanket of black, the only light coming from the iridescent blue tint of the wave he was riding. He loved the feeling, but still his nerves knotted up his insides, making him feel like a rag that was being wrung out.

Then a glance at his watch told him the three minutes were just about up. The air was beginning to change from cool to balmy, but since he was still chilled from the mountain, it felt good.

Suddenly the timer on his watch went off as Gus had programmed it to, and seconds later the wave disappeared. Just ahead, a thick cloud of Light illuminated the sky, which immediately caught Sam in its grasp as he sped forward in the darkness, and for a moment he was suspended in the brilliant blue cloud, his body tilting precariously in the Light. He felt himself descending slowly through the cloud at first, then faster until he was almost free fall plummeting toward the faint blue pool below.

Chapter Twelve: The Lightway

At the moment Sam braced himself for impact, another cloud of Light caught him from below, immediately slowing his descent downward. He gripped his backpack as he continued his descent, sending up a crude prayer to the sky above.

His body stabilized in the Light cloud, and soon the jungle-like treetops of the forest were visible. He could only watch as the Light chose his landing point—dead center in the pool below him. The dark water with veins of brilliant Lazuli light drew him downward, and suddenly he was under water, fighting to get to the surface of the iridescent blue liquid.

He instantly felt the eerie sensation of being in the water at night and made a beeline toward the shore, slinging his pack on his back so he could use his arms to swim. Silently, he thanked his foster mother Sylvia for forcing him to take swimming classes at the academy. As he crawled up on the sandy beach of the pool, the sound of the thunderous waterfall behind him was the first sound he heard.

The moon gave the only light on the beach, but it was enough to see his surroundings, which included a display of blue glowing insects that surrounded the pool just inside the tree line. He lay in the sand for a few moments, trying to get his bearings. The swim wasn't far to the shore, but he was panting nonetheless.

After a while of watching the strands of blue light lift peacefully off the water and drift past the moonlit waterfall to the hazy blue cloud above, Sam considered trying to venture into the woods to get a lay of the area, but thought it best instead to stay put and build a small fire until the others arrived.

He had been in the woods in the dark before, but only once as a Boy Scout. His leader was a good one and taught him to face his fear of the dark, convincing him to stand in the woods alone in the pitch black until he felt comfortable with it. It took several minutes, but he mastered it. This wasn't in the midst of the pines in the Manistee Forest, but the concept was the same.

He picked out a few pieces of wood and dug his matches out of his pack to start a fire. Just as the first few flames began to lick the top of the branches he had dragged from the edge of the woods, a flash

Chapter Twelve: The Lightway

of light soared above him and another form descended into the pool.

Wading into the water, he fished out a sputtering Emma with her backpack, who immediately fell in a heap onto the beach.

"I can't believe I just did that," she breathed heavily, inching her way to the now glowing flames in the makeshift fire pit.

"If you sit closer, your clothes will dry faster," Sam said.

She rolled over and sat up, prying off her sweater and laying it on the log Sam had dragged over from the woods.

"You know, I uh—don't like Sayvon," he said awkwardly, immediately hating himself for saying it.

Emma looked off toward the concert of blinking insects in the woods, her expression blank.

"I *was* worried at first," she said finally, her expression morphing suddenly into a smile that burst from ear to ear. "But now I can tell you aren't her type."

He pretended to be offended, but secretly he was just glad to have the whole thing past them.

"It seemed to me that you were pretty upset when I went on the tour with her," he toyed with her.

Emma laughed.

"Don't be sensitive. It's not your style," she said.

"True," he said, embarrassed, while poking a large stick into the coals. "I guess I was just more ... worried what you thought than anything."

A few moments later, another flash of light brought Lillia down into the pool with a splash. But seeing that she was a natural swimmer and immediately began splashing toward them, Sam let her come ashore on her own. She immediately kicked off her shoes and set them to steam next to the fire, then laid on her back in the sand and ignored the couple.

Gus finally arrived in a gurgling flop into the pool a few minutes later, and soon the group was together again, wet clothes propped up next to the blazing fire while they made plans to set up camp for the night on the beach.

"How far are we from old Lior City?" Emma asked to no one in

Chapter Twelve: The Lightway

particular, but all eyes focused on Gus, who was busy stringing one of Boggle's special cloth tarps that glowed a soft blue by drawing in small amounts of Lazuli light from any source it could.

"I think we are about a three hour walk through the forest," he answered.

"That's not too bad, I suppose. I figured it would be a lot farther," Sam acknowledged.

"No, the distance isn't bad," Gus agreed. "But I have been looking at the maps and we will have to skim the outer edge of the Darkness to get there, and the terrain near the City isn't the greatest."

"Excellent," Lillia rolled her eyes.

Sam was clueless about the Darkness, and from the looks of it, the girls weren't too excited to discuss it either. For Gus, however, the Darkness had been somewhat of a pet project. He was constantly reading about its effects in Lior or discussing the latest updates about where the patches remained from the last war with the Metim.

They thought it best to leave the details up to Gus because he knew the most, but that didn't mean they wouldn't notice when he showed concern about going near it.

They got to work on their tents, setting up camp around the fire Sam had built. They were a simple canvas setup, a bit heavy in the backpack but looking very comfortable after a long day.

Sam looked around for a suitable log to use as a stand to keep his shoes off the ground. Finding one, he plopped back down in front of the fire and added a few more pieces of wood to the dwindling flames.

"Are we safe here?" Emma was the first to ask when the rest of the group had their tents staked and were nibbling on some of the bread and turkey the young Outsider girl in the Light tower had packed for them.

Gus looked instinctively at the dark forest around him.

"I think we are. From the latest info on the wildlife, I would say we would avoid most predatory species in this area."

"What about the Metim?" Sam caught his gaze into the forest.

"Nope. No activity for—"

Chapter Twelve: The Lightway

"Fifty years, we know," Lillia shook her head. "But things sure look like they are beginning to unravel."

"We should set the lanterns around the camp boundaries like daddy taught us, right?" Emma said. "I know they can't protect us completely, but they do hide us, right?"

"The lanterns have saved many Descendants because they were never found," Gus offered.

"I suppose it's my job to set them up," Lillia stood and walked over to her pack, producing four small lanterns much like the ones Mrs. Sterling used at the cabin after they walked through the arch.

Sam watched her place the lanterns in a strategic pattern on the sand surrounding the tents. It made no sense that the light from the lantern would scare off Dark creatures of any sorts, but he kept his mouth shut. It was curious, however, to watch her carefully place one of the lanterns, then reposition it only inches away from its original spot.

"Can't you just put some sort of protective spell around the camp or something?" Sam asked.

Gus snorted and looked over the top of the book he was nose deep in.

"Ha! A spell?" He plopped the book in his lap. "Most of the 'occultish-type' who say they produce spells are more mental than magicians, and those that aren't couldn't do much more than light a candle! I mean, really, a witch? Humans claim to be witches but really they are just mixing a bunch of herbs together and chanting nonsense over glass balls."

"Unless those witches were empowered by a Dark Watcher," Lillia reminded him. "You of anyone should remember that the first humans were tricked into performing Dark magic by the Fallen Watchers."

Gus chuckled.

"True, but even they have had much less power lately. Dark Watchers don't have the access to humans in Creation like they once did, and even the ones that do can only possess humans—or Descendants—for short periods of time. There are only a few cases

Chapter Twelve: The Lightway

on record of true Dark Watcher indwelling happening in thousands of years."

Lillia poked at the fire with a stick.

"I'm just sayin' it's possible to be possessed, that's all," she said, more softly this time.

"So possession is real?" Sam stopped for a moment, hearing a rustling sound behind him.

It had ceased suddenly when he stopped talking.

"—like demons and stuff?" he said while motioning with his thumb behind him toward the noise, hoping not to give away the fact that he had heard whatever it was behind him.

But something *was* there, and it was getting closer.

****

The other three caught his signal and silently crawled over to his position, listening for any sound. There was no rustling, no movement—nothing.

Then suddenly, and to everyone's surprise, out popped a small creature, blue and green in color and looking much like a furry rat on stubby fat legs.

There were relieved sighs from the group as Gus stood and shooed the creature back into the forest.

"It's only a juvenile Lior possum, who, might I add, is probably lost from its romp."

"Romp?" Lillia laughed outright. "Seriously, Gus, you study too much."

"What? It's the name for a group of possum," he said.

"Forget it. You're just ignorant about your own strangeness, I guess," Lillia said with contempt.

At that moment, something in Gus became unhinged, which sent the creature waddling at a faster pace off into the brush. All of the insults, the backhanded comments and irritating expressions from Lillia had finally gotten to him.

He stood suddenly, his face bright red as he marched to where she

Chapter Twelve: The Lightway

had propped her feet up in front of the fire to warm them. Standing over her, Gus bent down and shook his thick finger right in her face and called her every name he could think of, from "self-absorbed bully" to "intellectual anarchist," all of which she took willingly while a look of silent fear began to emanate from her cringing form. When he was finished, he instantly broke down sobbing, plopping loudly back down at the fire with his back turned to them all.

Lillia looked as though she couldn't move, mouth open, a look of deep guilt and surprise splashed across her face. She then turned suddenly and slipped into her tent, trying hard to stifle her own sobs, which proved impossible.

Sam and Emma chose to sit quietly at the fire instead of trying to console Gus, which would have been impossible at that moment anyway. Instead, they listened to the waterfall pound the rocks below it and the occasional squawk from a bird calling into the night.

Nearly twenty minutes later, Lillia came stumbling out of her tent, cheeks red and damp from her tears, and she found her way over to the fire next to Gus, sitting just inches from him.

"Gus, I—" she started.

"Sam, let me show you something," Emma said quickly, grabbing his hand with an iron grip and pulling him off the sand.

She led him around the edge of the pool where the sand ended and the rocks began, and then seeing an exceptionally large flat rock that perched out over the water, she clambered onto the slippery grey surface, pulling him with her.

"I wanted to give them some space," she said, staring at the moonlit pool in front of her.

"I know," Sam said, feeling very relieved he was away from the drama. "Not that she didn't have it coming, but I am glad they are working it out."

"Yeah, I agree … about both statements," she smiled. Then she crawled on her hands and knees to the edge of the rock. "Come here," she whispered.

Sam obeyed, and when he peered over the rock edge, he was amazed to see thousands of little blue specks hovering just above the

Chapter Twelve: The Lightway

sandy pool bottom. Then they flitted like schools of fish toward and away from the edge of the rock, eventually coming to rest once again.

"What are they?" he said a little too loudly, and then instantly they were gone.

"Shh!" she hissed at him.

After a few moments of quiet, the tiny organisms reappeared a few at a time until there were once again thousands, sparkling like the stars in the sky on an exceptionally clear night.

Emma leaned into him, close enough that he could have simply leaned forward and kissed her. But she whispered into his ear instead.

"They are called Ori—tiny organisms that eat Lazuli."

Sam said nothing, just watched the strange organisms as they sparkled in front of them.

"Ori means 'light,'" she whispered softly. "Curious little creatures. No one can really figure them out. They are like ... the mystery of the animal kingdom here in Lior."

"Really? More than the giant flying dinosaurs in Jester's Pass?" Sam said again so loudly that the tiny specks of light disappeared again momentarily.

She smiled and held a hand over his mouth.

"The Ori eat Lazuli. The only organism that seems completely unaffected by Darkness. And when there is no Lazuli, they actually *eat the Darkness* too."

"That's strange."

"Miss Karpatch told me about a time that the Ori had eaten up all of the Lazuli in a pool she was studying and migrated to another pool where the Darkness had settled. They ate straight through the Darkness to get to the Lazuli in the pool."

"How can they migrate between pools? They're just fish," Sam said, attempting to understand.

Emma's hand touched Sam's momentarily, bringing a wave of warmth over him.

"Ori are some of the most versatile 'fish' in Lior. There's lots of strange stories and legends about them."

Chapter Twelve: The Lightway

Lior was truly a remarkable place. He had seen so many things already, and they had only been in Lior for a few days. No doubt there was so much more to explore.

They watched the groups of Ori move in waves like tiny ribbons beneath the surface for several moments before they saw Gus motioning them to come back to the fire. Sam didn't want to leave quite yet, but knew they needed rest for the following day, so he snatched up Emma's hand and led her back over to the fire.

When Emma and Sam sat down, Lillia handed them each a cup of coffee and a bowl of the soup that had been simmering on the fire. Her countenance had obviously changed. She had a quieter, more compliant attitude, and for once she was actually smiling. Other than the fact that her eyes were red from crying, she was a new person.

"We worked some things out," she said after the deathly silence couldn't be tolerated any longer.

Gus smiled largely, digging into his soup.

"There were some things that we both had bottled up for quite a while—but we are okay now," he said. "But we need to talk about something more important—our plan for tomorrow. As I said before, we will be going around a small portion of Darkness left over from the last war."

Emma let out a small whimper, but allowed Gus to continue.

"As stated before, there should be no encounters with Metim, but—just in case, we need to use any Light manipulation we can gather."

"Shouldn't be too spectacular," Lillia snickered.

"Lillia, you have shown the potential for some pretty good bolts, and you are pretty fast. Emma—you have done pretty well with the Light shield."

"Thanks Gus. I'm not that good though," Emma blushed.

Sam understood where this was going.

"I have no way to defend myself."

Gus looked at Sam, but didn't attempt to deny what he had said.

"I can't seem to have much success either. But getting you to

Chapter Twelve: The Lightway

respond to the Light is one of the reasons we are here, right?" He looked around at the others. "But until something happens, we need to do our best to make sure we are protected."

"But we are no match for trained Metim, Gus. How are we supposed to defend ourselves when we can barely make a bolt ourselves?" Emma asked.

"We will have to do our best to work together—to use our gifts and our brains."

"That'll be easy for you, Gus," Emma joked.

Gus smiled lazily at her, then continued.

"What I figured is that since none of our gifts are very strong, we can concentrate them together in the case of trouble. To do that, we must stay close to one another."

Lillia snatched another log from the pile and tossed it onto the fire.

"I honestly don't expect to see any, but we should be ready in any case," Gus said.

There was a question that had been plaguing Sam for quite some time now.

"Can Metim be killed? I mean—by stabbing them or shooting them or something?"

All eyes turned to Gus.

"Not easily with conventional weapons. They can be wounded, but it takes a lot for them to be killed. They are supernaturally indwelled with the Darkness and will heal if they are hurt."

"They must be killed with Light," Lillia said finally.

Sam wanted more coffee, but the pot was empty. Instead, he grabbed another honey roll from the napkin given to them in the tower. Part of him was only eating because this stuff was completely over his head and the slightest bit disturbing.

At that moment, Lillia reached over and waved her hand over the lantern she had placed next to her, which sat dark until her hand passed its exterior. As the lantern began to glow, suddenly beams of blue light shot from all four corners of the others she had placed around the perimeter, connecting each until a shield formed over the

Chapter Twelve: The Lightway

entire campsite, bathing the sand around them and everything else under the shield in soft blue light.

"Just thinking about all that Darkness made me uneasy," she said, reaching out and touching the milky blue dome next to her.

"What would we do without Boggle?" Emma said suddenly, watching the blue light swirl above her.

"Not be here, that's for sure," Gus said lazily as he yawned loudly, "and now, I think I will turn in. We have a pretty big day ahead of us and I'm already feeling the amino acids from the turkey kicking in. Not to mention the evening swim while getting here." Gus stood and dusted himself off, dumping the rest of his coffee into the fire.

"Me too. I'm out. Night, lovebirds." Lillia kicked the sand from her feet and followed Gus into the circle of tents.

Each of them disappeared into their canvas bivouac tents, leaving Sam and Emma alone once again in the darkness. As the fire died and their eyes adjusted once again to their surroundings, the Lazuli light that drifted upward from deep within the pool mirrored soft blue reflections on the water's face. Every so often a school of light-eating Ori would surface on the water and add to the spectacle of dancing light.

Scooting closer, Emma snuggled up underneath Sam's chest so that he was forced to wrap her in his arms, all the while her strawberry hair giving off intoxicating scents of fruit and lilac.

"I'm scared of sleeping alone," she mumbled into the shoulder of his sweater.

"I could sleep near you tonight … if you would like," he didn't hesitate to say, but his heart instantly thumped loudly in his chest.

She chuckled softly, putting her hand on his forearm.

"I would absolutely love to have you stay with me in my tent, Sam, but I can't—it's not the way we do things. I'm sorry."

Sam was somewhat relieved, but confused. It seemed like everyone he knew did that. Not that he was ready to do anything sexual with anyone. He hadn't really had the desire or the opportunity, but it seemed strange not to. He did know a few kids at his old school in Grand Rapids that were a lot like the Descendants, calling themselves

Chapter Twelve: The Lightway

"followers," and they didn't do a lot of things. But then there were a few of them that did … and other things much worse. It didn't seem like the name defined what you did or didn't do.

Emma stood, kissed him on the forehead, and then slipped off toward the tents, but before she disappeared into her own, she stopped for a moment, her face visible in the firelight.

"We are followers of Light, Sam … and of the Creator. And I would love to see you follow Him too," she whispered.

****

Crawling into his own tent for the night, Sam's head swam with emotions from the last few hours and what the day held tomorrow. Would they find any information on the Dark arch or the Watcher Stone? Would he find out he had Light manipulation gifts? Would they encounter any Darkness or Metim?

And then Emma's words about being a follower of the Creator—was that the same as the Christians he knew? He knew they claimed to be holy, but they were so confusing. They preached goodness and mercy but then did some things their own way.

His foster parents even called themselves Christian at some of the dinner parties where powerful people attended, but mostly they talked of Christian values as if they were requirements for being a politician.

Then there was the man Jesus that people would discuss as if He was God himself, the Creator of the universe, who came to the Earth to save man from their terrible acts. It was all so confusing.

He tried to push the questions out of his mind, but they persisted for nearly an hour while he tossed and turned on the cold sand beneath the tent floor. Remembering the blanket in his pack, he snatched it out of the pocket and tucked himself in tightly. The sound of the waterfall at the other end of the pool became rhythmic, almost hypnotizing.

He gazed at the soft glow of the shield from the lanterns above him. Focus on the Light, they told him.

Chapter Twelve: The Lightway

Open your heart to the Creator to guide you.

Sam focused on the light above him. It moved like waves rolling in a surf across the shield, rolling ever so slowly, as if the sea was stuck in slow motion.

,He could hear faint snoring from the direction of Gus's tent. Then it grew louder, as if someone turned up the volume in his throat. Why could he hear it so well?

Suddenly the sound disappeared and the sounds from the forest around him became the focus. A small flying insect—what was he chewing on? Then a scurry across the sand and into the water—tiny legs thrashing about in the water only centimeters from his head. He could hear it all so well. The feeling was almost like that day in the forest with old lady Wrenge.

He listened for a few moments and then covered his ears to shut out the sound, but found no relief, so he flipped over on his stomach and tucked his pillow around his ears. As he did, he thought he saw the slightest flicker of a blue spark from one of his fingers to the other, but it was quickly gone.

He let the pillow drop and stared at his hand. Did he just imagine that? He wiggled his fingers, hoping to recreate the phenomenon, but nothing would cause the spark to return.

It was all a dream, he decided. It had to be, because suddenly he noticed the waterfall had stopped making noise.

Impossible. He unzipped the flap slightly and stuck his head out into the cool air. There was only darkness and the occasional glimpse of Lazuli streaming out of the dark water. The moon had hidden itself from sight, showing no reflection on where the falls should be, nor on the beach. Vaguely he could make out the rock where the falls had originated, but no water.

Why would they suddenly stop like that? Some strange force from the Darkness? Metim?

He thought about waking the others, but then ignored the concern. There had to be an explanation.

Sinking back into his bedding, he listened to the forest sing for a while before drifting off to sleep. The last thing he remembered

Chapter Twelve: The Lightway

was flying through the trees on one of the Lightboards Boggle gave them and being chased by an unknown green glow behind him, while bursts of brilliant blue erupted from his palms.

****

The heat of the day was already upon them when they awoke the next morning. Sam forced himself out of the blanket into the chilly air after hearing someone clinking around at the campfire. The rest of the bleary-eyed group followed, clamoring out of their tents in search of caffeinated tonics.

They sat like zombies barely alive, staring into the crackling flames and waiting for oats to finish cooking in the pot that Lillia had started.

"Not quite like the feast at the City Center, but hopefully it will fill us up," she said, oddly cheerful.

"It will be great, Lil', really," Gus smiled at her, his hair wildly pointing in all directions.

Suddenly, Sam remembered the waterfall and looked toward the pool. The sun was just beginning to peek over the trees behind them, and a few rays shot through the canopy to make the pool sparkle as if diamonds were floating on the surface.

Sure enough, there was only a small trickle cascading down the ridge where the huge gushing of water once was.

"Hey, what happened to the waterfall?" He lifted a crooked zombie finger toward the opposite end of the pool.

The others peered toward the now dry falls. Gus pushed his glasses up on the bridge of his nose and squinted.

"I must say, I have no clue," he said.

"I bet it's a tide pool!" Emma said excitedly. "During the day the pool fills up and at night it drains back."

"A tide pool?" Gus echoed.

Emma laughed out loud.

"Gus, the expert on all things, doesn't know what a tide pool is? I will certainly enjoy this moment!"

If it weren't for the fact that he had just awoken, Gus may have

Chapter Twelve: The Lightway

well attempted a theoretical defense, but chose instead to fumble around for his coffee cup.

"Why don't we check it out when we head out?" Lillia suggested. "It's just around the other side of the pool anyway."

"Good plan," Gus said, taking no notice of Lillia's rare cheerfulness and picking up the pot of hot oat cereal to spoon an extra-large helping into his empty mug.

It was the first chance they had to get a good view of the area and their campsite, having arrived in the dark. The circle of tents was well placed in the center of the crescent moon-shaped beach that surrounded the pool, which was very modest in size, with clear emerald water that appeared almost glass-like now that there weren't hundreds of gallons of water gushing over the waterfall upon its surface.

The forest was dense around the perimeter of the pool except for the pure white beach, where lush green trees very jungle-like in nature grew tall and left little room for light to reach the forest floor below. Where it did, however, rays beamed through the vegetation and produced a mystic, golden glow to the humid undergrowth. It was a sight Sam had only seen in documentaries of the Amazon or in fantasy illustrations.

They all ate the sticky hot cereal in silence, Emma showing Sam how to add some "sweet root" to it, which resembled honey with its rich sweet texture. The cereal was not bad after drizzling a good amount on, which was fine to do since there were plenty of the trees that produced it nearby. Lillia passed a loaf of bread around as well, which also went well with the sweet root if spread liberally.

Then they dismantled camp, taking the tents down, putting out the fire, packing and repacking their backpacks, and dabbing on some Kararah root to keep the insects in the jungle at bay. Sam did his best to pack as fast as he could, but the others were experts at setup and teardown. He, on the other hand, had little idea what he was doing. But with a little cramming, he was able to fit it all into his pack.

Gus gathered the group into a circle and prayed before departing, which Sam was beginning to expect and enjoy now. It wasn't that he

Chapter Twelve: The Lightway

really felt a need to pray yet, but he felt comfort in the practice of it. It seemed to lighten the mood, and begin and end meals and events with formality and unity.

They edged around the outer lip of the pool, leaving the beach and their campsite for the first time since arriving. Although dense, the forest left an almost natural pathway around the waterline, all the way to where the dry falls now only spattered the pool from the water source above. The path led them into the mouth of the falls, which seemed to open up further into what looked like a cavernous entrance, which then opened through the throat of the falls leading to the top of the ridge line above. Seeing no other easy path to the top, they walked through the damp tunnel and climbed the rock side to the surface, half expecting the falls to suddenly come to life and flood the cavern while they were in it.

At the top without incident, they immediately saw what made the falls stop in the middle of the night. In front of them, above the first pool, was a second pool of water about the same size as the first, but noticeably deeper from the large hole between it and the falls, where a small stream poured into its depths.

From the hole billowed huge puffs of steam, along with occasional sprays of a blue fiery substance, producing hisses and sputters with each new bubble burst of liquid.

"It must fill up during the night with molten Lazuli, then harden and allow the pool to fill," Gus said, examining the hole from the safest distance from which he could see.

"... Which spills over and causes the waterfall during the day," Emma said.

Lillia was peering over the side of the bubbling hole.

"That's one hot pool of Lazuli," she said. "I bet there's hundreds of gallons of concentrated Light in there."

Then she reached out in front of her, closed her eyes, and a blue flash appeared before her—a jet of blue light erupting from her palm and instantly burning a hole through a large leafy tree to the side of the upper pool.

Chapter Twelve: The Lightway

"Lil! What are you doing!" Emma ran to her, a look of shock and fear on her face. "A-and how did you do that?!"

Lillia was as surprised as everyone else and tried to regain her composure.

"Uh … I was just seeing if this Lazuli was going to amplify our Light ability a bit," she chortled, "and I would t-think it does!"

Gus stood and squinted at the smoking hole in the tree, then back at Lillia.

"Wow. Have you been practicing your bolts?" he asked.

Lillia was still laughing and now added coughing to the mix.

"Actually—no, I didn't even t-try that hard," she managed to sputter out.

It reminded Sam of the old lady Wrenge in the forest. Her bolt had knocked him over, but it didn't leave a hole in his middle. He was rather glad it didn't.

"You could have killed someone!" Emma peered at the hole Gus was inspecting.

"Seriously—I'm sorry. I didn't—"

"It's fine, Lil', don't worry about it. No harm done," Gus immediately consoled her.

"Except to the tree," Emma pointed out.

Gus smirked.

"We probably should watch how we use our manipulation here. Obviously the effects are enhanced a bit."

"S-so that one really would have killed someone!" Emma laughed nervously, then looked at her own palms as if afraid of them.

"I would say so," Gus said, looking again at the now smoking hole in the tree. "But we must also remember that we need to be careful with how much we manipulate Light. Metim know when it happens if they are near, and since we are trying to stay on the lower key …"

"Keep it low key …" Lillia corrected him with a snicker, then burst out laughing finally. "Not stay on a lower key—*keep* it low key, Gus."

"Maybe you should stick with more sophisticated expressions, Gus," Emma joked.

Chapter Twelve: The Lightway

Lillia could hardly contain herself.

"Yeah, m-maybe you should keep your human slang low key!"

"Ha-ha," said Gus, who hastily tossed his backpack back over his shoulder and headed toward where the pathway picked up again into the woods. "We have a city to get to."

They followed him, laughing, but silence came over them soon as the faint path met the dense jungle undergrowth. Sam was glad they were more cordial and there was less drama, although no doubt Lillia would be back to her cheerless self sooner or later.

The way was clear, but there were numerous branches full of jungle insects and reptiles of many different colors that they had to duck under, crawl over, or circle around completely. Emma nearly lost it when a blue and green frog landed on her head and crawled down her pack. To make matters worse, Gus had finally figured out that the path they were following was likely made by a large animal, which put Emma on edge even more after the frog incident.

After an hour of fighting through the dense brush, the path seemed to open into sparser undergrowth, and the trees gradually reached higher and thinner the farther they walked. Some reached so high that they were some of the tallest pines Sam had ever seen. Their trunks were just as large, too—the smallest of which were almost an entire arm's width across—and they dropped long thick needles that carpeted the ground and crunched as they walked.

Soon the trees gave way to a small knoll that rose briefly out of the giant trees. At the top of the knoll was a lone craggy pine standing as a solitary beacon in the midst of a sea of forest.

"According to the map Miss Karpatch gave us, old Lior City should be another hour and a half walk through these trees." Gus stopped for a breath under an exceptionally crooked branch. "The path goes through there," he said as he turned to his left and pointed into the forest the other direction, "… and we need to go that way … away from the Dark—"

Gus stopped mid-sentence, for if one were not looking closely, they would miss the thick, black fog that seemed to hover just outside the tree line where he had been pointing.

Chapter Twelve: The Lightway

"—ness," Gus finally finished his sentence, mouth open, glasses crooked on his nose.

Inky, smoke-like tendrils of Darkness spewed silently from in between the now blackened trunks as they added to the cloud hanging just below the knoll. They stood watching it empty its bowels from the forest depths until Emma dropped her pack with a thud, jolting the others back into reality.

"Well don't act like we didn't know it was coming," Lillia said, a noticeable edge in her voice.

"We didn't know it was this big. Gus? Explanation?" Emma said angrily.

Gus adjusted his glasses and composed himself.

"Apparently I was wrong about its current vitality, I mean, after fifty years, most clouds dissipate ... even ones surrounding events this large."

"You're joking, right?" Emma was furious. "Gus, you're telling me there is *new* Darkness in this mass?"

Gus ignored her, turning the map around in his hands as if it was flawed.

"Nope. He's not," Lillia folded her arms. "Joking, I mean. And yes, it looks like it's expanding, not dissipating."

"According to the most recent maps, we should only have to walk through it for less than an hour or so." He then uncovered the lantern attached to his pack, which began to glow bright blue, even in the morning sun. "I will go first with the lantern. Lil', since you showed measurable improvement with your bolts, you follow up the rear?"

Lillia nodded, but showed little enthusiasm.

Emma uncovered her own lantern, adding to the light surrounding them.

"Daddy has told me about the effects of the Darkness," she said. "You start second guessing yourself—making you focus on your weaknesses."

Lillia looked down, her black silky hair glistening in the blue lantern light.

Chapter Twelve: The Lightway

"My dad said that you feel like you are being strangled—stripped of all life and purpose."

Her comment drew strange looks from the others, but they had come to expect them.

"I don't suppose we can't just go around?" Sam spoke up, looking around him as if there was another path to be seen. But he was already sure his words were meaningless and the only path was before them.

"Unfortunately, there is no other way. Because the City is on a plateau, going around is impossible."

Emma began grumbling under her breath again about how strange it was that her parents would allow her to do such a thing, and then repeated over and over how the "Council would be furious if they found out there were underage Descendants sent into Darkness controlled territory."

Most of what she said was only half understood, but everyone knew she was babbling out of fear on behalf of all of them.

Then she huffed around the clearing, cinching her backpack, tying and retying her shoes, and putting her hair up into a tight bun. They watched her stomp about for nearly a minute before she stood straight, facing the Darkness, an obstinate look now on her face.

"Let's get this over then, shall we?"

She ignored Gus's suggestion to lead and stomped down the knoll toward the darkened trees in front of them, the others falling in single file behind her until they reached the tendrils of Darkness spilling into the knoll, which they circumvented, entering the woods to the left. They picked their way beside the sea of black through the forest, around huge fallen timber and thick mossy rocks that poked out of the needle-laden forest floor. It was almost surreal to watch as the thickness flowed and oozed like it was alive, not unlike the Lazuli light of the pool below the City.

Then, as they pushed through the trees into another field, they gasped, suddenly unable to speak. There, rising out of the trees like a great monster, laid the source of the Darkness—a cloud greater by a hundred times than the first.

Chapter Thirteen
The Darkness

The massive wall of black stretched high into the sky and crested like a giant wave about to curl on top of them.

Frozen, the four stood watching the Darkness ebb and flow while it vomited out smaller waves near its base that rolled forward like a great tide into the trees behind them.

It was Lillia that made the first move this time, forcing herself to move forward into the field with the giant before them.

The rest followed after her, stepping forward cautiously, no one else daring to take the lead. The air was eerily calm and balmy as they walked toward the dark wave.

The few hundred meters to the wall were made in silence. The only sounds heard were the soft crunching of pine needles below their feet and the occasional bird behind them singing warnings of the danger they were about to behold.

As they moved closer, the wall of the cloud began to take on a curious shape, almost like that of many thousands of faces trapped in agonizing torture within the Darkness.

Chapter Thirteen: The Darkness

"Oh my," Lillia breathed, echoing the sentiments of the other three.

A few meters from the wall, they stopped, watching the oozing black belch out more agonizing faces. No noise came from the Darkness, but a curious odor was evident to all of them. Not a bad odor, but quite the opposite—an enigmatic smell that drew you in, craving more of whatever it was.

Before they would allow themselves the pleasure of it, however, they focused on where the Darkness was thinnest and quickly chose their path through.

"We have to do it," Emma said, watching an especially horrifying face emerge from the Darkness and contort its features into transitions of fear, anger, and rage before unwillingly dissolving back into the cloud. "We have to go through."

Sam couldn't explain what he did next. For some unknown reason—perhaps out of anger over his past, or because of the deception and confusion of being brought to this place, or maybe it was the appeal of the enigmatic smell of the cloud before him—he cinched his pack and walked straight into the Darkness.

He walked blindly, eyes closed, doing his best to block out the deafened calls and shouts coming from his friends behind him.

At first, the air choked him, doubling him over, expelling air and mucus from his mouth before allowing him a limited breath or two. He no longer heard the shouts behind him. There was only the thick, stifling silence.

For a few moments, he allowed himself to adjust, then forced his body upright to continue walking. He expected the others should be right behind him.

Inside the Darkness there was little light, similar to a cloud-covered moon at twilight, but he could see ever so slightly, and what he saw made the hair stand up on his neck.

Trees were only charred black remains of what they once were, and those that were alive barely clung to life as they were strangled by huge rope-like vines snaking up their trunks and squeezing the life out of their branches.

Chapter Thirteen: The Darkness

There were bones all around him—carcasses of animals once having the spark of life coursing through their veins, but now just remains of decaying flesh. He sat, closing his eyes for a moment to try and slow his breathing a little.

You will always be alone, a voice whispered softly in his ear from behind him.

He whirled around, searching for the verbal assassin, but there was no one there.

Your friends are using you, the voice jeered.

He covered his ears, but it was as if the voice penetrated his very soul.

Lies ... all of it.

Unable to breathe the vile air any longer, he vomited up the contents of his stomach and doubled over, sucking in the sickened air of the Darkness around him again. He had to get out.

He was so consumed with his senses that he didn't even notice the muffled yells of his friends behind him.

"Sam!" Emma ran to him, grabbing his head in her hands. "Are you okay? We were worried sick about you! Why would you run off like that?"

"I didn't run," Sam coughed, trying to fight his nausea.

For some reason, he felt sudden anger toward the others, almost like they were deliberate in leaving him in the Darkness alone. But he knew the truth, and still couldn't explain why he did it.

"I just walked through. You apparently didn't follow me."

Gus stood in front of him, blue lantern in his hand, hazily lighting the scene.

"Sam, you are almost a kilometer away from where we stood in front of the cloud. You have been gone nearly an hour."

"What?" He was confused, flopping exhaustedly against one of the trees that struggled to stay alive. "That's not true, I was only here for a couple of minutes."

Emma picked up his face and looked directly at him. Her emerald eyes were perhaps the only thing of beauty in the haze of Darkness.

Chapter Thirteen: The Darkness

"We thought we lost you. *I* thought I lost you," she said, fear splashed across her face.

"The Darkness must be altering time, perhaps distance as well. We will need to make sure we are staying very close to each other the rest of the way," Gus said.

Sam was instantly angry, but he didn't know why.

"You want to keep going through this? Have you seen the bones lying around?"

They were silent, except for Emma who was still holding his face in her hands.

"Sam, there are no bones."

He forced a look around and saw no sign of the deteriorated bodies or piles of white carcasses. What was this place? There were bones just moments ago—he saw them. Now there was nothing.

"*Sevel* ... Darkness. It is said to be a being of its own," Lillia whispered. "It affects everyone differently."

Gus's voice seemed suddenly more muffled than the others' as a particularly dense cloud settled around them.

"The Dark-ness affects all of us dif-ferently. It must be taking a larger toll on S—am for some reason," Gus's voice sounded distant, surreal.

"Well let's k—eep going so we can get outta here," Sam said, his voice suddenly sounding disconnected from his own body. He felt lightheaded once again, but found enough strength to hoist himself up against the trunk of the tree.

"Yes. Lu—cky for us, Gus kept track of which way we needed to go," Emma's voice was miles away.

Both Emma and Gus helped him to his feet, although he could see both of them were suffering from the effects nearly as much as he was. Gus's face was as white as a sheet, and he was sweating profusely. Emma's face showed more color, but she looked strangely tired and could not stop stumbling. Lillia looked as pale as she always looked, but her eyes were sunken and showed rings of exhaustion around them. She seemed to handle the Darkness better than all of them, but it still took its toll.

Chapter Thirteen: The Darkness

"The Dar-kness affects People of Light negatively—but Metim draw from it, us-ing it to wield just as we do with the Li-ght."

Gus talked as they stumbled along, mostly to keep the silence at bay.

No one was annoyed by Gus's rambling, for the small comfort of having someone talk as they pushed their way through the soupy black was better than the eerie silence that would take its place.

"When someone opens him-self up to the Darkness, there are all sorts of alterations they go through—physical distortions and such—that ultimately changes who they once were."

"Th-ey look like fre-aks," Lillia interjected, her voice weak and muted.

"Freaks, uh—yes," Gus said, "but ultimately they are just people—who have chosen the Dark over Light for one rea-son or another."

"Ha-ve you seen one?" Sam was able to walk on his own now, but still stumbled along with Emma holding his arm and him holding hers for mutual support.

"Only in the Watcher Press," Emma said. "A—guy a few years ago who brought a Met-im to the Council to try to convert him back to Light—but he ended up esca-ping in town and causing all sorts of havoc."

"Max Lemon—bout," Lillia recalled. "No one kn-ows how Max got the Metim inside the City, either."

"What hap-pened to the Metim?"

"They killed him," Gus answered. "Max got in the way of a PO agent who used a bolt on the Metim, and both were dead instan-tly."

"So Max believed he could change the Metim back to the Light," Sam said.

"Uh huh. When they turn they are gone for-ever. All hope of bringing Light back to a Metim is lost when they allow the Darkness in."

"I sti-ll think there's hope." Emma looked as though she would suddenly collapse.

"Look!" Lillia pointed off to the left in the black fog, her voice barely audible.

Chapter Thirteen: The Darkness

It was the first sign they had seen of a break in the Darkness. Clear, blue sky could be seen where she pointed, like a beacon of light guiding them out of the gloom. Sam could smell and taste the fresh air before they were even there.

They walked through the charred remains of trees, stepping over the oozing black vines littering the landscape. Every so often they could hear a strange combination of sounds coming from the vine's tree-strangling fingers that sounded like sticky sandpaper sliding over wet rocks as it reached out to snuff any remaining life within its grasp.

Sam knew the others were suffering as he was, but for him, it was a mix of emotions being in the Darkness—the strongest being loneliness. It was almost as if the others weren't even with him. Sam drifted between feelings of anger, emptiness, and deep resentment.

There is no such thing as real love. Everyone will always leave you. These things kept recurring like inaudible whispers in the back of his mind, and giving in to them would be so easy ...

When they neared the perimeter, the Darkness seemed to do its best to keep them in its grasp. The closer they came to the fresh sweet air, wave after wave of dense clouds descended upon them from above, forcing their every step to become labored and slow as if time was unhinging itself from its constraints in an effort to delay them.

They huddled together and walked through the thickness, unable to see or breathe in the toxic fumes as they gathered strength. The light from the tiny lantern was the only light to guide them, but even it struggled to offer any help. The air was like tar—when they tried to inch forward, more would close in around them, clawing at their eyes and noses, refusing to give any leeway as they pushed forward.

Just as they believed they would be prisoners of the unforgiving cloud for eternity, a brilliant flash flooded the group from somewhere ahead of them in the blackness, forming a luminescent bubble around them and quickly dispelling the Darkness that suffocated them.

Gus led the way with the shield as a cover the last few feet to the edge of the cloud. With a final push, they burst through the shell of

Chapter Thirteen: The Darkness

Darkness into the bright sunlight, the shield vanishing without a trace of Light anywhere.

****

Gus, Lillia, Emma, and Sam fell gasping for air into the tall field grass outside of the massive black wave of distorted faces. The sunlight hurt their eyes as they attempted to adjust them and search for the origin of the protective shield that aided them.

"Who's there!?" Emma called into the blinding rays of sunlight, but received no response. "Who are you!?"

Gus was wheezing loudly next to Sam, and Lillia was doubled over, coughing up phlegm. As the dizziness subsided, Sam reached over to where he believed Emma was panting heavily next to him and grabbed her arm. She immediately shook from the touch, but then sensing that it was him, gripped his hand tightly.

"That wasn't your shield?" Sam asked her.

Barely opening his eyes, he could see the sky above him was the purest of blues, and there were large rocks all around them. The wall of Darkness loomed darkly beside them, the cloud of faces looking even angrier now that the four had escaped its grasp.

"No."

Strangely, Sam felt an odd longing for something within the Darkness again. Even after he and the others were able to stand and have a look around, he couldn't shake the need to turn constantly and look again at the wall of faces. He tried to shut it out, but it kept returning. The only thing he could do to put it out of his mind was to keep focused on the map Gus laid out in front of them.

"Those trees here on the plateau ... they have to be the Woods of the Ancients. I recognize them from the map," Gus pointed at the large clump of trees near the City, the tops of which dwarfed the other trees drawn anywhere on the parchment. "From what I can tell, we are on the far side of the plateau from where the Old City sits. We are on the steepest side, so we may have a tough way of it ahead."

Chapter Thirteen: The Darkness

Emma pointed to another spot on the map near the left side of the Woods of the Ancients, just to the left of the entrance to the City.

"Isn't that the Light Springs?"

Gus nodded.

"Sure is. It's the second reason they built the City here—other than these." He pointed at a series of what looked like ponds behind the entrance of the City. "Large deposits of Lazuli, and the springs were just an additional benefit—known to be the best tasting water around."

"And that must be the Graves of the Renown," Lillia pointed to a circular spot on the map just beyond the trees where they were with many half-circle shapes inside of it.

"It must be!" Emma was regaining her excitement little by little. "Look! There is the Forever Lamp on that pillar in the middle!" she exclaimed, at which point everyone hushed her, and reminded her that they wished not to draw attention. "Sorry, I've just heard so much about it. Do you think it is still lit?"

"Not sure. According to records, it should be," said Gus.

Sam wasn't paying attention to the lamp, nor the graves. The closer they came to the Old City, the more his mind shifted back to the old woman and what she said, back to Julian Lawrence, Chivler, and the Dark arch from his dreams. Could what he had been seeing in his dreams really be a Prophecy? And why him? Was he considered a prophet like Julian? It didn't make any sense. He was no one of importance. He was only here because they thought him to be one of them, but he had shown no evidence of Light manipulation.

It was strange, however, because every so often Sam felt something deep inside him, like someone was calling him. To where? He had no idea. *Ayet Sal* she had said. *Boy with the shadows.* There was no way a place like Ayet Sal was calling him. That place was reserved for the imprisoned Dark Lords.

At the thought, the faces of the three Dark Lords popped back into his mind—faces of evil, of whom he hadn't told the others about, and the time may come when he may have to. One—perhaps the most dangerous of them, Kachash—was still at large, and according

Chapter Thirteen: The Darkness

to Mr. Sterling, they could be planning something terrible for Lior with him in charge.

Being on the Council and involved in the affairs of the Protector's Office, Mr. Sterling may know more than he led them to believe. One thing Sam knew for certain—this was more than he had ever had to deal with in his entire life.

But whatever called him did not feel like Darkness. The Darkness was different—alluring, yes, but provocatively, in a way that made him feel empty inside, almost *guilty*. No, this calling was strangely more subtle, like a whisper just beneath of the sound of waves crashing on the ocean. A whisper, calling him softly, gently toward it, whatever or whoever it was.

****

By the time they were ready to go again, the sun was just beginning to dip toward the afternoon. Emma had passed out a simple lunch of bread and honey butter, which they ate in silence, the black wall of Darkness still in sight from the spot where they chose to eat. A small spring bubbled happily next to them, converging with a small stream that eventually made its way to the Darkness where it faded out of sight in the mass. Gus had, luckily, mapped out the best spots to find water away from the terrible effects of the Darkness, so they made good use of the spring by filling their canteens while they could.

At first, the way toward the Old City was easy, and they wove their way up the grassy terrain toward the sheer face of the plateau. As they neared, the path took a sharp turn to hug the plateau's lofty rock wall, becoming more dangerous with every step. They wound their way up the once well-carved steps, now crumbling and blocked from loose rocks tumbling down the face until the four stood level with the height of the Darkness swirling beside them.

Finding a rock suitable to sit and rest, Gus took off his backpack and sat for a moment, sweat beading on his brow.

"There is a much easier way up the plateau on the other side of the City, but it would have taken us at least another day to hike to it,"

Chapter Thirteen: The Darkness

he said, taking a long swig from his canteen. "And the Darkness is much more intense there."

Sam dug in his backpack and found his canteen and followed Gus's lead, drinking deep of the cool water from the stream now far below them.

"I am always up for a death-defying hike," he said, wiping the water dribbling on his chin.

Emma had taken her shoes off and was in the process of emptying large pebbles from them. "

"I am surprised at you, Gus. You wouldn't normally have made it this far."

Gus turned red.

"Well, not as if you would have noticed because of my eating habits, but I have been trying to get in shape. I was thinking about trying out for the football team," he said with much insecurity.

Sam cringed, waiting for the outburst of laughter, but it never came. Instead, he saw that the two girls were truly happy for him.

"Really? You should have, Gus!" Emma said sincerely.

Lillia looked authentically surprised.

"Wow, that's cool ... Gus, a jock."

Gus puffed up his chest.

"I wouldn't be mean and self-absorbed like the other meat-heads, but I figured it would have helped me stay in shape."

"And perhaps find a girlfriend," Emma winked at him.

At that, he stood up, picked up his pack and put his canteen away.

"I would jump at the occasion, but too bad it's not possible," he said curtly, then turned and began up the path once again, with Lillia suddenly following right behind him, her face drawn down in an obvious frown.

Sam quickly put his own canteen away and waited for Emma to put her shoes back on. He wondered if Gus really thought he couldn't get a girlfriend. There were always girls that looked past the outward appearances, but it seemed like Gus was talking about something other than getting a girlfriend with his looks.

Chapter Thirteen: The Darkness

"Gus doesn't think he could find a girlfriend? With that brain, why couldn't he?" he asked Emma quietly as she laced up her shoes.

"It's not really that he couldn't. It's more like it would be frowned upon in Lior. We aren't really supposed to have close contact with people in Creation."

"You mean like you and me," he said flatly.

"Well, yeah, but you're ... different," she said defensively. "I know you're one of us."

Sam pressed her.

"How can you be sure? I haven't shown any signs of manipulating Light yet—or anything—so how can you *know*?"

She stood and picked up her pack.

"I just do."

Then she smiled and brushed past him, leaving only him and the grand vista before him.

The last stretch of pathway up the plateau was more littered with rocks than at the bottom, but they made good time anyway. With his new boost in confidence from the group, Gus was pushing himself even harder than before, ignoring the narrowing pathway beside the plateau, so much so that Sam and Emma had trouble keeping up with him. Perhaps the little time they had spent in Lior had given Gus a new sense of vitality.

As they crested the top, it was nearing late afternoon, and they took a few moments to look at the view overlooking the valley from where they came.

The Darkness sat like a great black monster below them, sinking its foggy fingers into any crevice of the valley it could find. Beyond it, the outline of the clear blue pools could be seen and the crescent beaches around them. Further to the left stood the majestic snow-capped Agam Mountains and somewhere among them, tower seventy-one's Lightbase.

Leaving the edge of the plateau, they crossed a series of grassy knolls before coming suddenly upon the Woods of the Ancients. Their trunks were easily two times wider than the large trees they saw

Chapter Thirteen: The Darkness

in the forest below, and they were nearly twice as tall. It was almost as if giants should be living in them and tending to them.

"They are the oldest living trees known in all of Lior," Gus started into his tour voice again for Sam's benefit as they approached the forest. But Sam wasn't the only one interested, as they had only ever read about trees this large, not experienced them up close.

They entered the forest timidly, as if the huge living skyscrapers would somehow uproot themselves suddenly and come crashing down upon them. Instead, the gigantic pine needles dropped loudly but gracefully as a gentle breeze surprised them from behind.

"They're huge! Look!" Gus held up a fallen needle that looked more like an arm-sized stalk of young bamboo.

It was alike to a normal pine needle in every way, except that it was a hundred times heavier. Sam picked up a needle, feeling the coarse, sticky surface. Then he snapped it in half, amazed at its frailty.

They moved on through the silent forest, the only sound made from crunching needles underfoot. It wasn't long before they reached a small stream that followed the trail until it broke off into a small green pasture, bathed in soft light from a break in the understory of the great pines above.

The stream flowed from a small pool in the center of the pasture, which was fed from a rock outcropping on the far side of the pool. The water flowed freely from the side of the rock and danced gracefully into the pool. Sam reached for his canteen and bent toward the cool, clear water.

"I wouldn't do that if I were you," Lillia said suddenly. "Look."

She pointed beyond the small outcropping of rocks, where Sam hadn't even noticed the grey half-circle stones poking out of the ground.

"Oh …" he said stupidly, seeing the ancient gravestones gleaming eerily in the sunlight.

Suddenly, Emma bolted from the group and, hopping over the small stream, clambered her way up the rock cropping and disappeared into the graves. A moment later, she popped her head out from the top of the rocks and motioned excitedly.

Chapter Thirteen: The Darkness

"It's here! The Forever Light! Come look!" she cried.

Lillia hopped over the small stream and ran to Emma, the boys following behind.

The three climbed up the rocks and onto the graveyard, which only numbered twenty or so graves. The markers were obviously ancient in nature, and all were only remnants of their former glory, now crumbling stones where once great memorials had been erected.

Most did not have any writing, either because it had been worn off or because it was never inscribed in the first place, but a few displayed short phrases in an unknown language.

"Shemitic," Gus said, looking at one of the stones, his breath winded from the sprint up the rocks. "The ancient Descendants spoke Shemite."

No one seemed to have a clue what he was saying, nor what Shemite meant, but hearing about the ancient languages from his geography class a year earlier, Sam thought he would take stab at it.

"Was that Hebrew? From the Old Testament Israelites?" he said as he ran his hand across a smooth, grey headstone.

"Good guess. Actually, Hebrew is a descended dialect from Shemite. Interesting, really, how so many dialects developed from the early attempts at writing," he paused, peering at the stone Sam was touching. "I think this was a name. Ara—something. Aram? Yes, that could be it … no … he would have been the son of the shipbuilder after the flood, but that would be more Hebrew."

Sam let Gus argue with himself and walked toward the outer edge of the graveyard where Emma and Lillia were. When he came upon them, they were peering down at a small circular stone buried half into the ground, a steady wisp of blue light rising up from a hole in its center like a flickering candle in slow motion.

"The Forever Light is said to have started after the first Descendant was buried here," Emma said, waving a hand over the wisp, causing it to divert around her hand like smoke. "They were the first of our kind to come to the old city—the first half-angel half-man."

Lillia sat in the soft green grass, tilting her head back to let the sun warm her face.

Chapter Thirteen: The Darkness

"Until the Giants killed them."

"Some of the children of the Watchers and women from Creation were born different than others. Bigger," Gus explained, joining them. "They were often children of the more powerful Watchers."

"Giants … of course," Sam said playfully, but fully believed them at this point. With all that he had seen since coming to Lior, the mention of larger-than-normal beings just seemed to fit right in.

"An angry lot, too," Gus said. "Personally I am glad they live in the eastern ranges."

Lillia stood and yawned loudly, then stretched.

"Boggle said there have been sightings around Warm Springs lately, though."

Gus whirled around to face her.

"There's no way that's possible!"

Lillia rolled her eyes.

"Uh, yeah Gus, I wouldn't have said it—"

"I'm sorry Lillia, I didn't mean to—"

"It's fine," she said. "I did hear Boggle correctly."

"Why you askin' Gus? Afraid of larger men?" Emma joked with him, hoping to lighten the mood.

"No … well yes—who wouldn't be afraid of large men—but that's not why I was worried," Gus said in a hushed voice. "The last time the Giant groups were found near Lior provinces was the last time the Dark Lords were building up their armies of Metim … when Old Lior City was attacked and destroyed. They moved West because the Metim were taking their territory."

They took in his words, Sam choosing instead to watch the soft wisps of the Forever Flame. It seemed as though the information they had been getting all along was turning out to be outdated. The Darkness, Metim, no return instructions to Lior … They were truly on their own, and the danger of the situation was beginning to mount.

Lillia broke the silence as the light began to fade from the opening in the trees above.

"I don't mean to cut this off, but isn't it getting late?" she said,

Chapter Thirteen: The Darkness

pointing at the waning light in the tree canopy. "Unless you want to spend the night in the ancient graveyard."

They all stood quickly as they gazed at the massive shadows projecting on the forest floor behind them. They didn't have far to go according to the map, but if they wanted to shelter inside the City, they needed to get moving.

According to Gus, the entrance to the City on the Grave of the Renown's side was the larger of the two and the most secure, and may require some finesse to get through as it led directly into the courtyard of the former City Center.

Upon leaving the gravesites, the massive trees began to thin out to reveal more open grassland. They passed two streams before leaving the woods completely, so they filled their canteens, unsure if any existed within the City walls.

Emerging out of the huge trees brought them the last bit of afternoon warmth, so they shed their outer layers before hiking up the small rise in front of the City. Two large guard towers greeted them first, and although tempted to explore them, they moved on toward the now visible wall of the City.

The closer they got to the City, the more they could see the damage to its exterior, including several crumbling portions of the wall and a large gaping hole in the center of its immense wooden gates.

"One of the lords—they didn't know which—was able to disguise himself as a merchant man under a special cloak that a mystic gave him to mask his Darkness. He walked right past the guards," Gus said, puffing up the last rise before the entrance of the City. "Then he unleashed a cloud of Darkness so powerful that the City was under total blackness. No one could see in order to fight the Metim being let in through the front gate. The PO was blindsided—couldn't mount any sort of attack. It was over before it began."

They traversed the stone steps to the gate entrance landing. Beautiful ornate stone statues several stories tall of carved winged creatures, much the same as those inside the City Center in Lior City, lined the walkway to the gate. Although most of it was overgrown with thistle and creeping vines, it was still impressive.

Chapter Thirteen: The Darkness

The hole in the gate seemed the best place to enter, even though it would require effort just to reach it because of the height. After a bit of arguing about who would be the first to climb into the hole, Lillia finally convinced them she was the one to scale the gate since she was the best climber.

It took Sam and Gus each lifting one of her feet high above their heads to get her to where she could reach the thick ledge where the hole began. They heard a thud, and then a loud call from the interior from Lillia that she was okay, and then they were left alone, waiting for her to return with a ladder or a rope of some kind.

The sun was setting quickly beyond the gigantic pines, and they would need to find shelter soon. No one, including Gus, knew what type of danger they would find if they were stuck outside the gates when the sun went down. Even though the Darkness was a good walk from where they were, it didn't appeal to them to test its boundaries.

Almost immediately, Lillia returned with an old wooden ladder, and after situating herself back on the ledge in the hole, she started maneuvering the ladder to the other side.

But as she worked the ladder, Sam thought he caught movement out of the corner of his eye behind them.

****

Slowly turning, Sam was shaken to see a large beastly-looking creature that resembled a wolf, disfigured in its face and body, but looking more fierce and bloodthirsty than an average wolf, stealthily creeping out of a small patch of brush only a few hundred feet away.

Another look behind the beast showed two more emerging from the bushes, identical in size, but different in their deformities, still equally as revolting.

A chill went up his spine. Sam knew this was horrible timing for an emergency, because to get everyone over the gate required time and finesse of the ladder from both sides.

He also knew from stories he heard while sitting on the front porch with his Grandfather that wolves sensed the best time to

Chapter Thirteen: The Darkness

strike—when panic struck its victim and it began to run. Maybe, if he pretended to ignore the wolves, it would take longer for them to get in their ideal stalking position, giving them time to get over the wall.

Sam connected eyes with Lillia, and he gestured silently toward the wolves while holding a finger to his lips to hush her. Quickly she sensed the plan and picked up the pace of maneuvering the ladder.

Gus and Emma were oblivious, and it was better that way. If the wolves sensed their panic, they would charge early.

The ladder in place, Gus climbed the wall slowly, testing each old rung to see if it would hold him. He did not yet know of the dangerous wolves behind him. Sam kept watch out of the corner of his eye as the three beasts crept silently toward them, their movements silent in the waning evening. His blood pulsed faster the closer they got.

Lillia pulled the ladder up quickly, nearly pushing Gus down to the other side. Then she yanked it out from under him and pulled the ladder back down quickly, which prompted a surprised and appalled look from Gus. She mouthed a quick "I'll explain later" to him, which seemed to satisfy him for the time being.

Next was Emma, but her keen sense informed her something was wrong. She saw the stifled panic in Lillia's eyes and how she kept glancing behind them at something in the distance. Emma turned around to see the three ugly creatures creeping up on them and let out a horrifying scream.

At the surprised scream from the girl, the three wolves leaped to the hunt. The fastest one was also the least disfigured and knew the sound well. Instinct told him to attack when discovered, or he would lose the edge and miss a meal. The ugliest and shortest younger male behind him only had three good legs and one good eye, so he knew he would get the best meat from the kill. Bounding, they covered vast space in only seconds. The easy prey were only a few dozen leaps ahead of the wolves, racing toward the wall.

Sam sprang as if by instinct and grabbed Emma, pulling her to the now dropped ladder in front of him. He knew the chances of both of them escaping were slim, but he had to try. But something inside him told him to save her first.

Chapter Thirteen: The Darkness

Emma would have none of it. After her initial panic, she calmed herself down and turned to face her attacker, slipping out of Sam's grip. She forced her eyes to close and sent out a bolt of Light from her outstretched palm. Lillia saw what she was doing and stood inside the hole in the gate and shot a bolt as well. But the two bolts were not perfect shots. One hit one wolf in the foot, causing him to stumble only briefly, and the other only singed an ear of another.

The front wolf didn't slow his pace and was almost instantly upon Sam, knocking him to the ground with his great paw. Then he stood triumphantly over his victim and snarled and smacked his tongue, ready to take a chunk of the delicious meat lying before him.

Emma's mind raced with how she could possibly help him, but then something took her over—a wave of calmness flowing inside her like a lake after a storm. She whispered the words, "Help me Creator" out loud, then lifted her hands to fire another bolt of Light. What came out of her palm was not a bolt, but instead a shield, large and round enough to cover her and Sam, and flowing with an intense blue light. She dared not move, but kept her hand as steady as she could. She discovered it was movable as well, and could allow her to force the wolves back until she was at Sam's side. Then she bent down and examined him, relieved to find only a small scratch on his right cheek where the wolf had just barely scraped him with its claw.

"Are you okay?" she said with a shaky voice, stroking his brown hair with her free hand.

He nodded at her, then looked at the shield above him.

"How are you doing that?" he asked, watching the fearful wolves edge further and further away from the Light, pacing and whining. One wolf even lay in the grass to nurse his burnt paw.

"I don't know," she said gleefully, helping Sam to his feet and walking him to the ladder. "Let's go up together," she said, walking him in front of her, careful to keep the shield behind them.

For a moment, the wolves acted as though they were going to make another attempt at the fleeing prey, but then trotted away when they realized it would soon be hopeless with the painful shield around

Chapter Thirteen: The Darkness

them. It was the cursed blue light that they feared the most of any predator or danger in the forest.

Safely over the gate, Emma put her hand down and the blue bubble shield faded into the air.

****

"I don't know. I told you already," Emma said for a third time to an exasperated Gus, who had nothing to do but listen to the attack from the other side of the gate.

"How did you conjure up that much Light?" Gus persisted, still pacing. "We are only on the outskirts of the City and there aren't any pools until we reach the Kingdom Hall."

"I told you—" she started to say again, then stopped out of frustration. "I don't know how it happened. It just did."

"Maybe she has been practicing," Lillia chuckled.

Emma turned red.

"You know we aren't allowed to practice until we go through Mentorship next year!"

"Oh, don't get your curls all tangled. I was kidding," Lillia scowled. "But it looks like you're obviously going to be in the Magen clan."

The mention of the Magen brought sudden fear among the group. What had they just done? Their first brush with the effects of the Darkness was not good. Sam was nearly lost in the blackness indefinitely, and then he and Emma were nearly devoured in front of the others by infested wolves. This truly was no place for inexperienced Descendants of the Light.

They may be facing more dangers within the gates of the City, but it was no time to reflect. There was plenty yet to do, fear or not.

Their attention turned toward the jungle-like garden in front of them. Behind the mass of foliage lay the old city's center, an enormous castle-like structure that attempted to keep the out-of-control vegetation at bay, but was losing the battle.

The garden was grossly overgrown as well, with thick green vines

Chapter Thirteen: The Darkness

forming a scraggly hedge that spanned nearly the expanse of the courtyard, choking out most of the color from the scattered flowers that clung to survival under the invasive weeds. In the center of the garden stood a crumbling statue of an unknown warrior surrounded by stone tables and remnants of benches that were too overgrown with vines to sit.

Emerging from the protection of the gate, they picked their way carefully through the winding hedges, looking very much like rats working their way through a maze of underground sewers.

Looking for a way through, they tried every possible inch of the hedge that would lead them past the statue, but to no avail.

Finding the thinnest spot in the hedge, Emma and Lillia were able to weasel their way through the twisted vines without too many scratches or torn clothing. When Sam's turn came, he did his best to slip through like the girls did, but his frame against the densely compacted vegetation made it more difficult to maneuver. At last, after a few tears in his new robe and a rather good-sized gash across the cheek, he freed himself and waited for Gus to go next.

The moment Gus thrust himself into the hedge, however, it became instantly clear he would become hopelessly stuck in the twisted vines.

They attempted to help him any way they could, but the vines would not let him go. Lillia tried her best to clear the area around him with a Light bolt, but it wasn't nearly as strong as it was next to the Lazuli pool, and she only managed to singe a few of the thicker tangles. Emma took from her pack a small knife and began sawing to remove some of the smaller branches, but she knew it was going to take much longer than they had time for. Gus was thoroughly stuck, and none too happy about it either.

It was Sam that came up with the plan to have Emma attempt another protective shield around Gus. Like the wolves, the shield would hopefully push the branches back enough to allow him to slip through.

"I don't think I can produce another one," Emma said sadly as Gus thrashed about in the thicket, attempting desperately to free

Chapter Thirteen: The Darkness

himself. "And that was different! Sam was in real danger—I didn't think, I just did it."

Grabbing her shoulders and spinning her to face him, Sam looked deep in her eyes, like she had done so many times to him before to get him to step out of the box he had created for himself. He had been so closed-minded, but now he was beginning to see so much more.

"You can. You did it before," he spoke softly to her, even as she began to show the initial signs of panic. "Now you just have to find that same passion to do it once again. Think about those wolves on the other side of the hedge about to get Gus. Use that to help free him."

She sighed and held up her hands in front of her, not exuding much in the way of confidence.

"I will try."

They all watched as a slow trickle of blue emerged from her hands, then sank back into her palm … emerging once again, stronger, and growing to a semicircle bubble around Gus. The branches resisted the Light, then parted slowly as if making way for a king stepping through the crowd.

Gus pushed into the Light and easily freed himself from the branches that bound him. Emma's eyes were closed, but something told Sam she could see what was happening anyway. They all watched her with fascination as she followed Gus through the opening with her shield of Light, then skillfully drew it back into her hands. Then she opened her eyes and a smile crept to her face.

"I think I'm getting the hang of it," she said.

It was the second time they had seen the shield flow out of her palms, but they were still stunned with the results. No one they knew of in Lior had been able to successfully manipulate Light as well as she did before Mentorship. It was a feat that was not only discouraged because of its danger that could come from inexperienced Light manipulation, but also because it was nearly impossible without extensive training.

After that moment, the others viewed her a little differently. She had saved Sam from the wolves, and now freed Gus from his

Chapter Thirteen: The Darkness

prison of vines. It had taken Gus and Lillia years to even produce a small amount of Light that emitted from their palms since they had first attempted it, but Emma had mastered it in only two separate moments. Although she tried desperately to hide it, there was an obvious glow on her face that followed her around, not out of pride but out of accomplishment.

With Gus back on his feet, they found themselves in the center of the overgrown garden. They passed the statue of the helmet-clad warrior, who was resolutely but gracefully holding his arms in the air as if producing a bolt of Light. Closer observance showed he was missing a hand, and his shield lay in pieces on the ground—dark green vines wrapped around the larger of them.

At the other end of the garden, the City Center loomed in front of them, and there were obvious signs of destruction from a simple glance at its exterior. Once a great magnificent architectural centerpiece, fortified with a thick brick and iron gate and dotted with numerous guard posts atop its now crumbling walls, the City Center now only lay empty for the mice and birds to make their nests.

They crept slowly along the vast exterior of the outside of the center, half out of the desire to explore the rest of the garden butting up to the structure, and half out of fear for what they may encounter. Ever since the encounter with the wolves, each was on edge and more aware. The wolves had been outside the gate when they attacked, but it was possible others could have entered through another route.

The center was sprawled throughout the City, which Gus had informed them was the model for a castle built in the mid sixteenth century in England.

"It was a conspiracy all in its own as to how the plans were leaked into Creation in the first place," he argued, which as he talked, suddenly gave Sam an idea.

Reaching into his backpack, he pulled out his journal that was given to him by the Sterling's and the others. He had written a few entries already since arriving, but as they traveled, he had felt compelled to write more. Now, he opened it to a blank page as they

Chapter Thirteen: The Darkness

walked and began tracing the outline of the Old City's City Center, including the overgrown garden.

When they had reached the end of the immense outer wall, another wall appeared, separating the center from the rest of Old Lior City. Fortunately, the majority of the wall was completely destroyed from the attack over fifty years ago, and the four friends easily picked their way through the rubble and into the heart of the City.

Chapter Fourteen
The Holobook

The Old City had seen destruction. There were only a handful of standing buildings, and the rest were either heavily damaged or completely demolished, leaving only outlines in the overgrown grass like remnants of ancient cities after a thousand years of erosion.

Sam wondered how powerful the Dark forces must have been to make entire buildings nearly disappear. He imagined the day when the Metim and Dark Lords walked through the streets, bolts erupting from their palms as they destroyed anything in their paths and murdered anyone they could see. Judging from the expressions of fear and sadness on the others' faces, he could tell they were thinking the same.

No doubt the others were also considering the fact that Dark creatures could still be lurking amongst the ruins, and he shuddered at the thought of being caught in the open with only one of them able to fight back with any true accuracy—a shield as her only weapon.

Moving through the City proved to be swift, even with the rubble from the buildings all around them. They saw no sign of life, and strangely, no sign of Darkness—not even the remnants of its deathly

Chapter Fourteen: The Holobook

effects. Gus pointed toward the town center where the remains of a large market once stood. In the center were numerous vendor stands, some still standing, like tiny miracles in the midst of certain destruction.

Just beyond the vendor stands, a lone white building high upon a grassy mound stood gleaming in the afternoon sun. It was taller than any of the other structures in the City, including the City Center, partially due to its domed roof with a majestic spire that rose well above the rest of the City. Much like the intact fruit and tea stands, it too looked curiously as if no damage had come to it. As they neared the white building cautiously, Gus echoed what all were thinking.

"I believe that temple is where we will find our library," he said, shielding his eyes against the brightness of the building's reflection of the sun. "I am surprised it is still standing, honestly."

Sam looked at the glorious building, which looked as though it could be dusted off and put back in operation. "Why would they leave this one and completely destroy everything else?"

Gus thought for a moment, then glared at the earth and rubble in front of the building. "Possible it was untouched because the pools of the City's Lazuli are beneath it."

"Dark Lords hate Lazuli," Emma added.

"That's what we are counting on."

It was simple in its construction, but magnificent nonetheless. Apart from the dome in the center, the rest of the design reminded Sam of a bland version of the Greek Acropolis. Atop its main columns near the stairway to the arched doorway were the words "*hen be'ene Yahweh*" chiseled into the stone above their heads.

"I believe it says 'Grace in the eyes of the Lord,' if I'm not mistaken," Gus said.

"The Creator Himself," Lillia added quietly.

They climbed its wide steps to the entryway then gingerly walked through the open door into the foyer, Lazuli lanterns out in front of them.

Inside, there was surprisingly more light than they had anticipated, which illuminated the large stone statue of a dragon in flight in

Chapter Fourteen: The Holobook

the center of the room. Below was a winged creature looking up toward the dragon, not as one would of a lower position, but in awe. Surrounding the magnificent stone creatures were four stone columns that glowed with flowing Lazuli light.

Both statues were completely intact, and except for the small mountain of dust that covered everything, the rest of the temple looked as though it had not aged one day since its last use.

They progressed through the foyer, pausing only briefly to look at the statue. Then they passed through another entry into a much larger room that contained a semi-circular amphitheater and stage, much like the one from the City Center. On the far end of the amphitheater was yet another entrance with a wooden door, and instinctively they headed toward it, a winged creature carved ornately into the frame above the entrance.

Gus stood in front of the entrance, staring at his journal he had been studying since arriving at the temple.

"I don't have the schematics on this building, but I would bet an electron's negativity that would be where the library is," Gus said with a snort, his voice echoing loudly off the stone walls.

Emma and Lillia rolled their eyes and shushed him, easily opening the wooden door to reveal another smaller room leading to a long hallway with many doors along its length. In front of them were stairs and another smaller hallway to the left of the stairs. On Emma's suggestion that the doors may be offices for Council members, they agreed to try the shorter hallway first.

Their guesswork paid off, for the shorter hallway led them directly to a balcony overlooking the rotunda library. Above them was a stained glass centerpiece, shining brilliant sunlight into the room. Along the walls below them were thousands of books, and from the looks of it, in perfect condition.

"I guess your theory was spot on there, prodigy boy-genius. The library is still standing," Lillia glanced sideways at Gus, who suddenly noticed that all of them were looking at him.

"I can only speculate, but I suppose that yes, the Darkness was

Chapter Fourteen: The Holobook

reluctant to attack the library because of the Lazuli reserves below it. The Office of Research must have overlooked it when they returned to study the City," he said with the slightest twinge of self-satisfaction.

Lillia hopped onto the railing and dangled her feet over the edge to the open floor below.

"Or they decided to keep it secret from everyone …"

Gus held his finger in the air.

"That was my second theory."

Emma furrowed her brow.

"But why would someone want to keep it protected—or hidden—enough to make up a story that it was destroyed?"

"It is strange," Gus said thoughtfully. "With the Lazuli pool directly below it, it would be near impossible for Dark creatures to get near it. Even Dark Lords would have trouble with it."

Lillia dangerously swung her leg back over the railing and hopped down.

"Well, there's a set of steps over there. Let's stop talking about it and see if we can go dig up some answers."

Gus smiled awkwardly at her.

"That's the Lil' I know," he said to her, at which she immediately rolled her eyes dramatically.

They walked down the marble staircase, marveling at the ornate carvings on the wall and the winged creature etched into the stained glass above them. The books were terribly dusty, but Emma discovered a few old scraps of cloth behind one of the desks to wipe books off as they searched.

After an hour or so of reading histories of Lior, legends of how dragons and dinosaurs came into existence, stories of giants, and how the Darkness had corrupted them all, they were getting frustrated. It was long, grueling work, even if interesting.

But they were discovering that most of the texts in the Old City's library were nearly identical to those in Lior City, or they were written in dialects of the old language, which Gus had trouble translating. Their next goal was to search for Boggle's lab.

🌲🌲 Chapter Fourteen: The Holobook

When her stomach growled loudly during an especially difficult translation, Emma put her foot down for a short break as they hadn't eaten much of a lunch.

"There's a spot with a table on the far side of the room where we can sit," Emma said cheerfully as she snatched up the backpack of food.

"I don't suppose we have any meat pies and mashed potatoes, do we?" Gus said jokingly.

"I could go for a cup of coffee too," Sam added as they sat down at the small stone table behind a particularly dusty shelf of books.

"I vote that tonight we find a house that's still standing and use the kitchen to make a late dinner," Lillia suggested, to which they all seemed to agree, but knew was unlikely.

"But for now, we get to eat honey and nut butter sandwiches," Emma said cheerfully while Gus pulled out a small bag of large red leaves and dropped one into his cup of water.

"Oh! You have Gunia leaves!" she dropped the knife she used to spread the mixed nut butter on the bread.

Gus smiled.

"I do … and I brought enough for everyone," he said.

Watching the others, Sam dropped one of the leaves into his cup of water and watched it suddenly begin to turn red, then bubble rapidly like it was about to boil over the sides. He took a sip gingerly, unsure of what to expect. The liquid was sweet, like a strawberry would taste, but the large carbonated bubbles exploded in his mouth, unlike any soda he had ever had.

"It's like nature's carbonation," Gus said.

"Good, isn't it?" Emma half hollered across the table.

Sam let one of the bubbles pop in his mouth before answering.

"Yes, I am not usually one for pop, but this isn't—" he stopped short. In the moment that he spoke, he noticed the large chips in the stone wall behind Gus, and then the outline of a hidden door behind a bookshelf that had been moved and then hastily shoved back into place.

Chapter Fourteen: The Holobook

"Where does that lead?" he pointed to the concealed door behind Gus.

They all turned to look at the hidden door behind the bookshelf, which was cleverly hidden if one wasn't aware of its existence.

"I wonder …" Gus trailed off, suddenly forgetting his sandwich and leaving the table to investigate.

They all followed him to the shelf. Sam was right. Behind the bookshelf, which looked as though it was made to be able to slide back and forth, was a small crack outline in the wall in the shape of a narrow doorway.

"Highly unusual," Gus said quietly.

"Could be the reason why you don't have a schematic of the library," Lillia suggested.

Without consulting the others, Sam attempted to pull the shelf back. Seeing it wasn't opening, Gus and Emma joined him, but it wouldn't budge.

"There has to be a secret switch or something," Gus conceded.

"Yeah, 'cause this is so a haunted mansion," Lillia snorted. "Why don't you try one of the book levers?" she said snidely.

The others ignored Lillia's skepticism and immediately began pulling out the books in the shelf. After a minute or so of examining each book and Lillia nearly laughing herself silly, they gave up. Dust now hovered like a cloud above them.

Emma began chastising Lillia for her lack of support, and they argued back and forth while Sam and Gus searched the shelf for more clues.

Letting out a muffled sneeze from the dust flying off the books, Sam was suddenly reminded of Chivler and his dusty old bookstore.

"The journal…" he thought aloud, remembering the strange drawings that now curiously resembled the old library tucked in the pages between the journal entries. He pulled out the old worn journal Chivler had given him from his backpack.

Gus poked his head out from the far side of the shelf and, before he could finish the sentence "What journal?" his expression turned

Chapter Fourteen: The Holobook

to a look of horrified surprise followed by child-like excitement as he saw the winged creature stamped into the cover.

"Oh wow! Where did you get that?" he yelled, snatching it from Sam's outstretched hands and then gently opening its fragile binding.

"Uh, Chivler gave it to me," Sam uttered, surprised at the sudden attention. "I haven't had a chance to read much of—"

Gus stood open-mouthed.

"I can't believe you have it!" he said. "It must have ... I can't imagine how ..." he stuttered.

"So what? He found a journal. What's it good for?" Lillia said.

"I believe it's the journal the PO has been searching for ... the one they think someone broke into Chivler's to find! The journal of Julian Lawrence!"

Lillia replaced a book neatly on the already disorganized shelf, for which everyone else eyed her questioningly.

"The banker with the dreams?" she asked. "The one they think was a prophet, right?"

Gus ignored her, his eyes searching the pages of the book he had taken from Sam.

"Other than his dreams," he paused for a moment, distracted by a certain page in the leathery contents, "it can't be ..." he trailed off, nose still buried in the dusty source.

"Gus. Back with us please," Emma said gently.

Gus was shaken out of his trance suddenly, knocking over the remainder of his Gunia drink, of which wasn't much left, but as it splattered across the floor, the cup bounced on the stone floor with a clang.

"Right! I knew it!" he exclaimed. "I can't believe it. Remember what Boggle said about his assistant 'Jules?'"

"Jules is short for *Julian* ... Julian Lawrence!" Emma exclaimed.

Lillia was dumbfounded.

"Didn't see that coming."

Gus paced in front of the dusty shelf.

"He must have been standing right here in this library over two hundred years ago."

Chapter Fourteen: The Holobook

"And?" Lillia stood.

Gus scowled.

"Well, then I would assume that the break-in and Chivler's disappearance would certainly now be the doing of a Dark Watcher or Metim."

"For the journal? Why would they care about it?" Lillia asked solemnly.

Gus didn't look up from Julian's journal, but after a moment, walked over to the bookshelf and drew out a series of letters in Light on the wall near the hidden entrance, a small sliver of Light trailing behind his finger.

"Because of this," he said with finality.

Immediately upon its last letter, the Light trail following his finger blinked out and a low rumble could be heard behind the bookshelf, which shook violently with the noise. Less than a moment later, the shelf creaked and groaned once again, then slid away from the wall to reveal the outline of the door in the wall. They waited, Gus's finger still in the air next to the wall, until a plume of dust blew from the outline of the door, then the door swung slowly inward.

A blue stone now glowed brightly above the frame of the hidden door, unseen to them when the shelf was in the way. Carefully they moved forward toward the dark entrance, covering their mouths to keep from inhaling too much of the dust cloud, which also stifled their congratulatory cheers upon Gus's accomplishment.

****

Emma begged to be first into the library's bowels, her renewed confidence from the wolves incident helping to quell some of her previous fears. She stopped in the door frame below the blue stone, holding her hand in front of her for a moment. At first, nothing happened, then, a blue glow began to emerge from her palm. It began to flow out of her hand, then as she closed her fist, it crept back, forming an irregular-shaped globe of Light that stuck to her palm, pulsing with flowing blue Lazuli light.

Chapter Fourteen: The Holobook

They all watched her in awe as the globe increased in size and intensity, then weakened, then swelled again to the point where it was nearly too bright to look directly at. Then she opened her eyes and turned, the globe still glowing in her hand.

"I was thinking I could do this in the garden. I guess it's not so hard after all," she smiled at them, then disappeared into the entrance, the glow following her and illuminating the long narrow hallway.

Lillia and Sam followed her, but Gus lagged behind, and out of the corner of his eye, Sam could see him holding his hand outstretched in front of him, attempting to produce his own Light globe. A small flicker shot from his hand, but then disappeared. He sighed heavily and followed them into the entrance.

The hallway was long and narrow, the walls made entirely of stone, but unlike the library where a dust cloud still circulated the disturbed books, this seemed strangely clean. No doubt they built it to withstand pretty much anything.

They followed the glowing globe from Emma's hand in front of them, seeing no doors or openings in the hall, but as they clomped across the echoing stone floor, they noticed the numerous picture frames that held paintings of various Chancellors throughout the years, all dressed in full white-robed attire. Some of them wore red cuffs as did the Chancellor back in Lior City, but others wore the familiar colors of their representative halls. Each frame was lavishly decorated and free of dust, as if they were hung on the wall yesterday.

They moved forward toward the blank wall of stone in front of them at the end of the hall, half expecting it to open up like the library entrance did once they approached.

Emma held the glowing globe out further in front of her as they drew closer to get a look at the wall they neared, but as she did, she took a step into nothing, and suddenly the light, the hallway, and Emma disappeared into the darkness below.

It was stifling darkness, as black as the cloud of Darkness outside the City. A scream rang out, echoing down the hallway.

Emma, Sam thought, but Lillia was already there, skidding to the edge of the abyss where she had disappeared.

Chapter Fourteen: The Holobook 🌲🌲

"Light! Gus, get a lantern!" she barked, peering down into the darkness. "Emma! Are you okay?" she called into the blackness, and suddenly the light from Gus's blue lantern lit the hallway where the scene was taking place.

Lillia was on her knees, peering into the hole where Emma disappeared.

"Emma! Speak to me girl!"

With the dim light now available, Sam and Gus searched the spot where Lillia pointed, attempting to make out Emma's form.

"Where is she? I can't see her! How can you see her?" Gus panicked, waving the lantern into the darkness.

Lillia snatched the light from Gus and held it lower into the hole. There, barely visible in the stone pit, was Emma's crumpled body lying face down. For a moment it looked like she was not moving, then slowly, she turned over on her back and stared at the three fearful friends above her.

"I—I'm fine ... I think."

She checked herself over, then stood up and looked around her prison.

"It seems I stumbled into an old stairwell, except there are no stairs. Oh! Hold on."

Slowly the secret of the stairwell began to become visible as a small blue light emerged from her palm once again. Set into the wall were steps flush against the stone, making it impossible to descend.

Emma then faded once again out of sight from the friends above her as she explored the bottom of the stairwell where it disappeared under the wall at the end of the hallway. Gus stood and hurried to his backpack a few steps away and immediately began emptying it, while Lillia handed Sam the lantern and disappeared back into the darkness of the hallway. Sam was alone to watch for Emma to return from the shadows.

Moments later and the contents of his backpack now strung all over the stone floor, Gus produced a rope from his backpack that looked just long enough to reach to the floor of the stairwell with some slack to tie it off. Looking around the bare walls, the two boys

Chapter Fourteen: The Holobook

searched for somewhere to tie the rope off. As Sam and Gus worked out how to get all of them down—and then up again—Emma reemerged from under the stairwell.

"Guys, you are never going to believe what's down here," Emma said.

"I don't think whoever built this wanted anyone to know what was down there," Lillia appeared suddenly from the darkness. "It's an optical illusion. The hole is masked so that if a person walks up on it, they can't see the stairwell."

"Not very welcoming," Sam said.

"No," Gus dropped the rope suddenly and looked around the hallway once again. "I don't think it was supposed to be a hole."

Then he walked over to the wall and began running the palm of his hand over the smooth stone.

"What are you looking for?" Sam asked, but Gus didn't answer. Instead, his hand stopped suddenly about midway up the wall, and he turned and smiled at them.

"Emma, back away from the opening!" he called suddenly, then he plunged his hand into the wall, his arm disappearing up to his elbow, and then he twisted something inside. Suddenly, the floor shook loudly, and a stone ledge emerged slowly from the side of the hole, locking itself into place, and thrusting itself upward to become level with the hallway floor. The hole where Emma had fallen was gone, and the floor looked like it was meant to be there the whole time, with not even the slightest crack showing.

Keeping his arm in the hole in the wall, he turned it again the opposite direction, and the hole opened up once again, and with another twist, ten stone steps jutted out noisily from the wall until a solid stairway was visible to all.

"Nice work, Gus!" Emma called from the bottom of the stairs.

"Yes, good thing we brought you," Lillia slapped him on the back and snatched up her pack just before bounding down the steps.

Sam followed her, but not before noticing Gus removing his hand from the wall, which too looked like an optical illusion, mirroring

Chapter Fourteen: The Holobook 🌲🌲

every other part of the wall. This was certainly a place meant to be kept secret.

Once all were down the stairs, they followed Emma into the darkness under the hallway wall, which at once she dispelled with the Light from her palm.

Emma led them through a doorway, and suddenly she didn't need her Light anymore. Inside the small but open room, there were lanterns of Lazuli, which lit up the modest stacks of books organized neatly in shelves built into each wall. On one side of the room was what looked like an elaborate workbench and a curious-looking box that strangely resembled a computer. Instead of a monitor, however, from the moment they entered the room, the shape of a woman dressed in long white gowns and a hood projected into the air above the box.

"Boggle's Holobook project!" Gus rushed over to the workbench, leaving the others to catch his backpack mid-drop and lean all their gear against the wall. "I can't believe it's still working after this long!"

Seeing they weren't going to pry him away any time soon, Sam, Lillia, and Emma decided they would have a look around the rest of the bookshelves in the small room. Unlike the larger library above them, the books that lined the walls in this room were smaller, less sophisticated in their bindings, and very plain. Numerous workbenches dotted the open spaces where there were no books, each littered with various parts and inventions for different projects. Quickly it became obvious that this was Jerma Bogglenose's secret lab, or a part of it at least.

Emma, Sam, and Lillia took it upon themselves to dig through the workbenches looking for the Watcher Stone, or evidence of it, but they had no luck and went back to the strange-looking books.

"I wonder why he would want it hidden so well?" Sam picked up a book from the shelf and scanned the dusty cover.

It was unlike any book he had ever seen. Although the cover was identical to a normal book, upon opening, the pages were like flexible glass with no words on them. When he touched the inside cover,

Chapter Fourteen: The Holobook

however, the first few pages suddenly came to life with words and images that literally leapt off the page in blue brilliance.

Emma was instantly at his side, having put her own book down on a small reading table where a Lazuli lantern sat.

"All of these books have been converted into Holobooks," she said, touching the words and letting them dance around her fingers. "I wonder if you can search for something just by asking. Say … the Watcher Stone?"

"No, you can't. The inside pages are locked by a passcode. You are only seeing the book's authorship information." Gus came up beside them and pointed to the hologram on the workbench. "But she can tell us …"

Chapter Fifteen
Incident No. 497

Standing in front of the hologram box, the four friends asked the image of the robed woman various questions about the library, the books, and ultimately the Dark Legend, Prophecy of Light, and the Watcher Stone. Each time, with the exception of providing basic information about her creation date and her model type, and with multiple apologies, she always responded with, "I will need to know your entrance passcode before I can search."

Frustrated, they sat down to give themselves a moment to collect their thoughts. Gus rifled through Julian Lawrence's journal looking for answers while they sat, but for a long while no one spoke. They had come so far, and yet they were being stopped cold suddenly by a simple passcode.

Sam was clueless about what to offer, having not been in Lior long and not having the same experiences as the other three, but he still racked his brain for some glimmer of promise that could keep them going forward.

"All this information right in front of us and no way to see it," Emma said glumly. "And no other doors in here that I can see."

Chapter Fifteen: Incident No. 497

Sam pulled out of his backpack a napkin of dried fruit and handed some to the other three. At the strange looks he received because the fruit was not on the "official packing list," and much to Emma's dismay, he sheepishly told them Sayvon had given it to him before they left.

Gus sighed, chewing on a piece of dried pineapple.

"Honestly, I am surprised we made it this far. It is quite an accomplishment what we have already done."

"Yeah, I kind of figured either we'd be dead by now or she would have lost her mind," Lillia chuckled and pointed at Emma, who responded with an angry look in return.

"What I don't understand is … why were people so wrong about the library being destroyed? You would think someone would have been out here to investigate regularly," Emma said.

"Only members of the Office of Research were coming out to the Old City after the destruction … not that it matters, because I haven't heard of anyone who has been out here for decades," Gus said.

"Oh, great. I'm sure we are breaking some law coming out here," Emma said with a scowl.

"Oh, well, I just figured," Gus stumbled over his words, "since your folks knew we were coming …"

"Yes, and that was probably before they realized there was new growths of Darkness around the old city," she sputtered.

Lillia leaned forward and drew in the dust that had accumulated on the stone floor.

"It just seems to me," she stopped, then sighed as if unsure as to continue her thought. "The whole thing just seems a bit off, that's all."

Gus was suddenly interested.

"What do you mean, Lil'?"

"I don't know …" Lillia proceeded carefully with her words. "I just keep thinking about the cloud of Darkness outside the City, how *big* it was. Gus is almost never wrong about these things, but there it was, right before our eyes."

Chapter Fifteen: Incident No. 497

"City leaders have been wrong about the Darkness before," Emma countered.

Lillia scowled.

"But if the Darkness was bigger—and newer than they thought, wouldn't the right people know about it? I just feel there's more to it, okay?"

While Lillia wasn't quite making sense, what she was saying was somewhat true. It was weird. And although he hadn't been here long enough to become comfortable with the way Lior did or didn't do something, there was something that felt amiss. Like Lior was engulfed in some mystical cloud that wouldn't let them see what was going on. Mr. Sterling was right.

Emma huffed loudly, sending a plume of dust that had settled on her arm into the air. "So you think there's some sort of conspiracy in the Council? There's no way. The leaders of our city would fight and die to help keep Lior safe. I trust them to make the best decisions for Lior, and you should too!"

"I'm not saying anything like that, but your dad did say—" Lillia understood that Emma was getting defensive and tried to change her tone suddenly, but it was too late.

"Yes you are!" Emma was now on her feet, her words reaching ear-piercing pitches in the small room as she stamped her feet in protest. "You have always said that there are people in the Council and Protector's Office that are corrupt! But you and I both know that hasn't been the case for thousands of years! The Council is a holy, very honorable position, and they know it. And you are tossing it off like they are a bunch of cheap politicians! You have always hated the Council!"

"That's not true, Em'. I am just saying that not everyone is perfect or can know everything, even your dad. He said there could be problems," Lillia attempted to defended herself, but there was no use.

"He was just being cautious. I'm sure Sam heard him wrong ..."

Suddenly an idea hit Sam like a bug hitting the windshield of a car. While only half listening to Emma and Lillia argue, he had pulled out

299

Chapter Fifteen: Incident No. 497

Miss Karpatch's instructions she had written from Gus' open journal on the floor and was glancing over it. *Road to knowledge,* he thought. No, it couldn't be. Could she have meant the library? "Known by the Creator," the note said. Was she telling them how to get the passcode for the Holobooks?

Sam attempted to block out the two arguing and focus on the problem, which to his relief seemed to be second nature now. He was glad too, because the stone walls were not meant to have so many emotions ricocheting off of them without inciting the slightest bit of craziness. At least it was Lillia who was the quieter of the two this time.

"What about other names for the Creator?" he interrupted their argument loudly, which was still in full swing, both girls now red-faced and stamping around the room.

Emma's tone shifted suddenly at Sam's question.

"Yes," she huffed, her face still red. "There are quite a few. What about it?"

"We tend to use the name Creator partially because the name has come to be familiar for what we know Him by, but also because Liorians have chosen not to use his names out of respect," Gus said. "You call him 'God' out of ignorance, but we know him by what he has *done* for Descendants."

Sam knew that Gus didn't mean to insult him by calling him ignorant, but it still stung a little. And it was true … the human race was ignorant about God, or at least what they knew about Him. But to be fair, no one in modern society had ever seen Him.

"So, what if we tried some other names of the Creator as the passcode? I was looking at Miss Karpatch's note and—"

"Brilliant," Gus stood suddenly, dropping dried fruit in Lillia's lap.

They made their way back to the workbench and called out various names they knew for the Creator, such as "Healer" for the gift of Light healing that was given to Liorians after the first great battle with the Darkness almost four hundred years ago, and "One who Hears" for guiding Descendants, and "Unknown Source" as the provider and supplier of Light.

Chapter Fifteen: Incident No. 497

Gus was able to come up with a few others that were in the old language, but none of them were accepted by the robed hologram woman. It was beginning to look like another dead end. No one wanted to admit it, but they were rapidly running out of ideas, and time.

But suddenly, the answer came again to Sam. If the information in the secret library was to be protected, from whom would it need to be protected? Who was the one group that would absolutely hate to say the name of the God of the Descendants? Right away, he knew the answer.

"What do the Dark Lords call Him?"

****

"Why would we want to say that? This is a city of Descendants, not Darkness!" Emma scolded. "Besides, they hate to call Him—" she stopped suddenly, a large smile creeping to her dirt spotted cheeks. "Oh …"

"They call him Tanash," Gus said quickly. "The Abandoner."

The robed woman turned and pushed an imaginary door open with her hands, then disappeared.

The room grew steadily brighter as the Holobooks began glowing shelf by shelf from words illuminating their pages. It was as though someone turned on under cabinet lighting.

The robed woman returned, asking them how she could help, to which they unanimously told her "The Watcher Stone." She then rattled off a warning about the content of the data being unsuitable for those under the age of mentoring and those without the proper authority to view secure official printings, then pointed to a shelf on the wall farthest from them where a single book glowed red among a shelf of blue.

Gus led them quickly over to the shelf where a book glowed bright red, even through the thin layer of dust. He cradled the glowing book in his arms and opened it gingerly, revealing its gleaming pages as the others gathered around him. As he touched the pages, the binding of the curious book turned suddenly back to an irides-

Chapter Fifteen: Incident No. 497

cent blue, except for one page, which still glowed red. He thumbed carefully to the glowing page and opened it up for everyone to see.

A peculiar scene glowed in full animation in front of them, with children running around a large tree, laughing and throwing themselves on the ground as if they were possessed by happiness. A sun had shined brightly in the background, but now began to melt into the scene, turning black like the ground below, and the tree. The tree twisted and turned where it was, almost as though it were captive to the darkening scene. The children lay perfectly still, and laughing at the twisting tree above them, which now began to take the shape of an arch.

The carefree expressions of the children changed to horror as dark fluid shapes burst from the tree-arch, billowing like a cloud above them and melting into the scene like the sun. Then the scene disappeared altogether, leaving nothing but words and a diagram of the black arch.

Not wanting to see it again, Sam turned away from the book and the other three to find a spot to sit down and catch his breath. It was the black arch and the dark swirling shapes, right there in real life for all to see. Emotion suddenly came over him, and all of the feelings, sleepless nights and anger he had been burying inside rushed to the surface, and tears began to make their way to the corners of his eyes.

Why did it affect him so much? Nothing had made him feel this way before, not even his foster parents leaving without so much as a gesture as they stood on the train station platform.

The image of the arch sank into the pit of his stomach and churned there. Something—he couldn't figure out what—was driving these feelings, like the calm before a storm.

Emma slid up beside him, putting her arm around his shoulders.

"Was the book like your dreams?" she whispered softly.

Her touch was deep and soothing, like a ray of sun poking through the cloud on a chilly afternoon. She looked deep into his eyes, able to see more of the real emotions he harbored than anyone else in his life.

Chapter Fifteen: Incident No. 497

He lied flatly, telling her the dust was getting to him, even though he knew she would see right through his attempted deception.

Instead of challenging him, however, she simply laid her head on his shoulder.

"You know, when I was old enough to understand what I was, not fully human, I felt strange, like I wasn't supposed to be in Creation anymore. I looked at everything differently—school, other people, even food, but my parents were always there for me, helping me to understand."

She held out her hand and a small blue light appeared, swirling in her palm like a trapped wisp of blue smoke.

"They told me not to be afraid, to embrace what lie ahead for me. My fear is what confused me, and I had to let go of it before I could understand. Now that I have embraced it, my faith has allowed my gift of Light to grow."

Even though he was only half listening, he understood her completely. She wasn't throwing his lack of faith in his face; she was sharing the wisdom she had obtained when she had feared her own future. It was valuable insight, and he treated it as such. Coming from Mr. and Mrs. Sterling, who he had come to respect highly, it was more than likely worth listening to.

Gus stood suddenly, looking perplexed, with his nose buried in the glowing book.

"I can't believe it," he said loudly. "It's here ... all of it. Sam's dream, the Sha'ar gate, the Watcher Stone, everything."

The three others were instantly crowded around him, staring at a page of glowing words.

"Look here," Gus pointed to the second paragraph. "It's from the Protector's Office daily records. It says—"

"Oh, just give it to me," Emma said as she snatched the book from his hands. "I'll just read it ..."

Chapter Fifteen: Incident No. 497

Incident No. 497 During the Creation year eighteen ninety-four, a young girl named Opus Wrenge was admitted to the Lior City Healing Center with dreams of dark flowing shapes emerging from an unknown arch into Themane. In her possession were sketches her parents, Mr. Jarston and Ginerva Wrenge, claimed to have witnessed her draw. Miss Wrenge was kept under watch for the time of one month by the Office of Seer Affairs, during which time no dreams occurred. Upon being discharged, however, her parents reported that the dreams returned, and thus also began daytime delusions. Reports were never investigated, but included unfounded warnings that the City of Lior would be infiltrated by the Darkness. No follow-up was initiated, as the Office of Seer Affairs did not give it credible thought. Mr. Jarston and Ginerva Wrenge have agreed that, in the best interest of Opus and the well-being of Lior City, Opus's condition would be better cared for outside the City walls ...

"Wow, newb. That pretty much sums you up—the dreams and being delusional ..." Lillia scoffed, but Sam ignored her, looking strangely at the name of the little girl from the account.

Wrenge. Where have I heard that before?

"Oh my," Emma said suddenly, staring at the glowing words on the page intently. "I am so stupid to not see this right away."

"What is it Em'?" Gus attempted to retrieve the book once again from Emma's hands with no luck, as she maintained her death grip on the binding.

"Wrenge," she repeated. "Old lady Wrenge from the forest by our hideout spot."

"What? Seriously?" Sam was floored. "That crazy lady in the woods?"

"Oh wow. I didn't see that coming," Gus smacked his hand on the wall behind them loudly, sending another plume of dust particles soaring through the soft blue light of the room.

"She had dreams just like Julian and Sam?" Lillia asked.

Chapter Fifteen: Incident No. 497

And one went crazy and the other one died at the hands of the Dark Watchers, Sam thought. *Not the best odds.*

Gus peered at the Holobook for a moment, then turned the page. "Look."

A crude drawing of a small stone took up nearly the entire page, obviously drawn in a hurry, but at closer look, the digitized image was turned into a three-dimensional holographic image that, when touched, would allow them to see all sides of the Stone.

Gus reached out and held the holographic Stone in his hand, turning it in all directions. On the face of the Stone, the four colors of the four regions of Lior began to become visible. A black marbling rippled throughout its exterior.

"These are some other drawings old lady Wrenge drew." Lillia pointed at the margin. "It says it right here."

She was right. Both the arch and the Stone were clearly labeled as evidence from incident No. 497, drawings from one Miss Opus Wrenge.

Gus turned and stared off into the corners of the dimly lit Hololibrary.

"Gus, what is it?" Emma pried suddenly.

Gus looked down at the journal and then back up at the other three nervously. "Seers that are found in Lior see events that are happening now, right now, as we speak."

"So?" Emma scowled. "There are many found with that gift and work in the Seer chamber. Why does that matter?"

Gus sighed.

"Prophets, on the other hand, can see events in the future."

Lillia and Emma gasped suddenly, but it took Sam a moment to understand what was going on. Then, it hit him. If Julian Lawrence and Opus Wrenge were prophets, according to the Prophecy of the Key, two of the three prophets would have already fulfilled their role in the Creator's Promise.

"Which would make *him* the third prophet," Gus said grimly.

Chapter Fifteen: Incident No. 497

****

Emma stared at the glowing image of the Watcher Stone Lillia was holding in her palm from the Holobook.

"This has gone too far," she gestured to Lillia and Gus angrily. "There is no way Sam is a part of this. Wrenge, I understand, she's crazy, and Julian worked with Boggle here in the City, but that doesn't make them part of the stupid Dark Legend, or the Prophecy, or whatever."

"We have to consider the fact that they could be connected somehow," Lillia interjected. "I mean, there are quite a few Descendants that believe the destruction of the old city started the clock to the Creator's return. Just because the Prophecy isn't what you think it should sound like doesn't mean it's not part of the Creator's plan."

"Yes, I realize that," Emma said flustered. "But the Dark Legend has no place in the Creator's Lior. It's just—not—right."

Lillia laughed.

"You think we are just impenetrable, don't you? Look around, Em'! This world isn't perfect!"

Emma's eyes dropped.

"I know … I just can't believe something like this could be happening."

In a strangely sensitive gesture, Lillia put her arm around Emma, hugging her tightly.

"I know you want Lior to be the way it always has been, Em', but you have to remember, our past has not always been so wonderful. There were dark days that we ourselves have never experienced."

"We also must remember that just because the Dark Legend came from their mystics, doesn't mean we have to believe it's true," Gus said. "Or at least the outcome."

"But the Council believes it," Sam said.

"Not—all of them," Gus answered. "But we must be ready for the possibility that the they may make the connection with Wrenge and Julian as well."

Chapter Fifteen: Incident No. 497

"What if their dreams are from the Darkness, and that is part of the deception?" Lillia asked pointedly.

Gus paced in the dark room, the only light emanating from the Holobook woman and the soft glow of the book they held. The Lazuli in the lantern had long since burned out.

"I don't know what to make of it at this point," Gus admitted.

Emma let out a frustrated huff, but none of them said any more about it. It wasn't a pleasant thought to wonder what the Council might think of the situation, but to not at least discuss it would be foolish.

Sam thought about the arch and his dreams. They were deeply powerful, and often he awoke afraid of what he had seen, but something about them did not seem like it was of the Darkness. Whatever it was still drew him, but the more he tapped into it, the less it seemed like a threat.

He stood suddenly and walked over to the holographic woman. For some reason, he kept thinking of the cloaked person at the gate in his dreams. He used something to open up the arch for the swirling dark shapes to pass through. It looked like a small stick, or maybe a stone, that was inserted into the leg of the black arch.

It had to be the Watcher Stone.

But what did Ayet Sal have to do with the Stone? It had to be part of it, but what?

Looking at the patient glowing image of the tiny woman in front of him, he decided to try something different, something he had feared discussing and was afraid to ask.

"Please search for Valley of Death," he told the glowing figure in front of him.

"I'm sorry sir. There is nothing found," she spoke softly.

"Search for 'Ayet Sal' please."

The woman didn't move.

"Valley of Ayet Sal," he tried. "Shadow Valley. Ayet Sal Valley."

None of them worked. He knew the term. Why wasn't it hearing him?

Chapter Fifteen: Incident No. 497

"Mind if I try?" Lillia was standing next to him and seemed to know right away what he was attempting to do.

"Ayet Sal," she said slowly, her pronunciation sounding more like a rush of wind than words.

The woman bent down, turned something in front of her, and then went silent once again.

Behind Gus, the outline of a door suddenly appeared with a great thud and a puff of dust. Gus, who was deep into a Holobook's pages, jumped at the noise. With a thunderous roar, the door slowly opened to reveal a brightly lit room on the other side. The blinding blue light stunned them at first, but as their eyes adjusted, they could see the many shelves lining its interior.

"How did you do that?" Sam asked with his mouth open dumbly.

"Its Hebrew. You say it without vowels. Boggle says it all the time," Lillia flipped her hair and walked straight up to the door and slipped inside.

"Yeah, well, too bad he had no clue how to get into his own dumb lab."

The others, dumbfounded, followed Lillia into the glowing room, where it took several minutes for their eyes to fully adjust from being in the dimly lit Hololibrary. The shelves of the tall, open room were filled with artifacts of all shapes and sizes, some made from gold, silver, or precious gems, and others from simple stone or clay. Three large stone tablets nearly the size of the door hung on the wall in the back, filled with writing in another language.

"It's not Hebrew or Shemite. I don't know what script that is," Gus said, looking very puzzled. "It is very complicated, from the looks of it."

"Guys, look," Emma pointed suddenly at one of the shelves underneath the center stone tablet.

A small Stone about the size of a quarter lay gleaming in the center of the carved shelf. It was walnut-black in color, with marbled streaks of differing colors crooking their way through the center of the Stone.

Chapter Fifteen: Incident No. 497

"It can't be," Gus inched toward the Stone. "It was here just like Mr. Sterling said ..." he trailed off.

"Gus, what is it?" Emma asked quietly, her hushed whispers echoing deeply off the stone walls of the tiny room.

"I *believe* it is the one and only lost Watcher Stone. No longer lost if this is the real deal, I suppose." Gingerly, he picked up the Stone and held it carefully in his palm. "See the four streaks throughout the Stone representing each region of Lior?"

"Unbelievable," Lillia added excitedly. "But too *easy*."

"So *why hasn't* anyone in the Council come for these things?" Sam wondered.

"Miss Karpatch said that the Office of Research indicated there was nothing left, remember?"

Sam remembered the night Mr. Sterling asked him to go. He had told him there was reason to believe that the library could still be standing even though the Office of Research said everything was destroyed. It was strange, but then again, with the Darkness around the City, who could blame them for fudging a few reports to avoid it?

Lillia reached her hand out to feel the soft ridges in the Stone that, at her touch, glowed slightly.

"I don't think—" Emma began, but then something made her stop mid-sentence.

Sam knew what had quieted her instantly, as he suddenly felt another presence sweeping over him like a rush of wind blowing throughout the room. He couldn't explain it, but mixed emotions poured over him suddenly, leaving him breathless. There was a longing, a heavy loneliness, and then there was hurt—deep, intense hurt. He didn't know who, or what, the feelings came from, but he did know that it originated from the presence in front of him.

Without thinking, he reached out in front of him to attempt to touch the presence, but it quickly rushed past his face, sending a surge of warm static electricity throughout his entire body.

It wasn't the feeling that made them afraid, but the unknown of what had happened that caused an uneasy feeling to come over them.

Chapter Fifteen: Incident No. 497

It was as though someone was watching the entire group in the room. Sam couldn't see anything or anyone, but he knew something was there—or had been there. A quick glance at the others was enough for them to call it a day.

****

"Guys, I think we should head back up now," Emma said.

"I agree." Sam heaved big breaths of air as if someone had just punched him in the gut.

"What—was that?" Gus was wide-eyed, his face sheet white.

"Maybe some leftover spirits were trapped here after the invasion of the City," Lillia snickered, but none of them were interested in her humorous remarks.

"Let's go, now, *please*," Emma pleaded with them.

Lillia nodded as Gus reached for the Stone and handed it to Emma, who pocketed it.

"I'd feel better if you kept track of this, Emma," he said quickly as they exited the glowing blue room to the dimly lit Hololibrary, where the door promptly thundered closed behind them.

Lillia suggested the temple just outside of the library for the night, but Gus reminded them that they needed water badly, and Lillia agreed that even if it meant sleeping outside of the comfortable library, it wouldn't be too awful to have water for coffee and a fire to fend off the night chill. Not to mention the rest were not too interested in spending the night that near to the strange wind they had just experienced.

After climbing back up the hidden stairwell, back through the library and out the giant temple door, they made a beeline for the nearest watering site, which Gus said from the map would be back near the old City Center. They agreed that the best spot from there to make camp would be the garden courtyard since it provided the most wood.

After setting up camp underneath the broken statue in the City

Chapter Fifteen: Incident No. 497

Center's garden, and dinner of rice and dried meat with root cakes was on the fire, they discussed their options for getting back to the Lightway and back home.

"We could find an arch," Sam suggested, noting the cylindrical map holder poking out of Gus's backpack. "Wouldn't there be an arch here?"

"There used to be, but they moved it to the new city. It was a big to-do with its size and all," he said.

"We could walk back," Emma offered, knowing instantly it would be a bad idea, as Gus reminded her of the Himalayan-sized mountains between them and Lior City, not to mention the nearly twenty days it would take to travel it, or the potential leftover pockets of Darkness that awaited them in the forest depths.

"I've been thinking about our options," Gus continued, "and I think that, unfortunately, our best and quickest route is to get to the Outer Dunes."

Emma frowned.

"You mean the outpost south of the Great Swamp that has been abandoned for years? Why would that station still work? No one has any reason to go there anymore."

"Not to mention the swamp is one of the worst places to be in Lior ... and most dangerous," Lillia added.

"I figure it's worth risking. Otherwise, we have a long hike over the mountains to Deep City ... at least a week," Gus sighed. "Plus, if the boathouse is still here in the old city's waterway, we can float through the swamp instead of walk. It would take us two days at the most."

Sam scowled.

"Why can't we just go back up to the Light station on Mount Halpa?" he asked. "It's got to be the closest one."

Gus nodded.

"True, but the cliffs of Mount Halpa are sheer three hundred foot faces on almost all sides—and below zero at night. It would be a nearly impossible trek for even a seasoned mountaineer."

Chapter Fifteen: Incident No. 497

"We don't have the gear for that, newb," Lillia pinched his cheeks in jest. "Wouldn't want to frostbite that pretty little face. Then Emma wouldn't be able to make out with—"

"That's enough, Lil'," Emma said suddenly, but the irritation she felt wasn't directed only at Lillia. The idea that all of them were stranded so far from the home they knew was disheartening, to say the least, but the fact that no one had left them clear instructions was the most frustrating.

"I just don't understand why they would have sent us out here alone." Emma accepted a cup of coffee from Gus. "I mean, we have only been through the gate three times in our lives! And never outside the City alone!"

"You're right. Princesses deserve better," Lillia joked.

"I'm not kidding Lil'!" she flashed an angry glance at Lillia. "This place is really dangerous!"

Gus sighed deeply.

"I just wish we could somehow help them locate the spy within Lior."

"If there is one," Emma retorted.

Suddenly the coffee no longer tasted good. It was now cold, and there was no sugar or cream to tone down the strong flavor. Sam wondered if a good night's sleep would do them all good, perhaps clear their minds a bit, and he was tired anyway from all the walking, and arguing.

Before he opened his mouth to suggest turning in, however, he glanced over at a very uncomfortable Emma Sterling, who was fidgeting with her coffee cup. From the little time he had known her, he could tell that something about the conversation was making her nervous.

"Emma, what is it?" he asked her calmly.

Her eyes welled up with tears instantly.

"I—um, I can't believe I forgot about this . . ."

Sam squinted over the light of the fire at Emma, whose hair glowed soft blues in the light of the moon overhead.

"Em', we really need to know."

"I overheard dad talking with some protectors," she blurted out.

Chapter Fifteen: Incident No. 497

"And there have been incidents of Darkness alarms going off in the City Center at strange times."

Sam scowled.

"That's funny. I remember that happening when I was there with …" he stopped suddenly, aware at once of the consequences his words would bring.

"With who?" Lillia demanded.

He didn't want to answer her, but after saying the words, he couldn't turn back. It couldn't be true anyway. The man was in their cabin circle, for crying out loud.

"When I was with Mr. Calpher," he said quietly.

Lillia snorted.

"Talister Calpher? High Council member and overseer of the Sons of Light? Wow, that's a conspiracy if I ever saw one."

"It's not true!" Emma thrust her finger in Lillia's face. "He's our friend and has done great things for the City! You can't just go around calling people spies!"

"I never called him a spy. I just said it would be quite a conspiracy if it was him," Lillia defended.

"She's right, Lil'. We can't call him a traitor from an isolated incident Sam saw," Gus stopped them, "but we can discuss it in the morning. We will need our sleep for where we are going."

No one argued with Gus' suggestion, with the exception of Emma, who didn't move. When the rest of them noticed, they stopped and turned to wait for her. She seemed as though there was something left to say, so they waited for her to spill it.

"I've been worried about Uncle Calpher for a little while now," she forced out. "He's been acting strange lately, leaving the City for days and—" she stopped. "I just can't believe it could be him."

"It's not," Sam lied. Lillia and Gus nodded along with him to soothe Emma's fears.

"I just can't help but think what could be happening in Lior while we are gone. It must not be good," Emma finished.

No one answered her, because they had nothing to offer. They had all been thinking it since the moment they stepped through the Lightway, but Emma had been their beacon of hope, their island of faith in a system that seemed to be quickly disintegrating.

Chapter Sixteen
The Outer Dunes

The next morning, over coffee, they watched the soft patches of fog lifting from the cool of the night.

Undoubtedly, Emma's discouraging words the night before hit home, to all except Sam. Since the fall of the old city, there had been no report of Darkness spreading anywhere in Lior. Metim were at their lowest numbers ever, and three of the four most dangerous Dark Lords were locked away. While rumors had been floating around for years about the growing Darkness, the ideas had been dismissed on account of the word of the Seer Chamber and the Protector's Office. But if one had the right access to some of Lior's highest offices, a grand deception was possible. Given the level of secrecy in the Seer chamber and the PO, it was conceivable that the right people could pull it off. But the thought that the point man for the conspiracy could be Talister Calpher was none other than shocking to say the least.

"When were they going to let all of Lior know about the alarms?" Lillia asked over breakfast. "And how could you just *forget* about something like that 'till now?"

Chapter Sixteen: The Outer Dunes 🌲🌲

Emma seemed in no mood to answer her, so instead she put her efforts into crumbling the dried meat into a pan with the edible plants Lillia had found growing near the castle. Sam was just now waking up and accepted a cup of coffee from a quiet Emma. Gus was sketching a copy of the Watcher Stone that sat in front of them all next to the fire.

Gus looked up from his drawing and took a sip of coffee.

"I've been thinking. We know it isn't logical that they would let us come alone without a meaningful reason," he said.

"Yeah, they wanted us out of the City for Sam's sake," Lillia said.

"I know that. But there's something more. Like perhaps they already know the perpetrator and we are part of a greater plot to catch him. Perhaps we are only to trust them. Maybe it isn't Mr. Calpher at all, and he has to play the part just like Mr. Sterling."

"Wow Gus," Lillia nearly choked on her breakfast. "You are starting to sound like a Mentor with all that faith."

"I've been—trying to see different perspectives."

Sam was watching Gus draw the Stone, noticing that he was taking detail to a new level. There were hundreds of books already in the library with drawings of it, but Gus was intent on looking for something specific, perhaps whether or not it was the real thing.

Gus' theory was good, however, it didn't explain Talister setting off the alarm before going into the Chancellor's office. Or perhaps it was the Chancellor that had dealings with the spy, and Talister was only waiting for the right time to expose him.

At that moment, however, instead of pelting Gus with questions, Sam decided to bring up the more immediate problem: how to get back to Lior City. While the options were already limited, he couldn't figure out for the life of him how they were going to get back down the plateau and around the opposite side of the City to where Gus pointed out the swamp where they would have to make their next leg of the journey.

"So what's our plan?"

Gus seemed to anticipate the question.

"According to the maps that you found in Lior's main library,

Chapter Sixteen: The Outer Dunes

there should be a boathouse ..." he pointed behind them, "*that* way, which I believe is a way out of the City to the swamp."

He pointed to the far end of the ruined city, past the temple where the edge of the buildings just seemed to drop off into the horizon on the other side.

"If I am not mistaken, there is an old underground escape route down the plateau—" he paused for a moment, then set his finished drawing on the large stone setting next to him, "—in an underground river, I believe."

Lillia shook her head in disbelief.

"First you tell us about the mosquito-infested nightmare of a swamp, and now an underground river? I'm afraid to ask where we end up next."

Gus chuckled nervously as he tossed the remainder of his coffee on the last of the coals in the makeshift fire pit.

"I promise nothing," he smiled.

They packed up camp, and after poring over the map and any alternative routes if needed, they set out to find the curious boathouse that should be resting on top of the plateau. It was quite a drop from anyone's perspective, and all four friends were a bit anxious as to how the boat would get them to the swamp below, if in fact the boathouse was still in functioning order.

With Gus' uncanny ability, it took only a few minutes to find hidden routes on the map that led them through the maze of broken rock and bricks that littered the streets of Old Lior. Before lunch, they had located a possible entrance to the boathouse and the escape route to the forest floor below the plateau, and Gus had estimated that they would hopefully be on the forest floor by late afternoon.

They were still skeptical that there would be a boathouse hidden inside the City since the City was perched high on the plateau with no visible waterways, but no one argued with Gus and his mapping abilities. If he had done the research and said there was a boathouse that would lead them out of the City, they trusted him. He had been right about most everything else so far.

Chapter Sixteen: The Outer Dunes

Dark and hidden in the side of a rock was a small stone opening that looked as though it had been heavily guarded in spite of its conservative design. While Gus was certain that this was the only way in, currently the entrance appeared to be merely a hole into a dark passageway to which all four were reluctant to enter.

"Alright, I will go first again," Emma stormed ahead finally, snatching a lantern from Gus's hands. "I swear I am with a bunch of cowards," she huffed, entering the passageway.

The other three shrugged and followed, unsure as to what had happened to give their friend such courage in such a short period of time.

It was intensely dark in the opening, even with the lantern Emma carried, and until Gus produced another from his pack, the meager light that extended from Emma's feet beneath her robe was the only light that could be seen in the stifling dark passageway.

The cold stone walls of the passageway seemed to go on forever as they climbed upward toward what felt like nothingness in front of them. They had caught up to Emma, but even with the extra light, they were eager to be rid of the feeling of being trapped in the depths of another secret hideaway of the old city.

On and on the passageway continued, twisting and turning in various directions, sometimes taking sharp curves to make them wonder if they hadn't just been walking in circles.

Just as they were beginning to believe they had entered an abandoned mineshaft instead of the entrance to a boathouse, a glimmer of light showed ahead of them and they hurried toward it, shuffling through the sandy floor as quick as they could in the darkness without risking a fall onto the unknown of what lie below them.

Blinking to adjust for the light of the room, the group emerged into a huge open cavern with a spectacular stained glass dome above them, partially broken but still retaining its original beauty, gracefully spraying blue, green, and yellow sunlight. In the center of the room were the remnants of a three-pronged stone structure.

Chapter Sixteen: The Outer Dunes

"This must be the arch room!" Gus said excitedly, pulling out his map and making marks in his journal as the others explored the cavern.

"And boathouse," Sam held up his hand for silence. "Water … that way," he pointed toward the far end of the cavern.

Gus sadly pried himself away from the arch remnants. Although the arch had been moved, the room still contained many exquisite stone carvings into the columns throughout the cavern.

"It must have been a fully functioning hideaway for many of the City's people in times of danger. Look, there's the kitchen, and the latrines," he pointed at the areas sectioned off within the massive room as they walked through the arch rubble. "I wonder why they didn't use this place when the City was burned."

"So many people died out there for nothing when there was a perfectly safe place in here," Lillia said gravely. "What a waste."

"I'm not sure they had time, Lil'," Gus responded carefully.

"Look, guys. Boats."

Sam didn't mean to rush them, but they were on a mission to get home, and he was ready to digest what they had learned and collected from the City, including the Stone. The adventure was exciting, but he didn't want to let Mr. Sterling down. He was skeptical, yes, but loyal to the promises he made.

The boathouse was hidden in a semicircular cove at the far end of the massive arch room where a small but manageable river flowed swiftly through the middle of racks and racks of tiny canoe-shaped wooden boats. Upon immediate inspection, there didn't seem to be any damage to them, but they were old, and certainly showed their age.

"Think those are seaworthy, captain?" Lillia punched Gus in the arm sharply.

Gus, who was going over every inch of one of the boats with a lantern, held up beside his nose, determined that he would see the positive side of the situation.

"Actually, they don't appear to have any reason they couldn't

Chapter Sixteen: The Outer Dunes

float," he said. "Not quite sea worthy, but able to traverse through an underground river? Certainly."

"I just can't believe there's an underground boathouse on a plateau inside the City," Sam stared at the water as it meandered past the sandy cavern floor.

Emma immediately began trying to wrestle one of the boats off the rack. With the exception of her seemingly undying courage, Emma, too, seemed ready to get back to the City.

"People from the Old City did it, and so can we," Gus muttered as he helped Emma with the boat, which looked just big enough for three people sitting in line.

"Yep, and they would rather brave the City being burned to the ground than join the death river ride," Lillia added.

"Two of us can ride in one, and two in the other," Sam suggested, reaching for another boat.

Emma was immediately at his side, slightly touching his hand to let him know she wanted to be the one to ride with him. He blushed at the thought that she actually felt safe with him. She, in fact, may be the only one that had ever trusted in him for anything. None of his friends back home had that kind of faith.

One partner positioned the boats in the river while the other partner got in each boat. Then the first partner counted to three before the other climbed in and let go of the loading ramp.

****

Immediately the river carried them into pitch black. Then began the queasy rhythmic flow in the dark current, pushing them swiftly through the curves and dips in the underground waterway for over an hour until each of them was forced to take turns hanging their heads over the sides of the boat.

"Why does this remind me of a theme-park ride?" Sam mumbled sickly as the boats slowed to turn an especially tight bend in the river.

"I hate rides like this," Lillia called out in the dark behind them. "Actually, I hate rides in general."

🌲🌲 Chapter Sixteen: The Outer Dunes

"As do I," Gus said with a burp.

Emma punched Sam suddenly in the leg, startling him in the worst of his queasiness, and finally sending up solid chunks in his throat.

"Cheer up you sickies! I think I see light ahead!"

Sure enough, around the next bend was an opening in the dark abyss. A beckoning light appeared in front of them as they approached, turning out to be another smaller cavern. The glass dome overhead spilled enough light into the room that even the darkest corners were as though the sun were shining directly into the room.

The river carried the riders in the boats in a snakelike pattern around the center of the cavern until they had passed through its interior completely. The water began moving at a more rapid pace the closer they traveled to the far wall. Enamored with the beauty of the various colors dancing happily on the walls from the dome above, no one paid attention as the boats made their way to the opposite end of the cavern. It was only then that they noticed the faded signs warning them of the danger ahead. The sign read:

**Make your exit sure,
or a certain end you will endure!**

"I think we were supposed to get out in the cavern!" Gus called back to Emma and Sam from his boat, which was already picking up speed.

Panic settled in the two boats as they hurdled toward the rushing water that disappeared into the pitch-black waterway in front of them. The opportunity for bailing out of the boats into the cavern was becoming increasingly impossible as they picked up speed.

The boats disappeared into the underground river once again, moving at such an incredible rate that even the intermittent blue from Gus's lantern as it clung to the side of the boat became only a distant speck that bobbed to and fro in the current.

Finally, after what seemed like an eternity of being slammed from one side of the boat to the other, scraping their hands on the sides of

Chapter Sixteen: The Outer Dunes

the wall sometimes just for balance, the river began to level out and the boats slowed to where they could just hear each other above the noise of the rushing water behind them.

As the second boat caught up to the first, Lillia pitched her head over the side of the boat just in time to heave into the dark water once again.

Lillia's sick floated by, bathed in eerie blue from the lantern's light, and upon seeing it, Sam did his best not to heave his own lunch again. It was at that moment, head over the side of the boat, that an even more eerie feeling swept over him.

"Uh ... do you uh ... what's that—" he could only manage to utter, hearing a soft dull roar reverberating off the water as he struggled to hold in his vomit.

"I can't take any more of this," Emma winced as she, too, looked green even in the blue glow. "Please Lord no more."

The dull roar grew louder.

"Guys, seriously, what is that?" Sam lifted his head up wearily as a tiny speck of daylight suddenly illuminated in front of them.

"What are you talking about?" Lillia started, then stopped suddenly. "Oh, I hear it too! Sounds like a waterfall!"

They began to realize their peril as the daylight ahead of them disappeared when the boats dipped into another stretch of swift current. At about that time, Gus' lantern smacked into a rock that jutted from the narrow river chute, sending glass and blinding Lazuli light bursting into the cavernous emptiness until it vanished into the dark water behind them.

Now in complete blackness, the boats leveled out once more. Sam and Emma's boat bumped sharply into Gus and Lillia's, nearly throwing Lillia out of the boat.

Panic set in as another bend in the river suddenly met them with a rush of warm fresh air and a distant soft light casting strange reflections on the violent water.

Sam attempted to reach out and grasp the walls that he knew were there, even though he still could not see them clearly, but they were

🌲🌲 Chapter Sixteen: The Outer Dunes

moving so fast that his fingers just bumped along until one struck a jutting rock, and instantly he felt the blood trickling down his hand and the searing pain that followed.

"Duck down and hold on!" Lillia yelled out suddenly in the darkness ahead of Sam and Emma, barely audible above the roaring falls, which loomed closer with every drenching wave from the growing rapids lapping against the boats.

Sam obeyed, and he felt Emma instantly curl into a ball and turn to lay sideways on his lap. He wrapped her up in his arms like a cocoon.

The boat hurled itself around bends in the underground waterway to the left and right, the rapids increasing in strength so badly that Sam found it difficult to hold on to the slippery makeshift handles of the craft and still keep Emma from bouncing around all over the place. Water gushed over them both, soaking them to the bone.

Suddenly the roar ahead of them was upon them, and sunlight pierced into the cavern through the opening in the side of the plateau that swallowed the underground river into the open expanse below. The boats slowed momentarily as they approached the falls, and they had only seconds to make a grab for the side of the cliff before the river spilled over the side to the rocks below.

Gus saw the chance and heaved himself onto the small ledge just inside the opening of the cliff, then snatched Lillia's arm before she tumbled over the edge, pulling her from the boat before it disappeared into the roar. Sam knew he would have to do the same with Emma, but he would have to hop in front of her first before he too could grab the ledge.

Fortunately, Emma let go of him out of instinct, allowing him just enough maneuverability to crawl over her before they reached the cliff. Gus reached out and grabbed his shirt as Sam grasped firmly on the ledge, and then he reached back to yank Emma from the boat.

Although she was stiff from fear, she managed to understand that she needed to hold on to Sam's arm instead of clinging to the boat. Together, Gus and Sam dragged Emma onto the ledge with them.

Panting heavily, the four laid on the ledge for a long while before attempting to sit up and survey the scene. They knew the closeness

Chapter Sixteen: The Outer Dunes

of their brush with death, and it kept them wary and quiet as they watched the thirty-story waterfall pound on the rocks below. Lillia pointed out the pieces of their boats swirling around the falls, the turbulence of the water churning them around like a blender.

When they had regained their nerves, Gus led the search for a way down the face of the cliff, but they didn't need to look long as a winding slender path presented itself near the back of the ledge.

"Who in their right mind would use this path of death?" Lillia muttered as they picked their way down the thin ledge.

"For once, Lil', I share your negativity," Gus acknowledged, his back pressed firmly against the rock behind him.

Emma had produced a rope that they used as a hasty lifeline down the path, but they still took their time getting to the bottom. It was almost nauseating moving so slow next to the thundering falls, and Sam looked forward to when they would get to the bottom and make camp for the night.

Gus had told them that they would need to stop again at the head of the swamp even though it would only be mid-day, because it would take them an entire day to travel through the swamp, and stopping in the middle, according to Gus, was a very bad idea.

"Other than the fact that Giants occasionally hunt down this way for the larger mammals, there are said to be monstrous reptiles of the dinosaur species that live in the swamp," Gus told them.

After what they had just gone through, a few extra-large lizards didn't sound so bad. But then again, upon remembering the razor-sharp teeth of the Sarse they encountered upon entering Lior, perhaps it was best to follow Gus' suggestion instead of trying to push through and get stuck having to set up camp along the banks.

Once down from the plateau, they fished their water-logged packs from the bank and filled up their canteens from the churning falls, then walked through the trees a short distance to where a rather large vine-covered stone boathouse sat proudly next to the river. Inside, there were more of the small canoe boats like the ones they sent careening over the falls, but there were minor differences, like a small hatch where they could place their packs—which were now certainly

Chapter Sixteen: The Outer Dunes

drenched—and a sail. They found two of the boats that were in the best shape and dragged them out of the boathouse to the bank of the river, then the four began setting up camp and drying themselves and their packs next to the fire.

Gus and Sam immediately gathered a stockpile of wood for the fire in hopes of warding off any larger animals that wandered in their direction. They circled the tents around the fire to make sure they didn't wake up cold and in the dark.

Emma got to work frying some dried pork and beans, while Lillia and Gus looked over the route they would take the next day.

"Looks like the river turns into the swamp not too far from here," Gus said over lunch. "I think the best route is through here," he pointed at a thin line running through the crooked body of water.

There were many fingers jutting to and fro on both sides throughout the great swamp, snaking like thick vines down a brick wall. For a moment, Sam had an awful feeling that they would get lost in the twists and turns, having to spend countless days eating turtles and insects and running from untold creatures who thought of them as a perfect midmorning snack.

"I heard it was really easy to get lost in the Great Swamp," Emma pushed her beans around her plate. "How can you be sure it's the right way?"

Gus shook his head sadly.

"I can't."

There was an uncomfortable silence while they all pondered the consequences, as they had already had many close calls. It seemed as though everyone was feeling the exhaustion from all they had experienced up to this point, and the added uncertainty about how they would get home was beginning to take its toll on their spirits.

Strangely, it was Lillia who brought them back around.

"It's okay," she cleared her throat. "We will just have to try the route and pray it's right."

Emma nodded wearily.

"As long as we do it together."

Sam leaned his pack against a rock near the fire and laid his head

Chapter Sixteen: The Outer Dunes

back and closed his eyes. Before long, the sun was beginning to edge down the far side of the treetops, and the shade was lending itself to a bit of cool in the breeze. The river bubbled and danced in front of them, the waterfall still easily heard deep and steady as it bombarded the rocks below it.

At some point, Sam must have nodded off, for instantly he was no longer at the river, but standing in a Lightbase overlooking the sun setting over the ocean.

****

He looked around him, and for a moment he thought he was alone, but then discovered he was not. There, standing in the doorway with their backs turned to Sam were the figures of two men standing in the shadows. The tall man was dressed in beautiful robes, but the smaller man wore a simple, bland robe. Sam could not see the faces of either of the men where the shadows fell, but he heard them talking in low, deep voices, and he strained to hear what they were saying.

"Have you considered my offer?" said the taller man with a deep, throaty voice.

"Do I have a choice, really?" said the smaller man just above a whisper. "Either we invite chaos into our city or endanger all of Lior."

"I have been told you have the ability to hide him," the robed man said.

"Yes, we have been able to hide ourselves for a long time now, but that doesn't mean that if the Prophecy is true we will be able to stop it from happening."

"We will deal with that later," the man turned toward the window facing the ocean, his robes swishing as he moved. "We need him gone from the City immediately. I have already set things in motion in the Council. He will be in your hands shortly."

The smaller man sighed.

"I suppose the fact that you will become Chancellor from all of this is only out of genuine concern."

The taller man turned sharply from the window to look at him.

Chapter Sixteen: The Outer Dunes

"I do what's best for Lior. Nothing more," he said sharply.

The smaller man nodded and then the scene slowly melted away from him, the voices fading into muffled noises.

I know that voice, Sam thought as his eyelids began to flutter open and he left the paralyzing effect of sleep, but while the dream still lingered, for some reason he couldn't pick out the person to whom the voice belonged. He strained to listen once again, but the voices were too distant to hear clearly.

****

"Have a good nap?" Emma said as Sam blinked in the evening sun throwing its last glimmers of light on his face.

She was stirring the dying fire, attempting to revive it as both Gus and Lillia slept on their packs. It seemed as though they all needed a long nap. Unwisely, they had not even thought about posting a watch, and Sam wondered if Emma had stayed up for that reason.

"It was good, thanks," he responded to her question. "Did you get a nap too?"

"Yes. Lillia and I took turns on lookout while you and Gus slept," she said as she placed another large branch on the fire.

"I'm sorry," he said genuinely, feeling suddenly bad.

"You both needed it," she said smiling. "But don't worry. You will return the favor sometime."

He smiled back, still blinking in the light. He couldn't take his mind off the dream that was still fresh in his mind. While he was glad it wasn't the same he had been having, it wasn't a normal dream either—if that was even possible. It felt as though he had actually been there, even after waking up—just like in the Dark arch dream. In any case, he was beginning to become accustomed to the dreams, almost as though he expected them to happen.

"You had another dream, didn't you?" Emma didn't even look up from the pot of coffee she was nursing over the fire.

"How can you know that?" he was stunned.

Chapter Sixteen: The Outer Dunes

"Call it a gift," she smiled again. "But you also wear your thoughts on your sleeve."

He thought for a moment about making up something to tell her instead of the real dream, but couldn't find a reason not to tell her the truth. He had always had trouble trusting—he knew that—but this was personal, his dream. It didn't seem important enough to talk about, but by the stubborn, anticipated look on her face, she wasn't going to let him drop it.

"I saw two guys in a tower," he started. "They were talking about getting some guy out of Lior and hiding him. He seemed important for some reason."

Emma considered his words, then went back to stirring the coals under the coffee pot.

"Who were they?" she asked quietly.

"I don't know. One was short and talked quietly but the tall one had shiny robes and had a booming voice like—" he stopped short, because he had just discovered where he had heard that voice before. "Mr. Calpher."

"Oh," she said quietly. "Did they say who the guy was they wanted out of the City?"

"No," Sam recalled. "Just some guy, I guess. But neither of them seemed too happy to have him."

The water in the pot began to boil as the sun continued to fall below the trees. Sam and Emma felt it best to wake Lillia and Gus up for some dinner and to gather some wood for the night before they settled down. It seemed like a safe place where they were, surrounded by the river on one side and on the other, a smaller rock ledge that made a horseshoe shape behind their tents. Before long, they had a good roaring fire burning with plenty of wood to keep it going for much of the night.

Not wanting to make the same mistake of sleeping without planning ahead for a guard again, Gus offered to take watch throughout the night while the others slept. With the sun gone, the breeze blowing through the tent was enough for Sam to slip under

Chapter Sixteen: The Outer Dunes

the blanket. The sound of the river was enough to put him to sleep for the second time that day. Exhaustion seeped into his eyelids once again, and before long, he had slipped into a deep sleep.

****

The next morning, camp was packed up quickly and the boats were loaded with the gear. Just to make sure they wouldn't have any mishaps, they strapped the packs down with a simple rope net they found in the boathouse.

They were getting a later start than they wanted to, but Gus informed them that his calculations didn't factor the river current pushing them faster than if they were in the still water of the swamp, and therefore they could make up some time.

When they were convinced the boats were river-worthy and they had enough provisions to make it through the swamp, they dowsed the fire and climbed into the boats, shoving off from the bank. Immediately, Emma shoved a napkin full of black and red berries into Sam's lap as they were paddling away from the bank, urging him to try a few.

"They are the best raspberries in the world. Trust me," she told him.

Sam tilted a few from the napkin into his mouth, letting the berries melt on his tongue. They were so sweet it almost tasted as though he had just eaten a jelly doughnut.

"They are great," he slipped a few more in his mouth. "When did you pick them?"

"This morning, when you were snoring like a moose," she chuckled, dumping a few more in his lap.

"There are moose here?" he asked genuinely.

His question made her break out into a snicker.

"Of course there are," she said. "Lior isn't that much different than Earth, except a little more well-preserved."

"But dragons?" he pressed. "Those aren't normal earth creatures, are they?"

Chapter Sixteen: The Outer Dunes

"They were, actually ... from Creation. But like all creatures after the fall, the Darkness changed them," she said.

"Made them evil, you mean."

She stopped paddling and sighed.

"Yes, sort of. But dragons are different. I believe the Creator gave them the ability to see the difference between Light and Darkness."

Sam turned on his bench to face her, lifting an eyebrow.

"Seriously? Like they can choose right and wrong?"

Emma picked up her paddle once again, pretending not to notice the doubt in his voice.

"Yep. I am sure of it. Some Liorians think they are of the Darkness, but I think we just don't understand them. I'm surprised the dragon was even at the opening parade this time. There was a petition to ban it last year."

"Do they live here? In the swamp?" he asked.

"No. They stay in the mountains to the north near the Giants," she replied. "Sometimes you can see them from Lior near the mountains, but that's rare. They only keep Orono in the City because they think he is one of the rarest breeds of dragon."

"Orono? That's his name?" Sam remembered the beautiful blue dragon walking down Main Street. He was jaw-dropping, even without all the glimmer and lights attached to his wings. Orono's eyes seemed to penetrate through the darkened street like golden plates reflecting the brightest of light, and even though it was in chains, the dragon seemed to understand its place among people—not one born out of violence, but of peace.

Sooner than they expected, only an hour into their journey, they rounded a small bend and came up on the swamp. The river seemed to melt right into its stagnant, murky water, disappearing below its dark surface.

The river pines changed suddenly into wide, arching mangroves that hung their dark, invasive branches over the water. They paddled into the vast abyss in awe, feeling suddenly very small and insignificant. Emma, who had really begun to do much better with her constant fear, was once again slunk down in her seat with her head on the pile

Chapter Sixteen: The Outer Dunes

of gear. Sam didn't mind, except for the fact that now that the river wasn't moving, he was having to do most of the paddling.

"I hate swamps. Their so ... so smelly and *swampy*," she made sure to verbalize.

Gus and Lillia slid through the black water to Sam and Emma's boat and caught up alongside them. Gus was already unfolding the worn map that showed the reaches of the massive swamp.

"While it isn't exact, I think whoever created this map may have been pretty thorough," Gus said. "I think we will be heading ..." he pointed somewhere in the distance ahead of them, "... over there."

Not knowing much about maps or cartography, the other three were perfectly content to let Gus take the blame for getting them lost, and therefore assume responsibility for all of their deaths should it happen. Normally there would be more protest and questions for showing resolute leadership in a time like this, but no one really had the desire to challenge him, nor did they have a better solution to offer.

They paddled into the dark, potent body of water, keeping to one side of the shoreline as the swamp began to widen. Deep patches of fog began to overtake their little boats the further they paddled, so to keep from losing each other, they tied a rope to the stern of each craft.

Scanning the banks for possible predators, they paddled earnestly for another hour before realizing how hungry they were. Instead of stopping for lunch to save time and avoid run-ins with any large predators, Emma put together a small lunch of dried meat and cake in the boat and handed it to each of the others before serving herself. Although it was neither hot nor enjoyed next to a roaring fire, it was filling and it kept them paddling.

Throughout the afternoon, they paddled for what seemed like eternity around endless stumps poking their massive heads out of the soupy water. They maneuvered numerous deceiving channels that led to the depths of one of the endless back channels. As the sun waned, they began to grow concerned about getting stuck in the swamp before the sun went down entirely.

Chapter Sixteen: The Outer Dunes

Another even more strange concern was suggested by Emma, who noticed that there weren't any animals, whether dangerous or not, to be seen anywhere. The sounds of a normal swamp had dissipated the further they paddled, unnoticed by them, leaving them with only their voices and the sound of paddles sloshing through the black water. As they listened and heard nothing, it was unsettling to say the least.

"I bet the Giants have wiped everything out," Lillia suggested.

Emma dipped her finger in the black liquid, half expecting it to come out looking the color of the water itself.

"It doesn't seem possible. The swamp is full of creatures. And there aren't that many Giants. They could never eat everything. And what about the frogs and toads and crickets? They don't eat those."

"It is odd," was all that Gus could say as he gazed at the milky air that enveloped the trees beyond the banks.

His unwillingness to explain his thoughts troubled the other three, but they said nothing. They counted on him for his knowledge and awareness, but now he gave them nothing.

"Well, there has to be something else wrong," Emma said, glaring at Lillia, who rolled her eyes.

Sam looked around at the thick fog that moved about the surface of the swamp like the settling cloud in the field by his grandfather's cabin on cold mornings. It seemed to move about and swirl, even though there was no breeze.

Suddenly, Sam caught a glimpse of something ahead of them nearly a hundred meters and to the left of the widening swamp. His heart skipped a beat.

"Didn't you say the cloud of Darkness surrounded the Old City from the time of the invasion?" he said quietly, eyeing what lie ahead of them.

"Yes," Gus said, looking around and scowling suddenly. "I did."

"Was it supposed to be this far out?" He pointed at the dark cloud that was quickly becoming visible through the clearing fog.

There, as though the soupy black water of the swamp had suddenly turned to a gas and settled along the bank, perched a dense

🌲🌲 Chapter Sixteen: The Outer Dunes

cloud of Darkness. While it wasn't the massive cresting wave like the one outside the Old City, it looked equally as threatening.

With the afternoon light deteriorating, they immediately dug in with their paddles and swung to the far right of the swamp, hugging the bank to avoid the cloud.

"This is a new mass," Sam said breathily, looking for any sign of the hollow pain-stricken apparitions in the cloud like the one they previously encountered.

"Yes," Gus said in awe of the cloud, which seemed to be slowly expanding even as they watched. "Maybe less than a month old, I would say. There aren't any dark souls that have been absorbed into it yet."

"So between the growing cloud we walked through, and now this, there is no doubt the Darkness is expanding again," Lillia reminded them.

Gus nodded.

"I'm afraid I have no other explanation than to agree with Lillia. We will have to alert Mr. Sterling of this."

For some reason, Sam could not take his eyes off the Darkness. He knew the intensity of the attraction having experienced the other, much older cloud, but the draw of this one was incredible. Everything inside of him told him to paddle straight into the inky mass. He knew the others felt it too, because they too, could not turn away.

He was glad that Emma snapped him out of his daze.

"It's unbelievably dense," she said.

"And the entire city is clueless," Lillia shook her head. "The Seers, PO, Sons—most of them have no idea this is going on."

It was true. Since arriving in Lior, nearly everyone who talked about the Darkness had said it was the weakest it had ever been, with virtually no new expansion since the fall of the Old City. Not that it was quite to the level of overwhelming yet, but there was no doubt it was gaining in strength. Mr. Sterling had been correct—something was deceiving Lior to hide the Darkness.

Sam peered into the cloud as they rounded the edge of the swamp where the Darkness had not yet reached.

Chapter Sixteen: The Outer Dunes

"What causes the Darkness to come into an area?"

Gus maneuvered his boat around where he could see Sam and Emma's face.

"Horrific acts, crimes against nature or anything within the Light," he said. "It takes something powerful to invite the Darkness into an area ... which is why the cloud is so large around the Old City. It was a very dark day."

"What exactly happened there?" Sam pressed. He knew many Descendants were killed, but something told him it was more than just an invasion. He tried not to imagine, but the thoughts flooded him anyway, almost as if he was there to experience it himself.

"About a third of the Descendants died in the initial attack. The rest of the City fought back and was eventually able to put down the hoards of Metim that stormed the gates, but not before the Chancellor of Old Lior was captured and tortured in front of the City's inhabitants," he whispered, his voice still carrying in the mist. "All the Sons of Light were killed except for one—Reuven Calpher."

"Unbelievable."

"Dark Watchers called in the Darkness, and no one of the Light has been able to expel it since," Lillia added.

"Maybe with the Watcher Stone it would be different," Emma said.

Gus nodded.

"I've been reading in Julian's notes where he and Boggle discussed it. He seemed to think that somehow the Stone lifted all Dark curses, regardless of how powerful they were."

"Such a tiny little thing. I wonder how it could be possible," Emma mumbled, refusing to gaze too long at the cloud beside them.

Sam had wondered that too. Would a powerful Seer or the Council figure out how to activate it? The library in Lior City had many books on the Stone, but they were inconsistent, and those that were only agreed that it contained colors representative of the regions of Lior.

He wondered again if the Stone was the object that the person from his dream put into the Dark arch. Could it be the key that opened the arch? The swirling shapes—were those creatures of the

Chapter Sixteen: The Outer Dunes

Darkness, making their way through the gate after thousands of years of being trapped? Mr. Sterling had said he believed the Dark Lords wanted to use the Stone to unite the Dark Forces somehow. Was this the way they planned to do it?

"What do you think happened *here*?" Lillia dared to ask.

The four looked at each other, and then back at the cloud, but no one answered. They could only watch the Darkness slowly morph in its invisible boundary, as though trapped in a bondage of its own doing.

The group watched it so closely, in fact, that they didn't even noticed the large bubbles of swamp water gurgling up beside their boats.

The bubbles surfaced slowly at first, but then more rapidly, as if something was about to surface …

Before any of them could react, a massive tail lifted out of the water and smacked the front of Sam and Emma's boat with such force that it threw both of them out of their seats and into the murky water.

Sam heard Emma scream as he hit the water, which drowned out the sound instantaneously as he plunged beneath the surface. He was instantly pulled under by something powerful, dragging him under with his shoe clutched firmly in its mouth. He screamed, but only air bubbles left his mouth, with more dark water being sucked into his mouth as he struggled for oxygen.

Down they went, the creature with Sam in its mouth, until they reached the bottom where both bodies hit the hard clay with a thud. Suddenly next to him was a large tree branch, and he grasped it and kicked with all of his strength. Although it felt like he was moving in slow motion, he managed to hit something solid on the creature that made it let go of his foot. Blood instantly colored the water everywhere from his shoe, but he felt no pain. Instead, he flung himself under the large branch he held, waiting for the creature to turn and try for him once more.

When it didn't, he kicked off from the floor of the swamp's depths and rocketed toward the surface. As he swam, he was met

Chapter Sixteen: The Outer Dunes

by a surprised Lillia. She grabbed hold of him and helped him swim upward through the thick liquid. It felt as though he had been under water for several minutes, and the surface only seemed to get further away the higher they went. His eyes grew heavy and his body limp somewhere along the way, and he felt himself drifting further into the black water.

****

"Get him up to the shore!" Lillia cried as she breached the surface with Sam in her arms.

Instantly, Emma and Gus sprang into action. Gus, who had pulled Emma into his boat, paddled to Lillia, and with her hanging on to the side, thrust his paddle into the water and towed them singlehandedly to the bank. Emma was stunned but unharmed, and eventually she snapped to and helped Lillia drag Sam's lifeless body up the muddy embankment. Lillia was at his side immediately, puffing large breaths into his lungs.

Sam opened his eyes for a moment, and seeing Lillia's face close to his own, reached out and struck out at her. Then he sat up, delirious, and struggled to regain his surroundings.

"Stop it! Sam! You are safe!" Emma screamed at him while Gus threw his arms around Sam to restrain him from causing any more harm to Lillia.

Slowly, the scene came back to Sam. He was no longer under the water fighting an unknown predator, but instead was watching a lone boat come into focus as it drifted back into the swamp without any passengers, and turning his head upright, blurry-eyed figures emerged around him frantically calling his name.

"What-happened?" he gurgled, spitting out some of the murky black water next to him that was sloshing around in his mouth.

Lillia had recovered from the blow and sat up, rubbing her temple.

"You nearly drowned, ignoramus," she spat. "You don't remember the giant disfigured lizard-whatever dragging you down to who-knows-where?"

Chapter Sixteen: The Outer Dunes

He nodded to Lillia, remembering the powerful jaws of the beast. Scanning the surface, he searched for a sign of the creature.

Sure enough, it was still in the water near the dark cloud, circling the abandoned boat in the middle of the swamp. Every so often it would poke its ugly disfigured head out of the water to reveal a monster, once resembling a large crocodile, with a drooping snout and twisted eyes that looked both up and down at the same time.

On its snout was a rather large gash that told Sam his kick under water hit home. Yet it was only a scratch, and the Croc ignored it while it watched the youths intently from the murky depths.

"I'm assuming the same thing happened to that as with the wolves?" Sam asked, still rubbing the muck from his eyes and dumping black water from his shoes.

"The Darkness—it alters not only the mind but the body as well. It makes them more aggressive and even causes them to be, well, bloodthirsty," Gus said. "Some even turn savage enough to eat their own young, and even themselves."

"Okay ... I think that's enough," Emma cut him off, rolling her eyes.

"Why didn't the Darkness change us when we went through it the first time?" Sam asked. "We don't look all crazy like that."

Gus looked cautiously toward the water once again, a large splash from the angry crocodile's tail distracting him briefly.

"That mass by the plateau slope on the other side is almost fifty years old, and not nearly as dangerous as it was when it first began. And, people of Light—Descendants that is—are protected for the most part from short concentrations of Darkness."

Sam didn't fully understand, but he let it go. There were too many questions already unanswered to try and add one more. Instead, they all got to work helping him, Emma, and Lillia squeeze the water out of their clothes before moving on. The afternoon was now nearly gone, and they were growing more and more concerned that they would not make it through the swamp by nightfall. One look at the dense jungle around them and the large predator tracks told them

Chapter Sixteen: The Outer Dunes

that where they sat would make them an easy meal for some large creature.

With the deformed Croc growing bored with the four, it snaked off beneath the surface in search of easier prey, leaving the friends to hurriedly shove off, all piled in the one boat until they could help Sam and Emma back into the abandoned boat, which was nearly a quarter full of swamp water.

When they were finally underway once again, the sun was on its way below the canopy of trees. Having skirted the cloud of Darkness, they had trouble regaining their bearings, and even started down a few fingers of the swamp in the wrong direction before Gus figured out the map once again. Every time they would try another waterway, Gus would turn them around and paddle them the other direction.

Emma was just beginning to panic, and Gus was furiously riffling through the map to see if they had paddled down another dead end, when Lillia suddenly saw a glimpse of what looked like a giant orange wave of sand just over the treetops in the distance.

"There are the dunes!" Emma exclaimed after Lillia pointed toward the huge mountains of sand. "We made it to the sea!"

For a moment, they all cheered loudly, partly from relief they would not spend the night in the swamp, and partly because it meant they were one step closer to home. Quickly the dark water began to narrow into a small channel that passed through the heart of the dunes, and the water began to clear as the moss-covered, gangly trees disappeared behind them. The channel widened briefly into a small inlet before opening up into full view of the sea.

There were no waves as they paddled out of the inlet into the clear blue water of the sea, and large fish could be seen swimming in the remaining light of the sunset as they searched for minnows and small fish near the shore.

Seeing the pointed peak of the Lightbase just south of the inlet on the beach, they hugged the shoreline, paddling until they reached the base, then pulled their boats up the sand, glad to be out of the water. The large stone structure loomed in front of them, the last bit of sunlight blazing its face.

Chapter Sixteen: The Outer Dunes

They emptied their gear from the boats, grabbing the small pile of wood they had thought ahead to carry with them from the swamp. As they approached the steps, however, Gus suddenly stopped dead in his tracks, holding a hand up to signal that something was amiss. Silently, the four listened as they heard voices echoing from the top of the tower.

"We will deal with that later," said a muffled voice. "We need him gone from our city immediately. I have already set things in motion in the Council. He will be in your hands shortly."

"I suppose the fact that you will become Chancellor from all of this is only out of genuine concern," said another distinct but muffled voice.

Sam waited, but then whispered the words along with the muffled ones at the top of the tower.

"I do what's best for Lior. Nothing more."

Gus and Lillia turned toward Sam with wide-eyed amazement, their mouths hanging open. Emma turned beet red, knowing she should have caught on the minute he told her.

"You will always look out for yourself, and nothing more, Talister," the man muffled.

"Don't flatter yourself, Jonathon. You couldn't begin to understand the complexities of being in the public life. Best keep to the better of your talents—cleaning up dragon feces."

There was a lull in the conversation, then a half-hearted exchange of parting greetings followed by a shuffling of shoes on steps, which prompted the four friends to disappear over a small sand dune beside the tower.

Emma's eyes widened and she began furiously tapping Gus' shoulder and pointing toward the beach, and then everyone saw what made her panic—the boats were still on the shore, in full view of anyone leaving the tower.

The short, athletic bald man walked from the stairway entrance and onto the sand, pausing a moment to watch the sunset. He was wearing a robe, but they were not the elegant robes of Lior City.

Chapter Sixteen: The Outer Dunes 🌲🌲

Rather, they were dingy brown and frayed at the edges, and underneath was a belt that carried a sword with a hilt that looked like it had been used often. Briefly, he seemed to gaze in the direction of the boat, but then circled the tower and disappeared over the dunes to the north.

Up in the tower, there was a blinding flash of light, and a blue beam lit up the cloudless sky toward the mountains, signaling that the man in the tower had just disappeared through the Lightway.

The four stood slowly and crept over the small dune toward the tower in the darkness, still wary of the eerie silence after the meeting in the tower.

Eagerness to get home delayed their conversation and forced them to overcome their fear of the unknown. As they crept quietly up the steps, a soft breeze brushed their faces and caused the sea to belch out small waves that licked the shoreline. At the top, Gus quickly worked at readying the Lightbase, using the coordinates he had found from the first Lightbase to plot a course back to Mount Halpa, and then hopefully home.

Because of the security precautions in Lior City, they wouldn't be able to simply dial in to the Lightbase at the City Center, but they hoped to somehow communicate with them once they reached Mount Halpa's tower. At least they would be closer to home.

Sam and Lillia assisted Gus with the preparations, repacking their backpacks to ensure the easiest travel while in the Lightway, and wrapping the Stone in a napkin to minimize the possibility for breakage. If it was going to help Mr. Sterling expose the curse shadowed over Lior, it would have to get there in one piece.

Emma stood at the window staring out into the ocean, and it took only a few moments for the others to notice that she wasn't helping.

"Emma, what are you doing?" Sam called out first.

At first she said nothing, but then turned slightly to face them, and back again.

"I d-don't know. I just feel like there is something—wrong."

Lillia and Sam stood and joined her at the window. The wind had picked up, and the clear night sky had given way to a massive dark

Chapter Sixteen: The Outer Dunes

cloud moving in from the north shore. The three watched as the cloud moved as though it was alive, spilling itself over the trees where the swamp lay, and moving quickly toward the dunes and the tower.

"Oh NO!" Emma exclaimed suddenly, surprising the others, including Gus, who was just about finished with the Lightbase.

Seeing that she had caused instant panic, she sheepishly hung her head.

"Sorry. I just realized I forgot my backpack in the boat. I will go get it."

"I'll go with her," Sam said immediately.

They silently descended the stairs, and pausing only a moment at the stairwell entrance, they hurried into the dark windy night toward the boat.

It was where they left it, but the increasing waves were now licking its stern. Emma snatched her backpack quickly from the boat, and Sam hurried her back up the beach toward the tower.

As they huffed through the cool sand, something caught the corner of Sam's eye, causing his heart to skip a beat. Emma saw it too, and she was instantly at his side. But it was too late to make it back to the Lightbase.

****

Suddenly, all around them were figures emerging from the crests of the moonlit dunes. The tower was out of reach, and in a moment, they were trapped and surrounded by horrific Dark creatures of the night. Emma's senses had not lied to her.

Deformed wolves with massive black fangs approached hungrily toward them, creeping along as though they were ready to pounce at any moment. Sam reached beside him and took Emma in his grip, pulling her close to him. There was no running, and nowhere to hide.

Feverishly, he looked for a weak point in the circle of wolves, but they seemed to read his every thought and closed in tighter, their eyes full of Dark fire and their fangs dripping with the anticipation of the

Chapter Sixteen: The Outer Dunes

taste of flesh. Just when Sam was about to throw himself on the sand and cover Emma with his body, six figures melted into sight from the darkness behind the giant predators.

One figure was cloaked in black, his eyes glowing iridescent green in the moonlight. He stepped in front of the circle of snarling creatures and held up his hand to them, and they instantly crouched to meet the sand, whimpering as if in pain.

The other five warriors slinked closer in the now scarce light of the moon, each showing the hollowed eyes and scarred faces of Metim. Their appearances showed they had seen violence, for their war-torn tunics were stained with blood and dirt. Each carried a sword at their waist, but they kept them sheathed as their leader approached the young Descendants.

The cloaked figure stopped only feet in front of Emma and Sam and removed his hood. Instead of giving into his fear, Sam forced himself upright to look into the man's glowing eyes. He was bald and clean-shaven, handsome, and showed the muscular stature of a man in his early forties. He seemed to peer directly into Sam's soul with his piercing eyes, and if it weren't for Emma's silent crying and tightening grip on his arm, he would have been unable to break the stare.

"Sar Samuel," his voice seemed to echo deep inside Sam's eardrums. "I have been waiting to meet you."

"Who are you?" Sam said shakily.

"I am Arazel," the man boomed calmly. "I am here to retrieve an item of great value that is in your possession."

Sam knew instantly what he wanted—the Watcher Stone. Emma had given it to Gus, who was in the tower. Perhaps he had it well hidden by now.

"Denying you have it would be foolish. I can see it in the tower clearly." The man didn't take his eyes off of Sam. "Your friends are surrounded. Please go and retrieve them and the Stone." He paused for a moment. "They will not be harmed."

"How will I know you won't hurt them?" Sam breathed harshly, certain by the way the man spoke there were no other options but to hand it over.

Chapter Sixteen: The Outer Dunes

"I am a man of my word," the man spoke, his eyes blazing. "But do not press me. I do not hesitate to end life if it serves my purpose."

Sam looked to the stairwell, and the man nodded that he would let him pass safely, but he held up a hand briefly, which seemed to force Sam to stand paralyzed mid stride.

"Do not try to use the Lightway. It has been disabled."

Once the strange force let go of Sam, he held Emma close to him and helped her to the stairs, and the great deformed creatures parted to allow them through. They glared with their terrible eyes at the two as if they were letting their last meal slip past their claws, and drool began to pool around their mouths, dripping all the way to the sand.

At the top, Gus was crouched behind the stone doorway and motioned to them to climb quickly. Emma said nothing, but moved with Sam as he moved. Her breathing was rapid, and she was pale even in the darkness of the tower.

Gus helped Sam move Emma inside, and then grabbed him and pulled him over to his backpack. Silently he handed him two small silver surfboard discs that Boggle had given them.

So they weren't going to give in after all. It seemed that Gus had a different plan, one that involved escaping. He just wondered if it would lead them to their deaths.

Sam nodded and slipped them into his pocket—one for him and one for Emma. Then Gus produced a velvet pouch from the backpack and took out two small round circles with an engraved inset button and handed one to Sam.

Sam recognized these as the devices that Boggle had given them just before they left his house. He didn't know what they did; he only remembered that Boggle said not to be too close when they went off. Sam slipped this also in his pocket as Gus took the Watcher Stone from the backpack to give to him.

It seemed to glow just slightly as Gus produced it, and for a moment the two just stared at it, as if mesmerized by its beauty but also taking the moment to think of an escape plan. It was too dangerous to speak with Arazel's wall-penetrating senses, so they

Chapter Sixteen: The Outer Dunes

would have to wing it. For all they knew, he had already seen them exchange Boggle's inventions and could be planning to kill them as soon as they descended the steps. But they had to take the chance. From what they believed the Stone to be, it was too dangerous to let go.

Sam battled his own fear of facing Arazel once again and thought about making a break for it alone. He thought of all that had led up to this point—from growing up in the city, to moving in with his Grandfather, to this. There was no going back now, no erasing what he had seen and experienced with his friends in Lior. He was somehow intertwined with them, and he felt it now more than ever.

He could not turn and run, however. He believed now he had to fight, if necessary. He would face Arazel, and he would do whatever he could to keep the Stone away from him, even if meant their deaths.

His face grew hot as he stood and led his friends out into the chilly night stairwell. The wolves had not moved from their spot, but they looked impatient, as if being held back by some restricting force. He knew they would be the first to tear into them when the fighting started.

Sam knew they would lose, but Emma and Lillia both silently agreed to use whatever Light ability they could get, although the Dark power that Arazel and the Metim had would likely overshadow any attack they made. Sam wasn't very knowledgeable on how the Light abilities worked, but he was capable enough to know they were outnumbered and out-skilled.

They made their way slowly to where the Arazel stood, trying hard to look as though they were giving in to his demands. No one knew the signal, but Sam imagined it would be him that started the resistance.

They stood in the cool sand in front of Arazel, who hadn't moved even slightly since Sam and Emma left him. He gazed searchingly into each of their eyes, as if attempting to detect some element of deceit. Finally, after a long silent moment, his bright green eyes focused back upon Sam.

Chapter Sixteen: The Outer Dunes

"Wise decision, Sar Samuel," he said.

"Why do you keep calling me that?" Sam said angrily.

The man had no expression, except perhaps a little more glimmer in his eyes at the question.

"You have been named for the Prince of Darkness, The Dark One, *Nasikh*, ruler of Sheba Haloth and Ayet Sal," his voice boomed. "The Prophecy says another will stand in *his* place to lead the Darkness. You are called Sar, for you have been chosen as second to the Dark One."

Sam felt the blood rush to his face once again, as he searched for the courage to initiate the fight without losing the element of surprise. His friends looked wide-eyed at him, waiting, and growing more fearful at every moment.

"And what do you think?" Sam said, afraid that he had overstepped his bounds. "Am I your great lord? Should you be bowing to me?"

Arazel's eyes blazed, and Sam was certain he was growing impatient.

"It is yet to be seen," he said with the slightest hissing sound emanating from his lips as he spoke. "Now, I believe we have talked long enough. Hand the Stone to me, and you will not be harmed—"

In the middle of the sentence, Sam saw his chance to act. As Arazel spoke the word "Stone," he saw him divert his eyes, only for a moment, as he searched for the artifact among them. At that moment, Sam pressed the button on Boggle's device in his pocket.

His pocket buzzed softly, and Sam grasped hold of the object tightly.

"You're right. You know nothing about me. In fact, you probably don't know that I like to surf," he said, and then tossed the object in the air in front of Arazel, diving backward and rolling into the sand.

Suddenly, three flashes of light erupted in front of him, as well as one from his own hands, as the Lightboards transformed. Gus, Emma, and Lillia were already climbing aboard before Boggle's device finally went off.

A huge explosion of blinding light from Boggle's device silently turned the night into neon blue daylight. The flash hit Sam like a

Chapter Sixteen: The Outer Dunes

bolt of lightning, compressing his chest and taking his breath away. Blinded, he searched for his Lightboard, feeling around him for its shape.

Three streaks of light had already whipped away from the scene, and Sam could only hope it was his friends. On the ground lay deformed wolves and Metim, writhing in agony from the flash. Arazel had disappeared.

He finally grabbed hold of his Lightboard as the Dark creatures were beginning to shake off the explosion and struggle to their feet. Sam climbed aboard the shimmering disc and tipped the nose of it down, which instantly propelled it forward.

He whizzed over the sand at breakneck speed, finding the controls easy to maneuver.

Leaning into a turn, he followed the three blue dots racing ahead of him. He tipped the disc down a little more and was amazed to feel the Lightboard accelerate to nearly double its speed. He kept up the incredibly fast pace until he caught up with the others, at which point Emma threw him a fearful but relieved look.

Ahead, the darkened outline of trees could be seen rapidly approaching, and further still were the cutouts of the enormous range of mountains shooting into the sky. *Safety just inside the tree line*, he thought. He wouldn't feel completely safe until they were deep within the cover of the forest and out of sight.

The cool coastal wind stung their faces as Sam and the others finally slowed in front of the trees facing them. They eased into the tightly-packed pines, picking their way through until they came to a small clearing in the woods. Gus jumped off his Lightboard and immediately smacked the button to return it to its smaller size.

Shivering from the cold ride, Sam did the same, unlatching his backpack to pull out a sweater. Both girls were obviously shaken but unharmed, and shivering in the night air. Sam immediately gave his sweater to Emma, and Gus followed suit with his own for Lillia. They considered making a fire, but agreed it was still too risky. Instead, they huddled together as Gus sent a meaningful prayer to the Creator.

🌲🌲 Chapter Sixteen: The Outer Dunes

****

It was Sam who opened his eyes first from the prayer to an unusual chill up his spine, unlike the normal feeling from the cold night. Hollow eyes from the five Metim, appearing out of nowhere, peered at them from just inside the clearing. Then, in the moonlight, a thick black vapor of smoke descended into the center of the clearing near the friends and rapidly morphed into the figure of a man with a smooth bald head and fiery green eyes.

Arazel's face was expressionless, but he held up his hand toward the four teenagers.

"You do not disappoint me, Sar, although I must say I expected it," he said calmly. "Your father would be proud."

"You knew my father?" Sam said loudly, the sound reverberating off the trees in the clearing.

Arazel held his gaze.

"He is well known among the Metim," he said impatiently. "Now I must retract my offer to allow your friends to go unharmed."

Emma began to whimper, and Lillia pulled her close to herself.

"You are afraid of me, so you must kill my friends?" Sam spat at him.

Arazel paused a moment, then as Gus reached slowly for his backpack, a burst of green light erupted from Arazel's fingertips, hitting Gus square in the chest. Gus lay motionless on the ground.

Arazel dropped his hand to his side, and the Metim lurking in the shadows of the trees rushed forward in unison, carrying with them vapors of Darkness in their open hands.

Suddenly, a blue beam of Light projected from Emma's hand, her eyes closed and her palm outstretched. The beam formed a shield, larger than any she had previously produced. The shield instantly enveloped three of the approaching Metim, pinning them and their fistfuls of Darkness to the ground.

Lillia sent a bright blue flash from her palms, sending a Metim

Chapter Sixteen: The Outer Dunes

flying backward with a gaping wound in his side. Before she could produce another, however, the last Metim was upon her.

Sam's mind raced, and without waiting, he unsheathed a small knife from his belt and pounced on the Metim that had pinned Lillia to the ground. Instinctively, he grabbed the Metim's wiry hair and exposed his neck, jabbing the knife into his throat.

The Metim spit foul blood and stumbled backward off of Lillia, his hollow eyes wide with fear. Darkness poured from his fingertips, swirling around his hands and concentrating into a pulsing, fluid form. He then reared his hand back, blood spewing from his neck, and attempted to thrust the Darkness forward at the two youths.

Lillia was too quick, however, and before his deadly mass of Dark poison could leave his hands, she sent another bolt through his heart, instantly dropping his lifeless form to the ground.

Then Lillia and Sam were at Emma's side. She still had the writhing Metim pinned under her Light shield, but her strength was quickly weakening and the Light from the shield was fading.

Lillia prepared herself for another bolt and Sam wielded his tiny knife toward them as the Metim began to get to their feet. Finally, the shield failed, and Emma went to her knees.

Instead of fighting, however, the Metim only stepped back out of the moonlight, their hollow eyes fading into the darkness surrounding the clearing.

Arazel was suddenly in the clearing, his eyes blazing. He lifted his arms up above his head, and suddenly Darkness descended upon them all, drenching them in a thick, fluid-like black cloud. Sam couldn't see beyond his own hand, so he quickly reached out for Emma and Lillia, grasping their hands and pulling them in to him.

Suddenly, Lillia froze in his hands, then her body went limp and she dropped to Sam's feet. Emma dropped immediately after Lillia, and Sam was left standing alone.

There was a brush of wind across his face, and then a voice whispered in his ear, so close it was as though it was inside his own head, and so painful it caused him to grasp his ears in agony.

There is nothing left but for you to do as I ask, the voice whispered.

🌲🌲 Chapter Sixteen: The Outer Dunes

There was nothing left but to give in. He would have been willing to die for the protection of the Stone, but Arazel wouldn't even let him do that. Instead, the Dark Conjurer had to take everything away from him to get him to submit.

He could have taken the Stone at any time, Sam was sure, but it was Arazel's way of showing his superiority. A game—and Emma, Lillia, and Gus were the meaningless sacrifices. And now he was going to give in and give him the Stone as Arazel had wanted all along.

****

But suddenly, there was something that welled up inside of Sam, through all of the emotion that built up to this moment—wonder, frustration, fear, shock of losing his friends—all wrapped up into the exhaustion of just wanting to get home.

All of it funneled suddenly into a great feeling of anger toward Arazel, the Metim, the wolves, and even Talister, who seemed to be selling out someone from the City of Lior for political pride.

The feeling rose so quickly that Sam couldn't control it, and suddenly everything around him faded except for his anger at the voice in the cloud of the one who just took his friends from him.

Suddenly Sam could see through the Darkness, the scene bathed in clear blue. Sounds were amplified, movements slowed, and his fear ebbed from his body. His hands grew warm as his fists clenched in pure violent anger, and then small blue sparks dancing from knuckle to knuckle began to glow a brilliant blue.

He raised his hands instinctively in front of his enemy, and blue Light exploded from his palms, drenching the entire clearing in a luminous display.

The Light hit Arazel square in the chest, and he stumbled backward, his green eyes wide with surprise and anger. Sam wildly aimed his palms at him once again, fighting to keep control of the powerful bolt.

It hit Arazel once again, and the Dark Conjurer, fighting to keep his balance, went to his knees. But the blast wasn't enough to keep

Chapter Sixteen: The Outer Dunes

him down, and the blue beam was suddenly met with an electric cloud of Darkness, slowly pushing the Light backward toward Sam.

He held the beam of Light still for as long as he could, but it was too difficult to control and seemed to be gaining in strength the more he tried to control it. As the Light from his palm increased in power, it became even more difficult to steady.

The whole scene was an enormous fight between Light and Darkness, sparks of blue colliding with dark, liquid clouds, each spraying their remnants everywhere around them. Sam felt no fear of Arazel in that moment, only the warm flood of blue Light that flowed through his body. It didn't seem to fade as Emma's did, nor did it drain him of his own strength. But the man with the green eyes was as strong and more skilled with his power of Darkness, and eventually Sam could not control it any longer.

He stepped to the side and lowered his hands, stopping the flow of Light to his opponent. Arazel lowered his hands at once, confirming Sam's suspicions that he would not kill him, no matter what he did.

Sam dropped to his knees near Emma and Lillia, the warmth of the Light fading into a mixture of hatred and sadness. He put his hands on Emma's forehead, feeling for any sign of life. She was cold and breathless, but curiously felt like she was still alive. A hand to Lillia told Sam she was in the same condition.

He looked to his enemy with contempt but with pleading his eyes. The man seemed to understand his unspoken question, and his face of surprise and anger turned expressionless once again.

"What do you want from me?!" Sam yelled loudly, his voice shaking.

"My master requires your service."

It was at that moment that Sam decided he would go nowhere with this man of the Darkness—alive, at least.

"I'm not going *anywhere* with you!" he shouted, and on a whim unsheathed a knife and held it to his own throat.

Arazel smiled devilishly.

"I am patient to allow you to go now, but I assure you there will be a time when the master will call on you," he boomed. "You may

Chapter Sixteen: The Outer Dunes

keep your precious life in Lior for now, but I will still need to collect the Stone."

Sam knew his attempt at resistance was over. If his friends were still alive, the Dark Conjurer would not hesitate to kill them, even if Sam took his own life.

Sam stood weakly, walked over to Gus' backpack and took out the Watcher Stone. There was no fighting any longer. Arazel was stronger, and Sam wasn't prepared to sacrifice his friends for a stupid rock, even if it was the key to somehow exposing the real threat of Darkness to the City. It simply wasn't worth it to lose those he had just begun to care about.

Perhaps it was part of Arazel's plan all along—follow the defenseless young Descendants into the forest and have them go through the Lazuli in the library instead of doing it himself. Maybe the rush of air past them was actually a Dark soul he sent in there to check on them. Or maybe it was Arazel himself.

Either way, it was better to sacrifice an object than a life.

Sam walked purposefully over to the cloaked being, trying his best not to appear afraid, but being so weak he stumbled as he walked. Arazel reached out and took the Stone, and Sam stood his ground, even though everything inside him screamed at him to turn and run. Arazel peered with his cold green eyes at Sam, as if searching him.

Sam turned back to tend to his friends, but he was suddenly caught by a paralyzing force, freezing him where he stood, just as the wolves on the beach had been restrained from ripping into them.

"Do not attempt to come after me, Sar Samuel. I will not be so forgiving with your friends the next time." He bore his eyes into the back of Sam's skull. "And there *will* come a day when you will subject yourself to the mercy of the Darkness."

Sam said nothing, only tended to his friends, keeping his back to Arazel purposefully. Anything that would have come out of his mouth would have shown how afraid he was, so it was better to keep silent.

The anger and confidence Sam had prior when facing the Dark

Chapter Sixteen: The Outer Dunes

Watcher was buried somewhere beneath the urgency to revive Emma and the others. Going after Arazel and the Stone was not even a fleeting thought in his mind at that time. He only wanted to get his friends home.

Then, above the clearing, there was a flash of blue, and a circle of pulsing Light opened up the night sky above them. Four beams of intense Light streamed instantly to the ground, and four figures materialized suddenly in front of Sam and Arazel.

Arazel's eyes grew wide at the sight, but instead of fleeing with his prize, something compelled him to face his enemies of the Light, as though bound by the Dark force within him.

Upon raising his hands above him, he called in three Metim hiding in the shadows to attack the four robed strangers that appeared before them.

Before the Dark servants had even taken two steps, however, one of the robed figures had rushed forward, and rolling gracefully to one side, dropped two of the Metim to the ground with a sword through the heart.

The remaining Metim stopped suddenly and, looking around at his dead companions, turned and attempted to flee. Another robed figure lifted his hand and blue fire shot from his palm and hit the Metim in the back, turning him instantly to ash.

Then Sam looked at Arazel, who seemed to have a slight smile on his face as the four robed people stood in waiting for someone to make the first move.

****

It was deathly silent as both sides sized up the other, but then one of the members of Light disappeared suddenly and appeared at the other side of the clearing, firing a bolt of Light toward Arazel, who blocked it in an easy stroke of the hand, simultaneously releasing a green bolt of light back at him.

It missed, but then Arazel outstretched his hands to produce a large swirling cloud of Darkness above them that began hurling thick

Chapter Sixteen: The Outer Dunes

black choking nebulas at the warriors, each containing haunting faces that struggled to be free of their evil prison.

Without hesitation, a massive burst of Light erupted from a warrior's palm, morphing instantly into a protective Light shield that settled neatly around all four warriors, forcing the haunting faces with their hollow eyes up into the night sky.

The shield was then concentrated toward the Conjurer of Darkness, the Light immediately taking hold of him and wrapping him into a thick, pulsing cage of Lazuli light. But the Light cage would not hold him, and quickly he was free in an angry burst of Darkness and green electricity that sparked violently around his entire Dark form.

Arazel then lifted his hands skyward once again in a fit of rage, where a violent cloud mushroomed up above the clearing, drowning out any moonlight that still shone through the thick air. It then descended down all sides of the clearing, dropping like a curtain until it surrounded them all in deadly black Darkness once again.

The haunting black cloud then took on life of its own, the intense green electricity sparking forcefully from one side of the curtain of Darkness to the other. The robed warrior with the shield rushed to where Sam crouched helplessly near his still unconscious friends, the Light shield from his palm shifting from the other Sons of Light to immediately bathe the young Descendants in the protective umbrella of Light.

While they fought, Sam felt for a pulse from Emma's stiffened body, but felt nothing. It was as though the very life was snatched from her, but without a scratch to be seen. He quickly moved to Lillia and to Gus, finding them in the same condition as Emma.

He feared the worst, and in spite of the furious battle being waged around him, he stood and lifted his hands up to the Creator whom he could not see.

Creator, Lord, I don't know if you can hear me, he began, *but I really need your help now. Please help us all.*

It was short, but the most meaningful prayer he had ever prayed. He only hoped the Creator would hear him.

He watched as the other three warriors outside the shield

Chapter Sixteen: The Outer Dunes

gracefully dodged the streaks of deadly green light in an almost rhythmic pattern, each returning deadly bolts of blue Light skillfully back toward the Dark Conjurer.

One spark of deadly strong electricity flashed within inches of one of the Sons as he attempted a risky maneuver to temporarily bind Arazel in a prison of chains made of pure Light, if only for the chance to give another an edge to fire a bolt from behind. The bolt nearly hit its mark, but with lightning fast movement, Arazel sidestepped the brunt of the bolt, catching only a grazing on his left arm.

Throwing off the chains of Light angrily, Arazel now stopped his barrage of Darkness for only a moment, ignoring the confused looks of his adversaries as he glared only at the four teens under the shield.

Sam saw the Dark Conjurer's eyes burning with rage, and he swallowed his fear enough to force a rigid smile to his face in defiance. But Sam knew at any moment he could turn his attention on him and his friends, perhaps destroying them all in one wave of his arm, if they weren't dead already.

Suddenly, Emma began to stir beneath his arm that he had laid upon her, and his heart leapt as he raced to her. She was still cold, but was alive. He looked to his other friends, hoping they would awaken like Emma, but they had not yet.

Like the brave warriors of Light, they too had been willing to fight—and die for something they believed in, and for him. Even in the midst of the pure evil before him, the compassion within him reigned supreme. He still held onto the anger he had felt when fighting the Dark Lord, but it had subsided and been replaced with the desire to see his friends healed. The same anger had slipped below the surface, and love had filled its place.

It was strange, the anger he had felt, as though it was purposeful and necessary for that moment, almost like it had been given to deal with the injustice of the Dark act before him.

Enraged, the conjurer of Darkness began his campaign of destruction once again, shooting twice as many twisted bolts of green electricity mixed with Darkness and forcing the Light warriors to use every possible move to dodge the deadly blows.

Delirious, Emma tried to sit up but could not. Sam placed his

🌲🌲 Chapter Sixteen: The Outer Dunes

pack underneath her head for support, and as he did, Lillia and Gus stirred. He sent a quick prayer of thanks to the Creator for answering his prayer, then still inside the shield, he watched the warriors battle with the incredibly fast Fallen Watcher.

As fast as the warriors were, Arazel was faster, and he knew it. Seeing his advantage, Arazel turned his palms silently upward and rolled his eyes back into his skull, at which point he was instantly surrounded by herds of lifeless creatures with hollow faces that rushed from the electric curtain of Darkness to destroy the Light warriors before them.

At the sight of the rushing hoard, however, the three warriors clasped their hands above their heads, causing a curious song-like noise to ring out throughout the clearing, and from each warrior immediately burst fountains of Light that sprung from their palms, radiating so brilliantly that the four friends had to shield their eyes.

From the fountains poured an untold number of magnificent creatures made of Light, some predators of the forest floor and others from the air.

As the hoards advanced, they were immediately met and overcome by the fountains of brilliant beasts, quickly succumbing to the incredible Light that radiated from the creatures. They devoured them violently, leaving only wisps of Darkness that could be heard screaming in agony as the Light devoured them.

Finally, as the army of Dark creatures began to disappear before him, in a grand show of power and force, Arazel lifted both hands into the sky and sent an atomic burst of Darkness and lightning so fierce into the clearing that it sent all four warriors flying backward into the Dark curtain, instantly dissolving the shield that covered Sam and the bleary-eyed friends.

They felt a deep compression in their chests as Arazel's Dark cloud imploded suddenly on itself, sucking the cloud, the curtain of electricity, and Arazel into a black hole. Then there was nothing but silence.

Chapter Seventeen
Amos

The warrior with the shield hurried to his friends, who seemed to be banged up but still in one piece as they stood to their feet. One warrior held his side, and another carried him over to where Sam and the others were, laying him down to inspect his wounds. He was cheerful and in good spirits, but Sam could see there was a nasty gash in his abdomen.

The sword-wielding warrior turned out to be a woman, who now knelt next to the wounded Son of Light, holding her hand gently over the gash in his side. The rest of the group watched a soft blue Light pulsing from her palms as she moved her hand lightly over the gash. The warrior winced in pain at first, but then forced himself to relax, allowing her to work.

Then she moved to Lillia, and then Gus, and finally Emma, passing the healing Light over all of them until they felt as though they could once again stand. Emma, upon seeing the destruction in the clearing and the wounded warriors, immediately embraced all of them, thanking them profusely.

Sam noticed all four warriors wore similar bracelets with marbled

Chapter Seventeen: Amos

blue stones on their left wrist like other Descendants, but all glowed brightly in the pale moonlight. Although they carried stains and rips from the battle, their robes were made with uniquely ornate black fabric with silver highlights. They carried a different aura about them, one of confidence and reserved strength, but genuine humbleness as well.

"You are the Sons of Light, aren't you?" Sam said weakly to the warrior that had protected them with his shield.

He sat calmly next to them as if he had just had a relaxing cup of coffee, although sweat beaded on his upper brow.

"My name is Tarmin," he said gently. "You're blessed to be alive."

"I know," Sam mumbled, still somewhat stunned at the intense fight that just took place before him. "I—*we* shouldn't be."

"Whoever summoned us certainly did it at the proper moment," he said.

Emma held up the small white button device that Mr. Sterling had handed Gus before they left.

"Gus handed it to me in the tower," she strained to speak.

"You were wise to use it. And although you are safe from the Dark Watcher now, we must be getting you all back as soon as possible," he told them. "More may come."

Gus spoke for the first time since he was hit with the bolt, but it was under his breath so that the others would not hear him.

"The Stone ... do we still have it?" he said, his voice shaky.

Sam bowed his head, knowing that if he could have only held out a few seconds more, they could have still had it.

"No."

There was silence as Sam's words sunk in. They had lost everything they had accomplished to this point. They had nothing to show for their journey to the Old City except for a few a few cuts and a good dose of exhaustion. Now Arazel had the Watcher Stone in his possession as well, almost as if it was planned.

Thinking back to the moment in the artifact room of the secret library and the strange brush of air they felt, Sam shuddered suddenly at the possibility that Arazel had followed them and was only inches

Chapter Seventeen: Amos

away ... but then, how could he have been there with the concentration of Lazuli so close?

Lillia walked off clumsily into the clearing at the news, throwing her sweatshirt on the ground as she left. Gus looked like someone punched him in the stomach upon hearing of the loss of the Stone. Emma hurried after Lillia, snatching the sweatshirt back up as she went, her strawberry hair sparkling in the clear moonlight.

He knew it wasn't his fault, but he still felt guilty for letting it go. What would the Metim and Arazel do with the Stone? Did they already have access to the Sha'ar gate? Were they already planning their entrance into Earth, and his giving up the Stone gave them the final piece into the rise of Darkness once again? Or was it just a legend that meant nothing at all?

Now that it was gone, there was only room to wonder how they could have done things differently. They wouldn't be the ones to determine if the legends were true; the creatures of the Darkness would be.

At the mention of the Old City, the Sons of Light gathered around Sam and Gus and began to ask questions of the youths' adventures into the abandoned area.

Gus wasn't up for storytelling much, so Sam offered the information to the warriors, who listened with keen interest as he told them of the wolves they encountered, the destruction of the City, and their narrow escape through the boathouse cavern. He did not, upon warning looks from the others, explain anything about the library, Holobooks, or the Stone.

"What was your purpose in going?" said one of the warriors named Parus.

Sam swallowed hard, feeling as though he was on trial. He knew there were spies in the City. Could any of the Sons be one of them?

"We had heard there was some Darkness around the City. We just wanted to see it for ourselves."

Another warrior, who was quiet before, now leaned in from where he sat.

"Even after fifty years, the Darkness is very strong in that area,"

Chapter Seventeen: Amos

he said softly but with authority. "It was a very foolish idea to do what you did."

Before Sam could open his mouth to defend himself, the girls came back to join the group, Lillia looking as though she had just finished crying. It was another one of the rare moments Lillia showed any sort of emotion other than anger.

Sam chose to keep quiet after that, accepting the blame for the group's foolish actions. He didn't want to keep the truth from them, but he was certain they could see right through his deceit anyhow.

"We need to get you back to the City," Tarmin said, patting Sam's shoulder gently. "I'm sure all of your parents will want to hear from you."

****

Gus struggled to his feet, favoring one of his legs from the fall backward.

"Will we be traveling by Ruach?" he asked them.

"Yes, we must. No other way is faster than the Lightsphere," said Nibetz, the woman carrying the sword. She winked at Gus, who promptly blushed.

"I can't believe it," Emma whispered to them as they gathered their packs. "I've never traveled with the Sons before—and by Ruach!"

The wind began to pick up and Tarmin hurried them all into the center of the clearing, at which point he gave them instructions on how to travel by Ruach.

"Most call it a sphere, but it's more like riding the wind, which is how you must think when you step into it," he said, obviously hurrying through his instructions, each of the warriors surrounding him and scanning the trees for any further signs of Dark forces.

"Think of it as asking the particles of Light to allow you to join them. With your spirit, you will join the Light. I will be calling the Ruach, but when it arrives, you will be on your own. Don't worry if it doesn't work the first time—we will come back for you shortly."

Immediately, Sam wondered what would happen if he wasn't able

Chapter Seventeen: Amos

to convince the Light to allow him to join it. They made it sound like it had a mind of its own, as if it could choose not to allow him, then leave him behind.

But it was too late to worry about it now, as Tarmin lifted up his hands to the night sky. Suddenly an incredible cloud of Light appeared above them, rapidly descending upon the clearing until they were all wrapped in its brilliant blue glow.

A quick glance at Emma's fearful expression told Sam he was not alone in his worry, so he reached out and grasped her hand, and then thinking quickly, with his other hand grabbed the hand of a very surprised Lillia, who in turn grabbed Gus's.

"Now close your eyes and allow the Light to surround you," Tarmin said, and then he disappeared into thin air, leaving only a small absence of the Light in his place.

One by one, the other warriors disappeared into the cloud, until only the four teens were left in the warmth of the Ruach.

Sam closed his eyes and concentrated on the Light surrounding him. He could almost feel the particles as they swirled around his body, blanketing him in warmth and comfort. The sensation of being pulled upward rushed over him immediately, and upon opening his eyes carefully, he watched as his body was pulled toward the thin tops of the trees above the clearing.

Suddenly, they were shooting through the sky at blinding speed, their bodies skimming along the cloud of Light in front of them, the trees far below them. Tarmin and the other Light warriors raced like blue shooting stars in front of them, streaking through the night air.

It was even more amazing than the Lightway. It was surreal—like swimming through an iridescent pool in the middle of a vast ocean of Light. It was as though he was just a boy again, dreaming about superheroes flying through the sky ... warriors against the worlds of Darkness.

Lior City quickly loomed largely in front of them, the brilliant spires pointing beams of Light high into the atmosphere, as though they were guides for lonely travelers looking for a place of rest. It was the most beautiful city he had ever seen.

Chapter Seventeen: Amos

Lior now felt more like home than anywhere he had lived with his foster parents or with his grandfather. He longed to stay, to make a life here, and perhaps never return to Earth, White Pine, or Mr. Wilson's crazy class.

And he had never felt so familiar with any group of people in his life as his friends and their cabin circle. Existing on the outside was all that he had known, until meeting his friends and their family. They weren't blood, but they loved him as if they had never known differently, and that was as strong as family, if not stronger.

The cloud slowed upon its arrival past the City Center, into a remote section of Lior, and finally to a small outcropping of older cabins that surrounded a large stone pavilion nearly buried in ivy from many years of growth. There was an enormous garden surrounding the pavilion that stretched far beyond the cabins, nearly to the boundaries of the City walls. A small stream danced happily around sandstone rock ledges and straight through the middle of the garden to the small Lazuli pool next to the pavilion.

Still high above the garden where the Ruach cloud now hovered, they could see the waterfall beyond the garden where the stream originated. The moonlight sparkled off the surface of the water, and Lazuli light beneath gave the stream a further fantastical glow that couldn't be reproduced.

The cloud lowered them gently into the garden between two large weeping trees and next to the pool, where the particles of the Ruach Light made one last swirl around their bodies before scattering into the night sky. It was peaceful, like being at the pools of Lazuli near the Old City. Sam believed it was possible that the Sons reconstructed it to mimic that very scene.

Tarmin and Nibetz walked over to the four awestruck youth standing on the edge of the pool. Nibetz offered her hand to Emma, then to the rest of them.

"Sorry I didn't get a chance to meet you before," she said quietly, her dark straight hair reminding Sam of an older version of Lillia without the oriental features. "My name is Nibetz. I am the one and only Son who is actually a woman."

Chapter Seventeen: Amos

"Nice to meet you," Sam said genuinely.

Tarmin pointed toward the blue spires beyond the pool and the trees, then looked toward Emma.

"You will find your path to the City through there," he said.

"Thank you ever so much, all of you," Emma suddenly reached out and hugged Nibetz, who hadn't expected it.

"We live to serve others," she responded, holding her gently while trying to detangle her now disheveled hair.

"I would make it a point to disclose what information you have not chosen to share with me to your father. He will want to know everything," Tarmin said sternly as they looked for their packs, which curiously they didn't remember taking up into the Ruach cloud with them. "And we would ask that the device that leaves us at your beckon call remain a secret, and be used sparingly."

"You can be sure we will," Gus said.

Nibetz produced one of the packs she had been holding and handed it to Emma.

"You will all want to go and see a healer as well," she said. "I would recommend a young lady named Darva on the Thalo Hall street. She is very gifted."

Tarmin handed Sam his backpack, which he too, produced out of nowhere.

"You would have forgotten this, I am sure," he said jokingly, then lowered his voice slightly. "If you should need help again, you may call on us. Now go and be blessed."

When Lillia and Gus found their packs, which were also held by the two other Sons named Josael and Grantham, the group thanked them once again and set off wearily, hand in hand, toward the spires of the City, leaning on each other both for moral support and out of sheer exhaustion.

****

Chapter Seventeen: Amos

"What do you mean you fought the Metim?" Mrs. Sterling sat on the edge of her chair after the four youths had reunited with the exasperated but relieved Sterling parents.

"And please elaborate more on the Stone if you would," Mr. Sterling added, asking for probably the third time.

Sam had been quiet up until now, but felt as though he might be able to help out an increasingly frustrated Emma.

"It was in the temple library in the City, hidden in one of Bogglenose's secret rooms created for the Holobooks," he told them.

Mr. Sterling shook his head.

"I can't believe it. The library was destroyed. I saw the official report from the Office of Research."

"I can assure you, Mr. Sterling, we had possession of it until Arazel took it from us," Gus yawned.

"I believe you. I can't imagine why the report on Old Lior would contain purposefully altered information. But I did have a hunch."

"Unless you have been subjected to some hallucinatory effects from the Darkness produced by the Metim?" Mrs. Sterling stooped to hug her daughter once more.

"We are fine, mom," Emma sighed as though she had been hugged entirely too many times since returning.

"I am fairly certain since we all saw the same thing," Gus attempted to explain, but was interrupted by a flustered Mr. Sterling, who now began to pace back and forth in front of the dying fire.

"There are only a few people that can be party to such conspiracies—" he began, but forced himself to stop at the danger of saying too much that could be considered confidential, but not until after Lillia shot a "told-you-so" glance at the other three.

Gus sipped his coffee that Mrs. Sterling scrambled to make upon their arrival.

"We think the Lazuli pool beneath the library provided some protection."

"Well, it was never made to be indestructible, but it *was* reinforced with Lazuli when it was built." Mr. Sterling put his hand on his chin. "I wasn't surprised to hear it was destroyed, actually. Most Metim

Chapter Seventeen: Amos

wouldn't have gone near the library, but with the vast number of Dark forces the day of the attack, the Darkness could have weakened the effects of the Lazuli."

"Mr. Sterling, I need to tell you something else about the night the Stone was taken," Sam looked into Mr. Sterling's eyes, hoping he would not take poorly the news he was about to tell him.

He had wrestled with telling Mr. Sterling about the conversation between Talister and the bald man in the tower, but with Talister's position, he felt it best to confide in him sooner than later before any more harm could be done.

"Certainly, boy. What is it?"

"We heard Mr. Calpher talking to another man at the Light tower in the dunes," he said, careful to not sound incriminatory. "He said there was someone in Lior that needed to be removed because they were dangerous. And … from what we heard, it sure sounded like Mr. Calpher was getting something political out of the deal."

Mr. Sterling listened carefully, but did not respond to Sam. Instead he smiled and stood to accept a piece of root cake that Mrs. Sterling was handing out, joking with her about the amount of frosting that layered the top.

"Thank you Sam. You were wise to tell me," he said as he dug into the cake.

Rather than pressing him, Sam let the rest of the evening unfold, as Miss Karpatch, Cooley, and Sayvon stopped by to see them. But he and the other three knew from their conversation that Mr. Sterling was hiding his true thoughts from them. Maybe Sam had gone too far, or sounded too accusatory toward Talister. It was, after all, Mr. Sterling's best friend.

"Do you think we shouldn't have told him?" he asked Gus later when they had a moment away from the others.

"I don't see why we would keep something like that from him," Gus responded, his yawns growing more intense. "We heard him speaking. While it's probable that we misinterpreted a conversation, it's still unwise for us to keep information like that silent."

"I guess," Sam responded, inheriting Gus's yawns.

🌲🌲 Chapter Seventeen: Amos

After a few more root cakes and coffee, everyone headed home and the Sterling household stumbled to their rooms. Gus agreed that it was good to be in their own beds again, and after a good shower and tooth brushing, Gus was heard snoring soundly in the dark upper floor of the cabin.

Sam lay in his bed too, exhausted, but unable to sleep once again. There were too many strange pieces to this puzzle that didn't make sense. Why was the secret library reported to have been destroyed, but hadn't? How did Arazel know about the Stone? There was no doubt he could have been following the group the whole time.

Sam remembered the rush of air that passed him and Emma while they were in the artifacts vault once again. Could that have been him? Or did Talister Calpher have a Dark connection with Arazel, and was he feeding him information all along?

An even more concerning question was, who was the person they were talking about removing from Lior City? Was that person the one who threatened to expose their connection to the Darkness?

Sam thought about his grandfather, and of White Pine. They had missed an extra week of school on top of the fall break—not that he had personally missed worrying about Bush lurking around every corner. But it had been nearly a week now, and his grandfather would certainly be getting worried. He wondered if Mr. Sterling had updated Amos while he was investigating Mr. Chivler's disappearance.

These thoughts made Sam question everything he had grown up believing now that he had seen Lior. What was the purpose of even going back to school if there was a celestial battle between good and evil that he was now a part of?

But he was just a boy from Grand Rapids, with a workaholic father and a drunk mother, not a prophet, or a leader of the Darkness, or anything.

Why did they choose him? They knew of Julian because of the journal, but how would they know about the old lady Wrenge? And who could have told them about Sam's dreams?

Hundreds of thoughts flooded his mind, and doubt overcame him. With these questions, the spy within Lior could be anybody,

Chapter Seventeen: Amos

including those he knew well, like Mr. Sterling, or Miss Karpatch, or even *Gus*.

He had forget about it. It would drive him crazy, and before long he would find something to accuse everyone about. Trust was not something he had ever really mastered, and to allow these thoughts would mean to destroy any trust he had built for these people who had loved and cared for him.

But doubt about his past still plagued him, and he fought with the idea that he would never truly become a Descendant of the Light, that he would be forced to live outside of the City, never to return home, and never to be with his friends.

Yet something happened in the forest with Arazel. He had found his gift of Light somewhere within, somewhere between emotions of fearlessness, anger, and determination. It gave him a confidence he couldn't understand, one that made him wonder if there was another person hidden inside of him, one who didn't even understand himself.

Although the incident was foggy now, he remembered producing an intense bolt he couldn't control, nor could he produce it again if he tried. It was more intense than any Light manipulation he had seen since coming to Lior, perhaps even more intense than that of the Sons during their epic battle with Arazel. Thinking of it made his heart beat more loudly, like a silent drum in the night. He knew the feeling it had taken to produce the bolt, and it was born out of a deep desire to protect his friends. They were his family, and seeing them hurt drew out something powerful hidden within. He couldn't help but think that only a true Descendant of Light would feel that way.

He knew sleep would not come easily for him again tonight, but he attempted it nonetheless. No doubt the household would be awake early tomorrow, with a grand breakfast and the Sterlings, Miss Karpatch, and others wanting to know more about their journey. Mrs. Sterling would likely take them to the healer, and would want to wash their clothes and make sure they were properly cared for. It would be a long day, and without sleep, it would be miserable, even if it was meant to be relaxing.

He drifted off somewhere between thinking about watching

Chapter Seventeen: Amos

the Lazuli creatures in the pools outside the Old City and shooting through the sky on the cloud with the Sons of Light. It was almost as if the entirety of the last few days could have been summed up as one crazy dream, but he knew it was much more than that now.

****

Gus and Sam awakened to the sound of bacon crackling in a pan and the smell of fresh coffee wafting throughout the house. They jumped up from bed like kids on Christmas morning, hurrying down the steps to get a cup of coffee and snatch a stray biscuit before the rest of the house could empty the first pot.

Mrs. Sterling was in the kitchen throwing dough onto a flowered pan when Sam and Gus walked through with their cups. She wasn't a large woman by any means, but she could surely fatten a person up from the size of the feasts she whipped up. Both boys greeted her and hugged her tightly just as Mr. Sterling came in the door, his face as white as a ghost.

Mr. Sterling filled up his cup with coffee, and then immediately asked the boys to join him in the living room. They obeyed, Sam sitting in the chair that overlooked the sea, while Mr. Sterling sat opposite him, and Gus on his left. At first, he didn't say anything, just stared out the window at the mist rolling in to the shore. Then he stole a quick glance out both windows and leaned in to Sam.

"We have an issue we need to discuss," he told them.

Sam felt the hair on the back of his neck stand up, even though he knew he shouldn't be afraid of Mr. Sterling by now. After facing Arazel, he should have been ready for anything. But because Mr. Sterling was Emma's father, Sam still felt the nerves working hard.

"I have some unfortunate news," he started, his eyes still darting around the room as if looking for someone that might hear them. Sam was fearing the worst, and a knot grew in the pit of his stomach. Maybe he could just tell him he didn't want to know. But then again, not knowing could be even worse.

"The Council has petitioned to see us, you and I, in a full session,"

Chapter Seventeen: Amos

Mr. Sterling said quietly to Sam. "While I have done my best to reason with them, after an incident that occurred this week with Opus Wrenge, they are growing concerned about the validity surrounding the legend and the Prophecy."

Old Wrenge again, he thought. *Why does this woman haunt him continually?*

"Why would they ever listen to her?" he interrupted.

Mr. Sterling sighed.

"Because she was the one that correctly predicted the attack on the Old City."

"Wow," Gus whistled. "She knew it was going to happen?"

"Yes. She tried to warn them, but to no avail," Mr. Sterling smiled. "I know you four were there the night she appeared at the City gate."

Gus looked at the floor.

"Mr. Sterling, I'm sor—"

"No reason to worry, Gus. I had a feeling you all would follow me after rushing out that night past you," Mr. Sterling smiled, putting a hand on his shoulder. "Actually, I was glad you were there, so you could hear it for yourselves."

"Sir?" Gus finally looked up from the ground.

"Because I believe time is short, for all of us. And for Lior. We need people on our side to help sway as many as we can away from believing the lies that are all around us."

"You think Wrenge is lying?"

Mr. Sterling shook his head.

"I didn't quite say that," he said, holding up a finger, "but the first thing we must understand is that the enemy—the Dark One himself—would have us believe anything other than the truth. We must weigh, discern, study everything, not give into every notion that comes our way. This is true with the Legend, and even the Prophecy as well. While we believe there may be something to the Prophecy, there are still those that would seek to twist it into something else."

"Mr. Sterling, there hasn't been a true prophet for a long time. How can we know when one is from the Creator?"

Mr. Sterling smiled.

Chapter Seventeen: Amos

"We have the most powerful resource of all—the Word of the Creator Himself to tell us that."

"The scrolls," Gus said quietly.

"Yes," Mr. Sterling nodded compassionately. "We must continue to study them, and pray the Creator shows us what to believe about what is to come."

Both boys were silent. They knew what Mr. Sterling was telling them was the best course of action. Many living in Lior, not to mention much of the Council, were headlong into the Legend or the Prophecy. While there could be truth in both, they could be completely false as well, fabricated for the very purpose of leading people astray. A sinister plot it was, and all you had to do was put a spin on the truth.

Mr. Sterling lowered his voice, leaning in so Sam and Gus could hear him clearly.

"Even though the Stone is lost, I believe we still have a case to make to the Council tomorrow about the growth of the Darkness, as well as your descendancy, Sam. You will be with me, of course, but it will be an official Council meeting, so they will be asking questions that may be quite difficult—"

"I'm not afraid, Mr. Sterling."

"Good," he smiled.

"Mr. Sterling, do you believe I am supposed to be part of the Dark One's plans?" The words sounded odd, but they were necessary.

Mr. Sterling turned suddenly, placing a gentle hand on his shoulder.

"Absolutely not. I believe in the sovereignty and goodness of the Creator. He would never use a boy striving for good to become a harbinger of Darkness. And you would do good to trust that."

As the words sunk in, the dining room of the cabin seemed to fill up with people from the cabin circle, many of them welcoming them back quietly from their journey to the Old City. Quickly it became clear that, unknown to Sam, Gus, Emma, and Lillia, many of them had been in on the planning all along.

Mr. Sterling was quick to shield anyone from invading Sam's space, as he knew he would need some time to consider their conversation

Chapter Seventeen: Amos

and impending Council meeting. Knowing there would be no one to interrupt them, Mr. Sterling smiled and pointed him into a chair next to his daughter, who, even after sleeping in, looked as though she could still win a beauty contest.

Although the breakfast was one of Mrs. Sterling's finest spreads, Sam had lost his appetite after the conversation. He did his best to eat what he could, but the eggs and chocolate gravy and biscuits tasted like sponges to him. Even the coffee tasted like hot ink sliding down his throat.

After breakfast, Sam quickly excused himself and went upstairs, trying not to give the impression that anything was wrong. It seemed as though he succeeded, because the rest of them stayed at the table for nearly an hour, joking around and talking as he slipped out of his silky pajamas and into a clean pair of jeans sitting on his bunk.

He just needed rest … and to sort this all out. So many beliefs in all sorts of ideas, just like the world he knew back home. Somehow he had hoped this world would be better, that it would have it figured out, but Lior seemed to have just as many problems as Creation did. Maybe more.

But there was no going back, no forgetting. He needed to see this through, to discover who he was.

Sam turned over his palm and closed his eyes. Concentrating on the same Light he had felt when going through the arch or riding the Ruach, he focused on his palm, gently calling the Light through his body to his fingertips.

He opened his eyes and saw the blue orb pulsing softly in his open hand. He watched as it flowed as if it had life, or as if something was directing its every move. It glowed a beautiful iridescent blue, like the Lazuli that was everywhere in Lior. It had an incredible quality to it—warm, and it just felt right for some reason.

Closing his palm, his mind wandered back to the forest with Arazel. His power was different somehow. Stronger, in a sense, and filled with raw anger. It was as though driven by some unmistakable surge of passion. In a sense, it was not unlike the way Sam felt inside when he fought him, sending a blinding bolt of Light straight at the

Chapter Seventeen: Amos

man who had incapacitated his friends. It came from deep within, as a monster that hid just below the surface waiting to emerge, just like the giant deformed crocodile in the swamp.

He considered slipping out and disappearing from the laughing voices downstairs to track down Arazel and the Stone. He knew it was reckless, but if there were any chance that the Dark Lords would be able to use it somehow to unite the Dark Forces, Sam would be responsible. He knew he wouldn't last long out on his own, but he considered it anyway. Perhaps it would be best another day when the attention wasn't so trained in his direction.

The rest of the day Sam spent quietly reading and relaxing, allowing Mrs. Sterling to pamper them with plenty of hot coffee and ham and cheese biscuits she had topped with a honey butter glaze. At noon she rounded them up to visit Darva, the slender young healer in town, as suggested by Nibitz. She put them in a spa-like medieval bath where they soaked for nearly an hour before she led them to an indoor botanical garden lined with cots among the foliage, instructing them to lay flat on their backs to stare at the diamond colored glass dome above them. Then she went from cot to cot where she began passing her hands over their entire bodies. Every so often Sam thought he could see a whisper of Darkness drift upward from one of them, which was immediately absorbed into the dimmed Lazuli lamps around the room. For the first time since their journey into Old Lior, Sam began to relax, allowing the warm Light to penetrate him as deep as it would go.

The next morning, Mr. Sterling was waiting for Sam when he came down dressed for breakfast. Sam had managed to keep the conversation between Mr. Sterling and him and Gus from the girls to not worry them, but it hadn't been easy. They could tell he was acting different, but he was able to pass it off as a stomachache. He wanted to tell them. In fact, it was the first time he had wanted to tell someone how he really felt.

Mr. Sterling knew he would be nervous about the meeting with the Council, so he had a steaming cup of coffee and a large piece of

Chapter Seventeen: Amos

root cake in front of Sam almost as soon as he sat down. He wasn't sure why they drank so much coffee in Lior, but today, like the other days, he welcomed it. The only other person he saw that drank as much coffee as the people here was his grandfather Amos.

"Good morning, Sam," Mr. Sterling sipped his coffee.

"Good morning, Mr. Sterling," Sam said nervously.

Mr. Sterling smiled.

"There is no reason to be nervous, boy. I believe this will be short and sweet," he said. "Just leave most of the talking to me."

"Yes sir," Sam said, relieved.

While everyone else was sleeping, Mr. Sterling and Sam slipped out of the cabin and walked down the morning mist-covered pathway to the Red Hall street. The sun was just beginning to make an entrance into the interior of the City while they walked, and stores were just beginning to stir as shopkeepers began to unlock windows and open up the canopies from their carts.

The guard, Achiam, greeted them as they entered through the Red Hall door, immediately closing it behind them. Mr. Sterling led them down the same hallway that Emma had taken him down when they were on the balcony, and then they turned and walked down the ornate wide steps into the heart of the Red Hall banquet center. The doors were closed to the center amphitheater in the middle of the four represented halls, but still the hall was open and large like Sam remembered. Somewhere below this one, Sayvon had taken him on a tour into the bowels of the City Center.

Nerves began to creep back into his body as they approached the stairwell that led to the Council waiting area and the doors leading into the amphitheater. He wished nothing more then to be back in the boring, dysfunctional living room of his foster parents, where his foster mom was most likely pouring a shot of whiskey into her morning coffee.

Mr. Sterling stopped at the wood door with the curious carvings etched into it and turned to Sam, holding his palm out toward him.

"Creator, we ask you for your grace upon our Samuel as we speak

Chapter Seventeen: Amos

to the Council, that you will cover him with your enabling power, as you have covered Lior with your great hand."

Sam closed his eyes, but could not focus. He, too, sent up a quick prayer to the Creator, whoever He was, asking Him to speak for him. They were hurried words, but he meant every one.

****

The wood door opened from the inside, which meant they were prepared and waiting for them. The Council amphitheater was full of colorful robes from the four regions, and the members were separated into the Telok, Themane, Nais, and Thalo seating quarters, represented by a large ornate cloth banner above each one. Almost immediately upon entering, Sam saw a massive three-pronged arch in the center of the room, its legs extending to three points in the room. At each leg stood a different white statue, each holding an object in one hand and a torch in the other. The statue closest to them bore a tablet that resembled the Ten Commandments from the story of Moses in the Bible.

Sam looked to the members from Thalo, their robes blending together like a sea of red. He didn't recognize any of them, but it seemed like all of their eyes were on him as he and Mr. Sterling were led immediately to the podium in front of the High Council's table. The nerves once again began to kick in, and Sam felt a bead of sweat trickle down his temple as the room grew painfully silent.

The High Council table was filled except for one spot, in which stood an exceptionally ornate chair in the center of the others. As Mr. Sterling and Sam sat down in front of the small podium, a small door opened behind the glossy cuffs of the High Council, and an aging man in a brilliant silver robe emerged from it.

Suddenly, the entire room stood to their feet, including Mr. Sterling, so Sam stood as well. As the Chancellor approached his seat, Sam noticed one of the High Council members taking more time than usual getting to his feet. It was a very tired-looking Talister Calpher.

Chapter Seventeen: Amos

"The High Council in the name of the Creator will now convene!" called a small man in the corner of the amphitheater that Sam hadn't even noticed, and suddenly, all three torches held by the statues surrounding the arch in the center lit simultaneously.

As the Chancellor took his seat, the rest of the members in the room did as well and began conversing quietly amongst themselves. It was the first sound of ambient noise that Sam had heard since entering, and he welcomed anything that would take the focus off of him.

For a moment the Chancellor seemed to stare down at the table in front of him, but then raised his head to peer down through his glasses at Mr. Sterling.

"Jack, are you choosing to forfeit your vote in this matter by standing with the boy?" the Chancellor asked, his voice booming throughout the room.

Jack Sterling stood and walked to the podium.

"Yes, Chancellor, that is correct," he said loudly, his voice echoing throughout the room. "I am here not only to vouch for this young man, but to stand with him."

"Very well," the Chancellor leaned back in his chair. "Samuel James Forrester ... is that your name young man?"

So they would choose him as their first target.

Sam tried to clear his throat but just ended up making some sort of awkward squeaking sound. He stood up and walked slowly to the podium to stand next to Mr. Sterling, who promptly put a hand on his shoulder.

"Don't be afraid, son. They just want to get to know you," he whispered to him.

"Yes it is," Sam squeaked at the Chancellor.

The Chancellor took off his glasses.

"We mean no harm here, Samuel. Just tell us the truth about everything you know. Can you do that?"

"Yes sir."

He put his glasses back on the tip of his nose and appeared to read something again on the table before him.

🌲 Chapter Seventeen: Amos

"It says here that you have never before been to Lior, is that right?"

"Yes that is right. This is my first time," Sam said, a little more confidently.

"How do you like our little city?" the Chancellor said, smiling an awkward but comforting smile at Sam.

"It's nice. I would like to stay here."

A soft rumble of chuckles could be heard throughout the chamber upon Sam's words.

The Chancellor turned his spectacles back on Jack, clearing his throat and lowering his gaze.

"Jack, you understand that in order for us to establish his true descendancy …" the Chancellor waived his hand as if dismissing the thought. "Regardless of his background, we must have solid evidence that he has received the gift of Light from the Creator," he said solemnly.

Jack opened his robe and took out a small silver device much like the surfing discs that Bogglenose had given them. He tapped the center, which immediately produced a blue hologram image in his palm. Then, as he placed the disc on the podium, the image suddenly sprang from the disc and portrayed a massive version of itself in the center of the amphitheater.

"The Protector's Office received this late yesterday morning," Jack told them.

Then the voice of the image began to speak, and out of the corner of his eye, Sam caught a glance of Harper Cooley stand halfway in his chair to glare at the image.

"It will be noted in the records that an event was captured by Chorim while in the Seer chamber," the man said calmly. "This is event number four hundred thousand six hundred twenty-seven."

Then the bald man disappeared and an image of the clearing back in the forest flickered into view. A blurry image of Sam could be seen standing in the clearing with a hooded figure in front of him. He was only the shadow of a man in the hologram, but Sam remembered the face of Arazel clearly. His heart leapt at the images, and his stomach

Chapter Seventeen: Amos

felt suddenly sick. Smoke shot from Arazel's outstretched palm to meet the large bolt of blue Light from Sam's palm.

The amphitheater erupted into hushed whispers and surprised chatter at the event. The Chancellor squinted at the hologram through his spectacles while Talister Calpher sat in his chair beside him, looking uneasy as the Council grew restless. Then, as suddenly as the holographic recording started, it ended.

Jack Sterling picked up the silver disc and the images disappeared.

"As you see, Chancellor, this young man has not only been gifted by the Creator, but he possesses extraordinary abilities that most Descendants at his age do not normally have," he said.

"I see," the Chancellor said once the room quieted down. "Does the boy have any previous experience with the gifts?"

Mr. Sterling looked down at Sam, nodding his head to answer the question.

"Uh, no sir. I never really knew about it," he said meekly.

The Chancellor sighed deeply, then looked around the amphitheater.

"As you may know, there are some who believe that there may be some truth to the Dark Force's claim on the Prophecy. While I don't share those sentiments, I must make inquiries on the behalf of the regions that are concerned."

The Chancellor looked down to Sam suddenly, a look of sympathy on his face. Then he once again looked around at the members in the room.

"Some of you have even expressed concern that this boy may even be connected to the Prophecy."

The room erupted in hushed whispers.

What? They actually believe it could be me? Sam couldn't believe what he was hearing. Sure, it was a fleeting thought, but now Council members were believing the nonsense?

Sam looked at Mr. Sterling, who had a downcast look upon his face. It was enough to tell Sam that he hadn't heard the whole story.

"I do find it prudent to inquire into the boy's past," the Chancellor continued, and the crowd was silent once again. "I have taken the

🌲🌲 Chapter Seventeen: Amos

liberty of doing some research on my own," he said, then looked down at the paper in front of him once again. "You grew up in a place called 'Grand Rapids,' with Phillip and Sylvia Forrester ... your foster parents, is that right?"

Sam was a bit taken aback at the information, but not surprised that they knew. They had the Seers, the Sons, and many other connections. Instead of questioning how they knew, he chose not to show emotion, only nod.

"I understand they weren't the best of role models, were they?" the Chancellor looked to Sam for an answer, but received none.

"What can you tell me about your true father and mother?" the Chancellor tried a different angle.

"They were killed in a car wreck when I was young," he said loudly, swallowing any emotion attached to the information because he had said it so many times before.

"I see," the Chancellor cleared his throat. "I am very sorry to hear that. You have been staying in White Pine with your grandfather ... Amos?"

"Yes."

"What can you tell me about him?" the Chancellor asked while looking down at the paper in front of him.

"Well, I don't know much actually," Sam began to say, but was suddenly interrupted by commotion from behind him.

He turned to see his grandfather standing behind him in the entrance of the amphitheater, wearing a flowing red robe of the Thalo hall.

****

"I suppose he could just ask me himself. Isn't that right, Almeous?" his Grandfather said loudly, causing more commotion from the amphitheater.

The Chancellor was obviously shaken by Sam's grandfather's entrance, and for a moment he had to move his spectacles around his nose until he could see him properly.

376

Chapter Seventeen: Amos

"Chancellor Ramis?" he said, which brought an immediate eruption of surprised conversation from around the room.

"It has been a long time," his grandfather said once the noise died down. "You have been foolish with your alliances I see."

The Chancellor cleared his throat and sat down in his chair.

"Ramis, we have been working to secure those alliances that best suit our needs as a people," he said defensively. "But politics cannot be why you have surprised us here today."

"No," his grandfather said. "I have come here to represent the boy you have put on display here, as his grandfather, Amos."

Hushed whispers once again filtered through the Council as they recognized the connection between the former Chancellor and Sam.

"You are the boy's grandfather he calls Amos?"

Amos nodded.

"For reasons I cannot divulge, I have been in hiding," he looked at Sam, "until recently."

Sam looked at his grandfather, who wasn't the same person he knew from White Pine. The flannel shirt and jeans were gone, and he showed remarkable confidence in the presence of so many people. The spirit about him was so powerful that when he spoke, the room grew silent.

The Chancellor stared silently at the three on the platform for many moments.

"We are merely surmising this young man's abilities, former Chancellor Ramis. He shows abilities that surpass most other Descendants."

"Of that, I am sure. I was aware that some of these possibilities exist, but let us get to the deeper question, shall we?" His grandfather stepped forward to the podium. "You are silently assessing his potential for fulfilling the legend of the Dark Prophecy—which, I should say, is a little premature, is it not?"

"Ramis, some on the Council are concerned with the boy's unknown past. It has been heard that the Dark Forces believe that one from Creation will become the second to the one called Nasikh, The

🌲🌲 Chapter Seventeen: Amos

Dark One," the Chancellor said, eliciting another round of rumblings from the Council.

"There have been many to come to Lior from Earth," his grandfather interrupted. "He is only one."

"Yes, yes," the Chancellor countered. "But the Dark Forces would have him—"

"Meaningless," Amos answered him.

Sam knew it was true, because Arazel told him that very thing in the forest. Believing it, however, was something he would never do.

"Ramis, you understand we must have full disclosure on the boy's past to be sure. What can you tell me of his mother and father?" the Chancellor pressed.

Amos looked to his grandson and a look of concern poured over his face. He then raised his eyes to meet those of the Chancellor.

"That is hardly the topic we should be discussing in a public Council, do you not agree?"

The Chancellor looked as though he was going to argue, but then paused and gave thought to the words.

"I agree ... but what of the gifts he possesses?"

His grandfather nodded slightly.

"Yes, they are powerful, perhaps rising out of some lost Descendant lineage somewhere. But they hardly mean he is to become the leader of a massive army of Darkness. They are undeveloped and in need of guidance. Guidance that could be found here in the City."

The amphitheater erupted into hushed chatter at his words, and the Chancellor stood and raised his hand to quiet them.

"Is there anyone here who wishes to speak for or against the boy at this time?" his voice boomed throughout the room.

No one spoke at first, but then a younger man with a blue robe stood and raised his hand.

"I wish to speak," he called loudly.

"The Council recognizes the Council member from Telok," the Chancellor boomed.

The man in the blue robe stared down at Sam.

"I know he is just a boy, but the people of Telok believe it would

Chapter Seventeen: Amos

be a mistake to allow the boy to go on unguarded," he said, but was immediately cut off by arguments around the room.

When the Chancellor stood again to stop the conversation, the amphitheater quieted down, allowing the man to continue.

"In the North, we have been experiencing more attacks than usual on our convoys to Nais, and we have heard reports that Dark creatures are more active, not to mention we have confidence that this activity is a result of the boy's arrival in Lior."

At his words, the room erupted once again, even louder than before. It took Mr. Sterling projecting a massive holographic map of Lior in the center of the room for the noise to finally die down.

"Friends, Chancellor, if I may answer that charge with a statement from the Protectors Office," Mr. Sterling said loudly from the podium. "While we too have been seeing a rise in activity around certain portions of Lior, as you can see by the chronological sequencing of the activity from the past until now, the map showing the sections of Lior covered in Darkness from the time of the fall of the Old City hasn't shown any significant growth."

The Chancellor peered at Mr. Sterling, then back to Sam.

"You know full well, Jack, that the events as of late have been unusual in nature. We must consider those as well," he said grimly.

"Yes, you are right, Chancellor. We believe at the PO that there is something covering Lior, like a shroud meant to deceive us into thinking we are immune."

Again the room burst into commotion, with some angry shouts being called out from various regions. Some even called out portions of the Prophecy.

"Jack, are you saying that we can't really see what is happening in Lior?"

At that moment, Sam understood the Chancellor's motive in the Council meeting. While it seemed at first that his request to see Sam and Mr. Sterling was an interrogation, it was evident that it was quite the opposite. Through the questions, he was merely making light of a larger, more dangerous situation, and he wanted the Council to understand the gravity of the situation.

Chapter Seventeen: Amos

"The PO is looking into the matter, Chancellor."

Chancellor Almeous sat back in his chair, waiting for the room to grow quiet once again.

"This land has been free from the threat of Darkness for many years. Many here say the Darkness is growing again, but there is no proof that I can see, and no word from the Seers of this activity. We must get this proof somehow."

Sam remembered the wall of Darkness outside the Old City, and the thick mass within the swamp. Why weren't the Seers able to see it?

"We have already sent out some PO agents to the spots the young people saw, but there was no sign of new growths—"

"Because there are none!" hollered a young Council member from Nais, at which point the amphitheater erupted into multiple shouting matches between members of different halls, as well as their own.

"Send him out of the City!" cried another. "He is a risk to Lior's safety!"

It took a massive eruption of Light exploding from the outstretched palms of the Chancellor to bring everyone to silence.

"As you can see, we are having trouble coming to a conclusion," the Chancellor sighed heavily. "I do remind those skeptical of the ability of the Dark Forces to orchestrate such a deception that only fifty years prior we were forced to build a new city simply because we chose to be blinded to their power. We buried many that day, some of whom were your family."

The Council remained quiet at the Chancellor's words, but one older member from Themane stood and looked compassionately at Sam.

"If there is one thing I have learned in my many years traveling back and forth between Lior and Creation, it is that young people have the incredible ability to see what we cannot," he paused to catch his breath, and still no one challenged his words. "Often we are blinded because we refuse to look past our own hands…" he held them up in front of him, "… and the Light which we hold is often the same Light that blinds us."

The man's words were stunning to say the least. He had incredible

Chapter Seventeen: Amos

wisdom that he had gleaned over the ages, and the Council seemed to calm at his words. Whether they believed him or not, that was a different story, but at least the tone of the meeting had changed.

"What do you suggest we do concerning the boy, Chancellor?" Talister Calpher spoke suddenly, his usual wide grin now only a smirk on his face.

The Chancellor peered at Sam.

"The High Council will make that decision, based upon their region's demands—"

Sam's grandfather stepped to the podium suddenly, as if to relieve Mr. Sterling from his quickly rising anger with some of the members of the Council who advocated sending Sam out of the City.

"Former Chancellor Ramis, unless you see another way?"

"I do, Chancellor," he said loudly, sternly. "My dear brothers and sisters of the Council, have we considered the dragon? He can determine the boy's true gift, can he not?"

Again there was chatter throughout the chamber as the Council members considered the former Chancellor's suggestion. Nearly all of the members from two of the regions, Telok and Themane, were in agreement, while large pockets of Nais and Thalo members held out with some concern.

Suddenly a light-skinned member from Nais stood and waited for the room to be quiet once again.

"The dragon's intuition on Descendants has not been called upon for hundreds of years. We only keep one here as a symbol of tradition and strength, not upon which to decide our membership!"

"Aye! I agree! Dragons are fickle creatures that can't be trusted! We must rely on research and the Council for making the decisions!" hollered a thin taller man from the Thalo section.

"What other choice do we have?" a younger member from Nais called out. "It's not like we can send him back into Creation with his knowledge of Lior! It'd be a major security breach if I ever saw one!"

A larger, older gentleman in the back of the Thalo region stood carefully as the arguing died down.

"Might I say a word?" he spoke feebly. "It may be noted that in

Chapter Seventeen: Amos

the cases in the past where the dragon has been summoned, the truth has always been revealed."

"And the other times have left that someone dead!" someone called out anonymously from the back of Thalo section.

Dead? What is he talking about?

Talister Calpher stood suddenly.

"Citizens and Council members, I want to welcome this boy in our City as much as anyone, but the dragon? Placing the boy at its mercy is foolish! We cannot trust the security of our City to a—a giant lizard that is thought to have spiritual insight, can we?" he steadied himself on the railing in front of him. "I implore you, former Chancellor Ramis, don't make this mistake. He is just a boy."

The Chancellor nodded at Talister's words, then peered at Sam's grandfather.

"Yes, it is dangerous, Ramis. Only Descendants with the true gift of Light come back from Ayet Sal on the back of the dragon. If the boy has any connection with the Darkness, he will not return."

Sam froze where he stood. There it was again. The name—Ayet Sal. The Valley of Death. Why does the name keep coming up around him? Unless the old woman, Miss Wrenge, was right. The Valley of Death ... It—whoever or whatever—was calling him, just as she had said.

"We can't just force a human boy to go to the most dangerous place in Lior alone. No, I suggest we continue in the search for the boy's ancestry, for his father. Try the earthly records another time." Other members tried to make their case from the various halls.

Sam was tired of hearing them talk about him. His safety, that he is just a boy ... he was sick of listening to it, listening to them decide his fate with him right there in the room. It was the same old politics, no different than Earth. The same diplomatic mumbo jumbo he had heard from his foster parents and their friends. It was easy to talk about someone else until it happened to you. Then it was amazing how fast things changed in the political world.

"I'll do it," Sam said suddenly, loudly, causing the arguing in the amphitheater to cease suddenly. "I'll go to Ayet Sal with the dragon."

Chapter Seventeen: Amos 🌲🌲

****

The grand hall of the Council was suddenly silent. Talister Calpher had stopped making his case for not sending Sam, and was now peering at Sam through his broken grin. Some other Council members looked puzzled, but there were also some that lifted their eyebrows in amazement at his words.

"Not possible," Talister dribbled out of his stunned lips. "You would never be able to resist the Darkness that place holds."

For some odd reason just then, Sam suddenly knew who Talister Calpher was talking about in the tower on the beach with the bald man. It was *him*. Sam was the dangerous one—the one that Talister believed would eventually destroy the people of Lior, and needed to be removed. Until now, he hadn't even considered himself the threat, but now it made sense. Talister wanted Sam gone before the Darkness won him over. He believed the Prophecy the Metim held to be true, and Sam was the major threat.

Perhaps Talister would obtain political support from regions wanting Sam removed. Maybe his goal all along was to divide the Council, and in ridding Lior of the threat that Sam posed, he would stand a better chance of becoming Chancellor someday.

But the real question was, if they removed him from Lior, what would the bald man from the tower do with him?

Sam looked over at Mr. Sterling, who was solemn in his expression. He wasn't sure if he was angry at Talister, Sam, his grandfather, or anyone for that matter. Either way, he seemed to be holding his words for some reason, choosing not to release what lay within. One thing was for sure—Sam was just glad he had someone fighting for him.

Sam's grandfather stepped to the podium once more.

"The boy is under my care, and it is his wish to go with the dragon to Ayet Sal, which means, with your permission Chancellor, he will go at once. That is, if the dragon is feeling up to the journey?"

The Chancellor nodded wearily.

"He is, Ramis," he said. "But it is not the dragon I am concerned about."

Chapter Seventeen: Amos

Following another few moments of commotion from the Council after the Chancellor's agreement to let Sam go, another member from the Telok section stood slightly and was acknowledged to speak.

"And if the boy somehow returns and he is successful in determining his gift, what then shall we do with him? Shall we wait another Creation cycle to welcome him as a true member of Lior?" he said loudly, which raised a few nods and grunts of agreement from the rest of the Council.

The Chancellor held up his hand.

"Nothing will be done with the boy until the start of mentorship classes, after which we can discuss the Lazuli Jubilee ceremony. As I am told, the Sterlings will be heading back to White Pine when the week is out. I am sure my fellow Council members will allow him to be welcome in the City until then." He looked around the room as if expecting resistance, but seeing none, looked to Sam. "I am sorry you have been caught up in this, young man, and I, personally, extend my promise to you that whatever is decided will be in your best interest as well as ours. Now as we adjourn, I would like to invite the High Council, former Chancellor Ramis, and Mr. Sterling to remain in my office for a few moments."

He then extended his hand and blue Light shot from his palm, dousing the large blue flames dancing from the three statues at the arch legs.

All at once, Sam was again alone in a sea of conversation and robes, members standing and leaving the amphitheater, and the slow lazy blue Light crawling up the spires of the City outside the windows. His grandfather and Mr. Sterling had abandoned him without a word, but they shot him a quick wink as they left the platform. Apparently they knew something he didn't.

His grandfather Amos, Ramis as they called him, had led him to believe he was nothing more than a small farmer getting by in a small Northern Michigan town. But no, he was a Descendant—*and* former Chancellor of all of Lior.

Why had he not told Sam about it? He knew Lior must be kept a secret, but why not tell him? Perhaps he was being protective. Although,

Chapter Seventeen: Amos

they hadn't been really close and he didn't see his grandfather as the sheltering type. Obviously, if he was sending him to one of the most dangerous places in all of Lior on the back of a dragon, he wasn't protecting him from anything.

He stood underneath the leg of the arch nearest the entrance to the amphitheater. He longed to talk with Emma, Gus, and Lillia, not about his future in Lior, but about the Council's take on the Dark Prophecy. But even more, something compelled him to continue the search for the Watcher Stone.

Turning and making his way out of the amphitheater and through the Thalo hall, he ducked past Achiam at the entrance to avoid having to explain why he was alone. Mr. Sterling didn't tell him to wait, but he may have wanted him to. He wasn't in the mood to talk, nor to pretend like he was pleased with what happened at the Council meeting.

No, now he was adopting his foster father's philosophy on going through difficult times—throw yourself into your work.

When he reached the cabin, the others were eating breakfast. Bleary-eyed, they greeted him when he sat down to a cup of coffee Mrs. Sterling had waiting for him. Mr. Sterling had already instructed Mrs. Sterling to let the others know what was going on, so as soon as breakfast was over, they nearly pushed him out the door and to the pavilion. He was immediately cornered by Emma, who was very concerned with the outcome of the Council meeting.

"So the whole Council met just for you?" she asked after he relayed most of the meeting details.

"Yeah, I guess so," he started to say.

"Kinda ridiculous to be afraid of you," Lillia interrupted. "No offense, newb, but you aren't that intimidating."

"Yes, I suppose they do that with every potential great leader of Darkness," Sam said.

"That's not funny," Emma stuck her finger in his face. "Usually they only take them to the Research Office for a background investigation, during which of course they find out their Descendant roots and that's the end."

"Maybe it's his massive biceps," Lillia added with a smirk.

Chapter Seventeen: Amos

"If we just knew where his father was," Gus added quietly.

Emma paced furiously behind them.

"So the regions are really going to accept this Dark Legend as real? What are they thinking? The Creator would never allow this to happen to someone like him! It's just not true!"

"We can't know the Creator's purpose in what He does, Emma," Lillia reminded her.

Once again, they were discussing him, not *with* him. Sometimes he felt that in doing the best thing for him, they overlooked his thoughts entirely.

Emma stomped around for a moment longer, then sat down next to him, suddenly sympathetic.

"I-I just don't understand after what happened in the forest they would still think Sam is a threat!" she stammered. "Why can't they just believe what we would tell them? That Sam fought Arazel with the Light! Not the *Darkness*!"

Lillia looked strangely at Sam.

"Yeah, newb, why didn't you tell them about that?"

"I didn't have to," Sam admitted. "A Seer saw it happen."

Emma threw up her hands.

"And they still think you are a risk?"

"I suppose so."

Gus looked Sam up and down, as if surmising his threat ability.

"I suppose they really don't have a choice but to be sure. If they don't know his lineage, he could have been infiltrated by the Darkness and still produce Light for a time," he said. "Maybe if you could tell us a little more about the outcome of the meeting."

Sam nodded and told them the whole story, how many of the Council members were concerned he may be connected to the Dark Legend, and how his grandfather showed up in the amphitheater and suggested sending Sam to Ayet Sal with the dragon to determine once and for all if he was truly a Descendant of Light. It wouldn't prove his lineage, but it would settle the Council's—and many others' fears of who he was. Return with the dragon, and they had no choice but to accept him as one of their own.

Chapter Seventeen: Amos

Initially, Emma took it well, but as the day wore on, she began to show signs of anxiety, as though it was her that would be going. But that was something Emma always seemed to do—take on the emotions of others, whether good or bad.

Both Lillia and Gus were silent the majority of the day, and instead of discussing the situation, they concerned themselves with helping Emma calm down before they were all called in to finish a few chores around the cabin.

As Sam predicted, he caught them eyeing him throughout the day with disbelief and the slightest bit of fear in their eyes, even though they hid it rather well. It was almost as if he was a new person in their eyes, much different than the bloodied boy who lay on the floor after being pummeled by a bushy-headed bully.

But there was a real threat out there, and now they knew it. The Council, buried in their own confusion over the validity of the Legend, was bent on sticking their heads in the sand. But at least now they had something to agree upon. If Sam came back from Ayet Sal in one piece, they would allow him to stay. It was a start.

But somehow, they had to get the Stone back. Since Arazel in the forest, Sam felt the Stone was the key to the lifting of the curse, even if he didn't know how. But something told him that the search for the Stone and its purpose was to begin at Ayet Sal with the dragon.

He couldn't explain it, but as the day went on, he felt more peace about the ordeal. Something was there for him to see, and he was committed to going. Perhaps it was the Stone, and perhaps not. Maybe old Wrenge was telling him of the place only so his curiosity would drive him crazy. Or perhaps it was a trap so Arazel could finish him off.

None of the scenarios made much sense, but it wasn't going to stop him from going. Risky or not, he was tired of not knowing who he was, and for whatever reason, he believed there was a clue that waited for him at the other end of the journey with the dragon.

It wasn't long before Mr. Sterling, Cooley, and Sam's grandfather returned from the meeting with the Chancellor. The dragon was being prepared immediately, and directly following Mrs. Sterling's

Chapter Seventeen: Amos

mandatory snack of coffee and cakes, Sam was to go and pack a small backpack, which he would take with him for the overnight trip.

****

It was surreal to sit at the table with everyone and listen to the cheery conversation. They all seemed reluctant to talk with Sam about the trip. Every so often Mr. Sterling glanced in his direction, but his grandfather didn't acknowledge him even once. Following the Council meeting, neither Mr. Sterling nor Sam's grandfather told him what they had met with the Chancellor about, and Sam resisted the urge to ask. He had decided to go to Ayet Sal—alone. It seemed once again he was on his own, which was what he was used to anyway.

His friends watched as he packed water, some root cakes and dried meat, a Lazuli lantern, and his leather journal into his backpack. There were a few other odds and ends, but they had told him he should return late that night or early the following morning, so there wasn't much to prepare for.

He gazed at a small note that Emma had slipped into a side pocket while no one else was looking.

I believe in you, was all that it read. But it was enough.

He could tell she was genuinely afraid, so he did his best not to show her he was too. There may be a time when he could show his true emotions, but now was not the time. He had to show resolve, confidence, and aloofness; otherwise those emotions would get the best of him. His foster father, Phillip, taught him that.

When it was time, Mr. Sterling, Sam's grandfather, Cooley, and Emma were waiting at the door when Sam came down the stairs. Gus gave him a rather awkward hug, and Lillia nodded to him from the living room. Oddly, when Sam glanced at her a second time, he thought she looked like she had been crying.

Mrs. Sterling rushed from the kitchen with another small package that smelled like hazelnut and wine, and she kissed Sam on the cheek while she handed him his robe. Instinctively, he threw his arms around

Chapter Seventeen: Amos

her and hugged her, feeling for the first time in his life like he had a mother figure that truly cared for him.

His grandfather put a hand on his shoulder, signaling that it was time to go, and the five of them headed for town. He didn't want to ask any questions, although there were a million to ask. He only wanted to walk in the quiet of the afternoon, and he sensed the others wanted the same.

They passed the City Center and through the trees to the same path where they had returned from the Sons of Light Center after battling Arazel. Before reaching the gate that led to the beautiful garden and ivy-covered pavilion, they forked left and headed down a steep path nearly to the shoreline. Behind them, the cliff that led to the great spires of the City Center towered over the grainy beach, giving a sovereign air of grandeur over the entire scene.

In front of them, propped up against the coastal horizon, in a clearing of a tall clumped-grass garden surrounded by thick pines, stood a large stone building with a spire protruding directly out of its deeply sloped roofline. Beyond the trees, the waves from the breezy afternoon pounded the shoreline just below the garden.

The massive dragon they named Orono stood calmly in front of the building, his iridescent scaled coat glimmering in the warm fall sun. There was no silver and white armor on his body, and no lights adorned his wings. The only unnatural item on his body was a large man-sized basket harnessed around his lower neck.

The wrinkled old Keeper with long silver hair and a thin braided beard that nearly touched his midsection stood just beneath the dragon's belly. With a hand on the dragon's mighty foot, he scowled as he watched the five persons emerging from the pathway in the trees. His red robe was faded, but he still looked the part of a distinguished professor or an aged wizard.

Sam's heart began to beat faster the closer they drew to the great beast, until he was sure it would beat right out of his chest. Somewhere along the way Emma had grabbed his hand, and as they got closer, she squeezed tighter. Something stirred inside him once again when

Chapter Seventeen: Amos

she touched him, forcing him to walk carefully so he wouldn't trip over his own feet. His knees too wanted to buckle with every stride. Perhaps it was anxiety mixed with anticipation of what he was about to do, maybe combined with a renewed affection for the girl walking steadily beside him in one of his most fearful moments.

His grandfather, Ramis, ignored the massive creature standing calmly above him and greeted the Keeper as if they were old friends. They kissed each other on the cheek and exchanged firm hand grasps before admiring the color and gigantic tail of the dragon as if they were judging a dog show.

As the old Keeper invited the rest of them to join in greeting Orono, Mr. Sterling pulled Sam aside briefly, a deep look of concern in his eyes.

"Samuel, you know I already consider you as one of my own …" he started, emotion quickly rushing to his face, "and I don't pretend to like this decision one bit, but this is, in fact, what is best."

"You, my grandfather, and the Chancellor planned all of this, didn't you?" Sam remembered their curious behavior in the Council meeting.

Mr. Sterling nodded.

"It was the only way to get the Council to agree to let you go."

Unbelievable. They set the whole thing up without his knowledge. They played the bad guys in the meeting so that the Council would have mercy on him.

"Mr. Sterling, what is this place—Ayet Sal?"

"As I am sure you have heard, Ayet Sal is dangerous. It is the place of untethered souls—of those who have chosen the Darkness over Light and have finally withered under the strain of the Darkness. They are now awaiting true death, a release from their pain," he continued. "Others have gone before you and never returned. The souls—the Darkness—will feed on any emotion you have, but most of all, they feed on *fear*. They will test you to the point of insanity—and lure you to their prison. You must not give in."

"I still don't understand why I must go."

Chapter Seventeen: Amos

"Ayet Sal is the only place that can reveal your spiritual or earthly identity. Since we do not have the records to prove your descendancy, this is the only other way of determining you're a child of the Light. The dragon will lead you to where you will be the most vulnerable and the most spiritually aware. If you are truly a Descendant of Light, the dragon will see it. The Watchers were very clear about not allowing Humans in Lior. It upsets the balance of Creation."

"Too bad I can't just produce a Light bolt in the Council chambers and be done with it."

Mr. Sterling smiled.

"Unfortunately, you can't," he said. "Mystics, humans, and even Metim have learned to mimic the gifts. They have an appearance of goodness, but in effect, are just the opposite. Dragons are the only creatures that can see Light and Dark in their truest forms."

"I just don't want to end up like Miss Wrenge."

Mr. Sterling laughed.

"More like her are showing up these troubling days, although no one will admit it, but don't you worry about it."

"Thank you for your help, Mr. Sterling," Sam said genuinely.

Mr. Sterling put a hand on his shoulder caringly while the wizardly-looking Dragon Keeper motioned for them to come closer.

"Do not worry, Sam. After today, we will see your true purpose in Lior. Then you can rest assured you belong here."

Sam followed Mr. Sterling as they approached the great winged creature. His grandfather and Emma were busy admiring the scales on the dragon's tail when the Keeper, with a glassy but coherent look in his eye, extended his hand to Sam. He briefly held a small grin as they shook hands, but it disappeared quickly beneath his grey mustache.

"So you are the one who will be riding the leviathan, eh?" he bellowed with a chortle.

"Yes sir, I suppose that's me—"

"Well then, you best get to know the beast, or he'll turn you into toast."

He snatched Sam by the collar and marched him in front of the dragon.

🌲🌲 Chapter Seventeen: Amos

"Orono! Please come and meet Sam!" he yelled up beneath the mammoth lizard's snout.

Instantly the dragon lowered his massive head to meet the Keeper's. His head was the size of a large garden shed, and his gaping nostrils were so large Sam believed he could easily fit inside one of them. As his great amber and jade eyes met Sam's, they glowed brightly, even in the afternoon sunlight, seeming to pierce Sam right through to the soul.

"Orono, if you please, would you formally greet our friend here?" the Keeper said.

Orono breathed out suddenly through his huge nostrils, and small puffs of smoke escaped in ring shapes, quickly becoming large clouds that engulfed Sam in eye-scorching smoke that left him in a coughing fit and forced him to bury his head in his robes.

Even after the smoke cleared, it took several minutes before he could even open his eyes once more, at which point he had already realized he was the center of a dragon and his Keeper's practical joke. The Keeper's belly laugh was contagious, and before long, the entire party was chuckling at Sam's expense.

"Sorry boy! I just haven't had the chance to do that in a very long time!" the Keeper continued to laugh, so much so that Sam thought he might split his side.

Sam brushed himself off and regained his composure, standing tall in front of the dragon once again. No fear—that's what Mr. Sterling told him whoever, or whatever, would be looking for. He was going to start now.

The dragon lowered his head once again to meet Sam's gaze. If he was expecting the satisfaction of seeing the human run from him, he wasn't going to get it. Sam met his gaze, and for a moment there seemed to be a power play for control. It was the dragon, finally, that turned and lowered his head first, his demeanor suddenly one of submission.

The Keeper gaped at Sam, in complete awe of what had just transpired. He looked the dragon up and down, then back at Sam.

Chapter Seventeen: Amos

But instead of demanding to know how Sam was able to get Orono to submit to him so quickly, he only bowed his head and extended his hand.

"I am Shatal, from the family line of Telok, and the last of the keepers here in Lior. Welcome to my garden," he said.

"Uh—well, it is nice to meet you, Shatal. I am—*my* name is Sam. I am from Grand Rapids," he said dumbly.

"Excellent," he said, then slapped him on the back. "It looks like we don't need any further instructions here with the dragon as you and he seem to be agreeing with each other. So we best get you right to it."

He led Sam over to the dragon's side where there were steps leading up to its huge shoulders. The others began gathering around as they approached the steps, and suddenly Sam was surrounded by the people he had come to love—each placing their hands on his head while bowing their own. Mr. Sterling began the prayer quietly, his hand becoming instantly warm to the touch. Then his grandfather spoke, his words showing obvious love and concern for Sam as he ventured out. Next came Cooley and his rigid, pious prayer, and finally Emma, whose voice shook with uneasiness and worry on Sam's behalf.

It was enough to make Sam's buried emotions come to the surface. Instantly he was so overcome that he could not hold back the tears.

When she saw his inability to control it, Emma grabbed him and pulled him tight to her. She didn't speak, or move, just allowed him to place his head on her shoulder. It was as if the floodgates of every dammed emotion he held since he could remember opened up. He tried to stop it, but the more he tried, the more he was unsuccessful. These people, the ones that seemed to initially keep everything from him, were actually trying to help him. He was not strong enough to face what he had seen alone, and he was grateful to have them here now. Truly the Creator was looking out for him when he sent him to White Pine.

Emma took her sleeve and wiped back the tears he attempted to conceal. Then she smiled at him, holding his face once again in her

Chapter Seventeen: Amos

hands, and whispered, "It's time to be strong now," so faintly that they were the only ones to hear it.

Mr. Sterling was still praying with his hand over his daughter and Sam, and it was only the Keeper's soft but booming voice that could snap them all back to reality.

"I hate to break up such a sweet moment, but the day is quickly escaping into the shadows, and if this young man is to return at all tonight, he will need to leave now."

Emma handed him his backpack, and Sam followed the Keeper to the steps silently. The emotions were still flooding his mind, but he felt as though a great weight was lifted off of his shoulders for the time being. He looked up at Orono, who seemed eager to be on the move. As they reached the top of the stairs, the Keeper hoisted Sam into the strange-looking basket strapped to the back of the great lizard. Then he handed him his backpack and slapped him on the back.

"Be sure to hang on. Orono here takes some pretty steep dives. There's a blanket in the front of the basket. It will get mighty cold up at some of the heights he takes you to."

"Thank you, Mr. Shatal," Sam told him.

Shatal shook his head.

"Don't thank me, boy. Thank Orono. He's the one that really chose whether or not to take you. Just be good to him, and he'll take care of you. You can count on it."

Sam looked down at the others. Emma clung to her father, half burying her head in his robes. Cooley's expression hadn't changed since earlier that morning, when at moments he almost seemed frustrated that Sam was going. Now he stood gazing into the depths of the sea in front of them.

Suddenly, from the trees on the boundary of the Keeper's garden appeared a young woman quickly making her way up the pathway. Shatal saw Sam peering into the distance and halted his descent on the stairs to get a better glimpse of the person.

Miss Karpatch's robes were flowing behind her as she hurried into the garden toward the dragon. Sam's heart leapt one more time

Chapter Seventeen: Amos

as he saw his once frustrated history teacher running to make sure she saw him off. Seeing the surprised look from Sam, the Keeper climbed the stairs once again and helped Sam out of the basket once more.

He descended the stairs with trembling legs to meet his teacher, who instantly took him in her arms. Sam accepted the embrace, clinging tightly to the woman who at one time was one of Sam's most despised teachers, but now, was a trusted mentor. In some ways, she even felt like the older sibling he never had.

"I believe in you, Samuel Forrester," she whispered in his ear. "I always have."

Sam forced the tears back for what seemed like the millionth time. "Thank you Miss Karpatch."

Once again, he climbed the stairs to the basket on the dragon, this time without help from the Keeper. He strapped himself in, situating his backpack, and nodded to the Keeper that he was ready.

****

Shatal lifted his arms up from the ground and made a gesture with his hands that looked sort of like he was waving to no one in particular, then moved quickly out of the way from the front of the winged creature. Sam felt a sudden lurch from the basket, and the dragon stepped forward from the stairs, stretching his wings out beside him, covering nearly the entire width of the garden. Then he lifted his head up into the air and belched out an incredible fireball, even larger than the one from the Light parade in the City. Sam felt the heat rush back toward him, bathing him in a foul burning warmth, and causing him to bury his head in the front lip of the basket.

With one leap the beast was in the air, pounding its wings against the air as it quickly gained altitude in the afternoon sky. The roar of the wings was tremendous, and other than the deep, rapid breathing of the dragon, Sam could hear nothing else.

He ventured an uneasy lean over the side of the basket and could see the tiny ant-like people of the City crowding through the streets of vendors. The Keeper's garden blended in with the trees and

Chapter Seventeen: Amos

surrounding cliff faces, and none of the group that had seen him off were visible.

The dragon circled the City, where the great spires rose like great white teeth coming out of the mouth of a great monster that appeared to swallow the City Center. They made a low pass just off the coast near Boggle's house on the cliffs before heading directly toward the mountains. They flew low, then climbed upward toward the sparse clouds, then swooped low once again into the forest lowlands, skimming the tops of the thin pointed pines.

He didn't believe it possible, but it was perhaps even more amazing to be flying with the dragon than on the Lightway, with it's euphoric feeling of shooting through the air, or on the Light cloud with the Sons of Light. The great beast beneath him was a master of the skies, using his great wings skillfully to catch updrafts and ride currents to speed their travel.

He had come a long way. Just two weeks ago he wouldn't have believed in God, and now he was flying on the back of a dragon. To place trust in a mythological creature he didn't know existed until coming to Lior was a complete submission of faith, and it was even more so to trust it to take him to a doomed place that could end up swallowing his soul.

The dragon banked toward the same valley between the mountains that brought Sam into this strange land, and sped toward the towers of rock and snow. Sam felt the air change to reflect a biting chill on his hands and face and was glad that Mrs. Sterling slipped an extra blanket into his pack before he left the cabin. They flew steadily upward as the forest gave way to the foothills, and before he knew it, they were passing over a small cabin nestled in the valley, the same cabin he first visited after walking through the arch for the first time, and where Emma had kissed him. It was snowing heavily at the cabin as they flew overhead, and drifts were piling up steadily against the pines. As he looked back at the scene, the small stream became visible for a brief moment, its icy banks reflecting the momentary sun in the breaks of the clouds.

Sam watched the picturesque scene disappear from view as

Chapter Seventeen: Amos

the dragon continued on through the thinning mountain pass, the massive peaks beginning to close in on them as the valley disappeared beneath them. Past the dragon's left wingtip emerged a glacier that wedged itself between two competing mountain cliffs, glowering over the valley and the curious pair of human and mythical creature as they passed it by. Sam considered its magnificence, having never seen a glacier up close. He had always admired them, even studied them, but had only seen them in pictures. It was beautiful.

Then, almost as if his thoughts were transmitted directly into the dragon's mind, Orono suddenly dipped left, racing downward toward the glacier as if he would fly smack into its face. Just before impact, he stretched his wings out and slowed, gliding calmly next to the wall of ice. It was as though they were suspended next to an incredible frozen wave, and at any moment it could come crashing violently into the valley.

The great dragon soared back up between the peaks of the mountain pass, effortlessly weaving through the narrow valley that soon would take them out of the mountains and into the steamy jungle-like forest. Even though he did his best to stay awake and take in every vista, at some point exhaustion overtook Sam, and he nodded off. Having no consequence, the dragon flew steadily onward toward a forbidden land.

Sam woke in the basket some time later, the sun beginning to disappear into the mountains behind them. There was no way of telling how long they had been in the air, but the cool breezes of the peak were gone, replaced with the misty warm air from the thick deciduous forest beneath them. Still exhausted, he thought about slipping back down into the basket to sleep out the rest of the trip. The dragon's steady beat of the wings was enough to put anyone to sleep, although something told them they were nearing a landing.

As Orono dipped slightly to the left, Sam caught a glimpse of a reflection below that resembled a grease spot on the road after a good hard rain, but after a closer look, Sam realized it was actually a body of water glimmering through the treetops.

The dragon headed straight for it, descending as they flew closer,

🌲🌲 Chapter Seventeen: Amos

until they were soaring only meters above the clear, blue water. There were no signs of life anywhere that Sam could see, except for a lone red and blue bird that steered clear of the great flying mammoth. By now, Sam had grown accustomed to the steep dips and gut-wrenching banks the dragon made, and prepared himself for landing as they slowed near a lone outcropping of rocks on the edge of the dense jungle surrounding the tropical lake.

The dragon bent his tail up suddenly, and the basket tipped upward, nearly dumping Sam into the water below. There was a tremendous beating of wings, and then they were safely on the ledge overlooking the lake. Immediately the dragon bent his long scaly neck down, burying his steaming mouth and nostrils into the sunset-orange water. Sam took a moment to do the same, drinking deep the cool water from the flask that Mrs. Sterling had packed. Then he removed the map from his pack that Gus slipped in his hands before leaving the cabin and attempted a guess at where they were.

The mountains were clearly behind them, putting them somewhere in the Anori Forest on the edge of Clear Lake. From where they stood, the lake looked fairly wide, but according to the map, it also stretched miles north into the region of Nais, where the tropical jungle turned back into alpine forest that led into the Descendant town of Sainia, nestled high in the mountains. They were heading east, straight for the coast of the Yahm Sea, although they could change course at any time.

Gus had shown him the land controlled by the Darkness and the Metim to the north, and just south of that lay the mountains where the Giants claimed their territory. Further east beyond the sea showed a huge chunk of land where rivers snaked every which way, and then the mystical mountains called the Sadak range—the edge of where Liorians believed lay the Divide, and beyond that, Watcher territory.

Somewhere between Lior and where the map ended lay Ayet Sal. According to Gus and the others, no one knew exactly where it was, nor did they attempt to find it. Most believed that it was only accessible by the dragon, and that finding it otherwise was impossible. But now, at age fifteen, a human from a small town on Earth was going to one

Chapter Seventeen: Amos

of the most dangerous places in Lior—*alone,* nonetheless—and his grandfather was the one that was sending him there.

When Orono had his fill of lake water, he spread his wings wide as if enjoying a great stretch, then looked back toward Sam in the basket, as if asking if he was ready to go. But before Sam could get the words out of his mouth, the dragon had already leapt from the ledge and was furiously beating his wings against the moist air.

Strange, he thought as they banked once again toward the east, flying away from the afternoon sun. It was almost as if Orono knew he was ready before he could say it.

They flew for nearly an hour before the dragon began turning to the north, where the slate grey peaks of the Shimshon Mountains where the Giants took residence were beginning to become visible. They weren't as tall as the Agam Mountains, but they rose up in almost straight sheer cliffs, almost resembling that of the City spires.

They would most likely fly to the north of the mountains, according to Gus, then across the narrow point of the Yahm Sea, where the mountains gave way to a long stretch of beach. But it was nearly another two hours before the glimmering evening sand could be seen stretching into the horizon in front of them. The dragon beat his wings to gain altitude as they left the cover of the forest, and suddenly Sam saw why.

Although small from the air, the dark-skinned Giants could be easily seen scattering like buffalo on the sand. It was difficult to tell exactly what they looked like from that altitude, but to Sam they looked exactly like normal people, just much larger.

Dragons were apparently not on the Giants' list of favorite animals, however, as a steady stream of abnormally large arrows began whizzing past them. A few struck Orono's wings and breast without harm but made the dragon climb even higher in the sky to avoid them. Soon they were high enough to see only the occasional arrow lazily flying by them as it lost momentum and began its downward descent. Sam wondered what it would take to bring down a dragon as impenetrable and as smart as Orono, and decided it would require certain speed and skill that most hunters did not have.

Chapter Seventeen: Amos

On they flew, and the night came quickly in the sky. Sam drew some deep breaths before nodding off to sleep again in the basket, listening to the steady beat of the dragon's wings as they transformed into a drowsy pattern of soft drums in the air, gradually becoming part of his dreams.

The arch was black as the sea at midnight as he stood in front of its opening, an overwhelming fear gripping him and forcing him to stand frozen where he was. The figure in front of him placed something into the leg of the arch. Immediately it began to glow a bright blue—but then morphed and dimmed into a deep, dull black cloud. He watched the green lightning as it climbed up the exterior of the arch, forcing it into submission much as a slave to its master.

The figure then stepped away from the arch, and thousands of liquid black shapes with hollow faces poured from the opening. They hovered desolately over him, and once again he was unable to run or scream for help. He writhed from the cold pain that emanated from the dismal spirits as they slowly descended toward him, their vacant eyes becoming hauntingly visible in the Darkness.

But suddenly there was one … a single hollow face that stood out to him. Who was he? Cold and lifeless, he pushed his way through the Darkness toward Sam …

Sam awoke to the pitch black and the sound of beating wings as Orono landed. He had no idea how long he had slept, but he figured it was a long time. As he wiped the sleep from his eyes, the listless feeling was quickly sucked away by an instantaneous fear, one that could only be brought about by a deep presence of Darkness.

For a few moments, he only found the courage to lay in the dragon's basket, listening to the sounds of deathly silence and the soft exhale of the dragon's breathing, waiting for something to make a noise … for something to happen.

The dragon did not move, but seemed restless in the dark scene

Chapter Seventeen: Amos

before them. The air had a thick quality to it, much like a humid summer night when nothing seemed to cool you down, not even a steady breeze. Sam felt the sweat beading quickly on his forehead and slipped his robe and heavy sweater off, folding them neatly next to him in the basket, partly to procrastinate getting out.

He wiped the sweat from his forehead with a handkerchief given to him by Emma, then cinched up his pack on his back carefully, slowly. He didn't want to leave the comfort of the dragon and the basket, but he knew it was the only way to find the answers he needed.

Now there was to be no going back, no ignoring it, no erasing what he would find out. He was going to face whatever it was that kept him from knowing the truth about himself.

He slipped down Orono's wing and hopped onto the hard surface below the dragon's feet. As his eyes adjusted, he noticed he was standing not only on a cobblestone road, but in the center of a very old village. An eerie glow from the moon above began to illuminate the stone houses and storefronts with wooden shingles and shutters through the thick mist, but the light had no seeming source, nor did it contain any warmth or feeling to it.

Then, out of the mist a figure emerged, hobbling down the street in front of the shops. It looked to be an old man wearing nothing but rags and no shoes, and as he drew closer, Sam saw his hollow face appear in the faint light. He didn't acknowledge Sam until he was very close, then stopped suddenly as if stunned by the stranger's presence, turning quickly into one of the store entrances.

Then more figures emerged out of the stores and stone houses, looking the same way the man did. There were young and old alike, all showing the same hollow faces, but not the same fear as the old man. Instead of disappearing back from where they came, they began amassing toward Sam and the dragon.

They weren't people anymore, but shadows of themselves, moving erratically as if they were fighting for control of their bodies, an unknown spirit warring within them. Their eyes were glossy and black like giant marbles, their hands scarred and bubbling with open boils. As he watched them lumber closer, past the crumbling shops

🌲🌲 Chapter Seventeen: Amos

and alleyways, he saw their faces momentarily distort into horrific demonic apparitions, then slowly re-form into their shadowed hollow selves with much effort.

An unholy fear welled up inside Sam suddenly as they approached, and Sam thought for a moment that he would run back to the dragon's wing and hide in the basket, but a flash of movement in the corner of his eye stopped him. Another figure was standing in the middle of the cobblestone street, bathed in a soft white glow. The light grew brighter slowly, until it overpowered the cold unknown light source and poured its warmth into the street.

The shadowed people suddenly dropped to their knees and wailed, clawing at their eyes as if poisoned by the Light. As the figure moved closer, the light began to blur his outline, bathing every corner of the cobblestone village in pure Light.

Sam stood frozen to the stone below him, completely unable to move even the slightest to turn from the inescapable brightness. Whoever was walking toward him was now in control of him.

Panic inched up through him as the figure drew closer, but all he could do was watch in horror as the Light enveloped him.

He expected to be disintegrated the moment the Light touched his body, but as it drew upon him, instantly his senses were calmed. The fear melted from him, replaced by the beautiful sensation of Lazuli light rushing over him.

The figure in the Light finally came into view—a middle-aged man with long dark hair and a soft tan face that glowed slightly as he approached. He wore a dark silver robe that illuminated him even more, and at his side he carried a large staff carved into a flame. The interior of the staff's handle held a soft blue flame that brought the carved wood to life.

Stopping directly in front of Sam, the man lifted his hand and smiled softly.

"Be free of your chains, Samuel."

Suddenly Sam was free of his invisible captor. He wrestled with the idea of still running while he could, but something about the man

Chapter Seventeen: Amos

made him feel at ease. He felt familiar. Burying his fear, Sam faced the man, his hands at his sides, but one wrong move and Sam would attempt to use the Light on the stranger like he did in the forest with Arazel.

"It is your fear that binds you, Samuel. Do not fear me," the man said softly, his voice carrying deeply, much like the Dark Watcher's.

"Who—are you?" Sam stuttered dumbly, attempting to regain his composure to appear confident. "If you are here for the Watcher Stone, I don't have it."

The man smiled again.

"I am only here for you," he said. "My name is Nuriel. I am from beyond the Sadak Mountains."

Sam was stunned. A true Watcher, here, in front of him. Gus had said there hadn't been an encounter with the Watchers since the Old City was destroyed. Now one was here, and for some reason, for *him*.

"What do you want?" Sam sputtered nervously.

"Not much confidence, I see," Nuriel said with a smile. "You are much like your father—stubborn, fearless, and untrusting. Qualities that can save you ... or eventually make you lonely."

"Why are you here? What do you know about my father?"

Nuriel's expression changed to one of compassion.

"I am your true father, Samuel, and I have been waiting for this moment your entire life."

****

No words came to Sam. He searched Nuriel's face for deception, or some sign that he could be trying to manipulate him, but found none. His mind raced, and he turned suddenly away from the man in front of him.

This man was claiming to be his dead father. But it was a lie, because he had the newspaper article to prove it. *It can't be. My father is dead. He and my mother ...*

Again Nuriel smiled compassionately.

Chapter Seventeen: Amos

"What you have been told was only to protect you."

Sam nearly choked from the man's words, unable to find his own words.

"No—I don't—believe it."

"I would certainly feel the same. I suppose I will have to prove it to you, my son. May I?" he said, reaching out his hand carefully toward Sam's head.

At Sam's reluctant nod, Nuriel placed his hand on top of his head, his eyes closed. Instinctively, Sam closed his own eyes, his heart pumping wildly in his chest.

Suddenly, there were visions blurring through his mind—a woman running through a field. She was carrying something in her arms. A baby. A cabin was lit up across the field, and lightning flashed dangerously near her. She stumbled—collapsing in the field, rain beginning to pour over her body as she shielded the baby from the elements. Then, a man held up a lantern from the porch of the cabin and hurried out into the storm toward the woman. He scooped her up and brought her back to the cabin. It was his grandfather ...

"This is how you entered into the world," Nuriel said, the visions in his mind ceasing immediately.

Sam fought back the tears.

"Was that woman—my mother?"

"Yes. A Descendant from Lior."

The tears began to flow. All of the stories about his parents were false. Lies, all of them. He knew that now, from a simple touch. Something he could never put his finger on had always been wrong about his past, yet he had fought the urge to question it. He had accepted that his parents died in the crash only to quiet his emotions, but there had always been that something—the silent voice that told him there was more. Now, there was nothing that could replace the feeling and the visions Nuriel had given him, because somehow he *knew* they were right.

Nuriel instantly held his son, his own tears staining the top of Sam's head. For several moments, they cried in silence, holding each other as tightly as they could. Neither the hollow, shadow people,

Chapter Seventeen: Amos

the mist-covered buildings surrounding them, nor the dragon entered their thoughts. The only thing that mattered was that father and son had reunited, and that the deepest and darkest of evil could not separate them.

****

"Why didn't you come to me earlier?" Sam sobbed, his emotions pouring from his body as he stood in front of his father.

Nuriel wiped his eyes with his gleaming silver robe.

"I was bound by the laws of Creation," he said. "Laws from the beginning of time that have been put in place—until now."

"I don't understand."

"At one time the Watchers walked the earth as humans did. They were sent to protect and guide them, even after the Darkness entered the land. The Creator's sole passion is, and has always been, to ensure mankind's survival," he paused, holding his hand open in front of him, a small but brilliant pulsing orb of Light dancing suddenly from his palm. "The Watchers are protectors of the Light, the shield for mankind from the Darkness."

"When the Dark One betrayed the Light, there were many who followed him, including many of the Watchers who followed the Creator. The Dark One's whole mission was to deceive as many as he could."

"Those that followed the Dark One married humans and created the Descendants," Sam nodded.

"The Dark Lords deceived the humans, showing them false forms of spiritual gifts that would give the appearance of the Light," he paused. "But the Light always finds goodness, even in acts of Darkness. While they were born out of the Darkness, some Descendants chose to follow the Light, forsaking the Dark One. Those who chose the Light were welcomed back by the Creator."

"He created Lior for them to live in," Sam understood.

"Yes, He did. The Descendants are in great contrast with the rest of Creation because of the abnormal physical qualities they inherited from celestial beings."

Chapter Seventeen: Amos

"Why won't the Descendants listen to the Watchers who still follow the Creator anymore?"

"Some of the Descendants believed that the Watchers were dangerous to their existence. They felt that since the Watchers had so much power, they were prone to being deceived once again by the Dark One, should he choose to awaken. In the best interests of the Descendants who feared them, the Watchers thought it best to withdraw from Lior, keeping only to the mountains beyond."

"Is that where we are now?"

Nuriel laughed.

"Not quite. I wouldn't want to step a foot in this place if I didn't absolutely have to."

"I can see why," Sam said quietly.

"Ayet Sal is a place where the Darkness has completely taken over the power of the Light. It is, in essence, where the ones who choose the Darkness will inevitably go, because of the constant lure of Darkness in their lives," he said sadly. "The souls that enter the Valley of Death have allowed the Darkness to rule completely, and there is no room for Light."

"How are we able to be here?" Sam wondered, seeing the choking black clouds just outside the little village, as though they were being held back by some powerful force.

"For another time, I'm afraid."

His unwillingness to answer frustrated Sam, but he wasn't really interested in what Ayet Sal was, but why they were there.

"Why have you called me here to this place?"

"Other than being one of the only places that is completely void of all gifts, including that of the Seers, it is the only place that would allow the people of Lior to truly let go of their suspicions of you. Ayet Sal is a place that, without a truly pure heart, one could not resist the call of the Darkness within."

"Then if I return, I must be of the Light, and not the Darkness."

Nuriel smiled.

"It is my hope that the Light is where you remain."

Chapter Seventeen: Amos

Sam was anxious to hear about his mother, whose image still flooded his mind from when Nuriel touched him.

"What about my mother?"

Sadness washed over Nuriel's face.

"Following the attack on the Old City, a few Watchers were sent to track the movements of the remaining ones who chose the path of Darkness—to follow the events of the land but not interfere. I chose to live among the Descendants in the new City of Lior, as one of them. It was there that I knew your mother, Sarias."

Sarias. The name of my mother.

Thoughts and questions flooded Sam's mind. He had believed a lie for so long that now it was difficult to understand the truth. But what he saw and what Nuriel showed him was real. Even more, he felt it was true. He was a Descendant, and his father was a Watcher. What did this mean for him?

"What happened to my mother?" he said suddenly, his voice choking with emotion.

Nuriel gazed beyond Sam, his eyes welling with tears that shimmered in the faint light.

"Your mother was abducted by the Metim just after your birth …" he stopped, turning his eyes from his son to hide the tears. "She escaped and made it to the Northern Gate at Jester's Pass, but was wounded by a pursuing Dark Lord before she passed through. She was trying to get you to her father, Ramis … who I believe is known better to you as your grandfather Amos."

"I can't believe he is the former Chancellor of Lior."

"Yes. And you are his grandson."

Sam scowled, trying to put the pieces together.

"Why didn't Amos—my grandfather, ever tell me about my mother?"

"I cannot tell you why he kept this from you, my son, but you must know that for quite some time, he was unaware of the truth."

"I don't understand."

"His wife, your grandmother Shoshana, was taken when she was

Chapter Seventeen: Amos

pregnant by the Metim during the invasion of the Old City. During her imprisonment, she escaped and found refuge in a small Outsider village until the Descendants rebuilt the City quite some time later. She had your mother while in their care," he paused. "She died not long after your mother was born in another Metim attack on the Outsider village. They continued to care for your mother Sarias, but constant fear of attack led the Outsiders to abandon her in the mountains when she was three. Strangely, a Son of Light named Reuven Calpher found her and raised her as his own. The entire time, your grandfather never even knew his daughter existed."

He thought for a moment, remembering the name *Calpher*. Could he mean *Talister* Calpher?

"Yes, what you think is true. Talister was raised as a sibling to your mother."

... making Sayvon my cousin—of sorts, he thought. *Maybe in some strange way, by kissing her, nature was telling me that.*

Sam fought the tears back with everything he had. As fantastical as it sounded, the whole of the crazy story felt more like the truth than what he had known.

"Why haven't you told my grandfather this? Don't you think he would want to hear about his own daughter?"

Nuriel held his gaze, a deep sense of compassion in his eyes.

"You must remember that Watchers were bound by the request made of the Descendants to not interfere," he spoke soothingly. "I can assure you, however, that Amos has known for some time."

"But you left Lior City again, didn't you? Why?"

"Sarias had the wonderful ability to see things, and she knew me for who I truly was—a Watcher, but Talister at that time was beginning his training as a Son of Light, and also began to grow suspicious of me. I left soon after to ensure there would be no confrontation."

Sam realized that was the point at which Sam was sent to live with Amos, or *Ramis*, who must have passed him off to his foster parents. It was another abandonment, but at least the truth was starting to come out.

"Why did the Metim abduct my mother?"

Chapter Seventeen: Amos

Nuriel sighed and looked above, where a large Lazuli light image of a Watcher wing appeared over them both.

"You are very special, Sam." His eyes twinkled even from the dim light of the moon above. "You are part of the Creator's Promise to both worlds, spoken long ago before the formation of Lior."

"The Dark Forces believe I am supposed to lead their army to unite the Darkness."

Even though the glowing wing disappeared, the Watcher continued to look above them, seemingly gazing into the sky above, which was invisible to Sam because of the murky mist circling their heads.

"There is more to the true Prophecy, more you do not understand ... and neither do the inhabitants of the City or the Council," he said. "The true Prophecy is spoken, and has been misunderstood through the ages. It is ancient, before any Descendant who walk these lands was born."

He held out his palm to instantly reveal a glowing orb that grew into a series of letters that formed phrases, and eventually Sam recognized it as ancient Hebrew. Then he began to read, his voice sounding as soft whispers on a still morning. Even still, Sam could understand every word.

> *In that day all of Lior will moan as the shadow is cast upon the lands. From the mortal world will come the last prophet, third to be called, who will seek the hidden gate to release the Dark One from his bonds. He will call unto himself the Darkness, and the shadow will be revealed. It is then the time is near and the Creator will return, destroying the Dark One and his servants forever! All praise to the one of the Light!*

Sam's heart was suddenly in his throat. *So it was true. The third prophet was in the Prophecy. Could it really be him?*

"The translation we have doesn't have the part about the Creator destroying the Dark One."

"One thing that will never change about evil," Nuriel closed his palm and the words of Light slowly dissipated, "and that is that it

Chapter Seventeen: Amos

can only ever imitate the Light. It has no ability to create, or even to grow. It can only take what is present and alter it to deceive those who have been weakened by it. In its truest form, the Darkness is only the absence of pure Light."

Sam understood now. Darkness imitates Light, it cannot *create*. The only thing the Dark Lords could do with the Promise of the Creator was to take a part of it away so it sounded like it favored them.

"The Council believes I am the third prophet because of the dreams I have." His heart pounded so loudly he wondered if Nuriel could hear it.

"To the Light, my son, you are called *Irin*, the *revealer* of the Darkness. The last of the third prophets before the return of the Creator."

A knot formed in Sam's stomach. It was all so much to take in at once. Not only was he the son of a Watcher, but he would also be the one to usher in the return of the God of both worlds, Creator of all things.

"How am I supposed to reveal the Darkness if the Dark One goes free?" Sam shivered, even in the humid air.

"One characteristic of the Creator above all others is the value of freedom. It is written in the laws from the foundation of Creation. All other aspects of Creation are built upon it. If there is no freedom, there are no other true emotions. Without it, there is no choice to love—or to hate."

Sam nodded.

"I understand, but …"

"Allowing the Darkness and the Light to coexist—it gives ultimate authority to the chooser to determine right or wrong. One must acknowledge the Darkness to allow the Light to prevail—if that's what is chosen."

Sam's heart beat so fast he felt as though he would fall over.

"So by releasing him, I will be letting them choose."

Nuriel held his hand out toward his son, placing his hand gently on his chest. Upon the warm touch, his anxiety instantly ceased,

Chapter Seventeen: Amos

allowing his heart to slow to normal. Sam stared open-mouthed at the man in front of him, unsure of what to say. It was as if this man knew him, inside and out, what he was thinking, what he was *feeling*. There was a connection there that even the most skeptical person could not ignore.

"You will have many questions, and I will be able to answer them for you in time. But for now, I do not have much longer with you," he paused, his eyes showing deep concern. "What I have to tell you is of utmost importance, and you must listen carefully before our time expires."

Sam nodded slowly.

"I'm listening."

Nuriel closed his eyes for a moment, as if contemplating what to say next. His young strong face showed traces of fear and anxiety, even for an immortal being.

"Even though the Creator has promised to restore all things as they were before the fall of Watchers and men, many will turn to the Darkness and will become lost to the Light forever."

He paused, turning and pointing at a deformed young man cowering from the intense Light just inside the edge of the alleyway.

"For them, it is too late. They will never be able to choose the Light, for they have hardened their hearts to the Creator. But for many, they must see the Darkness for what it truly is."

Sam scowled.

"Why can't they see the danger of the Darkness?"

Nuriel smiled.

"You have had some wonderful guides along the way to show you the dangers of living in Darkness, but others, I am afraid, are not so fortunate."

"What can I do?"

"The Council is blinded from a deception about the reaches of the Darkness. Kachash, the fourth Dark Lord, has orchestrated a plan to deceive all Descendants into believing the Darkness is no longer growing," he paused. "It is, in fact, greater and more dangerous than it has ever been."

Chapter Seventeen: Amos

Sam remembered the horrific faces of the Dark Lords Sayvon showed him in the secret tower of the City Center. Kachash, the Lord of Deception, was the only one not imprisoned. He wondered what part of Ayet Sal held the Dark Lords.

"The Creator's Promise of restoration is indeed true, but the people of the Light must unite to defeat the Darkness, in Lior and in Creation. Without their help, Lior will be destroyed."

It was strange—an immortal being of the spiritual realm, asking him for help.

"Why not just tell them they are being lied to? Can't you meet with the Chancellor and join forces?"

"It was the Descendants who banned us from interfering, not the Watchers. I assure you that I did everything I could while in the City to convince them otherwise. They will not listen because the curse is just too strong," Nuriel paused. "And we believe there are some Descendants within your city who have aided the Darkness in their deception."

Now there was no doubt a spy existed. The question was, what could Sam do to help?

"What do I need to do?"

Nuriel gazed compassionately at his son.

"The Sha'ar gate was the first arch ever to be opened between the two worlds," he told Sam. "The original gate for the spiritual world, allowing the passage of all celestial beings to and from Creation."

"Yes, I know. The Dark arch."

"Yes, the first true test of the Creator's power over the Dark One."

"I'm not sure I understand."

Nuriel smiled.

"Long ago, when the Creator first banished him to Earth for his acts upon humanity, the Dark One and his followers mounted an attack upon the gate. He did all he could to reopen it, sacrificing many in the destruction, but was unsuccessful."

"What happened to the gate?"

Chapter Seventeen: Amos

"It was imprinted with the souls the Dark One sent to attack it, but it was otherwise unaffected."

"It turned the arch Dark, didn't it?"

Nuriel nodded.

"Shortly thereafter it was hidden, never to be used again … until now."

****

Sam looked at the man before him, and even though he had just sent images and emotions flowing through his mind that he could not deny, for a moment he doubted Nuriel's intentions.

Mr. Sterling said there would be some that would try to take advantage of his weaknesses, but he never expected this, nor was he prepared for it. Emotions of all kinds raced to the surface, and even though he contained them, no doubt Nuriel could see right through it.

"It is time for the Sha'ar gate to be opened once more," he said genuinely.

"Why is that necessary?"

"It is the only way to remove the curse that has blinded all of Lior and show the true face of the Darkness."

"But the people of Creation won't stand a chance if the Dark Forces are able to unite again," Sam sputtered.

Nuriel looked at his son, seeing the doubt he reserved.

"I understand your concern, and you would be correct if …"

Suddenly Sam knew. Freedom. People must be given a choice to follow the Light or the Darkness. Yes, opening the gate would give the Darkness a chance to regain its strength, but in doing so, it would also reveal itself to humanity, and to Lior.

"The opening of the gate removes the deception," Sam whispered in the stale air. "And the Watcher Stone is the key to opening it."

"Yes. It is the one and only gate stone of the Watchers," Nuriel said quietly. "As you are the only one to open it."

Instantly, he knew what his father implied. Yes, the stone was the

Chapter Seventeen: Amos

key to the gate. But really, *he* was the key to opening it. He was the *true* key of the Watchers.

He felt sick to his stomach. Turning behind him, he heaved his afternoon's lunch onto the stone street. This ... all of it ... was more than he could take.

His father helped him upright, once again placing his healing hand upon Sam's head, instantly removing the queasiness from his son's body. Then he glanced behind him as if hurried for time.

"There is a war coming, son, and it will be the war to end all wars. All of Creation and Lior will fight the forces of Darkness, and they will fight for their *lives*."

He had no response to his father's words, and yet he didn't need to. Sam knew this wasn't something he could say no to, because there was no other way.

The Council and the people of Lior would not understand this strategy, and he had a feeling his father would ask him to do it without their knowledge, specifically for that reason. If they knew his plan, they would likely lock him up until it was sorted out.

But there was still the problem of the Stone that Arazel had taken from him. How could he get it back?

Again Nuriel smiled, seeming to already know his thoughts.

"Fortunately, son, what Arazel has taken is nothing but a replica. When I found out Kachash sent Arazel for the Stone and for you, I planted it there shortly after you arrived in the Old City."

Again Sam remembered the rush of wind past his face in the vault. He wondered why he would have to plant a bogus Stone in the library to fool Kachash, but then it hit him. He shuddered to think what would have happened if he wouldn't have been able to give Arazel the fake Stone.

"Was that you in the Old City library when we were there?"

"Yes."

"And the one who produced the cloud of Light outside the Old City?"

"Of course! You think I would pass up an opportunity to spend time with my son?" he laughed, making Sam smile through his tears.

Chapter Seventeen: Amos

It was a sound that was familiar to him, even though he had never heard it before.

"The real holder of the Key is unaware he even has it in his possession. I spent much time with Talister Calpher ... enough to ensure that with the completion of his mentorship, *he* would receive the Stone as his own. You will need to retrieve the real one from him."

Sam nearly choked as he remembered the Stone in Talister's bracelet. It was nearly identical to the one they had retrieved from the artifact vault. *How could I not remember that?*

"But it will need to be done quickly. You may take your friends with you, and you will only need to say my name to get the Stone from Talister, but do not tell anyone else. The truth will come out in its own time. Don't delay. The gate must be opened soon. Any delay and there may be no stopping the Darkness."

"Father, I don't know where the gate is."

Nuriel smiled widely at Sam's calling him father.

"Trust Gus, son. He will help you find the gate. I must go now."

"When will I see you again?" Sam tried to ask, but as he did, the soft glow around Nuriel suddenly began to grow steadily brighter until it looked like it had completely absorbed him. Suddenly Sam's father was gone.

****

Sam reached out into the essence of Light that remained, but it vanished before he could touch it. He stood, listening for a moment to the silence of his once again absent father, but heard only the rhythmic sound of the dragon's breathing behind him. With the Light gone, the hollow figures began to emerge from the darkened buildings and, in zombie-like fashion, slowly started to make their way toward him.

Sam turned to find the dragon bending his long neck down toward him, his gleaming eyes level with Sam's. He then lowered his giant wing to the ground for Sam to board.

Sam glanced once more toward the street where Nuriel had

🌲🌲 Chapter Seventeen: Amos

appeared, but saw only Darkness and more Dark figures as they poured from every crack and opening in the haunted village.

Eager to be away from the place, Sam clambered up Orono's wing and into the basket. He was instantly very tired, as though he had been given a massive dose of drugs to put him to sleep. He lay down in the basket as the great reptile leapt from the cobblestone street and soared into the air. As they cleared the mist, the last sight Sam saw before drifting off was a vast moon casting eerie shadows into the night sky. There was so much to work through in his mind, so much to consider.

Chapter Eighteen
Sha'ar Gate

Sam awoke to the soft thump of Orono's feet on the tall grass. It was daybreak, and right away Sam recognized the large weeping pines of the Keeper's garden.

Shatal emerged from his cabin and hurried to the dragon's side, clasping his hands in the air and calling out excitedly in a language Sam could only guess was Hebrew.

Bleary-eyed, Emma, Gus, and Lillia emerged from the Keeper's cabin and, upon seeing the dragon and Sam climbing out of the basket, broke into a run through the grass toward them, stumbling as they attempted to wipe the sleep from their eyes.

Sam slid down the dragon's wing and hit the grass just as his friends reached them. He scooped Emma and Lillia into his arms in one swoop, then grabbed Gus around the neck and squeezed him. Emma cried softly as they all four hugged in a circle, and even a misplaced tear could be seen falling down Lillia's cheek. This was the only place he wanted to be, and he knew they felt the same.

"Welcome back lad!" Shatal slapped him on the back. "You did good bringing Orono back safely!"

Sam turned and shook his hand.

Chapter Eighteen: Sha'ar Gate

"Thank you sir, but actually, it was Orono that brought *me* back safe."

The great dragon turned his massive head toward Sam and bowed slightly, as if to say thank you. Sam nodded back toward him. They definitely had a connection that Sam didn't quite understand yet, but he welcomed it.

"Samuel!" Mrs. Sterling called as she, Sam's grandfather, Mr. Sterling, Miss Karpatch, Cooley, Sayvon, and Talister Calpher walked up the pathway toward the Keeper and the four friends. Sam made greetings all around, including one rather awkward hug from Sayvon and an animated handshake from the wide-grinning Talister.

Sam gazed at the tall man's wrist, watching the Watcher Stone as it glowed softly.

"The dragon's return has shown us enough, m' boy. We would like to formally welcome you to the family of Lior," Talister said while still shaking his hand. "Personally I had my doubts, and I would be grateful if you forgive me, dear boy."

Sam remembered his thoughts about Talister, that he could have been the one that was deceiving Lior, feeding false information to the Dark Lords. But after talking with Nuriel, something about the man was truly genuine, and now Sam understood the connection he had with him. Only a few days before, Sam had believed that Talister was making a promise to an unknown man to abduct him from Lior based on a prophecy, but now he was sure there was something behind his motive, something purer. The tall man before him in the long silky robe was his uncle, after all.

Who else could Talister have been talking about to the man in the tower? Certainly not the Sterlings. Perhaps another member of the Council who could be helping to hide such a great deception that much of Lior would believe the Darkness was, in fact, weaker than it had ever been?

Then it hit him all at once. *Cooley*. He was the head of the Seer Chamber, and the Seers were the only ones that could see events throughout Lior. Could he see have seen the growing Darkness outside the City? Was he perhaps also responsible for the deception of the condition of the library in the Old City?

Chapter Eighteen: Sha'ar Gate

Cooley would have been the one to report all incidents with the Seer chamber to the Council and the PO. Could he have hidden it from the other Seers in the chamber so easily?

The story was somewhat forced, but what else could make sense? There was only one way to find out.

****

Sam waded through the people toward the silent Cooley as his friends chatted with one another, each slapping him on the back as he passed. Sam reached out his hand, and Cooley reluctantly took it in his own, his hands ice cold even in the morning sun.

"Why haven't you told the Council about the threat of growing Darkness?" he took a chance, gambling on his instincts.

Cooley glared at him, his eyes as cold as his hands. Immediately he withdrew his hand and put it at his side, backing away slightly. From his expression, Sam suddenly recognized him as the same man that stormed out of Chivler's the same night he met his friends for the first time. No doubt Cooley had something to do with Chivler's kidnapping.

"Why would I listen to an accusation made by a simple boy from Earth?" he said darkly.

Sam didn't back down.

"Because you know I'm right. I've seen it in Ayet Sal. You are keeping information from the Council and PO."

Cooley smiled casually.

"You are blind, as all of Lior is. A fool, on a fool's errand."

"Did you also lie to the Council about the library in Old Lior being destroyed?"

Cooley laughed.

"You really don't know anything, do you? Except for that little mistake in the swamp where I killed a Giant and forgot to cover my tracks, the Darkness is less of a threat than it has ever been."

"Maybe, but I found you out."

Cooley's eyes leveled, a look of sheer hatred crossing his face.

"You may have evaded the Metim in the forest when you first

Chapter Eighteen: Sha'ar Gate

arrived *and* escaped Dark Lord Arazel, but now we have the key to open the gate. You *will* submit to the Darkness, and to the Dark One when he calls on you."

Sam felt the blood rushing to his head, much like in the forest with Arazel.

"That's where you are wrong. I will never submit to the Darkness, or to the Dark One. I will never lead the Metim anywhere."

"You are mistaken, and it will cost you your life!" Cooley said angrily, suddenly drawing attention from the others around him.

"What's the problem here?" Mr. Sterling hurried over to intervene.

Sam refused to take his eyes off Cooley, who was just beginning to break a sweat in the morning heat.

"I met a Watcher in Ayet Sal. He confirmed to me there is a curse over all of Lior to hide the truth of how strong the Darkness really is."

Mr. Sterling stared at Sam, his expression unchanging, as if expecting more explanation. When he saw that Sam refused to take his eyes off Cooley, he turned to him.

"Harper, you have been silent regarding any Darkness related events. Would you care to defend this accusation?"

While Sam was indeed surprised that Mr. Sterling would question Cooley first and not Sam's accusations, he continued to do his best to remain emotionless.

Talister was suddenly with them, his hands out in front of him, facing Cooley.

"Out with it, Harper. We have suspected some foul doings for quite some time."

Mr. Sterling lifted his hands toward Cooley suddenly, following Talister's lead, as though something about Cooley's manner said he would not easily submit.

"Fools. All of you," he hissed, a slight hint of a black smoke-like substance beginning to encircle his body. "You think you are safe, protected by your precious Creator, but He will do nothing for you when the Dark One returns."

Suddenly Mr. Sterling put his hands down to his side, as if purposefully showing Cooley he was not a threat.

Chapter Eighteen: Sha'ar Gate

"Jack, it's too late, he's gone too far," Talister urged, but Mr. Sterling continued to show his desire for peace.

"Harper," Jack said quietly. "We can work through this. We have help waiting for you with the keepers."

"Jack," Talister repeated, but his words were ignored.

"We have been working on a rehabilitation program with the Tanniym that could—"

"He's too far, Jack," Amos touched Mr. Sterling on the shoulder gently, refusing to take his eyes off of Harper Cooley.

"Last chance, Harper," Mr. Sterling said with emotion, but his words were met with empty hollow eyes.

Cooley said nothing, but raised his hands suddenly, firing a blue-green bolt from his hands toward Talister, who, though surprised, blocked it at the last moment with a Light shield.

Jack Sterling and Amos sprung into action, bolts firing from their palms, as Miss Karpatch flung a makeshift shield over the others in the middle of the fight. Cooley blocked both bolts easily, then threw his hands to his side, and a bright green light erupted around him, igniting him in a massive ball of fire. Then he was gone.

****

"Put the council on alert!" Jack Sterling yelled back to Talister as he searched the scorched grass from where Cooley disappeared. A blue light shot from the sky where Talister stood, and he was suddenly gone. Panic surrounded the group as everyone tried to figure out what had just happened, but it was Sam's grandfather, Amos, who was finally able to calm them down.

"Please may I have your attention!" he bellowed, which caused everyone to pause from the chaos. "We must remain calm at this moment! Please! Thank you. I know you are surprised at the altercation with Mr. Cooley, but Jack, Talister and I have, in fact, been suspicious of Mr. Cooley for quite some time now. We have been unsure how to proceed until now, but thanks to my grandson, Samuel, we have all the proof we need to continue." He paused while they gathered around him. "We will have much to do to sort this out, but after a bit

Chapter Eighteen: Sha'ar Gate

of proper sleep, as I believe after the night we have had waiting for the lad, we will all need it."

As they all filtered out of the garden talking of the crazy confrontation with Cooley, Sam walked purposefully to his grandfather, determined to get answers.

"You knew about my father, didn't you?" he met Amos's gaze, although he was nearly a foot shorter and not quite as broad. "And about me being connected to the Prophecy."

"For now, all I can tell you is that I have known who you truly were your entire life, but until now it was not necessary to tell you who I am."

Sam understood, and was not angry with him. No doubt he had a story to tell, much like Sam did, but now was not the time to tell it. This man had ruled a world full of celestial beings, and if he didn't think it was wise to tell him more, then it was probably best for all.

It was strange, being in his grandfather's presence, when all Sam ever knew about him was from their time in White Pine. To Sam, he was Amos, simple man who lived in a small northern town in the woods—farmers, copper mills, and small-time merchants, just trying to make a life.

He had kept so much from Sam, and yet Sam did not worry. He knew he was in good hands, and now for the first time since moving in with his grandfather, he trusted the man fully. And he respected him.

His grandfather leaned in toward Sam, lowering his voice.

"What *he* told you, you must keep absolutely silent, but do not delay. While you have friends and family here who believe in what you have been called to do, the Council is not yet willing to accept our path. The request you have been given is your decision to make, but if you decide to heed the request, then you will need to do so quickly."

"Thank you," Sam told him.

"Now go," his grandfather seemed to choke up, suddenly overcome with emotion, which he attempted to hide. "We … all of us, believe in you."

Sam nodded and hugged his grandfather. He could wait a little longer to hear the whole story from him about his past. He had kept

Chapter Eighteen: Sha'ar Gate

secret an incredible lie for so long, but he understood why. There was no way Sam would have ever believed it without seeing it for himself. And now, it was obvious he had some thinking to do.

Upon returning to the circle of cabins, Sam and Amos were met with cheers from a packed living room, including two other families in the circle—Harben and Sommy Baswaller and their eight year-old son Gabriel, and old Rali Harrowroot and his wife Janna (both hard of hearing and both very eccentric).

"'Bout time ya stop foolin' around and join us, eh?" Rali slapped Sam on the back rather hard, earning a harsh scold from his wife.

"Yes sir," Sam said, knowing that after telling the Council something other than what really happened, he had to keep up the story.

To the Council and everyone except his friends, Mr. Sterling, Talister, his grandfather, and the Chancellor, the story was that he arrived in Ayet Sal, produced a bolt to defend himself against a small group of lost Metim souls, and then returned on the back of the dragon.

The Council accepted the story, but they were not ready to let Lior know the details of their concerns regarding the spread of the Darkness quite yet. They only admitted to the general public that Harper Cooley had been persuaded by the Darkness and had falsified some visions. Stories filtered in from everywhere about Sam and Cooley, and all of them different. Some said that Sam would become the one that would someday free Lior from the Darkness forever, while others said it was just another legend. Most still believed there was little threat with the Darkness at all, because there was none to see.

With Cooley, some thought he was only a wayward Descendant who had decided the life of Light wasn't for him, but others took on a more serious approach—that there were others just like him still hidden in the City. Some even believed Cooley was acting under the Dark One, Nasikh, himself.

One thing was certain from the trip to Ayet Sal—Sam was now welcomed as a Descendant, though some still believed him to be the third prophet and thought he should be watched carefully.

Chapter Eighteen: Sha'ar Gate

Later that day, the Chancellor himself, walked through the door of the cabin with his personal entourage of four other rather large-looking Protectors. He ignored all of the hushed surprises and walked directly to Sam, who set down his plate of biscuits to greet him. The Chancellor stuck out his fair-skinned hand to him, and the entire room grew silent as they watched the interaction.

"Samuel, my dear boy, it is good to see you again," he said, a large smile splashed across his face. "I think that all of us are a bit astounded at your accomplishments today—discovering your Descendant gift and aiding in the exposure of a danger to our City. And for that, I must say, we are most in your debt."

"Yes, uh, thank you. I am just happy the Creator told me what to do," Sam fumbled for the right words.

The Chancellor smiled and clasped his hand again, this time shaking Sam's hand vigorously with both hands.

"Yes, yes, and I think we will need to keep an eye on that gift of yours as well," he stopped, then raising his voice, turned to face the rest of the cabin. "And, you will all be happy to know that the Healer's Office just sent word that Mr. Chivler is going to be just fine. He will still need a while to recoup, but I assure you he is in good spirits."

The words brought sighs of relief and cheers from around the cabin, including from Sam. While they weren't close, he was still happy to know that the old bookseller was okay.

At that news, Emma came out with a rather large stack of root cakes, coffee, and Jurana juice sent out by Mrs. Sterling from the kitchen. Before long, a heaping bowl of eggs, potato cakes, more homemade biscuits, and berry pancakes made their way to the table. Again, there was an abundance of food and friends, and it was long into the afternoon before everyone had overfilled their bellies and laughed at old Rali's Metim-fight'n stories before the cabin was silent once again and the Chancellor had left.

Talister walked through the door just after the Chancellor's departure and immediately pulled Sam aside as the others called for another round of coffee at the table.

"Samuel, my boy, I wonder if I could perhaps explain myself from the meeting yesterday afternoon."

Chapter Eighteen: Sha'ar Gate

"You don't need to, sir."

Talister smiled.

"I believe I must, I am afraid," he breathed loudly. "The man you heard in the tower was from the territory held by the Dragons ... a friend of sorts. At that time, Jack and I were concerned with Cooley and were hoping to send him to the Dragon Keepers to rehabilitate him."

Dragon Keepers aren't too fond of politicians, Sam thought.

"The Council is not the best at keeping secrets, so we had to keep our suspicions rather quiet, which meant that only someone who wasn't closely watched by Cooley would have to be the one to go to the Old City. You are the first to be there since its fall."

Unbelievable.

"Why hasn't anyone gone?"

Talister sighed.

"The Office of Research never sent someone to the Old City to investigate in the years following the attack. Guess who was head researcher at the time?"

"Cooley."

"We figured he found out about the Watcher Stone some time ago and had been making plans to go get it himself. We believe that is the reason the Darkness from the initial attack on the City was growing again. They were attempting to limit the Lazuli so it wouldn't affect them."

"He didn't stay with the research office, though. Why not?"

"His goal in the Seer chamber was to make sure that no incidents surfaced that would give any hint to the City that the Darkness was growing."

"He's been hiding this for awhile, hasn't he?"

"Quite right, my boy. Nasikh's curse is, I am sure, very potent, but not perfect. Cooley was no doubt recruited to make sure it was foolproof, until you four came along."

"How did you figure out it was him?"

Talister laughed.

"It was the old inventor, Bogglenose. His invention, actually. It wasn't abnormal to see Darkness alarms going off throughout the

Chapter Eighteen: Sha'ar Gate

City when there are so many of us that travel about Lior, but it began to become clear that whenever one of us visited the Seer chamber, we would come back with trace amounts of Darkness."

Now the triggering of the Darkness alarm upon entering the Chancellor's office made sense. Talister worked closely with the Seer chamber.

"He's also been working on some other methods to detect the Darkness."

"Eccentric, that man is, but brilliant. I think by the time we suspected Cooley, he was suspicious that something was amiss. But please do not think of all Descendants as—well—how do you say, crazy?"

Sam chuckled as he remembered Boggle. He understood why Lillia liked him so much.

"Mr. Calpher, do you think there are more like Cooley in Lior?"

Suddenly Talister's face crept into its typical grin, but Sam could tell instantly it was not out of smugness or egotism, but perhaps the slightest bit of fear.

"Of course," he grinned. "With the allure of the Promise of the Dark One's return, many will be seeking out evil in order to earn his favor."

It was so strange to think that both sides—Light and Dark—waited for a Promise of their Lord's return, both of very different paths, but each retaining a striking resemblance. Only cosmic fate could arrange something so ironic.

"Mr. Calpher, what if I choose not to choose a side? To remain independent, free of allegiances …"

"I think you should know this, being an intellectual."

"I can't remain neutral, can I?" Sam lowered his head. He knew the answer before he even spoke the words.

"By not choosing, you are choosing yourself. And like the rest of us, you are conflicted without a perfect Creator to make you truly free."

Finally, he understood. By choosing not to decide whether or not there was a God, Sam, like all the others on Earth who were

Chapter Eighteen: Sha'ar Gate

undecided, was already making a choice to reject Him. There was only one other choice.

"What will we do when the Dark One returns?"

"The only thing we can—go to war and defend ourselves and humanity to our deaths."

"Thank you for the help Mr. Calpher."

"Dear boy, stop calling me that. I am *family*. Call me Uncle."

Sam nodded, but knew it would take time to see them all the same way Gus, Emma, and Lillia did. Sam never really had family that cared about emotional bonds. It was all so foreign.

Talister slapped him on the back loudly.

"Good! And now I probably don't have to remind you that you need to keep our conversation between our little group … or I will have to turn you into dragon feces."

Sam laughed.

"Of course I will."

****

After helping Mrs. Sterling with the dishes, Gus and Emma coaxed Sam out to their usual meeting spot around the fire pit in the pavilion, where Lillia was poking at a log that was spitting out a lazy flame.

"Spill it, newb. We want to hear about your *dad*," Lillia said, not taking her eyes off the fire.

"Wait—what? How did you find out what happened in Ayet Sal?" Sam was surprised, having kept Nuriel a secret thus far.

Emma punched him in the shoulder playfully.

"Your grandfather told us."

"And Gus helped," Lillia said quietly.

Immediately Gus blushed.

"I—uh just found in Julian's journal that apparently after being snuck into Lior by none other than Chivler himself, Julian was also visited by a Watcher. It was all in code, but with a little effort—"

"He was awesome," Lillia said genuinely, making Gus blush once again.

🌲🌲 Chapter Eighteen: Sha'ar Gate

In a strange turn, Emma rolled her eyes at the flirting couple.

"And now everyone is going to know tonight that you are formally to be known as a Descendant of Light."

"They're going to *announce* it to *everyone*?"

"At the closing ceremony," Emma said with another punch to his shoulder. "You were found in Creation. It's kind of a big deal, you know."

"Not many have been to Ayet Sal either," Gus added.

"Now spill it," Lillia scooted closer, her eyes widening.

Sam told them the whole story—about his father the Watcher, his instructions to open the Sha'ar gate, everything. He had considered attempting to keep it from them, but it would have been impossible. His father even knew that, having given him permission to tell his friends. Eventually they would know what he was doing, and they might not understand unless he explained it first. And he needed their help.

In turn, Gus told them about Mr. Sterling and the PO's suspicions about Cooley, and the Council's response to the deception. The Council hadn't fully embraced the idea that the Darkness could be in fact growing again, but at least their eyes were open.

Emma stared at the fire while Lillia attempted to work through the details of Sam's story out loud. Gus immediately began thumbing through the journal that Chivler had given to Sam while he listened.

Gus stood suddenly as the others continued talking, a huge smile on his face.

"I think I found it," he said.

"Found what?" Emma peered at him.

"Sam's story about his father the Watcher reminded me of something in the journal. Something Julian said to Chivler …"

"Gus, what is it?" Emma smacked his knee to get his attention again.

"Oh my," he said quietly, looking around as if fearing eavesdroppers. "It's the original gate, it has to be …"

"Gus!" all three said in unison.

"I know where the Sha'ar gate is."

Chapter Eighteen: Sha'ar Gate

****

"Sam, are you sure this is what's best?" Emma began her pacing routine around the fire once again to calm her rising nerves. This time, by the expression of horror on her face, she was truly afraid of what Sam was considering.

"No, I'm not," he said quickly. "I have no idea what to think anymore. I'm just going to hope that it's best."

"I believe ... that is called faith," Gus smiled and patted his shoulder. "But that is all we can do, right Emma?"

She let out a frustrated sigh as she plopped back on the bench, glaring at Gus and his newfound trust. She said nothing, and once again it was the fact that her father, Talister, Miss Karpatch, and Amos had been involved from the beginning that caused her to believe what they were doing was right.

Gus even suspected that the Chancellor knew the inner secrets of those who orchestrated the four friends' journey to the Old City, and even of Sam's true experience with Nuriel in Ayet Sal. It didn't matter, however, because they all seemed to let Sam be the one to make the decision to go through with it, and he knew it. All of the people involved, regardless of their age or position in Lior, trusted *him*. And Sam believed the opening of the original gate was what they thought was necessary, even if it sounded as if all hell would break loose with it. It was, they believed, what the Creator would have them do.

At some point in the conversation, Emma left the fire and headed toward the cabin with Lillia trailing behind her. Even though she said she wasn't upset, Sam could still see her demeanor had changed. He knew she was afraid, but then again, so was he.

Gus flopped into one of the chairs overlooking the spires of the City while reading through the journal, leaving Sam alone with his thoughts.

Laying down on one of the long benches, however, Sam decided to get a little bit of a nap before the ceremony that evening. He was just so tired ... just a few minutes would do him good. After such a huge meal, it was impossible to keep his eyes open.

Chapter Eighteen: Sha'ar Gate

He awoke to the booming of a large firework exploding above him. It was nearly evening, and he had slept the day away. He began to assume that no one had bothered him while he had slept, but as he looked around, he found Emma curled up in a chair not far from his bench. She was sleeping soundly, her strawberry hair fallen partly over her face. The last of the evening sun was shining gently on her shoulders, and a shiny stream of drool cascaded down the corner of her mouth. When he sat up, she awoke suddenly, wiping the drool from her lips.

"What was that?" Sam pointed to the remnants of the firework in the sky.

"One hour till the ceremony," she said sleepily, sitting upright and putting her hair back in a ponytail.

"You drool when you sleep," Sam said playfully, drawing a sleepy frown from Emma.

"Leave me alone," she tried to force back the smile, but couldn't.

"It's cute, that's all."

She stood and brushed the ashes of the dying fire off of her, then forced Sam to stand with her. She hummed a tune Sam didn't recognize, pulling him close to her and swaying slightly in his arms.

Far in the pools the Ori hide
Graceful they move like streams of Light
Then moonlit night gives way to day
Deep below the Ori stay
But dark may come and night return
To bathe in rays of Light they yearn.

They held each other for the few minutes before Mrs. Sterling called them in for dinner and to get ready for the ceremony.

Following dinner, they were instructed to go directly upstairs and pack, as the plan was to take the Lightway back to the gate after the ceremony and head back to White Pine for the remainder of the school year. They weren't expected to see Lior again until the following year's Light Festival.

Sam wanted to stay, but knew what his father had told him about

Chapter Eighteen: Sha'ar Gate

being quick to open the gate. He would need more than courage to finish this task. It would require help, and not just from his friends. He needed help from the one they called the *Creator*.

As he slid his over-packed backpack to the stairwell, on an impulse he asked Gus to come downstairs to talk to Mr. Sterling with him.

"I know I am a Descendant now, but you have all told me there is more to the Light, specifically uh—with the Creator. I have thought about it, and I think I want to understand the Creator—like you all do," Sam said to Mr. Sterling, feeling awkward with his words.

"You want to become a follower of the Light! Sam, that's great!" Gus exclaimed.

Mr. Sterling put his arm around Sam as they headed into the living room.

"With all of the Darkness and evil that has a grasp on these worlds, it is easy to see only the Dark, completely missing the Light. You must trust the Creator with everything, believing that only He will be the source of Light for your life. Can you?"

"Yes, I mean I want to," Sam answered. "I mean, I do."

"That's all any of us can do," Mr. Sterling said genuinely.

Mr. Sterling held his hand out, and suddenly a small orb of blue began growing in his palm.

"The Light is different from the Darkness because it is not about compliance, or blind obedience. The Light is a gift, and only requires one who is willing to reach out and take it."

Sam remembered how closely this related to the story of the man that was killed for the sin of humanity. The man they called Jesus offered His life so that others could be free.

"So the Creator—does He see any Darkness in me?"

"Never. He chooses to look past your faults, your past, everything. He only wants you to be free to choose the path of Light."

Sam paused. It was a completely new concept for him to submit his pride to anyone willingly. He had always believed respect was earned, not given. But he saw the way they acted—the love, respect, and desire to do what was right. Even if they weren't perfect, they seemed to see a different path than those that muddled though life searching for truth and happiness in everything but God.

🌲🌲 Chapter Eighteen: Sha'ar Gate

"I'll do it. I will believe in the Creator of the Light."

"*Barakhi nafshi et Adonai!*" Mr. Sterling and Gus said simultaneously. "Bless the Lord of the Light!"

Instantaneously, it seemed the whole cabin had crowded into the living room where Sam, Mr. Sterling, and Gus were, hugging Sam and sending up thanks to the Creator. He had been ready to become a follower for quite some time now, but the words of his father and the love of the people around him had reminded him how important it was. It was the only thing that would separate him from the Darkness, even if he was to allow its hatred on Earth through the opening of the gate.

He knew there was much to get past—anger, fear, and most of all, mistrust—if he was truly going to be a follower, and they were things he believed he made great strides in. But for now, it was as if a great weight had been lifted off of his shoulders, and a large hole in his heart had been filled. He was now a follower of the Creator, and a Descendant.

****

The stadium was packed for the closing ceremony. Their own winning Thalo Kolar Ball team paraded around the stadium in bright red suits and red and silver-trimmed luxurious robes. The Sons of Light made an appearance as they zipped around the crowd, inciting eruptions of cheers as they passed, then disappearing into a Light cloud above the stadium. Next was the commencement of Helel Malach—the graduation of those who passed the School of the Shining One training. After that was the orientation and send-off of a much larger mass of students enrolled in the mentorship school that was about to begin.

"We will be attending mentorship next year," Emma said loudly over the cheers.

Gus overheard and raised his eyebrows.

"And now Sam will be invited as well!"

The next thing Sam heard was the sound of the Chancellor's velvety voice from the center of the stadium. He stood solemnly at

Chapter Eighteen: Sha'ar Gate

center field, a lone light shining on his brilliant white robe and long silver hair.

"As you may now know, one of us was found to have been deceived by the Darkness." He stopped to allow murmurs from the crowd to dissipate. "Harper Cooley was a long-remembered friend and ally to the Descendants, not to mention the head of the Seer chamber here in Lior. He was lured by the enticing schemes of the Metim, and is now no longer a part of the People of Light. But we remember him for who he was, not for what he has done."

More murmurs rippled through the crowd. Suddenly Sam felt as though he was the center of attention, and although no one was looking at him, he still felt the imaginary stares on the back of his neck. Slinking down on the bench, he waited for the next announcement and his name to be called.

"And, I would like to extend my personal gratitude to our newest Descendant, Samuel Forrester, for his valiant efforts to expose the Darkness within the City. Welcome to Lior, Samuel," the Chancellor held his hand out toward the Thalo section in the stadium.

Sam slunk down further on the wood bench. Mr. Sterling had told him earlier that the announcement would happen, but somehow he forgot until that moment. Now it happened, and the entire stadium stood and applauded him, the boy from Creation turned Descendant. He turned bright red even in the cool air as they clapped on, Mr. and Mrs. Sterling and Miss Karpatch some of the loudest. It was truly overwhelming.

As they exited the stadium at the end of the ceremony, it was nearly impossible to wade through the crowd without someone congratulating or welcoming him, hugging him, or shaking his hand and introducing themselves. Eventually they were able to break free and make their way back to the cabin.

****

The group had planned to leave that evening, taking the Lightway to the cabin and crossing through the gate while it was still dark, as long as the Lightway was in working order. It was customary to

Chapter Eighteen: Sha'ar Gate

protect their identities by entering and leaving Lior while most people in Creation slept.

Sam was sad to leave the cozy circle of cabins and the fire pit in the pavilion, but he knew it had to happen. Before they could be accepted to mentorship, they were required to finish up to their ninth year of education. Most Liorians studied at home as a family unit, but as arch protectors, Lillia, Gus, and Emma went to the traditional school, one that Sam wasn't too fond of returning to.

The trip back was eventless, although one could never really get over the feeling of the Lightway or the transition back to Earth through the arch. Exhaustion took hold of all of them when they finally walked the pathway from the cave, past Orvil's, and sadly parted company. Before the group split up, however, Mr. Sterling gathered them together in the early morning darkness beside the building.

"Parting words, I am afraid, are never the easiest, and in this case, come with a warning as well," he said quietly. "With the discovery of Cooley, the PO has uncovered a few anomalies from the Seer chamber that were never reported. One report is being investigated about the three original Lords of Darkness escaping from Ayet Sal."

Gasps filtered through the group as Mr. Sterling paused for them to digest his words.

"There are also reports that some Dark Watchers who have recently fallen prey to the Darkness still have access to the gates."

"Meaning that by association, the Dark Lords have access as well," Miss Karpatch scowled.

Emma's eyes gleamed in the nearly full moonlight.

"You don't think the Storm Lord *Sar Sehrah* could be responsible for the storm before we went into Lior that night?"

"There is no doubt," Mr. Sterling nodded. "And even more now, we must be watchful because we have been targeted by the Metim."

"Oh no," Mrs. Sterling whispered as the rest of the group fell silent.

"I do not mean to make you fear, only aware," Mr. Sterling held up his hand. "Amos and I have discussed it with the Chancellor, and he has agreed to lift the ban on practicing Light manipulation while

Chapter Eighteen: Sha'ar Gate

in Creation—even for those who haven't gone through mentoring. I recommend the rest of the year be spent learning how to control it."

The four youths nodded.

"Now, I believe it is time for the Sterling's to get on home and get some sleep. I know I could sure use a few hours of shut-eye," Mr. Sterling said as he snatched up Sam's hand and shook it vigorously.

As the rest of the group hugged and said their goodbyes, Gus made a point to pull Sam aside.

"I suppose you will want to know where the gate is," he whispered solemnly, "and I found out where the Sha'ar gate has been hidden all these years ... if you still want to know, that is."

Sam nodded.

"Inside Chivler's Bookstore. Julian uncovered it and built the bookstore around it."

"Unbelievable," Sam nearly choked. *Right in the middle of White Pine.*

"I believe it is the reason that the Metim wanted him so badly. They must have found out about Julian's journal, or they figured they could get the information from him about the gate, or the Stone, or both."

"It was almost like this journal was meant for us," Sam thought aloud.

"True."

Then Gus peered directly in Sam's eyes.

"There's something else I found in here too, about the third prophet."

Sam's heart skipped a beat. He almost didn't even want to know what Gus was about to tell him.

"Julian believed that the third prophet would be—well—*conflicted.*"

Sam watched the others as they disappeared from the road toward their respective homes.

"What does that mean?"

Gus did not take his eyes off Sam.

"Julian called the third prophet the one with the *shadows*, which I assume means he they would be more susceptible to the Darkness."

Chapter Eighteen: Sha'ar Gate

Somehow Sam already knew that. There had been clues everywhere, including inside Sam's feelings deep down. While he knew he wanted to be of the Light, something about the Darkness kept drawing him closer …

Sam tapped Gus' backpack where the journal was most likely tucked, ignoring Gus's subtle warning.

"You know you will have a giant target painted on your back as long as you keep the journal."

Gus nodded.

"And now so do you."

They bid their goodbyes and disappeared down separate paths from Orvil's, each member of the group exhausted from the journey. As Sam silently walked back to his grandfather's cabin in the light of the full moon, he prayed to the Creator for guidance. He was in charge of his decisions now, not Sam. His prayer was awkward, but it was real.

As he prayed, the answers to his questions became very clear. While he still had his doubts about it, he knew what choice he must make, because the Creator had spoken. He felt it, deep down. It was the right thing to do. Did Amos know? Perhaps it was the reason his grandfather chose to stay in Lior a few more days to meet with the Chancellor. Maybe he was giving him the chance to complete the task on his own.

It was now or never.

Turning suddenly toward town, Sam kept to the shadows to ensure no stray midnight walker would see him. His heart beat soundly, and he attempted to calm himself as his father did by placing his hand upon his chest. He couldn't tell if it had worked because he was nearly running down the street, in a hurry to be done with the whole thing.

He thumbed the small Stone Talister had given him as he walked past the police tape over the splintered door of Chivler's. It looked as though no one had moved so much as a torn book from the littered, dust-covered floor since the kidnapping.

He didn't risk turning on the lights in the store as the police could be patrolling by at any time, but he didn't need to. Directly above him,

Chapter Eighteen: Sha'ar Gate

with the columns and ceiling built around it, stood the outline of a coal-colored four-pronged arch.

He walked over to one of the ornately carved legs, which seemed to blend in flawlessly with the bookshelves around it. Reaching out, he ran his hands over the rough stone, feeling the outline of the many hollow-eyed faces that barely swelled from its surface. How many people had passed through this store and never even knew the arch existed? It was hidden well, and he believed there was more to the story behind why it was hidden.

In front of him was a small round hole set in one of the legs of the arch, perfect for the Stone he now held in his open hand. At the mention of Nuriel, Talister had removed the Stone from his bracelet and given it to Sam, without question.

Sam closed his eyes, fingering the smooth Watcher Stone in his palm as fear began to creep over him. Arazel's piercing green eyes flashed through his mind, his words rolling in his ears as if he were right next to him. *The Prince of Darkness, the ruler of Sheba Haloth.*

It was about to become true, for he was about to open the floodgates of all Dark creatures into Earth from the spiritual realm. He would be the champion of the Darkness, the hero of the Metim. What if his father was wrong? Maybe he was only hoping it would help the Light, but what if he was mistaken? What if the curse was not truly lifted and the Darkness still hid until they grew too large to stop? What if ... his father wasn't who he said he was? Ayet Sal was the place of deception. What if this whole thing was a lie? Could it have been Arazel disguised as his father? Dark Watchers could manipulate Darkness just as Descendants could the Light ...

But he remembered the sensation when his father touched him, and the visions of his mother running through the field. He couldn't deny the powerful feeling it left him with. But wouldn't it be possible to mimic feelings as well?

He fought with these thoughts in the dark bookstore, the moonlight casting an eerie glow through the window, while particles of dust danced around the quiet moonbeams. Once he made a decision, there would be no going back. There was only the aftermath

🌲🌲 Chapter Eighteen: Sha'ar Gate

and consequences from his choice, whether good or bad. Who would suffer because of his choices?

He remembered the moment he met the Chancellor, and the power that the curse had over Lior, even to the point of deceiving the Protectors guarding the Chancellor. The guard who let them into the Chancellor's chamber had seen a moment of the Darkness that Talister had carried back with him unaware from the Seer Chamber, but chose to believe the status quo instead of challenging authority. A moment, one moment, where the Darkness reared its ugliness, and it was dismissed. How much more would be revealed because of the opening of the gate?

He breathed in and out, soaking in the silence of the moment. He lifted his face upward toward the heavens, opening his eyes once again. His heart beat a million miles a minute, and he reached out in front of him toward the opening in the arch, placing the small smooth Stone in the opening…

****

Nearly a thousand kilometers from the Jester's Pass arch in Lior, another figure wearing a deep blue cloak walked up the stone steps to the gleaming white castle of stone. Instead of waiting for the guards to stop him, he immediately withdrew a brilliant steel sword from his belt and, in one sweeping motion, removed their heads from their bodies. Then he casually strode into the great hall and threw his sword down in front of the platform where a robed man with glassy eyes was reading from an ancient scroll.

At the sight of the man with the deep blue cloak, the robed man's eyes blazed suddenly with lustful surprise, almost as if he had seen his greatest enemy being slain in front of him. The man in the blue cloak stood, palms outstretched, as if surrendering himself. His eyes showed defeat and deep resentment, but he stood his ground.

Kachash stood and strode carefully to the edge of the platform as throngs of guards emerged from the entrance to surround the man in the blue cloak. When he held his hand up to stop them, they slunk

Chapter Eighteen: Sha'ar Gate

back away from the scene, looks of surprise on their faces at the sight of the man.

"I must say, this is a surprise. To what do I owe the pleasure of a great Watcher's company like yours? Did you find no hope in the Light?"

The man in blue did not look up at the beautiful man standing in front of him, but his face showed intense anger as he choked out his words.

"I have come to surrender to the Darkness. I cannot fight that which is in me."

Kachash's eyes blazed with sadistic excitement.

"Nuriel, the great warrior of legions of Watchers, has surrendered himself to the Dark One? Oh the thrill of this moment! Oh how the Darkness will rejoice! And what do you have to offer as a token of your pledge?"

Nuriel did not take his eyes off the white stone floor. Images of his son raced through his mind as he fought the urge to snatch the sword and lop off Kachash's head right then and there. It would certainly silence him. But it would not be for the greater good for Descendants and Watchers alike. For the segulla—for *mankind*. This was something he had to do, without question.

"The Sha'ar Gate has been opened."

About The Author

A first time author, Troy is excited to launch his new series, The Descendants of Light, which premiers with the first book The Watcher Key.

Having loved fantastical and science fiction novels, the time was right for a Christian fantasy to be brought to those searching for exciting worlds and creatures of the Light and the Dark.

Troy lives in Dayton, Ohio with his wife Stacy and two wonderful daughters, Maddison and Sydney.

His desire is to continue bringing those worlds to fellow fantasy lovers everywhere, because there is something always beneath the surface...